Vanquished

4/09/04

Indebted

Paper Billionaires
Book 2

A novel

by:
Ainsley St Claire

Dedication & Thank You

This is my 30th book! I'm so grateful to have a husband who supports and encourages me. Sweetheart, I love you when I leave my dirty clothes on the bathroom floor even though you may disagree. Toujour et pour toujour.

Thank you readers for your wonderful notes and kind words of encouragement. I wouldn't be able to do this without you. Writing isn't always easy and those comments keep me going when the characters have different ideas than my plot.

To the army behind me that encourage and help to get these books in your hands: Jessica, Courtnay, Nancy, Linda, Iris, Diana, Chas, and Candi.

To my author friends who meet with me most mornings to write over Zoom (we actually do this!) thank you for your encouragement and support:
Nala, Janna, Kathy, and Maggie.

CHAPTER 1

Jaxson

"Billionaire Busts Tessa's Heart," Grantham Wilks, one of the board members at Honeycomb Games, the company I founded, announces as he stands and drops a tabloid on the conference table. "Billionaire Bancroft Breaks Tessa Sky's Heart." He drops a second. "Billionaire Playboy threatens to share naughty pics of Tessa Sky." He drops another tabloid on the table. "Tessa Sky's Untold Story: in her words." He tosses another on the pile.

He looks up, and I realize he has at least ten different tabloids with Tessa Sky and me plastered all over the covers.

"Do you know what all of these articles have in common?" he asks.

I shake my head, despite knowing where he's going with this.

"Each one has quotes from people who are deleting our games from their devices and burning our merchandise."

"I didn't break —" I start.

"It doesn't matter," he interrupts. "She's spilling her broken heart out to the media, and it's going to affect our IPO."

I lean back in my chair and take the beating. I don't blame anyone in this room for this mess. Tessa Sky is a pop icon, and she has legions of fans. She started out as a teen star on one of those singing talent shows, and she's swarmed everywhere she goes. A while back, a friend told me she wanted to meet me. I thought she might do some sponsored social media posts for Honeycomb or something, so I agreed. But our afternoon together led to two days of a down-and-dirty one-night stand. Then she had to tour for her latest album, and I was—and remain—knee deep in getting a new game out and preparing for Honeycomb's IPO.

Tessa invited me to see her shows in New York and Boston, so we enjoyed a week together, which landed me—for the first time—in the tabloids. After that, we dated for three months. And the tabloids are her life. She loves it.

I hate it.

For three months, our every move was chronicled in the media, from romantic dinners to weekend getaways. It was overwhelming, and after a little while, I found it painful and exhausting.

In the end, I guess I was kind of a drag, because she dumped me. I didn't mind so much, except the tabloids went from her being pregnant with my child and watching for wedding bells to all-out terrorizing me.

Her fans blame me for the breakup, and as Grantham has helpfully pointed out, they've started boycotting our games. It's a disaster, and my reputation is in shambles. We've even lost three of our female developers because of this.

I've spent the last month living at the Fairmont Hotel with security around me twenty-four/seven. Tessa's fans have come from far and wide to tell me how I hurt their icon's feelings.

Never again.

10

Before Tessa, I dated Melanie. I liked her… She was an elementary school teacher, and I took her to the wedding of one of my closest friends last summer, Grayson Blackstone. We had a great time, and then we went to her best friend's wedding a few weeks later, and I stepped out for a phone call from my development team. I returned to find her making out with one of the teachers she worked with. That was a real gut punch.

My introduction to Tessa came shortly after that breakup.

Now my board of directors isn't happy, and they've called an emergency meeting.

"You need to settle down, like, yesterday," Veronica Vance, another board member, stresses. "We want you to present a more stable image to the public. That's the best way to protect the company and its impending IPO."

I look at her, confused.

"You'll present a general non-disclosure agreement to a woman and pretend to date her," Dominic Valente, another board member chimes in. "After a while, you can move her into a guest room in your home, and you can even pay her to marry you for a year or so."

I sit up straight. "What?"

"Come on. This happens all the time in these circles," Dominic says. "Plus, once this is behind you, you can say you've done the marriage thing and you don't want to do it again."

I roll my eyes. "I'm not going to get married just because my ex is dragging me through the tabloids."

Mason Sullivan, the chairman of Sullivan Healy Newhouse, Honeycomb's venture capital firm, clears his throat. "I don't think you need to actually get married. You just need a stable relationship that will get the world to stop thinking you're a playboy."

I shake my head. I can't believe he, of all people, agrees with this. "Why can't I just be seen around town with the same woman for a while?"

"Because that's still the playboy image we need you to lose," he explains, without even looking at me.

"And you think me settling down with someone will change how people feel about the company?"

The meeting goes a little sideways after that. I thought dating Tessa Sky was a weird experience. Now my board wants to take over my life. But there's nothing I can say to change their minds. They leave me understanding that if I can't pull off a fake relationship that looks serious, I might lose my company. And that is bad on so many levels. This has happened to me before — under entirely false pretenses last time — so my business partners from that venture and I have a plan for revenge. And losing this company would definitely derail it. I can't let that happen.

After the meeting, I head back to Honeycomb's offices. I have fires to put out.

When I arrive, I get straight to my office without stopping to talk to anyone. I shut the door behind me and message my two closest friends.

Me: Can you all meet me at the hotel tonight? There was an emergency board meeting today, and we need to make sure they don't fuck up all our plans.

Gray: What time?

Nick: I can reschedule with Olivia.

Me: How about 8 in my room?

After a few minutes, they both agree. I lean back in my chair and look out the window. From this vantage point, I can see the Golden Gate Bridge, the Bay Bridge, and everything in between. I love San Francisco. Growing up outside of Detroit, I never thought I'd live anywhere like this.

There's a knock at my door.

"Yes?" I call.

My assistant, Alicia Cummings, pokes her head in the door. "Mr. Bancroft? I was wondering if you had a moment."

"I don't, but what do you need?"

Alicia has worked for me for the last two months, and she's finally getting the hang of things around here.

"I'm really sorry to do this, but I need to give my two weeks' notice."

My eyes go wide. "Why? You just started."

She nods. "I'm sorry, but before I interviewed here, I met with the Mindworks Ad Agency for an account manager role. They called me again last week and have extended an offer. The pay is less and the benefits aren't nearly as good, but it's my dream job."

I don't even know what to say. She's dead to me.

She sets an envelope on my desk. "I've alerted human resources, and they've posted the job. If you hire someone in time, I'll happily train them."

I don't respond. If I say what's going through my head, she'll walk out the door and go right to a tabloid and that will be a whole new story to contend with.

I clear my throat. "Thank you for the notice. I have to get back to work. Can you pull together Julia Willis and the development team working on Spy Game? I was playing it last night and found some bugs."

"Of course, Mr. Bancroft."

"Shut the door behind you," I say as she goes.

I stare at the closed door. This office is all glass, so there's no real privacy. I pick up the phone to call HR.

"Natasha Zhu," she says as she answers.

13

"Tasha, Alicia has quit."

"She told me. I've already posted the ad, and in less than two hours, fifty people have applied."

That makes me feel a little better. "Okay, at the end of the day can you—"

Suddenly the line fills with the sound of hammers pounding and an electric saw's whine.

"What the fuck?"

"They're working on the new space for the development team," Tasha explains.

"Why aren't they doing this after hours?" I ask as my blood pressure soars.

"They don't have anyone willing to do that. The disruptions should only last a few weeks. Most people are working from home."

"Why didn't I know about this?"

She pauses a moment. "Um…Stacy mentioned it at the staff meeting, and they sent out emails," she says.

I pinch the bridge of my nose. I'm behind on everything. Stacy Bragio is my head of operations, and we have discussed this, but I thought it was months out. "Thank you, Tasha. If you could send me info on the top five candidates by the end of the day, I'll go through and let you know who to set up interviews with."

For the next two hours, I'm serenaded with a barrage of nail guns, electric saws, rap or dance music, and banging. It's giving me a headache, and it's enough of a distraction that my brain keeps going back to this morning's meeting.

Eventually, I realize trying to accomplish anything here is futile. I pack up my things and pass Alicia's desk on the way out.

"I'm going back to my hotel room," I tell her. "I can't take the noise any longer."

She pulls earplugs out of her ears. "I'm sorry?"

I repeat what I said and add, "I'm very happy for you and your new job. I'm just disappointed that you're leaving."

14

She gives me a shy smile. "I think you need someone a lot firmer who can do a better job of blocking people who demand to be on your schedule."

"Duly noted." She's right. I've ended up with a few meetings I hadn't expected because she was bullied into putting vendors and prospective partners on my calendar. Thankfully, I have no problem telling people no.

Well, except for my board. I still don't know how I'm going to make this fake-relationship thing work.

I have my bodyguard and driver, Christophe Broussard, stop at a café not too far from the hotel, and I pop in to grab some food to take back to my hotel room.

"Well, if it isn't the world's biggest heartbreaker," I hear behind me.

I prepare myself to be verbally abused, but when I turn around, I find Rick Shula. He was a developer at my first company, Quick Reels, and he's now a multimillionaire living the high life. "Rick," I say. We shake hands.

"Man, I saw about you and Tessa Sky." He shakes his head. "How the hell did you meet her?"

I shrug. "She asked. What about you?"

"No one's putting a ring on me."

I nod, understanding exactly what he means. When there are so many beautiful women out there, why limit yourself to just one?

"I can't believe you dumped her," he continues. "She's sexy as all get out."

"Despite what the tabloids say, she dumped me. I guess her fans don't want to see her as the bad guy."

"Ah. Well, there are plenty of fish in the sea," he says.

I roll my eyes. "It's difficult to date after being in the tabloids. Who wants that mess?"

He leans in. "I may have a solution for you. There's this place I know. The women are discreet, and they can be dates or just spend some quality time with you. They know it isn't anything else."

15

I hold up my hand. "I'm not sure I want a prostitute."

"It's not like that. These women enjoy that kind of fun, and they usually just want a gift."

I raise an eyebrow. "A gift?"

"Sure. They'll leave you information for a store where they're registered, and you have something sent over to them."

I'm still not sure I want to go there.

He pulls out his wallet. "Before you completely close the door, go to this website. The password on the back will get you in and let them know you were referred by me. Please don't share it. They're picky about the men they'll work with."

I weigh his suggestion and roll it around in my head, liking it more and more as we catch up and order lunch.

Rick tells me a bit about what he's doing these days. He's sold most of his stock at Quick Reels and is working part time for the company. He'd like to be out completely, and he says he's tried a few times to quit… But then he overshares that the new people Mandego has hired are not the strongest. Peter Mandego worked with Zack Villefort to sabotage my friends and me at Quick Reels, and in return, he was made CEO. Too bad he's not actually qualified for the job.

I school my face, but knowing Mandego continues to fail is great information.

When we finish our meal, I wish Rick well and return to the hotel with Christophe. I spend the afternoon working through the issues I've discovered with the Spy Game developers via Zoom. If we can't fix the bugs, this game can't be released. And we've committed to dates on the various platforms. If we have to push back, we won't get prime placement with our next release, and that's yet another thing that could affect our IPO.

I'm trying hard not to put too much pressure on Julia and her team. But I'm beginning to wonder if they're so busy counting the money their stock options will yield that they've forgotten this game affects those prices.

We've finally ended our session, and I'm deep in thought, trying to figure all of this out, when there's a knock at the door. I look up, and it's dark outside—when did that happen?

I open the door to Nick, who's holding a nice bottle of bourbon. "Come in." I stand aside while he shuffles past me. Suddenly, I realize I'm hungry. "Have you had dinner?"

"No. So I'm down with ordering something in."

I walk over to grab the room service menu. "We can get a couple of Wagyu rib eyes or go simpler and order a pizza from Anthony's."

He thinks for a second. "The rib eyes sound good."

"Should we order for Gray?"

"I'll check."

I pour us drinks while Nick texts Grayson. He's recently married to his second wife, Scarlett, who he met while she was taking care of his twin boys. She's perfect for him, and now, she takes good care of the three of us.

Nick looks up. "Scarlett had dinner for him. He's offering to bring leftover lasagna."

"It's up to you."

"You got me thinking about rib eye, so let's do that."

I use the house phone to place our order, adding a few appetizers. They tell me we'll have our meals in twenty minutes.

"How are things going with the release of your new game?" Nick asks while we wait.

I shake my head and fill him in on my maddening afternoon. I'm just finishing up when our dinner arrives, and Gray is right behind it.

We get a drink for him and all sit at the dining room table. We chat as Nick and I eat.

"So how's your dating life, Mr. Tabloid?" Nick asks as we're finishing our steaks.

"It's not that easy these days, thanks to Tessa. The entire world knows how much I'm worth, and they're either out to skewer me or propose. There's not a chance in hell I'm going to just get laid again."

"Well, there are NDAs that can help with that," Gray offers.

I think before he met Scarlett he had a few relationships no one knew about because of an NDA — at least it wouldn't surprise me.

I groan. "It's so much worse than that."

I tell them what my board of directors said this morning.

"Mason Sullivan was in favor of that?" Nick's eyes bulge.

"They believe the IPO rate for Honeycomb has gone into a freefall."

"Has it?" Gray asks.

I shrug. "I don't know. Right now, lots of media are reporting about people deleting our games."

"What are you going to do?" Gray takes a sip of his drink and sits back.

I tell them about running into Rick Shula today. "Maybe I'll hire someone who can give me the girlfriend experience."

Gray nods his head. "That might work. It's *Pretty Woman*. And you can save the hooker."

I narrow my eyes. "Rick says they're not prostitutes but women you have on your arm for photo shoots and other things that typically require a date. Then you give them a gift in return."

"Where are you going to go for sex?" Nick asks.

I hold up my right hand. "I don't know beyond this."

After we have several drinks in us, Gray suggests we check out the website Rick told me about. We sit together on the couch, and I balance the laptop on my lap.

We pass through several security measures, and I enter the code Rick gave me, and then finally, up comes a website featuring beautiful women in a broad spectrum of ethnicities, shapes, sizes, and hair and skin colors. I click on a beautiful blonde with long, straight hair and green eyes. Her name is Katherine, or so it says. This opens up a resume with everything from her height and weight to favorite foods.

"Click on her pictures." Nick points to the folder.

I do, and it's like we've opened a spread in *Playboy* or *MAXIM*.

"Holy shiiiiiitttt." Nick whistles. "I have a feeling the girlfriend experience isn't what you think it is."

"Rick says they want gifts, not money."

Gray points to a different folder. "There's her wish list."

I open the file, and there's a list of jewelry from designers like Cartier and Bulgari but also furniture and high-end cookware.

"It says she's a student at Stanford, studying electrical engineering," Nick says.

"No offense, but she looks nothing like the women I went to school with in electrical engineering," I say.

"Agreed," Grayson says.

After ogling a bit more, we shut down the computer and hang out for a while longer. I'm disappointed that my friends are also pushing for me to follow what the board says. I can't believe that's really my only choice and my personal life, which is not even being portrayed accurately, is a factor in the professional performance of my company.

But I guess I have to get this done. I owe these guys that much. Gray took his company, Firefly, public last year, and we've all benefited greatly. I want to return the favor, and more importantly, I want to continue making progress with our next goal, which is revenge on Zack Villefort and the people who helped him cheat us out of Quick Reels. We need Honeycomb to go public and on schedule as planned.

After the guys leave, I go back to the website and look again. Several of the women are very interesting to me, but a little voice in the back of my head whispers that it could be bait and switch. I have nothing but photos and resumes to go on here. There's no guarantee these women are who's actually going to show up once I agree.

I close the computer again, but I can't stop thinking about what Wilks said today as he went through all the tabloids. People are deleting our games, and I need to repair my public image. Maybe the only way to solve this is a fake girlfriend who grows into a fake fiancée, and maybe a wife — for a specific amount of time.

The more I think about it, the more I think one of these website women could be the answer to my prayers. I have no one else I can reach out to, and God forbid I contact anyone I've already gone out with. There's a reason I'm not seeing any of those women anymore.

I click on the contact button and carefully put in my request.

I'm interested in the girlfriend experience. Recently I had a very public breakup, which is affecting my company's value. I need a woman who can appear as my date at public events, and then possibly enter a contractual relationship or marriage for a predetermined amount of time. Please contact me to discuss.

I press send and close up for the night. It's nearly midnight, and five and a half hours from now, I'm meeting Christophe, who is going to kick my ass as we run the boardwalk and lift weights. Tomorrow is abs.

My phone lights up, and I don't recognize the number. Yet for some reason I answer. "Hello?"

"Hello, this is Sarah Beck. You left a message on my website?"

Her voice is silky smooth, and my dick twitches.

"Um, yes. This is Jax Bancroft."

20

I hear her chuckle. "You *have* had a very public breakup."

I don't know quite what to make of that. "Yes. I'm curious about your girlfriend experience."

She's quiet for a moment. "You need someone long term?"

"If they'll sign an NDA," I respond.

"That's not an issue," she assures me. "But I think you need one of my new hires — not one of my regulars."

I knew it. Bait and switch. I'm ready to thank her and send her on her way.

"I'm thinking of a beautiful natural blonde. She's five foot nine inches tall and the daughter of a U.S. Senator."

My interests are piqued. "Why not someone like Katherine?"

Sarah pauses. "I think you'll be more successful with someone who isn't on our website and hasn't worked with other customers."

"Do you think this woman would go for something like that?"

"I'll reach out to her. I think you should start with a first date. Maybe she could meet you somewhere?"

"I'm very visible right now. But I'm living at the Fairmont for a few more days. Would she feel comfortable meeting me in my hotel suite?"

"I'll talk to her, and I'll tell her you come as a referral. Rick Shula mentioned you might call."

Agh. "If he asks, do you mind telling him I never reached out?"

"My business is all about discretion," she agrees smoothly, "which is the reason I think you need someone no one has met."

"When are you thinking we should meet?"

"Her schedule should allow her to meet you at two on Friday afternoon at your hotel. If something comes up, please just send a text. You have my number."

That's two days away. It will be worth the wait if she's the right person for the job. "Thank you. If this works out, you'll really be saving me."

"I have a feeling you're really going to like Laura."

"I look forward to meeting her."

"Have a good night."

We disconnect, and for the first time today, I feel like there might be a way out of this. *Tessa Sky, you can't screw with me any longer.*

CHAPTER 2

Harper

My phone buzzes like crazy on my desk at work. I pick it up and quickly count eight emails from my bank. My stomach drops. Opening the first one, I see that my rent check bounced. I shut my eyes. This can't be happening.

I switch over to my banking app and look up my account. My paycheck isn't in there. It definitely should be.

I've spent the last two years working for a coupon startup. We work with retailers to produce coupons that will increase purchasing for overstocked items or simply bring in foot traffic. But business has been slow lately. Our biggest retailer pulled their business a couple months ago because of an error we made. The salesperson set the coupon at an eighty-percent discount, when it was only supposed to be thirty. It wasn't pretty.

I look up and survey the office. A lot of people are out today, including our CEO, Travis Edgar. I walk over to Monica, the office temp, who is sitting outside his door. "Do you know when Travis is due back?"

She shakes her head. "They don't tell me anything."

I wander over toward the company accountant. Maybe I can ask her. But I stop short when I realize her office is completely empty.

What. The. Fuck?

I look around the office again and realize *many* people have cleared out their things.

I've been applying for various other graphic-design jobs, but no one is calling. *Shit.* This is not good.

Since no one here can help me, I go back to my desk and shift gears to seeking encouragement from my best friend, Amy. I met Amy Brighton shortly after I moved to San Francisco when I got lost trying to get on the right bus. I had just graduated from Massachusetts Art and Design. I'd lived at home while I went to school, and I was ready for something different. I wanted to make it on my own. But my problem has been dependable work.

"Hey," Amy says when she answers.

"Hi. I just got hit with four hundred dollars in overdraft fees because my paycheck bounced."

"No!" she says with horror in her voice. "What are you going to do?"

"I don't know. Travis isn't here to tell me when he'll make good on the check." I look around again. "But, Amy, I'm not feeling too good about this. There's hardly anyone here, and the accountant has emptied her office."

"Oh no!"

I sit back in my chair. She's not making me feel better.

"Okay, the last time this happened, I was dating Geoff, that lawyer?"

"I remember." They had like three dates, and he ghosted her.

"He said you should file an unemployment claim immediately. That way you'll get any money from the company before it goes to creditors."

I sigh. "Okay. But Travis made good on payroll last time—and the late fees. You don't think he will again?"

"Try calling him. If you can't speak directly to him, you need to file. I know you're already looking for work, but you may have to open up your requirements and take a job that doesn't include as much graphic design."

"That's what I'm afraid of. Let me call Travis, and I'll let you know what he says."

"We're still on for drinks tonight?"

"Yep. Bar None six o'clock. Be there or be square."

"Ciao!"

I call Travis, and it goes to voicemail. Travis is a good guy. He's always made sure we're taken care of. It's just hard running a startup. I'm sure he's trying to get some money from our vendors.

"This mailbox is full. Please try your call again later," the recording says and then disconnects me.

My stomach flops around like a fish out of water. *Where is Travis, and where is my money?*

I have Lisha Rogers, one of my coworkers, in my contacts, so I try her. She's not here today, so maybe she knows something I don't. I'm relieved when she answers.

· "Hello?"

"Hey, this is Harper Lockwood. Do you know what's going on at the office?"

She snorts. "Yeah, Travis has taken all the money and done a runner to South America."

My eyes pop wide. "Are you sure?"

"Well, I know some people heard yesterday that he was gone. Did you go in today?"

"Yeah. It's a ghost town."

"I'm so pissed at him. I have overdraft fees all over my bank account," she rants.

"Me too. What are you going to do?"

"I had a second interview today, so I'm hoping I can just move on to something else. Otherwise, I need to borrow money from my parents, and that always comes with strings."

I groan in sympathy, but inside, I wish that was an option for me. My parents are both teachers, and with four kids still at home to feed, they don't have a lot of money to spare. "Okay, thanks for the info," I tell her. "Good luck."

I hang up, dreading what I may have to do. San Francisco isn't cheap, and I only have one account left — my old 401K. I worked through college as an assistant at a local software startup, and I'm proud to say that with each paycheck, I put the maximum into the 401K. Now, I may have to drain the account, and that sucks about five different ways. It was only ten thousand dollars, and more than half of that will go to taxes and penalties.

I pack up my desk and walk out to take the bus home. It's not in the best neighborhood, but it's more affordable, and I love my neighbors.

When I get to my place, my landlord is waiting. "Your rent check bounced."

I consider my words carefully. Calling him slimy would be an insult to every amphibian and lowlife I can think of. "I know. My paycheck bounced, and my boss is apparently on his way to South America. I will find the money, and as soon as I can, I'll deliver it to you."

"You call me, and I'll come get it. There's a hundred-dollar fee each day you're late."

"My rent is already two thousand dollars!" I screech.

"Then you shouldn't give me checks that bounce."

"I'll get you what I can as soon as possible."

"If I don't have your rent by the fifteenth, I'll change the locks."

My shoulders fall. "Okay."

I shut myself into my cockroach-infested apartment, pull up my banking website, and direct it to liquidate my 401K. I'll have to work twice as hard to replenish my retirement savings. A few clicks and the internet promises that the money — what's left of it — will be in my checking account in forty-eight hours.

I click to another site and search through the job postings. There's nothing for graphic design I haven't already applied for. I expand my search and apply for several admin jobs. I'll be lucky if any of them call me.

I can't think of anything else to do, so I lie back on my bed and have a good cry. Whatever happens, I don't want to move home. But I have to be realistic. If I can't get a job soon, I'm not going to have much of a choice.

I look at my watch. It's after school for Mom, so I call her.

"Hey, baby, what's up?" she answers.

Already I feel a little better. I tell her about my boss taking off with my paycheck.

"You can always have your old room back," she promises.

"Thanks, Mom. I'll keep that in mind. I just don't feel ready to give up on San Francisco yet."

She catches me up on each of my brothers and sisters. We're four boys and four girls, and I'm number five in the mix. Once my baby brother finishes high school in three years, my parents say they're going to retire. I'll believe it when I see it.

When my call waiting beeps, I interrupt Mom. "Hold on, please. My other line is ringing."

I switch over to the new call. "Hello, this is Harper Lockwood."

"Ms. Lockwood?"

"Yes?"

"This is Natasha Zhu from Honeycomb Games. We've received your resume. Do you have a minute?"

"Let me just get off another call. I'll be two shakes." I flip back to Mom. "Mom, this is a company I applied to for a new job. I gotta go."

"Good luck," she singsongs and hangs up.

I take a deep breath. "Thank you for holding."

"Yes, I see you've been working for Couponing Inc. Why are you looking for work?"

"Unfortunately, they ran out of money, and they didn't make payroll."

"Oh no. You didn't even get a final check?"

"Unfortunately, no."

She talks me through my resume. The job she's explaining is in admin, not graphic design, but I'm desperate, and I can't afford to be picky. I explain what I did for the CEO of Symmetry Software while I was in college, and she gets very excited. "Our founder, Jaxson Bancroft, is a little high maintenance. He'll have you get coffee and probably do some personal errands, but it's mostly managing his calendar and keeping all of us out of his office. Do you think that's something you would enjoy?"

No, but I can't afford to be hungry either. "That sounds right up my alley."

"Wonderful. Our offices are under construction, and Mr. Bancroft is working from the Fairmont Hotel. Would you be willing to meet with him tomorrow afternoon, say, two o'clock?"

"In his hotel room?"

"He's actually working out of the penthouse suite. I promise it's nothing nefarious. You'd be meeting in the living room — no beds to be had, and chances are others will be in and out."

"Oh. Sure. Can you tell me what the job pays?"

"We're about six months from going public, so there are a few stock options included, and the pay is eighty-five-thousand dollars annually."

My eyes go wide. I was making barely half that at Couponing. Suddenly, this job sounds much more in line with what I want to do. I clear my throat. "Okay. That sounds fine."

I'd rather be doing something else, but I can at least get my foot in on the ground floor. I pull up Honeycomb Games' website and find I play two of their games on my phone pretty regularly. Maybe if I can impress Mr. Bancroft, I can move into graphic design.

When I finish the call, I float around my apartment as I get ready, and then I practically skip to Bar None to meet Amy. I see her immediately when I arrive. She's flirting with Tom, the bartender.

"Guess what?" I say after I hug her.

"You got a new job?"

I smile. "I have an interview. So that's a step in the right direction."

She raises her arms in triumph. "Congratulations."

"What can I get you to celebrate?" Tom asks.

"I'm afraid it needs to be some of San Francisco's finest tap water on the rocks, please."

He gives me a strange look.

"My paycheck bounced today. I have nothing to pay you with."

He grabs a glass, scoops up some ice, and fills it with water. "What a bummer."

I give him an appreciative smile. He gets it.

"One of my other customers had something like that happen," he adds. "They were all invited to the conference room after lunch, where they were all let go. They couldn't even go back to their desks. It took the police coming and escorting people back in to even get their keys, wallets, and purses." I watch as he pulls a champagne glass, pours something into it, and then adds champagne and a cherry.

"That would be terrible!" I shake my head. "This was the second time our checks bounced, so most people didn't even come in today. I have four hundred dollars in overdraft charges."

He sets the champagne cocktail in front of me. "It's on the house. You can't celebrate with water."

I lean over the bar and hug him. "Thank you so much!" I exclaim. "This job may not be my dream job, but it will pay well, and I can get my feet back under me."

I sit down at a table with Amy, and we dig up everything we can about the job. She Googles Jaxson Bancroft.

"Oh my gawd," she announces after a moment.

I look up from my phone. "What?"

"He recently broke up with Tessa Sky."

"What?"

"That's what it says here." She looks at his picture. "Holy hotness, Batman. I bet women give him their underwear."

She turns the phone around, and I kind of agree. He has dark brown hair, mysterious eyes, and in every picture, he has scruff.

I fan myself. "It will be hard to work with him, but someone needs to do it. And I volunteer."

She nods. "I will be coming by often to meet you for lunch, and I fully expect an introduction."

"Consider it done," I say. Amy is the best, but she's had a string of bad luck with men. If I could introduce her to a great guy, I would do it in a heartbeat. Maybe I can at least introduce her to Jaxson Bancroft.

We talk our way through two drinks each—she insists on covering my second one, since she's still employed—and then we head back to our apartments.

As I lie in bed, my mind bounces through the many possibilities ahead. Despite everything that happened today, I believe things are going to work out just fine.

CHAPTER 3

Jaxson

By mid-morning Friday, I've had three potential-assistant interviews over the last two days, and the candidates are getting wackier and wackier. I call Tasha at the office. "The last one is a no-go, too. Her hairband had kitten ears, her nails were pointy, and I swear she meowed. No way."

Tasha chuckles. "If only those things were clear on their resumes. Don't worry. I have two more coming at you today. We'll finish out the week strong. I just emailed you their information."

I open the first email and find info about a Harper Lockwood. She's been working as a graphic designer and went to art school. I sigh. "Go ahead and cancel Harper. She wants to be a graphic designer. She'll only stay until she finds work doing that."

"I think you should meet her. Maybe you can tempt her with working in our graphics department in a year or so."

"No. I want someone who's dedicated to working as an assistant."

"Okay, but she's the strongest candidate we have."

I make a growling noise, but it's not worth the argument. I'm not changing my mind. Moving on, I open the next resume... *Oh, this one might work.* His name is Kevin Woods, and he's been working as the executive admin for the head of marketing at Salesteam for the last two years. "This Kevin guy looks interesting. I like him."

"Great. He's coming to you shortly, so let me know how it goes," Tasha says.

When we finish the call, my meeting with Kevin is an hour out, which gives me enough time to get an early lunch. If Kevin worked for me, he could pick up lunch. Instead, I'm stuck doing it rather than returning calls. I'm also eager to meet this Laura person later this afternoon. Sarah confirmed that appointment last night. I've tried looking the woman, Laura, up online, but she's nonexistent—not even a picture with her father. So I guess this could be fantastic.

I wolf down my sandwich and make it back to my hotel suite just as Kevin arrives. He's wearing a suit, which is a little overdressed, but it's an interview. And I now know that's better than the alternative. He does not have cat ears.

We shake hands in the hallway, and I usher him into the living room of the suite. "Honeycomb Games is pretty casual," I tell him. "We typically wear jeans and T-shirts."

"Hmmm..."

"Have a seat and let's talk."

He smiles as he takes a chair, and I'm already feeling good about this. "So, why are you looking to leave Salesteam?" I ask.

He takes a deep breath, but then his face seems to crumble. Tears pool in his eyes. "I...I made the mistake of sleeping with my boss. He's married, and it's so ugly. He needs me to leave, but he's the love of my life. I don't know if I can stand it. What we have, it's so amazing. So hot. But I can't listen to him tell people about his fabulous family without wanting to stab him in the heart."

My mouth opens and closes as I attempt to formulate a response. *Okay, Kevin is not the candidate for me.* Still, somehow I let him ramble for almost forty-five minutes before I finally find a window and stand to signal him to leave.

He reaches for my arm. "You know, you're very easy to talk to. I hope we get the chance to work together. It could be so much fun."

I smile. "Tasha will be in touch. Thank you for coming to meet with me."

"Anytime," he says in a seductive voice.

Nope. No way.

I return to the table I've made my temporary desk. I'm not even going to bother calling Tasha about that one. I'm working my way through my inbox, making a list of things to follow up on, when there's a knock at the door. *Ooh!* This interview I'm looking forward to for sure.

I get up and answer, finding a beautiful brunette with a dazzling smile waiting. I thought she was supposed to be a blonde, but I guess women change their hair color all the time. She's even more beautiful than Sarah mentioned.

"Welcome," I tell her, gesturing for her to enter. "I'm so glad Sarah sent you over."

She smiles. "Thank you for your time."

"Can I get you water, maybe a glass of wine?"

"Uh, no, thank you. I'm good."

"So Sarah explained what I'm looking for?"

She nods. "I think so. It's pretty standard."

Standard? Sarah must have done a good job selling this. I guess I should cut right to the chase. "How would you feel if we were intimate?"

Her eyes bounce wide. "Excuse me?"

"If we're going to be linked to one another for a year or more, and we need to present as a couple, it makes sense that we'd be intimate, doesn't it? I'm just wondering how you handle that. The profile I got from Sarah says you're up for fellatio—both giving and receiving, though you don't want to kiss except in public. And I think I remember that sex toys are okay, but no whips or paddles. Though you don't mind rough sex."

She looks like a deer in headlights. "I don't think I'm the person for the job. I understood this as an interview to be your assistant. In my book, that doesn't include seeing each other naked."

My eyes go wide. "I'm sorry. What is your name?"

She stands and picks up her purse. "Harper Lockwood. I appreciate your time, but I'm not the person you're looking for."

I shut my eyes. Tasha was supposed to cancel this one. Fear grips my heart. "*Shit.* I'm so sorry. Please…I beg you to forget everything I just said."

"Trust me, that won't be an issue." She essentially runs out the door and slams it behind her.

I look up at the ceiling. *What the hell?*

I call Tasha. "I thought you were going to cancel the interview with Harper Lockwood?"

"I thought you were going to give her a chance. She's by far the strongest candidate."

I can't tell her what's happened. "Well, uh, we're going to need more candidates. Kevin cried through his interview and is in love with his previous boss, who he's having an affair with."

"Oh, that's not good," she says.

"No. It's definitely not. And I thought Harper was someone named Laura, so I thoroughly confused her, and she ran out of here in a panic. Can you send me her home address and phone number? I need to track her down."

"Harper? Sure, no problem." I can hear Tasha typing. "Are you sure? I can smooth it all over."

I breathe out a deep sigh. "No. I think the only person who can fix this is me."

She gives me the info, and when we hang up, I call Sarah next. "What happened to Laura?" I ask.

"She didn't show?"

"No, she did not."

"Okay, my apologies," Sarah says. "Let me find out what happened. Maybe she got lost or something."

"Thank you. Please let me know. I have to go out for a while, so if she's still on the way, we'll need to reschedule."

After we hang up, I call a car and have it take me to Harper's address in the Tenderloin neighborhood of San Francisco, which is certainly not the finest. The apartment building she lives in looks okay, but who knows?

I ring the buzzer. Fortunately, after a moment, she answers. "Hello?"

"Harper. This is Jaxson Bancroft. I'm so sorry. I thought you were someone else earlier this afternoon. Please forgive me. Will you talk to me for a moment?"

She's quiet.

I forge ahead. "My life is chaotic right now, and I'd love to tell you it's never like this, but it is. Honeycomb is six months from IPO, and my board is giving me grief about being in the tabloids. Please?"

She sighs. "I'll be right down."

I wait a few minutes, and she walks out of her building wearing jeans and a T-shirt. Her face is freshly scrubbed, and I realize she doesn't need any makeup to look beautiful. But that's not why I'm here.

"Is your board giving you trouble over your breakup with Tessa Sky?" she asks, sizing me up as the door closes behind her.

"Uh, shall we walk?" I ask.

She nods, and I follow as she heads down the block.

35

I decide to tell her the truth. I've told her way too much already, so it seems the least I can do. "Tessa broke up with me, not the other way around, although I probably would have done it eventually. She lives a much more public life than I want to."

"And your board wants you to have rough sex?"

I must turn fifty shades of crimson. "No. They want me to settle down and at least appear to be in a stable relationship. But it might have to be fake."

"Why would you want that?" Her eyes go wide. "I'm sorry. That's none of my business. Thank you for taking the time to explain it to me. I really wasn't sure what to think."

"I know we didn't sign an NDA or anything, but I'd appreciate you keeping my mistake earlier to yourself, and I'd like to offer you the job."

Her steps falter. "I don't know you well enough to be your fake girlfriend," she blurts.

"No!" *Why do I keep messing this up?* "I'd like you to be my assistant. I noticed from your resume that you're a graphic designer. Maybe after a year or so I can move you to the design team for one of our new games."

I'm not sure why I promised that. I have no idea if she can do that kind of design, if she'll fit with the team. I don't know anything about her.

Her eyes grow wide, and she comes to a full stop. "Really?"

I stuff my hands in my pockets, suddenly not sure what to do with them. I manage a nod. "But I will need an NDA signed."

"I can do that. Okay. Great. When would you like me to start?"

"Monday morning? We should be good to go back in the office by then." I pull out my business card and hand it to her. "How about eight o'clock?"

"I'll be there. Would you like me to pick up coffee on the way?"

I smile. *That's what I'm talking about.* "That would be fantastic. I'll take the biggest nonfat latte you can buy." I open my wallet and hand her a twenty. "Get yourself something, too. We'll get you a company card for the next time."

"Great. I'll see you on Monday."

"Thank you, Harper. See you then. We'll have all the paperwork ready for you to sign."

I leave her standing on the sidewalk. She could go to the tabloids before she gets to the office on Monday, but I'll just have to pray she doesn't.

CHAPTER 4

Harper

I arrive at the Honeycomb Games office a few minutes late on Monday but with coffee in my hands. I've been doing this for a month now, and every day Jaxson has something to gripe about. But beyond that, this is turning out to be a pretty good job. The paychecks appear in my bank account like clockwork.

I pass out cups to the ladies around the floor, including Louise Harvey, who sits next to me, assistant to the director of operations. I put one on my desk and deliver the last one to Jaxson.

"You're late." He doesn't even look up at me.

"My apologies, but the line for coffee was long."

"You need to plan your time better," he quips.

The phone rings on his desk, and I lean over and answer. "Jaxson Bancroft's office."

"This is Grantham Wilks. Please put me through to Mr. Bancroft."

"I'll check to see if he's available."

I place him on hold. "Grantham Wilks is on the phone."

Jaxson's eyes move to the blinking line.

"I'm happy to tell him you're in a meeting."

He takes a loud breath. "No, he'll only be angrier when I talk to him later. Can you shut the door on your way out? And if you have the feedback from the game testers for Spy Game, that would be great."

"No problem." I walk out to my desk, pull the file, and return to his office, knocking lightly as I enter.

"—I don't know what to tell you, Grantham," he's saying into the phone. "Her fans will eventually move on to someone else."

I hand him the folder, and he nods.

At least there's some sort of acknowledgement.

When I took over as Jaxson's assistant last month, things were a mess. I'm not sure what was happening before I arrived. But since I did, I've reorganized Jaxson's office, his calendar, and his life. In a short time, we've become a well-oiled machine. His weekday calendar is booked from eight a.m. to eight p.m. And who's right there with him?

Me. That's who.

I return to my desk and sit down in my chair when up pops an email notification about Couponing Inc. and the money they owe me. The State of California is involved now, and they've seized assets and completed most of the liquidation, so they're finally sending me some cash. It isn't everything I'm owed, because they're not paying the overdraft and late fees, but at least I got my final check. The money I'm making at Honeycomb now is good, and I feel like I have my head above water.

Jaxson appears next to my desk. "What are you doing?" he asks.

I look up at him. "What can I do for you?" I ask, rather than answering his question. I glance at the clock on my computer. "Your next appointment is in three minutes."

"I need you to put some time on the calendar for lunch today. Make a reservation at Waterbar."

"Sure. I'm on it. What time? And how many people?"

He looks at me strangely. "Two. And whatever works on my calendar."

I quickly go online and make the reservation for twelve thirty. I text Jaxson the details and go back to my work. Today, my project is to read through Honeycomb's sales numbers compared to projections and put them in a pretty table that's easy for people to read. The numbers have been down since Jaxson dated Tessa Sky. I'm sure that's why Grantham Wilks called. He calls a lot, and Jaxson is always in a bitter mood afterward.

I'm busy moving data from one form to another when the phone rings again. It's Jaxson on his cell phone. I hope I didn't screw up the lunch reservation. "Yes, boss man?" I answer.

"Where are you?"

"I'm sitting at my desk. What do you need?"

"You're supposed to be at Waterbar for lunch."

"What? Why?"

"I told you to make a reservation for us at Waterbar."

I roll my eyes. What is this even about? "I don't want to argue with you, but at no time did you ask me to join you."

He sighs. "Well, just get over here."

I look at the ceiling tiles, willing myself to remain calm. "What should I bring with me?"

"Just get here."

"Okay, I'll try to get a rideshare."

"I'm sending Christophe. Be outside waiting for him." He disconnects the call.

Who is this man, and why does he make everything so crazy? I grab a pad of paper and make sure I have several pens in case one runs out of ink. You think that won't happen, but it could. It's happened to me before.

On the way downstairs, I look at my yellow floral dress and green sweater and hope I'm dressed well enough for Waterbar. But I suppose Jaxson knew what I had on when he had me make the reservation.

40

Christophe arrives in the Land Cruiser, and I hop in the front seat. I know it drives him crazy, but I feel silly sitting in the back of the car. "What has his panties in a knot today?" I ask.

"You, apparently," Christophe says in his delightful French accent. In addition to driving, Christophe is also Jaxson's bodyguard. I've heard rumors he was in the French Special Forces. I wouldn't mind a few days alone with him on the French Riviera — or even my little apartment.

"What else is new? He's always upset with me about something."

Christophe snorts. "You definitely get him going."

"I don't do it on purpose."

Christophe smiles. "I like you much better than Tessa."

"Wow. That's very kind of you. This is not at all the same kind of thing, but Tessa seems so nice and sweet to everyone. Her fans love her."

Christophe has signed the same NDA I have, and while he waits for Jaxson outside his office, he occasionally tells me things I normally wouldn't know, just because we can't talk to anyone else. "She is not what she seems," he informs me.

I nod, considering that. "They say you should never meet your idol."

He doesn't respond, and we ride in silence until he pulls up to the restaurant.

"Thanks for the lift," I tell him. "Do you think he's firing me today?"

Christophe smiles. "I don't think he'd take you to a fancy restaurant to fire you. You're safe for now."

"Darn it! Could have been my lucky day." I smile at him and wink.

Losing my job would *not* be a good thing. But, maybe today, I can talk to Jaxson about a career path that will take me back to graphic design. They have a huge graphics team at Honeycomb, and some of them are not that good if you ask me. Which absolutely no one is doing.

The hostess takes me to Jaxson's table, and he looks at his watch as I approach. "You're twenty minutes late."

"I can't be late to a meeting I didn't know I had," I say as I smooth the napkin in my lap.

There isn't a menu, so I guess I'm not eating. I take the pad of paper and a pen from my bag and look at him, ready to take notes.

"I ordered you the seafood salad," he says. "I notice you eat a lot of salads for lunch. You eat seafood, don't you?"

I nod. I love seafood. I'm from Boston, and my uncle works for a seafood distributor. But here in California, who can afford it? I'm lucky when tuna goes on sale and I can buy a few cans. "I like seafood. Thank you for ordering for me."

I can see why the women flock to Jaxson. His chin is chiseled, and his T-shirts show off some nice muscles. He's more than six feet two inches tall, and I know that because, in my best stilettos, he's still taller than me.

For a while, he looks everywhere in the room except at me. Finally, he seems to settle in. "When we first met, I thought you were someone different," he begins.

I snort. "Yeah, that was pretty obvious. We've been over this." I've wondered a few times if whoever he thought I was ever showed up to meet him. He doesn't seem to have a girlfriend—fake or otherwise.

"Honeycomb's board of directors has been unhappy since my breakup with Tessa Sky," he continues. "It doesn't help that last week she gave several tabloids recordings of our phone calls, which I never knew she'd made."

I nod sympathetically. He's getting a lot of attention, and it's been several months. If the feeding frenzy slows down for even a minute, something else pops up.

Jaxson clears his throat. "When we met, the board had given me direction to find someone to settle down with."

I snort. So typically male. Like that's a simple thing to do. I guess that's why he was willing to go the fake route. "How can I help you with that?" I ask. I'm not sure I'm ready to be his wing woman, but I can try to do what he needs.

"I'm glad you asked," he says with a nervous grin.

He'd better not expect me to ask women the questions he asked me.

"I've tried working with a service, but they've not been able to provide me with anyone I like. I need someone who is discreet and willing to be my fake girlfriend. It would mean she goes places with me and is photographed with me. Eventually, we'll get engaged and possibly married. And there would, of course, be generous benefits. Beyond living in my house in Pacific Heights, I can offer a generous clothing allowance, bonuses, trips, and whatever else might be required."

I frantically take notes. I don't know who he thinks I know. We work a ton of hours right beside each other, so it's not like I have a vast network of friends and outside resources I'm keeping up with.

When he stops talking, I look up at him. He seems to be waiting for me to say something.

Thankfully, our meals arrive. My salad is so big that I'll take probably three-quarters of it home. Jaxson's plate has an entire fish.

"What did you get?" I ask, grateful for the change in topic.

"I went with the sable fish in a white wine sauce."

Without asking, I steal a bite from his plate and moan my satisfaction. He knows he owes me. "That is amazing."

He lifts his plate. "Do you want mine instead?"

"Nope. The salad is perfect." I take a bite, and it too is heavenly, with a lemon vinaigrette that's delicious with the seafood. "I can see why you like this place. The food is amazing."

He has a strange look on his face.

"What? Do I have food on my chin?"

43

"No, I'm just waiting to hear what you think of my proposal."

"Oh. I don't really know anyone who seems right, but I can look around."

His brow furrows. "I'm not *looking* for anyone. I was thinking it could be you."

My bite of salad goes down wrong, which leads to a nasty coughing fit. By the end of it, eyes all over the restaurant are staring. I wipe my mouth and try some water. "What?"

Jaxson leans in. "You know everything there is to know about me. You're beautiful, smart, and it would be believable."

I shake my head, brushing right past his compliments. "No, it wouldn't. I don't think this is a good idea."

"I will give you five thousand shares of Honeycomb stock, which will make you a millionaire when we go public in a few months."

My eyes pop wide.

"And you can move out of that cockroach-infested apartment. I'll buy you clothes and jewelry, which you can keep. I know you have a school loan. I've seen the paperwork on your desk. I'll pay that off too."

All I can do is shake my head for a moment. "Why would you want to do this with me? You don't even like me."

He looks confused. "I like you just fine. Why do you think that?"

"Because you're always upset with me." I look down at my lunch, which no longer seems appealing. *What on Earth is happening?* I don't even know how to evaluate this offer. "I don't know."

"What will it take for you to say yes?"

My mind goes right to what I truly want and what he promised, yet every time I've mentioned it, he steers me away. "I want a job on the graphic design team."

"But you're so good as my assistant."

44

"You promised me — on the sidewalk when you showed up at my place. I didn't spend all that money in art school to be an admin."

He sits back. "How about when it's all over, I finance you for a freelance business and work on getting you a list of clients?"

"Why can't I work for Honeycomb? You need better designers."

"I don't disagree, but if we're in a relationship, it isn't fair to put a manager between us. They'll never succeed."

"I have to think about it."

"Come on, Harper. You could move your things over this afternoon and stay in the guest room in my house."

"That seems extreme."

"Look, people do these things all the time. Let's examine the pros and cons."

Of course he knows how I make big decisions.

"The pros? You will live rent free and have someone who cooks and cleans for you."

"A con is being at your beck and call twenty-four hours a day," I point out. And that's a big con.

"Another pro is that you'll make good money and have zero expenses," he counters. "Think of all the things you can do with the raise you'll get."

"A con is that you and I will forever be linked. I'll always be known as the rebound from Tessa Sky."

Jaxson picks up his fork. "Okay, in three years you'll be a millionaire and able to afford almost any house you want in the Bay Area. You'll also have a thriving graphic design business."

"Three years?" I gasp. "I'll be putting my life on hold to further yours?"

He puts his knife and fork down. "What will you be waiting to do?"

"What if I want to have kids?"

Jaxson turns green.

"Well… We haven't talked about your expectations there. When I met you the first time, you were looking for an intimate relationship."

He holds up his hand. "This is different. She was a *professional* girlfriend."

"I guess that's one way to say it. Will you visit professional girlfriends often? I mean, if we're supposed to be in love, how is that going to look when you get caught?"

"There are plenty of discreet agencies I could work with."

I blanch at the thought. "That's gross. And you already told me the agencies aren't working for you."

"I've never used one for, uh, short-term purposes." I swear he might be blushing. "I just hear people talk about them. Look, the ugly side of being successful is that you sometimes want the release but not the commitment. If it's more transactional from the beginning, everyone is on the same page."

"It's still gross."

"What do I need to do to make you say yes? More money? More stock options?"

"If we're boyfriend and girlfriend, that means you'll need to meet my family and attend family events, like my brother's wedding next month."

He nods. "That seems appropriate."

He gave in to that too easily. "I need to think about it."

"I thought we'd detour by my house on the way back to the office. You can see the room you'd be staying in."

"You're playing dirty."

He smiles. "Maybe a little."

He picks up his fork again, and while we eat, I steer us far away from any more discussion about his request. Instead, we talk about work, and he shares his frustration with our sales numbers.

"Do you think it's still Tessa Sky and her fans?"

He shakes his head. "I don't know. Spy Game is our next release, and with all the bugs, it isn't resonating with some of the advance players we've given it to. Have you played it?"

I shake my head. "I can't afford to play games."

"As an employee, you should have an account that allows you to play any of our games without cost."

"Oh. Well, I guess I can try it out."

A little while later, we finish our lunch and walk out to the car. I fight the urge to sit with Christophe and instead join Jaxson in the back this time. Without any instructions, Christophe drives us to Jaxson's home. It's on Broderick Street, and the view of the Golden Gate Bridge and the Bay are beautiful. The weather is also fantastic, which makes this all seem so romantic.

Except it's not. I look over at my boss and wonder why I would even consider something like this. But I know why. The money he's talking about would pay all of my brothers' and sisters' college loans. And I could fix up my parents' home, make sure they actually take a vacation sometime. There's so much that money could help with.

Jaxson leads me into his house. An older woman appears as we enter the foyer.

"Helen, this is Harper Lockwood," Jaxson says.

Her face lights up, and I can tell I'm going to like her. "Welcome," she says. "Please let me know if you need anything."

"Thank you."

I follow Jaxson up the stairs. The view continues to be nice. His home is fairly masculine and contemporary. It doesn't look lived in at all.

On the second floor, he opens the door to a white room. It's beautiful, but there isn't a speck of color anywhere. The bed has a cherry headboard, but it's mostly covered by decorative white pillows. There's a white leather couch, a white desk and chair, and a white dresser and side tables.

"I'd need to sleep with sunglasses on," I quip.

"You are welcome to redecorate however you want. No limit on a budget."

He really wants me here.

He shows me the ensuite bathroom, and it too is all white. "Your designer really likes white."

"My sister was getting her feet wet in decorating. She lives in Michigan, close to my parents."

Oh God. Now, I've insulted his sister. I'm a train wreck around this guy. "Good to know. I wouldn't want to insult her."

"She did better with my room."

We step back out of the bathroom, and Jaxson opens the shutters. The view stops me short. I look north to Alcatraz and the North Bay, and east I can see downtown and Berkeley. "That's not fair," I tell him.

He smiles.

Next, he walks me across the hall to show me his room. It looks a little more lived in, but it's still incredibly neat. It's also rather close to the guest room. That sends butterflies flitting around my stomach. But I don't have much time to worry about that because next on the tour are his home office, his game room, the indoor gym, which has more equipment than the Y, and a movie room. "You can use any of these things," he assures me.

This house is incredible. But I still don't know what to make of all of this or even exactly what he's proposing. It would certainly help me financially, but it's a lot.

When we're back in the foyer, he looks at me expectantly. "What do you think?"

"I honestly don't know." I look around. "Where is your red room of pain?"

His brow furrows.

"You know, where you keep the whips, canes, and handcuffs."

He nods knowingly. "That's a secret."

I chuckle.

"Please think about it," he says, his smile fading. "I have the utmost respect for you, and this is not intended to take advantage of you in any way. This entire relationship would be mapped out in a legal document. No surprises."

CHAPTER 5

Jaxson

Harper walks into my office with my Friday-morning coffee. She's been avoiding me all week, so this is one of the only times I'll likely see her today. And that's unfortunate. I need her to be willing to spend more time with me, not angling for less.

She gives me a curt smile, sets the cup on my desk, and disappears right back out the door.

Just like the first time, when I did it by accident, it was probably a mistake to ask her for what I did. But I really think she's my best option—and possibly my only hope. Over the last few weeks, I've met with three women Sarah sent me, but none of them interested me enough to pursue even a fake relationship. Plus, despite Sarah's assurances about professionality, they wanted more than I'm willing to give. I never even broached the subject of sex, but they were looking for me to pay generously, open some doors for them, and one made it clear that we wouldn't need a prenup. That's a red flag if I ever heard one.

Even Laura, who I did finally connect with last week, was a disappointment. For a senator's daughter, she wasn't very polished. Sarah said she got lost getting to the Fairmont, which I find hard to believe, so I think she might have chickened out the first time. Regardless, she wasn't right for this job.

I think I might be comparing them all to Harper, honestly. She's the best assistant I've ever had, and I know her heart isn't even in it. She has talents that go way beyond managing my schedule. But she does it with a smile, and despite all the hours we spend together each week, I continue to enjoy her company.

And, when I allow myself to think of her that way, which I try not to, she's gorgeous. Her laugh is a melody, and she makes everything she wears seem so sexy. She's the right person to help me navigate this ridiculous situation with my board of directors, but I'm at a loss as to how to convince her to make the leap.

In the meantime, if Grantham Wilks doesn't stop pestering me about it, I'm going to lose my mind. I'm meeting with the guys tonight to strategize some more.

My phone rings, and I practically jump, I'm so lost in my thoughts. "Hello?" I answer.

"Hey, baby bro," my sister, Ava, says. "What's poppin'?"

She's the mother of three teenage boys and tries to keep up with the lingo. It often goes right over my head.

"The sky hasn't fallen yet."

She laughs. "I was in the supermarket today, and you're still dominating the headlines. I like the latest transcription of your phone calls. Tessa Sky sounds like a whiner, and you weren't putting up with that."

I groan. "Every time I think this is about to fade away, she does something that puts it right back in the tabloids."

"My kids love it. They tell everyone they were that close to greatness."

I snort. "Greatness? She only has six Grammys."

Ava laughs. "Yes, only. And you own one of the most popular gaming companies, at least for now."

"I know. Spy Game isn't yet ready for release, which is a huge problem. Between that and Tessa Sky, it's going to kill our IPO."

"I have three kids going to college," Ava reminds me. "You gotta fix this because I'm counting on my stock options." She and my parents each have five thousand shares. It was the least I could do. After Zack Villefort pushed Grayson, Nick, and me out of Quick Reels, I went into a serious funk. Ava and my parents supported me while I licked my wounds, but when I was ready to move on, they wouldn't take any money. Fortunately, they did take shares.

"Even if the IPO isn't as strong as we would like, I'm pretty sure you won't have any problem paying for college," I assure her.

"And to think of all the years I took you out for lunch at Taco Bell," she muses.

"Who would have thought all that generosity could manifest into millions of dollars in stock?"

"I really just wanted to check on you." Ava's voice turns soft and caring. "I know you broke up with this woman months ago, but have you talked to her at all?"

"*She* broke up with me, and no, I haven't spoken to or texted with her. She's not interested in being reasonable. And anyway, I'm seeing someone else." I lie too easily.

"Your new woman must be a saint. But maybe if you talk to Tessa, you could get her to back off."

"I probably need to call a lawyer. My board is going crazy over this."

"I'm sorry, and here I am putting pressure on you about my options, which you kindly gifted me."

"Don't worry about it," I assure her. "I know you're only teasing."

"Well, if you need to get away or want to bring this mysterious new woman to meet us, you know where we are."

"I *don't* know. Do you still live at the same address, or have you moved uptown?" I tease.

She laughs. "You have no idea. I'm painting the living room with actual gold."

I cringe and give her a belly laugh. She lives in a small ranch, which is stuffed full of kids, their endless video gaming devices, toys, games, two dogs, a cat, and her husband. No gold for her. Her house was the perfect place to stay when I fell apart after Quick Reels. I slept on the floor on an air mattress in my youngest nephew's room and figured out my first game, Chocolate Crush.

"Well, enjoy your golden room."

"Have a great day," she singsongs. "Come visit us soon."

"I'll try." We disconnect, and I call out to Harper's desk with the intercom. "Can you please come in here?"

"Yes, sir."

Watching her enter my office—today she's wearing a pencil skirt and a men's white shirt—just sets me off. "Close the door, please."

She hesitates, and I can tell she's nervous. After closing the door, Harper sits down across from me, ready with a pad and paper.

"What's it going to take?" I ask.

Her brows jump. "Excuse me?"

"What can I do to convince you to sign a contract?"

She sighs. "I don't know. I'd be lying to everyone, and I'm not a liar by nature."

I purse my lips. That she's not asking for more money further convinces me she's the right person for the job. "Do you know about my relationship with Quick Reels?" I ask.

She shakes her head and gives me a skeptical look.

"My two best friends and I founded Quick Reels. We were young and stupid when we got our funding, and in our excitement, we signed a bad contract. It had a stipulation that said they could terminate us and we'd lose our stock options if we violated an ethics clause. And sure enough, that's what happened. Grayson Blackstone, who was the CEO, was accused of assaulting a coworker he never touched. Nick Maywood, our CFO, was pulled over for a DUI, which was later dismissed, and I was accused of harassing an employee I was in a consensual relationship with."

Harper's eyes grow wide.

"The venture capitalist who funded us in exchange for forty percent of the business brought us all into a room and explained that we were being fired and losing all of our interest in the company. We'd given that work almost ten years of our life, and we have nothing to show for it."

"That's awful," she gasps.

I'm grateful she agrees because it was shitty and below the belt. "My new funding agreement has nothing like that in it, but I have a board of directors who hate watching Tessa Sky and me continue showing up in the tabloids three months after we broke up. She's had us in the tabloids longer than we dated."

Harper looks out the window, and I can see her wheels turning.

"I see this as a business arrangement," I continue. "But I really need your help. I think I'm out of other options. We don't have to sleep together, and I know you're someone I can trust. The board is nervous. I need to look like a normal guy, not some whipping boy for a pop star. I need to show the world I've moved on. So I'll ask again. What will it take for you to commit to being my fake girlfriend?"

Harper shakes her head. "That's the easy part. It's the lying to my family and to everyone else when we get married."

"It may not come to that," I remind her.

"But the option is there."

I nod. "I know this is asking a lot, and there's really no way around the secrecy. If it were ever to get out that this was a ruse from the beginning, it would affect the stock prices for sure."

She sighs. "I've read the contract you sent over. I figured as much."

"How about this..." I think for a moment. "You move into my place. We announce to the company that we're seeing each other. That should make things calm down with Tessa. Then we'll get engaged. I'll buy you a stunning diamond from Cartier or wherever you want. We'll announce our engagement and ride out the IPO, and then we'll quietly break up. I'll set you up with an apartment here or wherever you want to live, and I'll make sure you have some graphic design clients to start with and several million in the bank."

"I don't care about the money—" She stops herself. "Okay, some money would be a big help to my family. But why won't you let me work for Honeycomb's graphics department?"

"I can protect you better if you're outside my office, and I'm offering you much more by setting you up with several clients."

She shuts her eyes and tilts her head to the ceiling. "You said this is a six-month commitment. Or is it three years?"

"I suspect six months would be the minimum and three years maximum. It could be less."

"Why up to three years?"

"Because I don't know how long it's going to take for everything to calm down and my board to feel Honeycomb is on secure footing."

"And you don't think we'll need to get married?"

"I'm not taking it completely off the table, but you'll be involved in deciding if we need to go there."

She looks at me carefully. "My family doesn't believe in divorce, so that has to be a hard no."

I wish I could be certain it wasn't necessary because I'd rather we not marry too. Makes everything so much more complicated. But for now, I just agree. "Okay. I understand. We can write that in and initial it."

"I want to tell one person, my best friend."

"Okay, as long as she'll sign an NDA and you trust her. I'll also tell my best friends, Gray and Nick. They have NDAs because of their Honeycomb stock options. And the board will know."

She stands. "I'll review the contract, make the changes, and get it back to you. One of my older brothers is getting married next month. You'll come with me?"

"I will."

"I've brought no one home before," she warns me. "My brothers will be tough on you."

"I'm up for the challenge," I assure her. "So I'll send movers for your things tomorrow."

She looks back at me and slowly nods.

"You won't regret this," I promise. "You're going to love this so much you'll fall in love with me."

She laughs. "Don't make promises you can't keep."

"Promise you won't fall in love with me," I call after her.

While I spend the rest of the afternoon working, I have Christophe make plans for movers to get Harper's things. I also call Nordstrom and request a personal shopper to select some clothes that will be delivered to my house. I love Harper's style, and I want to show her how much she'll enjoy this.

When seven o'clock rolls around, Harper sticks her head into my office. "I'm going to meet my friend Amy for dinner. I'll see you tomorrow. Christophe says the movers will be at my place by ten."

"Are you giving Amy the NDA and telling her about our plan?"

She nods. "Yes. She's my closest friend. I already told you I'd be telling her."

I nod but raise a brow at her.

"I won't tell her everything. I know I signed the NDA. Your rough sex will remain a secret. I'll only give her the broad strokes. That way, if I kill you in your sleep, she can testify on my behalf. Plus, she agreed to sign the NDA."

"Okay. I don't know this woman. Please be careful. If she were to go to the tabloids, this could blow up."

"If you can trust your friends, plural, then you can trust my friend."

I dip my chin in acceptance. "Tomorrow, since it's Saturday, I'll work from home, so I'll be there when you arrive. And I'll get us reservations for dinner somewhere nice to celebrate."

She nods. "Okay."

"Harper, this is going to be fun," I assure her as she moves toward the door. She gives me a tight smile, and I can tell she doesn't believe me. I'm determined to change her mind.

After she leaves, I pack up and head over to Bourbon and Branch to meet the guys. This place is always fun, and they have a revolving menu of creative cocktails — if you're into that sort of thing. What I like most is that you need a password to come in, and you can't use your cell phone. That affords plenty of privacy.

"We were going to send a search party out for you," Nick says as I slide into the booth next to him.

"Where's Scarlett?" I ask Gray.

"She'll be here a little later. She's getting the kids taken care of and doesn't want to hear all our moaning."

"I don't want to hear it either," Nick says.

We all chuckle.

"Did you get your problem figured out?" Gray asks me.

I nod. "I did." Thankfully we won't have to hash out another potential plan this evening.

"Are you sure your admin is the right person? I mean, wouldn't someone professional be better?"

I shrug. "None of the women I met through the agency seemed very professional to me. They all had an angle. When I offered Harper more money to sign the deal, she said she didn't want more money. She's worried about lying to everyone."

"Whoa," Gray says. "She sounds like a keeper."

"Let's not get ahead of ourselves," I correct.

"What are you going to do if she turns into a stalker?" Nick says.

I shrug. "Maybe then I'll get laid."

"Wait. This is business only?" Nick asks.

The server puts a glass of bourbon I didn't order in front of me. *Did she get the wrong table?*

"That's the Old Rip Van Winkle twenty-five-year Kentucky straight bourbon," Gray explains. "I figured you were on the way, so she was holding it until you arrived."

I lift the glass in toast as I thank him, and we settle in to catch up for a bit. Nick has been dating Olivia for over a year, and she gives me the same vibe as the women Sarah presented me with. To be blunt, Olivia's a gold-digger, out to get what she can from Nick. He's bought her an engagement ring, and he said he was planning to propose on some vacation she wanted. But that was a while ago. Now, I don't know what's happening. We're trying to be supportive, but Gray, Scarlett, and I are not fans.

"Olivia and I are leaving for Napa in the morning," he announces. "We'll do some wine tasting and exploring this weekend."

"Are you going to propose?" Gray asks, as if reading my mind.

Nick seems uncomfortable. "Probably not. I don't know. Something feels a little off. She hinted at it, which is why I bought the ring, but since then, she's not brought it up, and she keeps changing her mind about when we can do the over-water villa in Fiji. That's where I was going to propose. I don't know what to think."

"You think she's going to break up with you?" I ask. I don't think she'd go without a settlement. She moved into his house after the third date, and she seems constantly unhappy.

"No. I think we're just having a dry period. This weekend will be our chance to reconnect. If it goes well, I'll get back on planning that trip to propose."

"And if it doesn't?"

"I guess the ring will remain in the back of my safe."

"I know you're not asking me," Gray says, "but if you're this blasé about getting married to her, you shouldn't do it. You should only propose to a woman you can't live without, and you know she can't live without you."

CHAPTER 6

Harper

I open my eyes this morning and realize immediately that my head is killing me. Amy and I had too many drinks at Martini Happy Hour last night. I think everything was fine until we came back here to go over the contract. We opened a bottle of wine after too many cosmos, and we talked about it until way too late.

I had her sign the NDA, and I wrote all the things Jaxson and I discussed into the contract. But then I didn't sign it.

Amy thinks I should. She says if it ends up that I can't take it, I can walk away. It's not like he'll sue me—too much publicity. So I'm not sure why I'm hesitating. I can do this, right? It's just like the other work I've been doing lately—not my dream job, but it's going to be a huge financial win for my family. I just feel overwhelmed.

My stomach rolls, and I wonder if I'm going to need to run for the toilet. I take a deep breath and look at the clock. It's already after nine. Christophe is going to be here in less than an hour, and I have done nothing to pack. Should I even be moving?

Suddenly, I'm feeling a little panicky. But then a roach scuttles across the floor. *Ugh.* Jaxson wants me to move in, and I want some sense of whether this can work. Like Amy said, maybe being with him in his own space is a good way to try it out?

I take another deep breath, and my stomach feels a bit calmer. I can do this. I don't have much to move, so it won't be hard to undo if I have to. This apartment was furnished, so it's just a few personal items and my clothes.

One decision made, I drink a large glass of water with four Advil, hoping they'll kick in sooner rather than later. Food is not appealing right now, so I pull out my suitcase and start loading my things. I'm mostly interested in packing up my underwear. I hate the idea of strangers touching them. I pack them in Ziplock bags when I fly in case someone needs to open my bag. I shudder at the thought of someone touching them. *Gross.*

I dress in my favorite gray fleece pants and a comfortable Boston College sweatshirt my brother got when he was there, and after organizing a few more things, I'm as ready as I'll ever be. At exactly ten o'clock, there's a knock at my front door.

I open it to find Christophe with two giant men standing behind him. "I told you I don't have any furniture."

He nods. "They have some boxes for your hanging things, and many hands make light work."

"I packed the clothes that were in the dresser and my toiletries."

"Great." Christophe nods again, and the men head inside.

We take less than an hour to empty the apartment of my things and get them loaded. I feel silly that they have a giant truck for my dozen boxes.

I ride with Christophe over to Jaxson's.

"You know, you're going to have to sit in the backseat," he tells me on the way.

"Why?" I ask. I don't want to be that person.

"Well, now that you're dating Mr. Bancroft, you need to be safer."

"What does sitting in the back have do with my safety? I'm closer to the air bags here."

"True, but in the front seat, you're visible."

"Who's going to care about me?"

"Anyone trying to get to Mr. Bancroft."

I sigh. I don't think Jaxson has any enemies, but I guess just being successful makes him an enemy to some. "Okay. I hear you. I'll try to be better, but know that I don't believe I should have to sit in the back and would rather be sitting with you."

"Duly noted."

When we arrive, Christophe pulls around to the alley and parks in the garage. "We'll get your things up to your room. Welcome to Broderick Street."

I get out of the car and walk into the mudroom behind the kitchen. The guys have already unloaded most of my things and are delivering them to my room.

Jaxson watches them bring it in. "That's it?"

I shrug. "My apartment was furnished, and I arrived in San Francisco with a single suitcase, so I have a lot more than what I came with two years ago."

He pulls four crisp hundred-dollar bills. "Thanks for your help, guys."

The two giant guys light up as they accept the money. "Anytime," they say in unison.

After the door closes behind them, I stand next to Jaxson, not sure what to do. "Well, I guess I should go unpack."

"Catherine from Nordstrom will be here after lunch to go through some clothes she's picked out for you."

"What?" I ask, feeling my eyes go wide.

"I promised I would buy you clothes, and she's going to bring some options — work clothes, some clothes to go out in, and a few other things you might need. We'll be able to augment as we go, and then when summer arrives in a few months, we'll start over."

"That's not really necessary."

He shoves my shoulder. "You're doing me a solid. It's the least I can do."

"Okay…" My mom taught me to sew, and I love doing it, so I've made a lot of my dresses. I'm not sure what someone would pick for me. How is she going to know what size I am? Jaxson is still looking at me, so I force a smile. I'm not going to worry about it.

"Helen will have lunch ready shortly," he says. "She makes a wonderful tomato soup with grilled cheese sandwiches, and we have a reservation at seven this evening at Sotto Mare."

"I don't know that place, but I'm sure it will be fantastic. And Helen's lunch sounds perfect."

I walk upstairs and begin to unpack the boxes. Just as I'm finishing up in the bathroom, Helen knocks on the door frame. "Lunch is ready when you want to come down."

"Oh perfect. I'm almost to a stopping place."

"Take your time."

"I'm sorry if I'm disrupting your routine."

She makes a funny face. "It will be nice to have you here. Mr. Bancroft doesn't require much, and I love to cook. We can talk this week about what you like to eat."

I smile. "I'm not picky. I grew up with seven brothers and sisters. We learned that we'd go hungry if we didn't eat what was served."

"Eight kids? Wow! Where did you grow up?"

"The south shore of Massachusetts, in Weymouth."

"I don't know that area."

"It's not far from Boston."

I walk with Helen downstairs, and we chat easily. She's from eastern Oregon and has a sister who lives in Los Angeles. She's worked for Mr. Bancroft since he bought the house during his days at Quick Reels.

When we reach the dining room, Helen disappears. Jaxson is at the table, looking at his phone.

"Oh, I'm sorry. I didn't realize you were waiting for me."

"That's okay," he says.

I don't know what he wants from me, so I hesitate.

"Please sit with me. I promise I'll only bite if you ask me to."

I smirk. "I suppose Helen and Christophe know what's going on?"

"If you're wondering what I said to them, it wasn't much. I told them you'd be moving into the guest room."

"Christophe mentioned me being your girlfriend, so he's pieced a few things together."

"He and Helen are both discreet. You have nothing to worry about."

I smooth the napkin on my lap. "Thank you." I slurp a spoonful of soup and moan. "This is so good."

Jaxson's spoon is halfway to his mouth. He's frozen in place.

"Sorry." I wipe my mouth with my napkin.

"No... You're fine."

My stomach flutters. Part of my hesitancy about doing this goes beyond the idea of the contract. I'm insanely attracted to this man. I've replayed our first meeting in my mind so many times, and I know I could easily make a mess of this. I need to keep my wits about me and be careful.

"What do you like to do with your weekends?" I ask.

"I work, work out, hang with friends, and date a bit."

I snort. "A bit?"

He shrugs. "You can't believe everything you read in the tabloids."

"I haven't signed the contract yet."

"I'm painfully aware of that." His eyes bore into me.

I take a small bite of the sandwich, holding myself back from inhaling the delicious ooey-gooeyness in three big mouthfuls. "What are you going to do about your dating life?"

He shrugs. "Go out with you. What are you planning?"

"Oh, I wasn't planning on dating anyone. I was... We didn't... You know..."

He smirks. "You mean we didn't define the intimate aspect of our relationship?"

How can he be so direct? Of course I mean that, but it's more than that. "You're my boss—at work and now at home, too."

He stops with a wedge of the grilled cheese inches from his mouth. "Yes, and I'm guessing you're even less cooperative at home than you are at work."

"I think that's a fair assumption." I take another bite, and in no time, I've finished the last of my lunch.

Jaxson looks at his watch. "Catherine should be here any moment."

"Is she just going to look at my style and take measurements?"

He shakes his head. "No, I gave her your sizes and some parameters of what you need."

There's so much to unpack in what he's just said. He knew my sizes, and he wants to dress me?

"Before you get worked up, I guessed on the sizes," he continues, likely reading my face. "I told her about your penchant for floral-print dresses. We have a nice dinner tonight, a fundraiser in a few weeks, and your family wedding. As part of the contract, I agreed to buy you clothes."

"Do you have right of approval on these clothes?"

"I wasn't planning on it. Would you like my approval?" His eyes twinkle.

I laugh. "I wouldn't want to embarrass you."

He nods. "You could wear a burlap sack, and I wouldn't bat an eye."

"What's my spending limit?"

He tilts his head. "Buy whatever you want. I assure you, I can afford it."

The doorbell rings before I can reply.

Christophe appears in the doorway and looks at Jaxson. "Ms. Catherine Collins from Nordstrom has arrived."

"Send her up to my room. There's privacy in the closet for Harper to dress, and I can sit on the couch in the sitting area."

Christophe nods, and a moment later, Catherine walks in. Christophe and another gentleman pass by behind her, taking four racks of clothes and multiple boxes upstairs.

She extends her hand to me. "Good afternoon. It's so nice to meet you."

Helen appears and raises her brow curiously.

"Let's go upstairs and see what Catherine brought," I suggest.

Helen smiles. "I'm sure you can handle that all on your own. Catherine, would you like something to drink?"

She shakes her head. "I'm good. I'm terribly clumsy, and I'd hate to spill anything on the clothes."

I suppress a giggle. This is my kind of lady. We head upstairs to Jaxson's bedroom, and it feels a bit strange being in here. He's sitting on a brown leather sofa, as if he's about to watch a show. I guess he sort of is.

Catherine claps her hands together. "Okay, right here, we have everyday wear. How do these look to you?" She shows me a pair of white linen pants and a pink floral blouse. She then opens a box with a nude stiletto sandal inside.

This is something I would choose for myself. Stepping into the closet and away from Jaxson's view, I change into the clothes. At least I have on one of my prettier bra and panty sets. Everything seems to fit perfectly.

When I come back out, Catherine has set up some mirrors. Jaxson looks up.

"What do you think?" I ask.

"That looks great on you."

I nod. "Okay, I'll put this in the possible pile. I love these sandals, though."

Jaxson's eyes heat. I think he likes them too.

I try on three more casual outfits, and I like them all. It's going to be hard to pick just one.

"Catherine, you have an amazing eye," I tell her. I look over at Jaxson. "And I don't want to know how you guessed so well on what sizes I wear."

The corners of his mouth turn up.

Catherine takes out some evening wear next, and I gravitate to a black dress, nice and understated — until I realize it has slits that go essentially to my hip. Catherine must notice my shock and suggests a simple light blue gown instead.

Once I have it on, I'm pleased with how it looks, but Jaxson shakes his head.

"It's okay. I know you like it, but what else did she bring?"

I try on a pink strapless dress, but it has a train, and we all agree that at a fundraiser I'd be dealing with people stepping on it all night.

Catherine hands me the black dress. "I think we have to try this one. Can I help you put it on? It's a little tricky at first."

"Sure." When we get to the closet, she takes it off the hanger and I can see that there are two pieces of chiffon fabric that make giant loops from waist to shoulder, leaving the back open — and much of the front. I can't wear a bra, and I'm not even sure about panties.

Catherine opens a package. "These are great," she says as she peels the backing from a pear-shaped piece of silicone. "Now, put this on your areola and use the tab to pull the breast up."

I struggle to understand what she's directing me to do and feel a bit silly.

"May I?" she asks.

"Sure."

In two quick moves, she has both the girls sitting nice and high. I slip the loops of fabric over my shoulders, and she hands me a pair of three-inch heels before helping strap me in. I want to hate this dress, but it's pretty damn sexy.

Jaxson takes one look at me and adjusts himself. "That's the one."

"Are you sure? The light blue one is more my speed."

"No. That's definitely the right one."

After that, we go through some dresses I could wear to the wedding, and I end up with several I like. I quickly change back into my own clothes and I walk out and find the gentleman who came with Catherine pushing out the racks with the clothes we agreed weren't working. She seems to be gathering all her things.

"Wait. I haven't decided which of these to keep," I say, gesturing to the rack with things I liked.

Catherine just smiles.

"I told her we'd take it all," Jaxson says.

That has to be several thousand dollars. "What? No. I don't need all these clothes."

Catherine steps over and points to a bag. "In here, you have matching panties and bra sets you might like. I enjoyed meeting you."

With that, she's gone.

I turn to Jaxson, still just sitting on the couch. "You didn't have to do that."

He shrugs. "I don't mind. And if you ever want to model what's in the last bag, I'm happy to give you my opinion on those, too."

I roll my eyes. "Keep dreaming."

"Trust me, I am."

I look around at everything he's bought me, and it's too much. This is all happening so fast. My heart races.

"You should wear the white pants and pink blouse tonight. You look beautiful in that."

"Umm…thanks."

He finally rises. "I'll give you some time to get settled. See you downstairs about six."

He descends the stairs, leaving me standing in his bedroom. When I woke up this morning, this was not how I envisioned my day.

I take the racks across the hall and slowly look through the clothes as I hang them in the closet. These are designers I've only seen in magazines. They're almost too nice to wear. When I've put them all away, I sort through the lingerie — La Perla, Agent Provocateur, and Fleur du Mall. These are so far outside of my price range. But they're so pretty and soft.

I look over at the clock. I have two hours before I need to be ready. I might as well go all out.

CHAPTER 7

Jaxson

Our reservation isn't for an hour, but I can feel myself getting anxious. I don't know what's bothering me. Everything is going great. Harper moved in this morning, she seemed pleased with the clothes, and we're on track to go to dinner and begin rehabbing my reputation. The contract makes it clear she'll live in my house, but we'll lead separate lives and make social appearances together. That's exactly what's happening.

Though she still hasn't signed the damned thing. Is that what has me all in knots? I have to believe we're on the right track there too. She wouldn't have bothered to move if she wasn't planning to sign it. Right?

I pace in the front room. Music plays faintly upstairs, but I can't make out what it is. Then it goes silent. *She's on her way.* My stomach flutters. I take a deep breath, and I wait. And wait some more.

Where is she?

I glance at my watch. We're cutting it close. Restaurants in San Francisco run tight kitchens. They'll fill our table with a walk-in if we're even ten minutes late. I mean, that's never happened to me. But it could happen. I should let her know.

"Harper? We need to go, or we won't make our reservation."

After a moment, she appears at the top of the stairs, and my breath catches in my throat. She looks amazing, like herself times ten. How is that even possible?

"I can't find my purse," she explains.

"You don't need your purse."

"What if they card me or something?"

I raise an eyebrow. She's not that young. Plus, she'll be with me. That will never happen. "I think you're fine."

She walks down carrying one of the new handbags. "I thought you said you couldn't find your purse."

"This just has my lipstick. I meant the purse I brought over here. I don't even have a key to the house."

"You shouldn't need one. Christophe will always have one."

"What if I want to go out with Amy?"

"Christophe will take you and bring you back."

She rolls her eyes.

My cock stiffens. *Shit.* What is wrong with me? "Don't roll your eyes at me."

"The contract doesn't say I won't have a personal life."

Keep it professional, I remind myself. "I'll get you a key."

"Thank you." She bows her head slightly and walks past me.

Christophe is waiting for us outside. He opens the door, and she gives him a brilliant smile as she slides in, which he returns.

I glare at him, and his smile disappears.

The restaurant isn't far, but traffic is terrible. We inch along, and I look at my watch. Our reservation is in three minutes, and we've just passed the busiest road, but we still have to make our way up Nob Hill to Sotto Mare. It's going to be close.

I take a deep breath and try to distract myself. "Have you eaten at Sotto Mare before?"

71

She shakes her head. "No. This will be my first time. Any recommendations?"

"No, but I don't think I've had a bad meal there."

When we pull up, I jump out and take Harper's hand as we walk in. "Sorry," I tell the hostess. "Getting across Van Ness was hard this evening."

She nods. "Mr. Bancroft, we've held your table."

We follow her to a high-back booth in the corner. It offers wonderful privacy. With a typical date, I might take advantage of that, but that's not what this is. And anyway, Harper hasn't even signed the contract. I'm trying so hard not to put pressure on her to sign it, but I would feel a lot better about what we're doing if she would. I can't take another woman going to the tabloids about me. My reputation and my company can't take it either.

We sit down next to each other, bumping knees in the process. There's a spark of static, and we both jump. Harper laughs. What a great sound.

"I really like hearing you laugh like that," I tell her. "You should do it more often."

She smiles, and we pick up our menus. When the server arrives, I order us a bottle of pinot grigio.

"Everything looks so good." Harper takes a sip of her water.

"You'll love whatever you order."

She nods, still perusing. "The only problem is I'm a slob. I'm wearing white pants, and there's a chance I'll splash dinner across my lap."

I suppress a snort. "You have a napkin for your lap."

"Oh I know, but it was the running joke when I was growing up. My older brother used to ask if I was saving it for later."

This time I laugh. "Your brother sounds funny. Is it just the two of you?"

She chuckles. "There are eight of us."

"Eight?" I sputter.

The server arrives with our wine and pours me a taste. When I approve, he then pours a glass for Harper before topping off mine.

He asks if we're ready to order. Harper nods and looks at me.

When I gesture for her to go ahead, she orders the lobster ravioli.

"And I'll have the seafood risotto," I add.

The server disappears, and I turn back to Harper. "Where were we? Eight kids?"

"My parents are both good Catholics — and teachers. It's my oldest brother who's getting married next month. His fiancée was a friend of mine. They've been together since high school."

"How does someone find the person they're going to marry in high school?"

"I have no idea, but they did. They just seem to click. She's a teacher with my mom, and my brother works for a bank. It works for them. I bet she'll be pregnant by the end of the year."

I try to school my face and not show her my horror. "Did you grow up in Boston?" I ask.

She nods and reaches for her glass.

"You don't sound like you're from there."

"My mom teaches Language Arts, and she insists that there's an R in the alphabet."

I smile. "Everyone else in town must slaughter your name."

She nods sheepishly. "I respond to Happa."

"Where are you in the mix of kids?" I ask when I'm done laughing. "The second?"

"No, I'm fifth, and we're between the ages of fifteen to twenty-nine," she says. "What about you?"

"I have an older sister, Ava. She's married and lives with her husband and three boys outside of Detroit."

"Is that where you're from?"

I nod. "I went to high school in Troy. It's a northern suburb of Detroit. My dad worked on the assembly line at General Motors. My mom worked for Kelly Services."

"What's Kelly Services?"

"You know, Kelly Girls? The temp agency?"

Her eyes light up with recognition.

"Its world headquarters are not too far from where I grew up."

"How did you get into the tech world?" she asks.

"You haven't read all the articles on me?" I raise an eyebrow.

"I've read a few, but they never say the same thing. I'm looking for the truth."

"My mom would tell you I was one of those kids who took apart home appliances to figure out how they worked. I loved it. When I discovered the circuit boards had software, that was it for me. Nick and I were drunk one night in college, and we brainstormed Quick Reels. Gray was there, and he added the way to make it addictive with the psychology behind moving from reel to reel."

She nods. "People spend hours on Quick Reels."

My stomach flips with excitement, like it always does when I talk about this with someone who seems to get it. "The algorithm isn't static. Each video someone looks at adds to their information, and the program shows them more that fit their profile."

"It's like those books you read as a kid—Choose Your Own Adventure," she says. "The algorithm keeps revealing the adventure, and three hours later you've done nothing but watch videos."

"Exactly. After we lost the company, I went to my sister's house for a while, and I slept on the floor of one of my nephews' rooms. We talked a lot about the different games they were playing. They liked shoot-'em-up types, but that didn't go well with Ava. I started playing one of their Tetris games with them and got the idea for Chocolate Crush. I didn't have any funding, but somehow I got it off the ground on my own. After about six months, things took off, and I used that money to bring on a team of developers. When we were ready to expand to other games, I got venture capital funds—and a better contract this time," I add.

She laughs as the waiter arrives with our food. "Everything you touch becomes addictive—Tessa Sky, Quick Reels, Chocolate Crush. You know how to get into someone's soul."

She's looking into my eyes, and I'm sure she can see my soul. I look away, feeling a little off balance. "I wish I had the power you're describing. Nick, Grayson, and I have only figured out how to make software do that. And Tessa just craves publicity, regardless of whether it's good or bad."

Harper nods thoughtfully, and we start in on our food. It's good enough that we eat in silence for a few minutes.

"Look." Harper points to her leg, and there are three drops on her pants. "The napkin is perfectly across my lap. And yet the sauce was a magnet."

This woman is nothing like my usual dates. "We'll get the pants cleaned," I assure her. "And the spots are so small no one will notice."

She shakes her head, dabbing gently with the napkin. "I should have gone with fettuccine Alfredo so it would be less obvious."

I raise my wine glass to hers, and we continue eating. When we're entirely stuffed, the server takes our plates and offers dessert, but we pass. Instead, we head out to the car, and I ask Christophe to take us home.

"I thought we'd have a drink and work through the contract," I tell her on the way.

"What's there to work on?" she asks. "I've read through it, and I've told you I agree. I want to work in Honeycomb's graphic design group, which you promised, but now you have other ideas. There's nothing more to say."

"I want more for you than slaving away for a bunch of incels who will be rude as well as create a sexual harassment case for the company. I'm offering you something better than that."

"Yes, I understand," she says. "I'll sign it. I just don't want to talk about it."

"We still haven't discussed intimacy."

She looks at me, her eyes narrowed. "I won't be sleeping around with anyone. Don't worry. I won't be anywhere near the tabloids. This is a big job, and I'm taking it seriously."

That isn't what I meant, but I realize now it's a good thing she interpreted it that way. That's how I *should* have meant it. *Why do I insist on pushing things with her?* She looks out the window, and the back of the Suburban is suddenly twenty degrees colder.

"I appreciate that, but—"

"You're my boss, both at work and at home now. You don't have to worry about me."

Christophe opens the garage door and pulls in. As soon as we've come to a stop, Harper opens the door and exits.

My head falls back. *Where did I go wrong?* We were having such a nice time at dinner. Why am I even worried about this? Keep it simple. That's clearly what she wants. She said she'd sign the contract, and I have no reason not to believe her. I should quit pushing before I dig myself a bigger hole.

Christophe returns to the driver's seat after seeing Harper into the house. "Where to?"

I guess I am still sitting here. Doesn't seem like I'll be hanging out with Harper this evening. "How about the San Francisco Club?"

Christophe backs out of the garage and drives me over to the club. This place is a little snootier than I normally prefer, but Gray, Nick, and I got memberships back in the Quick Reels days because it's one place I can always drink in peace, without any prying eyes or unwanted company.

I text Gray and Nick.

Me: I'll be at the San Francisco Club if you want to meet me.

Nick: I'm on a date. How about tomorrow?

Gray: Scarlett and I just put the kids to bed. Tomorrow?

I look at the ceiling of the car. Looks like I'm a pity party of one.

Christophe drops me off, and I walk in, show my membership card, and sit at the bar. I've never been here on a Saturday night, so I'm surprised to see that most of the guys are old timers—like, over seventy. They're drinking and playing chess or cards.

The server arrives with a glass of good bourbon. I like that they know what I drink.

"Mr. Bancroft?" An older gentleman sits down next to me.

"Good evening. How can I help you?"

"I'm a friend of Mason Sullivan."

My ears perk up. Mason's investment firm, SHN, is Honeycomb's major funder, and he's on my board of directors.

"I thought you should know that Green Light Games is struggling. They need an infusion of money. You could make a move and bring them under Honeycomb's umbrella."

I look him over—diamond-encrusted Rolex and tailored suit. I shake my head. "I'm not interested in being involved with Zack Villefort. I trusted him once. And you know the old saying—first time shame on you, the second time shame on me."

He shakes his head. "You're misunderstanding. Villefort is looking to unload them, to take his money and run."

"And how do you know this?"

"I'm one of the board members for Green Light." He shakes his head. "Villefort's made some risky investments, and his house of cards is about to fall."

"If Mason Sullivan isn't interested, then neither am I."

"I believe Mason is coming to you about it this week. Running into you tonight was just luck."

I finish my drink. "Well, thank you for thinking of me."

"Just listen to what Mason says, and be open to the idea when you see him."

I manage another polite smile. *Not likely.* Zack Villefort has already profited from stealing ten years of my work. There's no way I'd let him anywhere near my company again.

I signal to Christophe that I'm ready to leave. He heads out, but the club doesn't allow cars to sit out front, so I'll have to wait for him to circle the block. I step outside and scroll through the names in my contacts. There are any number of women here I could call, and they'd come running. But that isn't particularly appealing. Also, I've just moved someone into my house.

I've got to walk the straight line until we go public. I've gone to all this trouble to do what the board wants. No reason to put it in jeopardy. Too bad Harper didn't end up being one of Sarah's professional ladies.

That thought sends my mind to a very dangerous place. Fortunately, Christophe pulls up, I get in the back of the car. "Let's go home."

He pulls away from the curb, and I rest my head on the back of the seat and watch the crowds go by. San Francisco is a wild mix of people—every color, size, and brand of crazy—but I love it here. The energy is on overdrive, and it's the place to be for what I do. I wouldn't live anywhere else.

When I come into the kitchen from the garage, I find Harper at the table, reading. She's changed into flannel sleep pants and a T-shirt, and I'm pretty sure she's not wearing a bra. She looks up at me. "Where did you go?"

"Out for a drink."

"I thought we were going to have one here."

I... Oh. Dammit. "I'm sorry," I begin, wondering how to explain this since I don't really get it myself. "I guess I don't know how to do this. I've never had a fake relationship before. And to be honest, I've never been out to dinner with a woman I didn't have sex with after."

"So you went and found someone else to have sex with?"

I can hear contempt in her voice.

"No. I went to a club I belong to—it's a men-only club, and I know I won't be bothered there. I thought you were done with me for the evening. I mean, I guess you should be done with me for the evening. We're not in public anymore."

She looks down at her lap. "Maybe this is a mistake. I can get my old apartment back."

"I don't want that. I want this to work."

"As a professional arrangement," she says. She can't look at me. I don't know what she's getting at.

"I, uh, I can't lose another company. When Villefort took Quick Reels from us, it broke us all in different ways. I can't go through that again. That's what's driving me to put on this big act. I know it's ridiculous, and I want you to be as comfortable as possible with the process, but I just need us to make it work."

She sighs. "I signed the contract and left it on your desk. If you don't like what I added, then cross it out. I'll live with your terms."

79

"Thank you. You won't be sorry. I'll help you any way I can, and you'll be financially set for the rest of your life."

"My goal is to cover my siblings' tuition debts and provide money for my younger brother and sister to go to school, and if there's anything left, it'll go to my parents."

I stop and look at her. "The contract gives you five thousand shares. That will be worth at least forty million dollars on the low end. You'll be able to do all of that and anything else you want to do."

Her eyes go wide. "I want to renegotiate."

My stomach drops. *Here it is, and there's likely no way out for me now.*

"I don't want your stock options. I want you to pay off my siblings' school loans and provide money for the two that still need to go. But that's it. Nothing more."

"What about you?"

"I don't want anything."

I don't know what to say to that. I'm not sure I've ever heard a woman I've gone out with — or who worked for me — say that before. I've just offered Harper a life without wanting for anything, and she's thinking about her family? Even if she did cross those things off in the contract, I know she's giving up a lot for me and I won't take advantage of her.

She stands and is halfway up the stairs before I can form a coherent thought. "I'm getting up to go running tomorrow morning, and I thought afterward we'd go over to the farmer's market."

She stops and turns around. "Are you asking me to join you?"

I nod. "You don't have to do the running part, but maybe the farmer's market. It's, ah, it's a good chance to be seen in public. Helen has a list of things she'd like, and I told her I'd get them."

"Oh, sure. And I'll go running with you."

I smile. "Are you sure?"

"If I'm too slow, you can always go on ahead."

"I usually run the three blocks over to the Lyon Street stairs, and then I run up and down once or twice."

"Oh, I'm totally down with that. Stairs are my thing."

"Great. What time? Seven? Eight?"

She looks at me. "If we're doing this for show, I would suggest that we want people to think we've been up half the night having sex. So going at eight is better."

I nod. I see where she's going with this. "You're not a morning person. You just want more time to sleep in."

She shrugs. "I work for this asshole who has me in the office twelve hours a day. My weekends are the only time I can sleep."

"See you at the base of the house stairs at eight. Christophe will most likely join us."

She nods.

"Goodnight."

"Goodnight," she says softly.

I watch her go up the stairs, feeling entirely disoriented, although once again, everything seems to be going to plan. My board will be thrilled. But this woman is going to drive me crazy.

CHAPTER 8

Harper

My eyes fly open, and I remember my alarm went off ten minutes ago. I jump up, splash some water on my face, get my hair into a ponytail, and put on running tights and a tank top. I looked up the Lyon Street stairs last night, and I shouldn't have any problem with them. The run over there is another story.

I'm not a very good runner. People talk about running in terms of being fast or slow, but I'm not either of those. I can't seem to run a straight line, and I stumble all the time. I can't explain it. I obviously have two left feet.

I walk downstairs with one eye open.

"Are you ready?" Jaxson asks, seeming wide awake.

"Barely," I say as he swings open the door to a beautiful, bright day. I hold up my hand. "Wait! I need sunglasses."

"Good thinking."

We both grab glasses and then head out, with Christophe behind us. I bump into Jaxson twice within the first few feet.

"I'm sorry. I'm terrible at running in a straight line."

Jaxson's brow furrows. "What?"

"I don't know why, but I can't run straight."

He throws his head back and laughs hard—I mean, really hard. I urge him to go on ahead, but he shakes his head. Somehow, we finally arrive at the Lyon Street stairs.

"Are you going to be okay on the stairs?" he asks at the top.

"I'm fine with stairs," I assure him. "Are you ready?"

"After you." He opens his arms.

The stairs are pretty busy, but we start down, and I count as I go. Three hundred thirty-two stairs.

Jaxson takes a big breath at the bottom. "Take these as you can. We're in no hurry."

I look back up to the top. "I take the stairs all the time at work. I'm ready."

He once again gestures for me to go ahead, so I take off. I don't sprint up the stairs, but I move quickly. I can hear Jaxson panting loudly behind me.

When I reach the top, I turn to see he's fallen back a bit. I wait for him with my hands on my knees, trying to catch my breath. "Ready to go again?" I ask when he arrives.

"You want to do that again?" He's breathing harder than I am.

"If you figure there are sixteen steps per flight, this is just under twenty-one flights. I could probably do them four times."

His breathing has become more normal. "Let's try it once more."

I smile as I work my way back down. This is a great workout. I have to weave around people a little, and I notice several women looking at Jaxson behind me. Some smile at him, and I give them the evil eye. They don't seem to notice.

When we get to the bottom, I turn to Jaxson. I can tell he's talking himself into this.

"Ready?" I ask.

He blows out a big breath of air. "Let's do it."

"Do you want to lead the way?"

"No. I find if I concentrate on your ass, I don't think about the incline."

"What?"

He shrugs. "I now see why you have a great ass."

I roll my eyes and start back up the stairs. Even Christophe seems winded now. At least I'm good at something.

When we get to the top, I walk in a small circle with my hands on my hips. A slender blonde walks up to Jaxson and hands him her card. "Call me sometime. I promise to make it worth your while." She winks at him.

I step forward. "I'm sorry, but he's not available."

She steps back, her eyes wide. "No worries." She holds her hands up and smiles.

Jaxson gives her back her card, and I lace my fingers with his for a moment as we start to run home.

"Can I tell you how hot that was?"

"The nerve!" I bristle.

"I kind of like that you didn't want her giving me her number. By the way, I wouldn't have called her."

"Let me guess, because you never call women who make the first move?"

He shakes his head. "No, most of the time women make the first move."

I shake my head, amazed at his ego.

"I wouldn't have called her, because she wasn't my type," he explains.

I look over at him. *Not his type?* "This should be good."

"She didn't care that it would be cheating, and I don't cheat. I never have. I never will."

"We have a business relationship."

He moves in close and his voice drops. "You see it as business, but the point is that others see it as real. We're rehabbing my image, remember?"

He reaches for my hand and clasps it in his. "Can you walk a straight line home?"

I shrug. "I can try, but there's no guarantee I won't bump into you."

"I can handle it."

When we get back to the house, I start up the stairs to get ready.

"You realize most people at the farmer's market will be dressed in what we're wearing now," he calls after me.

"Okay, but let me at least wash my face."

"I usually make a smoothie after running. Can I make one for you?"

"What do you put in it?"

"Coconut water, pineapple, banana, blueberries, spinach, maca powder, cinnamon, and quinoa."

"What is maca powder?"

"Maca is a plant found in parts of South America. Is root is a superfood. The powder nourishes the body's endocrine system and helps with stress. Maca also energizes naturally, without the side effects of caffeine. And it supports hormone balance and reproductive health in women."

"Do you own a company that imports it?"

His head tilts to the side. "No. Why?"

"Sounds like you just recited the marketing materials."

He grins. "I have a good memory, and I like it."

"Sure, I'll try it."

"If you don't like it, I'll drink yours too. It's my favorite."

I head upstairs as he goes to the kitchen, and just a few minutes later, we pile into the Suburban. The man behind the wheel is introduced as Wyatt Carlson, and Christophe is in the passenger seat today.

Once I have my seatbelt on, Jaxson hands me my smoothie. I take a tentative sip as he watches me carefully.

It's not bad, so I take a deeper pull. The coconut water and pineapple provide a sweet and tangy base while the banana adds creaminess. I take another taste and catch a hint of the blueberries and cinnamon. I honestly can't complain. "This is excellent!"

Jaxson preens. "Thank you. You can't taste the spinach. I saw the way you made the face when I mentioned spinach."

"Yeah, I wasn't so sure about that. But I like this, even with your weird powder in there."

When we pull up at the Fort Mason Center Farmer's Market by the marina, we hop out with Christophe and the driver disappears around the block. It's still pretty early, but the crowds are thick.

"Here's our list from Helen," Jaxson says, handing it to me. I look it over as he leans in. "If anything goes crazy or you're uncomfortable, just let Christophe know and he'll get you out of here."

"What are you expecting?"

"Nothing, but I want you to be safe."

"And you?"

"I'll be right by your side."

"Okay." I look back at the list. "Do you have any preferred vendors for these things?"

He shakes his head. "I rarely do this. But I thought it would be a great way to show you around the City."

I nod. It's sad that I've lived here for two years and have never done this. I need to get out more. "What are your other plans for today?"

"I have to work this afternoon. You saw my calendar for the week."

"Okay, I can join you."

He shakes his head. "I'm not expecting you to join me. You asked what I was doing, and I told you. You can do what you want. Hang out with Amy. You're living at my place now, so have her come over."

"You're okay with that?"

"Of course. I hope you'll introduce me to her, and sometime, I'll introduce you to my friends."

We pick up the fruit, vegetables, and loaf of sourdough Helen wanted, but she also asked for fresh basil, which we're not finding. I stop to gape at a stall filled with stunning flowers. I wouldn't have the first clue how to arrange them, but I love them all.

"Don't you think the table in the entry would look nice with some flowers on it?" Jaxson asks.

"Sure," I say.

"Jaxson!"

I hear a woman's voice behind us, and I'm ready to go to war again. But then I realize it's Caroline Sullivan. *OMG.* She's famous—almost as famous as Tessa Skye. She owns her own cosmetics company and recently took a member of Congress to task who didn't believe in a living wage. I've watched that video so many times. I can't even believe this. Behind her is a man with a bright grin. That must be her husband.

CHAPTER 9

Jaxson

"Hey, guys," I call as Caroline and Mason Sullivan approach through the crowd.

Caroline leans in and gives me a hug. "We're running into everyone this morning!" She looks over at Harper, and I can feel her question forming.

"This is my girlfriend, Harper," I announce. Harper jumps. *Shit*. If we're doing this, we have to do it. I don't know why she's so nervous.

Caroline chuckles. "Apparently you haven't talked about that."

"No, we have," Harper says smoothly, shoving my shoulder. "I just didn't expect him to be announcing it to the world."

Caroline jacks her thumb at Mason. "This one was dating everything that moved, and it took him five years to ask me out."

Harper and I laugh, and Mason rolls his eyes.

"How did you two meet?" Caroline asks Harper.

"We work together." She tucks her hair behind her ear and studies the ground.

Mason catches my eyes and nods. This is perfect. Now, he knows the plan is in place.

Caroline asks Harper to look at flowers with her, and Mason moves closer so we can talk. "I like her," he says.

"You've met her multiple times," I point out.

"Yes, she's your assistant. She's the one who organized your life after a string of terrible help."

I can't disagree there. "She did. She's been really great. She was hesitant to do this, even after I threw money at her. Turns out she wants a job in a different division."

"Really?"

I watch Harper move through the buckets of colorful flowers. She looks back at me and smiles. "She wants to be a graphic designer," I explain, ignoring the flip in my stomach.

"Interesting," he says with a nod. "Well, like I said, I like her."

"I like her a lot more than I should," I confess. *Why on Earth did I say that?*

Fortunately, Caroline returns before Mason can respond or ask any more questions. "What are you two gossiping about?" she asks. "Are you telling him about what's going on at Technology Startup Fund?"

I turn to Mason. Technology Startup Fund — or as some people refer to it, TSF — was founded by several venture capitalists, including Villefort, and they've been acting more like a bank than an investment fund, taking in deposits and letting people withdraw money for expenses and payroll. "What's going on there?"

He sighs. "We're telling all of our investors to move their money out as soon as the markets open. We were on the phone all day Friday and yesterday."

"Why would you do that?" I ask, my head spinning.

"Friday morning TSF had a call with investors, and they shared that they'd lost one-point-eight billion dollars because part of their portfolio is locked in treasury bonds and mortgages."

"I'm no financial wizard—that's Nick—but the Feds have been talking about interest rate increases for months," I point out. "Why didn't they move their money earlier?"

"I think mostly because they thought funding from venture capitalists would continue to flow during the downturn and it wouldn't be a problem to have that cash locked up. Unfortunately, we're not seeing many good ideas right now, so we're not making many new investments. We're waiting for Honeycomb to go public, along with a dozen or so other companies."

"If they're struggling, I would think there's an opening there."

Mason nods. "Maybe the gang should get together tonight?"

I nod. "Great idea."

"Caroline?" Mason asks.

A grin spreads across her face.

"What do you think? Just a small group for tonight—the Healys, Blackstones, your brother and Sara, these two, and Nick Maywood?"

"All the kids too?"

Mason nods. "Sure. That will make it easier for everyone. We'll set up a movie downstairs, and Tina can stay with them."

"That sounds great," she says. "Let's do burgers. I'll need to pick up a few more things, and you can let everyone know."

"Done." Mason turns to me. "Can you get Grayson and Nick to my place about six? Tell Gray to bring Scarlett and the kids, and if Nick wants to bring Olivia, that's fine too."

I nod, already composing the invite to Gray and Nick on my phone. "Sounds good."

Gray and Nick report back that they're in almost immediately, and I let Mason know.

"Sara is in, as is Dillon and his family," he tells me.

"Wait, is Sara married to Caroline's brother?" I ask.

"Yes, and Dillon is married to Caroline's best friend. We're an incestuous bunch."

I chuckle. "That's another way of keeping it all close."

"Cameron is married to another good friend. I'll include them as well."

This will be quite the last-minute party. "That all sounds good, and I'm glad we're moving on this quickly. I have to believe there's a lot of room to grow right now."

Mason nods. "That's what I'm thinking. Very few of those invested with TSF will be able to get their funds out for a while, and the money isn't covered by the FDIC."

"That will make some public entities very vulnerable," I muse. "Can I include David Fleming this evening? He's a lawyer and has been doing some work for Nick, Gray, and me in the background."

Mason nods. "That's fine."

"He's also been dating someone he put in Villefort's office," I add.

"That would be quite interesting to hear more about," Mason says.

Speaking of interesting to hear more about, that reminds me of the man who approached me last night. "I stopped by the San Francisco Club last night for a drink, and a gentleman spoke to me about needing to be open to you when you suggest we buy Green Light Games from Villefort."

Mason looks at me, surprised. "You ran into Adam Backus? That's something we can talk about tonight."

Harper returns with a bouquet of flowers in her hand, and we now have a full evening ahead of us where we can talk freely as a group, so we say our temporary goodbyes and go our separate ways.

"What were you and Mason strategizing about?" Harper asks as we walk back toward where the driver will pick us up.

"Remember I told you about the asshole who took Quick Reels away from Gray, Nick, and me?"

She nods.

"He's an owner of Technology Startup Fund, and they've run into some bad luck."

"What does that mean for you?"

"That there really is karma out there."

She raises an eyebrow. "What happened?"

"Villefort and his friends at TSF have been acting like a bank, even though it isn't. It's almost like a co-op. All these different startups put their money into the fund, and they can borrow from it, as needed, but mostly it grows interest, almost like a credit union. But it's not regulated like a bank or credit union, and now, they're having a cash-flow problem. All the companies that have their money there may be in trouble if they can't get it out, because it's not protected."

"But Honeycomb isn't invested there?"

"No way. We'll never voluntarily be involved with something that includes Villefort in any way."

"Sounds like you dodged a bullet with that decision."

"I agree."

After the farmer's market, I drop Harper at the house and go in to the office. She's planning to get organized and have Amy over for the afternoon. And we agreed we'd walk the two blocks over to Caroline and Mason's house together just before six.

I spend the afternoon combing through work, and I get a surprising amount done without all the interruptions of a typical workday. When my phone rings, it's almost five thirty. No wonder Harper is calling.

"Hey, I'm just leaving," I tell her when I answer.

"Okay. Just thought I should check. I worried you'd work two more hours without noticing the time or that it was dark outside."

I laugh. "You know me well." I slide my laptop into my bag. "I'm walking out. See you in a few."

I take the elevator down and walk out to find Christophe waiting at the curb.

When we make it back to the house, I have five minutes to change before we need to walk over.

When I come back downstairs, Harper has a grocery bag. "What do you have?"

"Everyone will bring something, so I offered a dessert."

"What did you get?"

"I *made* Boston cream pie, of course."

"You can cook?"

She narrows her eyes. "Don't look so surprised. We all took turns cooking growing up at my house, and we never ate out."

I open the door and usher her through. "You never ate out?"

She shakes her head. "Ten people on two teacher salaries? Eating out would be an entire paycheck."

"I never thought about it that way."

Christophe is waiting for us on the sidewalk.

"I smell the rain coming," Harper notes as we begin to walk. "It must be raining somewhere already."

"How do you smell the rain?"

"The humidity is high, and the petrichor smell is out."

"What is petrichor?" I ask. *She thought the maca powder in my smoothie was weird?*

She beams. "My dad is a science teacher, so he would drop this kind of knowledge on us all the time. Petrichor is the earthy smell that comes from the moistening of the ground when it rains. It's a real thing."

I reach for her hand. "You're very hot when you get all sciencey."

She laughs, and I point her to the Sullivans'.

"I can't believe they live so close."

"It really isn't that big of a city. It's just densely populated."

As we reach the porch, Mason opens the door. "Welcome!" He steps aside, and we walk into a room already full of people. "Caroline is in the kitchen with most of the women, pulling all the last-minute things together."

"Great," Harper says.

He points her in the right direction, and I follow Mason into their living room. I've been here once before, after we signed the paperwork for Honeycomb's funding.

I shake hands with Dillon Healy and Cameron Newhouse, the two other principals at SHN with Mason, and then Grayson.

"This is Trey Arnault," Mason says.

He extends his hand. "Thanks for letting me join you."

"Of course," I tell him.

Trey Arnault is Caroline's brother, and he runs a company his parents founded. The Arnaults are considered some of the original Silicon Valley elites. I'm impressed that he's here, and I'm kicking myself that I didn't put together that Sara Arnault, Trey's wife, was related to Caroline.

Sara comes in and sits down with us as Nick arrives — without Olivia. I'm not going to ask. We're a big group, but everyone settles in. Mason turns to Gray. "Why don't you catch everyone up?"

Gray nods and stands. "Mason called me yesterday with rumors of several people moving money out of Technology Startup Fund following their investors call Friday morning. I checked with our lawyer, David Fleming, and he got back to me a few hours ago. He's not able to be here tonight, but his friend who works at Villefort Investments said things yesterday were very harried. Villefort was in a shit mood and yelling at everyone. They were scrambling to make sure TSF didn't fold. They didn't expect interest rates to jump the way they have, and they have too much money locked in long-term investments and not enough new money coming in."

"Were they not watching television or paying attention to the financial news?" Dillon snipes.

Mason shrugs.

"Apparently they're now bracing for most of those that used TSF to withdraw their money tomorrow morning in favor of something federally insured," Gray continues. "They seem to have been surprised by this reaction to the loss. They have nearly two-hundred billion in deposits and lost just under two billion."

"I don't know," Cameron says. "Makes sense to me. Some companies that have payroll running tomorrow are already having issues. Are any of you invested with the fund?"

"Never," Gray says.

"How are you guys sitting at SHN?" Nick asks.

"Most of our startups will not be affected by the sell-off," Dillon says. "We've never recommended the Fund, but a few of our clients still banked there."

"I met with them but wasn't impressed," Gray notes. "Especially after Villefort bought in. Firefly is at American Bank."

Mason nods. "That's smart. Some of their fees are a little high, but they're stable."

"Honeycomb is there as well," I add.

"As is PayFriend," Nick says.

"Dillon, what do you think will happen to the Fund?" Gray asks. "It's pretty big to just fail. And there's still a significant amount of money there."

"I think there are a lot of meetings like this going on tonight. Companies who have money tied up there need cash. There's a lot of opportunity to invest." Dillon sips his drink. "We're not super liquid, but I wouldn't want to make rash decisions about companies I haven't done enough research on anyway."

Cameron nods. "And I would hate to dump cash into a company when I'm not comfortable with their software."

"Yeah, I'm not feeling a big draw to this," Sara says. "Investing in companies like this runs counter to the way we do business. We want to be involved with their development from the beginning, not just throw money at them when they need it."

"That makes sense for SHN, but what should we do?" I ask. "Anything at all, or just sit back and let it work itself out?"

"Good question," Mason says as he pulls out a folder and hands Gray, Nick, and me a sheet of paper. "The situation is definitely a little different for the three of you. These are twenty companies that are going to have a problem this week because their money is trapped in the Fund. They also run parallel to the work one of your companies is doing."

When we've had a moment to peruse our lists, he continues. "The companies on the left are great startups that would be something Firefly might consider acquiring. The middle companies are all in the finance world. And those on the right are gaming companies."

I see three of the biggest domestic gaming companies on the list, and each of them started around the same time I did. Green Light Games is here. Like the other larger companies, they've grown through acquisition. Their profitability is not as good as Honeycomb's, but they're making more money than I am.

"What should we do?" I ask. "I wouldn't mind poking the bear and making an investment in at least three of these companies."

Dillon stands and presents me with a file. "These are the only ones I think you should consider. This is our internal research and cannot be shared outside this room."

I nod and open the folder. He's not suggesting my competitors. He's suggesting companies that complement our business — a gaming-device company, a payment application that could help us avoid banking fees, and a company with a very interesting algorithm that could have some gaming applications.

Dillon hands folders to Nick and Gray.

"I never would have considered these companies," Nick says after a moment.

"That's why we're suggesting them," Dillon says. "If you invest through your personal fund, it's blind to Villefort. If we work together, we can really undermine him."

"I like it," Gray says. "Tell me more."

"We'll invest through our personal fund in some of the entities that have viable applications to companies we have interest in," Dillon explains. "And we'll have the SHN fund invest. Between the three entities, we can combine to grow to major shareholder status, and then we'll have real power."

"Every one of Villefort's investments is impacted by TSF struggling," Mason points out.

We talk a bit longer and decide we're going to have David reach out to the companies in the morning on our behalf. He'll approach them as head of a consortium of wealthy individuals. We agree on the amount of money we're able to invest on our side and theirs, and we agree not to deviate from our list. We have eleven companies as possibilities, and if we end up with only one, that's fine.

Caroline appears in the doorway. "Are you guys done talking business?" she asks as she walks in.

"Dinner ready?" Trey asks.

"Yes. We've fed the kids, and they're all set downstairs in the media room playing games."

I stand and walk over to Harper. "How are you doing?"

She smiles. "Everyone is very kind and welcoming. All good. Scarlett and I will have lunch one day this week, since you and her husband are so close. And Caroline has given me more cosmetic samples than I could ever use, so I'll take them to my brother's wedding and spread them around with my sisters."

"I'll give you more if you're going to share them with your sisters," Caroline pipes in. "How many do you have?"

"You don't have to do that," Harper says.

"Don't even argue with her," Emerson, Dillon's wife, tells her. "She won't listen."

Harper shrugs. "I have three sisters and a soon-to-be sister-in-law."

"Perfect," Caroline says. "You'll be helping me. They don't live here, so they can market for us by telling friends about our products."

We make our way through the buffet, and even though I haven't had a bite of dinner yet, I have to take a piece when I get to Harper's Boston cream pie. I can't wait to try it. Dessert is my weakness.

Harper smiles, and I realize I may be developing another weakness too.

We sit down together at the Masons' giant table, and there's so much talking going on.

Gray catches my eye. "Are you okay with these investments? I feel like I'm pushing you and Nick into this."

"I'm fine," I assure him. "Seems like an opportunity we can't pass up. And we're on track for my IPO."

After that, we're done talking business, and the evening is light and fun. Harper seems to blend right in. She is absolutely the perfect person to help me out with the board.

It's after ten thirty when the evening winds down, and it's also raining. Christophe brings the car for us, rather than making the walk back home.

CHAPTER 10

Harper

I sit down with a harrumph across from Amy and immediately a bellini with a cute little plastic monkey on the glass is placed in front of me. "You knew exactly what I needed. Thank you."

It even has a sangria swirl, perfect for the week I've had. I wouldn't mind a dozen of these, actually. Christophe is here with me at Bar None, currently lurking close to the door, so I know I'll get home in one piece regardless. But I'm not that careless.

"How's it going?" Amy asks.

Where to begin? "It's been a week, but it feels like three weeks, and it's only Thursday night. Let's start with you. Tell me what's up. If we have time, I'll tell you about my week."

"At least tell me you got between the sheets with him."

I shake my head. "No. This is business. You recall that there's a contract and everything."

"I don't recall that it had much to say about the bedroom," she notes, giving me a look. "You have so much self-control."

I shake my head. She's messing with me. She's been out on several dates lately and hasn't slept with any of them. She has plenty of self-control too. We have to be smart about these things.

When I don't say anything further, she sighs. "Fine. This week I went out with Eric. He has a daughter from a previous relationship, and he must have asked me a thousand questions about my feelings on birth control and whether I'd want the father to be involved if I got pregnant."

My face distorts. "I'm hoping every single question inched you closer to the door."

She nods. "Pretty much. Thank goodness it was just a lunch downtown."

"What about your date last weekend?" I ask.

"Didn't I tell you about him?"

I shake my head.

"He was great."

I smile encouragingly. *Ooh!*

"He works for SalesTeam as an instructor. He's from Colorado Springs, which is about an hour south of where my parents live. We're the same age. We talked about going for a hike at Mount Tamaulipas as we walked down Market Street and around the Battery. It was great..." She shrugs. "And then he went MIA."

I sit back and groan. "The men in this town are such jerks. But keep at it. You just haven't met the right one."

"I'm not ready to give up," she agrees. "But I might be giving this town another year. If I can't meet anyone, I'm moving home."

I sigh. I hate that idea, but I guess I can't blame her. "It'll happen, and maybe it'll be a guy who will want to go back to Colorado with you."

"Maybe." She doesn't sound convinced.

This whole dating thing for Amy is new. She met a guy named Brett Price right after she moved here, and they really hit it off. They dated for two years. Then one day, she asked him a casual question about his future plans for his career, and he explained that he was going to make his millions here in Silicon Valley, then move home to Chicago and meet a nice college co-ed to start a family.

She was devastated. I tried to tell her at least he was honest and didn't string her along, but it still felt awful. Despite all that, though, she likes being in a relationship and has been looking for a replacement ever since.

I finish my first drink and feel relaxed for the first time in days. The server asks us if we want another round, and we nod.

"Now, tell me about your week," Amy says when my next frozen delight has arrived.

"Did you see the news about Technology Startup Fund?" I pick up my drink and take a sip.

"It's all anyone is talking about."

"Well, Jaxson and some friends invested in nine of the companies affected by the frozen funds. That way they could help them out of a jam and get people paid."

"That's really kind of them."

In a way, she's right, but they're also doing it for reasons I'm not able to share.

"Yeah, I think it was. But that means we've been vetting nine companies and going through a whole process with each of them. And meanwhile, we're still stepping closer to Honeycomb going public. I had lunch with Caroline Sullivan and Scarlett Blackstone this week." I pause for dramatic effect, and Amy gives me her I'm-impressed face in return. "They're helping me organize some IPO parties, with the help of a party planner, thank goodness."

"Phew, that will help."

"I think so. But I'm glad to at least know what I need to do."

"Any word about moving to the graphic-design team?"

I shake my head. "That wouldn't be immediate, even if it happens. Honeycomb has a hard time keeping designers. I've met several of the current group, and they're the type who think their shit doesn't stink, just giant dicks. I think Jaxson means it when he says he doesn't want to put me in that situation."

She nods thoughtfully. "The contract did say he would set you up with your own company."

"But building a company isn't easy, and I'll be out of the game for a while. My skills will get rusty. I can't be an admin forever."

"Who's doing the marketing materials for the IPO?"

I perk up. "I hadn't thought about that."

Amy gives me a silly grin.

"I like it."

We chat a bit about how it could work — not like I have a ton of free time since I'm still Jaxson's assistant, but I think I could at least do some of it.

A little while later, I'm staring at my second empty glass and contemplating a third when my cell phone pings.

Jaxson: Time to come home.

Heat rushes through me. Who does this guy think he is?

Me: You don't have control of my personal time. I'm out with Amy.

Jaxson: I think you'll find the contract states that you can't be drunk in public, and a third drink will have you drunk. If you and Amy want to keep drinking, come home and do it here so the tabloids don't splash you all over for your friends, family, and my board members to see.

My shoulders fall. There's always another facet to working for him I haven't considered. I drink my water and tell Amy I need to head out. I offer to have Christophe drive her home, but she opts for a rideshare.

Once we're alone in the Suburban, Christophe looks in his rearview mirror. "I'm sorry."

I shake my head, feeling a little embarrassed. "People are looking for me to screw up. I need to keep that in mind. Jaxson was right to remind me."

He nods. "He sometimes forgets what it's like *not* to be under a microscope."

When we get home, I march right up to my room. I don't want to talk to Jaxson or even see him until we drive into work tomorrow or meet to work out.

I drop my things on the bed and start the tub. At least, I can have a bubble bath without the tabloids judging me.

I set the temperature nice and hot and inch my way in. I've just gotten settled when Jaxson comes running into the bathroom.

"Oh, thank God."

My hands fly to my breasts. "What are you doing in here?" Thankfully, the bubbles cover all my lady bits, but what the hell?

"You didn't come find me after you got home to yell at me, and you didn't respond when I was knocking on the door."

"The water was running. I didn't hear anything. And I didn't bother finding you because there's no use yelling at you. You're right. I wouldn't want my parents to learn about us dating and me being drunk on the cover of a supermarket tabloid."

He nods and turns a little pink. "I'm sorry. We had a shitty week."

I lift my hand and let bubbles drip off my fingers. "We did. Is that all you need?"

He jumps. "Oh. Sure. I'll give you some privacy." He turns around but then turns back. "I forgot. Your mom called the office looking for you after you left."

My heart races. "What did you tell her?"

"That you had gone for the day and I thought you were meeting a friend."

"Thank you. She wants to know about my brother's wedding. You're still planning to join me, right?"

"That's the plan, but how does my calendar work?"

"We just need to move some internal meetings."

He nods. "Then let's do it. Book a NetJet."

I blanch, and I can see him in the mirror watching me. "I can't afford a NetJet. I'll just book you a first class ticket, and I'll ride coach."

"We'll want Christophe and Wyatt with us. I'll book the NetJet. I haven't used it recently, and I pay the fees regardless. We'll be fine."

"Will they be at the wedding?"

"They're security. They go everywhere we go."

I sigh and look away from him. *How am I going to manage this?* "My parents will want to pick us up."

"Tell them I'll rent a car. And since things are tight at your house, I'll book us a room downtown."

"Okay. Thank you, but my parents live in the suburbs. It's actually a good thirty minutes outside of downtown. Maybe the Residence Inn in Braintree... Or there's a big Marriott in Quincy on the interstate."

"I'll find something that can accommodate us, and I don't mind. We can stop at my parents' in Detroit after the wedding and meet them. Let's take the week off."

I stop playing with the bubbles and look at him. "This close to IPO?"

"We'll announce to our parents that we're engaged, and we can then send out a press release. We have a PR agency on retainer, and I'll let them know."

My stomach sinks. I take a deep breath. "That seems kind of fast. We've only been dating a week."

"Well, you moved in a week ago, but I thought we'd present ourselves as dating a bit longer."

Right. This is fake, so I guess we can say anything we want. I take a deep breath. *Here we go.* "I guess that's settled then."

He nods and disappears.

I pull the plug and wait until all the water is gone. Then I rinse off the remaining bubbles and pull on a pair of flannel sleep pants and a T-shirt. I catch a glimpse of myself, and I look like I belong in a grunge band. Turning the television on in my bedroom, I lie back and fall asleep. When I wake up, the TV is off and it's dark.

I roll over and see that it's after five. I pull the covers up. I don't want to work out this morning.

What seems like seconds later, there's a knock at the door and Jaxson sticks his head in. "Are you coming?" he asks.

Now, it's five thirty. I stifle a sigh. "Give me five, and I'll meet you downstairs."

I throw the covers back and get myself dressed and ready like my life depends on it — or my livelihood at least.

Jaxson looks at his watch when I come downstairs. "Call me impressed."

I give him a half smile, and we walk out front. We stretch in silence and then start down the street with Wyatt behind us.

Jaxson bumps my hip. "Sorry. I can't run straight today."

I realize he thinks I'm mad at him. But I'm not. I'm disappointed in myself. How did I get into this situation? Just because I'm female and organized doesn't mean my life's destiny is to cater to someone else.

We get to the stairs, and I look over at Jaxson. "How many times?"

"No more than three," he says. "I worry I'll get shin splints if I do any more."

106

I laugh as I start down the stairs. It's really not surprising that I'm better at this than Jaxson and the security guards. I have smaller feet and a lower center of gravity.

At the bottom, I notice a gentleman standing off to the side, fussing with his sneakers. I avoid running into him as I circle around and prepare to start back up. I nod at Wyatt and Jaxson, and we race up again.

When we get to the top, my heart is pumping, my pulse is racing, and I'm feeling great.

We complete the second descent, and the guy is still there. This time I hear some kind of repetitive click. I can't quite place it. I turn and start up again. When we get to the top, Wyatt asks us to stop. I suspect that these mornings are tough for him. This is probably a different workout than he's used to.

"Getting too old to do the stairs, old man?" I tease.

He shakes his head, and I realize he's barely out of breath. "I just think that's enough for today."

Jaxson looks prepared to argue, but then Wyatt speaks again. "The guy at the bottom is taking your picture."

I close my eyes and cringe. Photographs are part of the deal, but not like this. And if Wyatt is concerned… "Let's get home."

We usually walk back, but today I'm angry, so I run. I knew this was going to be a part of my life. I just didn't realize it was going to feel like this.

After we've showered and changed, the ride to work is slow. Jaxson scrolls through his emails, and I watch the people on the sidewalks. San Francisco is so different from Boston. I see blondes everywhere here. Boston seems much more brunette than blond. And most people here seem happy. I really like it. I miss my family, but I enjoy being so far away from their chaos.

When we get to the office, we hit the ground running. We're still dealing with the new investments. Jaxson is moving money around, and I've had all sorts of paperwork going back and forth to his lawyer and to Mason's company. I can't keep it all straight, so I'm hoping Jaxson has it buttoned down.

When I look up, it's after one, and I haven't had lunch. I step into Jaxson's office. "I'm going to step out and grab some pho. Would you like me to pick you up something?"

He looks up and sits back in his chair. "Please. Pho sounds perfect. Chicken, and get it as spicy as they'll make it."

"Are you trying to burn off all your tastebuds?"

He laughs. "I like a lot of spice."

"And I'm going to call my mom before she sends a search party."

He nods. "She's worried?"

"Oh yes. She's not happy that I'm so far away, and I haven't talked to her in a bit. She'd much prefer that I find a graphic-design job right in Weymouth. Boston might even be a little too far."

Jaxson nods and waves as I step out of his office.

I head outside and turn toward the pho place. It's after four her time, so Mom should still be in her classroom. The phone doesn't even ring before she answers.

"Sweetheart!"

"Hi, Mom. I got your message."

"I hadn't heard from you for a while and thought I'd check in."

"Everything is fine — just busy. I'm enjoying my job with the gaming company. I work long hours, but I like it. Oh, and I've met someone. I can still bring a plus one to Hudson's wedding, can't I?"

"Of course, sweetheart. I'm so excited you're bringing someone with you. He must be very special."

"I think so." *Just not the way you're thinking.* "How are the wedding plans going?"

"Very nice," she says. She doesn't even seem to notice the subject change. "Father Murphy has been wonderful. He's done all the Pre-Cana with Hudson and Hannah. The reception is coming together, and we have a good plan for the rehearsal dinner here at the house."

"How are you doing?" I ask. Mom suffers from depression, so sometimes she hides in her room and doesn't do any peopling.

"You know me. I have my days. Some are better than others. Don't tell Hannah, but I'm ready for the wedding to be over. She's a little high maintenance, and it's hard."

Despite teaching thirty fifteen-year-olds and having eight kids, Mom really wants everyone to manage their own stuff. That's why as we grew older, we were responsible for a younger sibling.

Mom spends the next forty-five minutes regaling me with various details about the wedding, her classroom, and her friends. Much of it doesn't interest me, but I don't want to rain on her parade. I just sit down outside the restaurant and take it all in.

"Well, I better run," I finally tell her when there's a lull. "I'm picking up lunch for my boss and me. I'll talk to you soon."

"We can't wait to see you and meet your special someone. What's his name?"

They already know Jaxson is my boss, so I'm not ready to get into that. "Oh, Mom, I have to go. I'll call you soon. I can't wait to see you."

I walk into the pho place and order two chicken pho, one extra spicy, and I'm back within my hour.

Jaxson is on the phone when I return, and he watches as I cross the room and leave his soup on his desk. He snaps his fingers and points to the conference table in his office. Because I was gone so long, he must figure I already ate. I hold up a finger and return to my desk for a pen and pad of paper so I can take notes.

I sit down at the table as he finishes his call.

"Thank you for running out." His brow creases. "Did you already eat?"

"I can eat later," I explain. "I had to call my mom, and she wanted to catch me up on everything."

"Go get your lunch," he tells me. "That's why I was gesturing to the conference table."

Now, I feel stupid. This situation is just impossible to navigate. I forget who I am at any given time. But I smile and nod and retrieve my soup from my desk.

"Did you tell your mom I was coming to the wedding?" Jaxson asks when I return.

"I just told her I was bringing someone. I didn't want the lecture about dating my boss."

"That's fair." He slurps his soup, and I do the same.

"What about you? Have you told your family about me?"

He nods. "I told them we'd stop by on our way back from your family wedding. My sister is very excited to meet you."

"Really? They don't think I'm after your money?"

"They know I'm very careful about who I let into my circle of friends. I don't really have a lot of friends. Anyone I bring home is someone I trust."

"Great." I nod. I take another slurp of soup.

Jaxson studies me a moment. "You know, we're going to need to have a more realistic personal relationship when we're out with our families. They're going to expect some PDA and lots of longing looks."

I snort a laugh. "I'm aware." The idea makes my pulse race. I mean, the man is gorgeous. But doing those things will be like playing with fire.

CHAPTER 11

Jaxson

"What's the password?" the woman at the door asks.

"Hedgehog fever," I reply.

Her lips curve into a smile. "Good to see you again, Mr. Bancroft. Your friends are in the library."

"Thank you." I step into the dimly lit speakeasy. The library at Bourbon and Branch is my favorite. It's a private room with a big round table in the middle, so no one is obstructed from view.

I give a subtle nod to Grayson and Nick as I enter. They seem to be deep in conversation, so I slip into a chair between Mason and David Flemming, our lawyer. "Gentlemen."

David shakes my hand. "I'm glad you're here. I have a few things to talk to you about after this meeting if you have a moment."

"Sure. What about?"

"Green Light Games."

I nod, though my heart lurches. *What could that mean?* "I'll be sure to stick around."

The door to the room opens again, and in walk Cameron Newhouse and Dillon Healy.

Gray looks around the room as the server arrives with my bourbon and a tall glass of ice water. "Looks like we're all here," he says. "Mason? You had news for us?"

"On behalf of SHN, thank you for having us." Mason stands and passes out a small bound booklet to each of us. "We had Clear Security do a background check on Villefort and his company. If you turn to page three, you'll see the start of the information."

I scan the page to his net worth and my eyes pop wide. He's in the negative. I look up at Gray, and his face tells me he saw it too.

"This says his assets are negative," Nick says.

"It does," Mason confirms. "It seems during the downturn with Technology Startup Fund, he leveraged his stock options for Quick Reels and Transcend Biosciences."

Holy shit. Those are two of the most successful startups in the past few years, and they probably earn him the lion's share of his personal income.

"What does that mean?" Gray asks. "Is he bankrupt?"

Mason's eyes twinkle. "Yes. He's been talking to bankruptcy lawyers about starting the process."

"What does that mean for all his investment companies?" I ask.

Dillon puts his glass down. "He used TSF as his bank. All of his investments shouldered the money within the fund, and after the collapse, forty-two percent of his investments collapsed as well. They were unable to get further funding, mostly because his process of validating a good investment is crap."

"And he's taking the CEO of Quick Reels, Peter Mondego, down with him," Mason adds.

Gray's the one who hired Peter, so I'm sure that makes him happy. I look across the table at Nick. He got stung twice when we lost Quick Reels. When everything fell apart, we learned his girlfriend at the time, Mercedes McCloud, had been having an affair with Mondego. There's a silly grin on his face now.

Good. Karma is a bitch.

"So Mondego is also looking at bankruptcy?" Nick confirms.

Dillon gives a curt nod.

Grayson gives Nick a fist bump, and I follow suit.

"I know it's rude to celebrate someone's misfortune, but after everything they did to us, we can't help it," Grayson explains.

"You don't have to tell me," Mason says. "They've given all venture capitalists a bad name."

I nod, but on the bright side of having everything ripped away from us, between the three of us we now have a robust online retailer, a thriving gaming company, and an ingenious way of moving money that wouldn't have existed had Villefort not been so ruthless.

Don't get me wrong, losing Quick Reels took years off of my life, and I hate them for that, but we came out ahead. I'm celebrating because they cut corners and the universe is slapping back.

I lift my glass. "To great friends," I offer with an eye roll. Villefort and Mondego are anything but. "May they get everything they deserve and then some."

"Amen!" My real friends in the room all lift their glasses.

We toast, and I feel a weight lift from my shoulders. I can't wait to tell Harper about this.

For phase two of our meeting, Mason and David go through the list of our personal and group holdings that affect Villefort. Mason has also compiled a listing of other entrepreneurs who had their businesses stolen from them by Villefort, including Tom Ackerman of Transcend Biosciences. He's an impressive person, so that makes me feel the tiniest bit less stupid about what happened to us. Tom is now working with another venture capital firm for his new company. Good to know he's landing on his feet as well.

"We currently have control of these fourteen companies," David says. "When the eight companies on the next page announce their earnings, we could buy the next set of options, and we should have control of them by the end of October — end of January at the latest. I think it's time we make our move."

With nods around the table, we all agree that we're ready for the next step, which is not only destroying Villefort's business, but also making sure he can never take advantage of anyone again.

"How much more do you need to secure our positions?" Gray asks.

"I think if I can get ten million from the three of you, that will cover our part," David replies, looking at me, Gray, and Nick.

"And SHN will be going in with twenty million to drive the purchases," Dillon says.

"And as long as things go off without a hitch with my IPO," I add, "that will be another nail in their coffin."

"Knock on wood," Cameron says.

Everyone at the table knocks with me.

"Any concerns?" Mason asks.

"I think you're a better person to answer that than I am," I reply.

"The board isn't chattering about the tabloids anymore," he reports. "Grantham was pretty hot under the collar there for a while after Tessa Sky released tapes of your conversations."

"It's so kind of him to be concerned about my privacy," I tease.

Gray rolls his eyes. "You know this is about the IPO, but you can hope it's your privacy and not his wallet."

"Good luck with that," Dillon snipes.

We talk for a short time longer, and once everyone knows the game plan, the meeting adjourns. I get another drink and meet David over in the corner.

"So what's up with Green Light?" I ask. My stomach has been iffy since he mentioned it.

"Have you invested with them?" he asks. "I haven't seen paperwork."

I shake my head. "It was brought to my attention, but I think, with all the craziness of the Technology Startup Fund collapse, I'll let that go for the time being." It wasn't on the recommended list Dillon gave me.

David's shoulders relax. "Thank goodness. My girlfriend found out that Villefort knew a board member who was close to Mason, so they planted their weakness to try to get into Honeycomb."

Our revenge is close. That thought makes me a little giddy. "David, you take that girlfriend of yours out for a very expensive dinner and charge it to me."

His brow furrows.

"There was something about that whole thing that didn't smell right, particularly because of Villefort's interest in the company. I'm glad I didn't get sucked in."

"Looks like you dodged a bullet." David clasps my shoulder. "I invested what I could with you guys, and I'm grateful you've brought me along."

"I appreciate all your help," I tell him.

With a smile, David says his goodbyes, and I pull Mason aside to tell him what David's girlfriend has learned.

Mason closes his eyes. "I don't want to let Adam Backus know David's girlfriend is a mole with Villefort, but we need to somehow let him know he was played."

"I'll leave that for you," I say, and he bobs his head. "But please don't say anything about David's girlfriend. We can't afford to lose him."

"Maybe I'll wait until we've taken control and ousted Villefort's dumb ass." Mason drains what's left of his drink. "All right. I need to get out of here before Caroline makes me sleep in the guest room because I'm late again."

He heads out, and then all that remain are Gray, Nick, and me. I groan as I stretch.

"Too many late nights?" Gray teases.

"Maybe…" I won't give him any details.

"How are you feeling about your admin?" Nick asks.

"She's fantastic. We've got the office down to a real science."

Nick rolls his eyes. "What about the request with your board?"

"It's coming along."

"Are you still in the friend zone?" Gray presses.

"We're going to Boston next week. I'll meet her family and on the way back, we'll stop in Detroit and meet my parents and probably my sister and her family." I smoothly avoid his real question. They don't need to know that Harper's in the guest room.

"That should be fun." Nick's face distorts in horror.

"Was meeting Olivia's family a little disappointing?" I ask.

He shrugs. "I like her sister just fine. Her dad left them when she was young, and her mom worked two jobs to support them. I bought her a small house in Reno."

The server returns and offers us another round, but I shake my head.

"What is your actual plan with Harper?" Gray asks, circling us back. "Are you going to get engaged and married just to please your board?"

"I would prefer that we get engaged and then have the relationship quietly end when the coast is clear with Honeycomb, but if things are still a little off on the stock value, we may have to have a wedding."

"Not that it's any of my business, but what are you paying her?" Nick asks.

"It's not your business, but every time I offer her big money, she turns it down. She just wants me to cover her brothers' and sisters' college loans and pay for college for the two who haven't gone yet."

"How many brothers and sisters does she have?"

"There are eight of them."

"Eight?" Gray takes a pull on his drink. "Are her parents wealthy?"

"Quite the opposite." I explain what I know about her parents.

"And she didn't ask for a boatload of options?" he asks.

"I tried to give her stock options, but she's refused them." I shake my head. "I don't know how to talk people into doing things without money."

"How shallow does that make me?" Nick muses.

That's how everything works with Olivia.

"Thank goodness Scarlett was similar to Harper," Gray says. "She didn't want my money either." He raises his fist for a bump.

"I hope you have a good time," Nick says. "I guess dealing with the families will determine how well you can at least pretend you're together."

I nod, and we say goodnight. He makes a good point. On the drive home, I keep playing it through my mind. I don't know anything about Harper's brothers and sisters. She's going to need to brief me so I can be prepared. I was just going to show up, but now, I think I need to impress them too.

When I walk in, Harper is on the couch watching *Ted Lasso*. "I've never seen this before."

"It's pretty good."

"It is! It's really making me laugh."

I heat up some leftover lasagna and sit with her. As I'm shoveling the food in my mouth, she asks, "How did it go this evening?"

I bounce my head side to side as I swallow. "I'm almost afraid to say this out loud, but I think it went really well. We're getting closer to having Villefort be just a bump in the road behind us. I'll feel better once we go public, though."

"That makes sense." She looks at the frozen face of Jason Sudeikis on the screen. "Is anything you're doing illegal?"

I shake my head. "No, definitely not. We've just been slowly working our way into his companies using corporations that can't be traced back to us. Eventually, we'll own the majority of shares. Our goal is to take over the boards, fire Villefort and his allies from all of them, and force him out completely. We'd love to see him go to jail, but I don't know if that's possible. What he's done to us and others was legal, but it certainly wasn't ethical."

"What will you do once he's out of business?"

"After we finish celebrating—" I do a little happy dance on the couch to demonstrate. "—we'll go back to what we do best and use the money we make to help struggling entrepreneurs discover their dreams."

She leans in and gives me a kiss on the cheek. "You're a good man, Jaxson Bancroft."

"I'd love to *show* you how good I am."

She laughs and shoves my shoulder, picking up the remote. She seems to think I'm kidding.

But I'm not.

CHAPTER 12

Harper

It was hairy getting everything done so we could get out of town, but we finally did it. We worked until after one o'clock in the morning yesterday to get it all finished and agreed to try to leave first thing in the morning. That kind of flexibility is definitely a benefit of the NetJet.

As I headed to bed, I warned Jaxson that there'd be no stairs workout for me in the morning, and he agreed, but I still planned to get up and get going.

However, when I open my eyes to a knock on my door, the clock tells me it's nearly nine.

"Are you getting up?" he asks before I can even form a coherent thought beyond *Shit!*

"I'm sorry." I wipe the sleep from my eyes and stretch.

Jaxson stands in the doorway. Fortunately, I think he seems slightly amused.

"I haven't really packed yet. But I can be ready in an hour. Promise," I say with a big yawn.

"That's fine. I'll let the pilot know so he can file a flight plan." He shuts the door, and I jump out of bed.

Racing around the room, I dump everything I could possibly need into my suitcase and race into the shower. *How could I have overslept, today of all days?*

I have my suitcase at the top of the stairs in slightly *over* an hour, but thankfully, Jaxson doesn't seem miffed. Christophe walks up the stairs to bring my bag down. He groans as he lifts it, and I can feel myself blush.

"I hope you left a few things behind to come back to," Jaxson says.

"I did. But with the wedding and the rehearsal dinner, and all the activities before and after, I packed for all sorts of weather — even snow."

"Boston gets snow in May?" he asks as he ushers me out the door.

"Well, not normally, but my luck is such that if I'm not prepared for it, it will happen."

"I didn't pack for snow."

I wave that away as we get in the Suburban. "You agreed to wear a suit for the wedding, and what you're wearing now is good for the rehearsal tomorrow night. I'm all over the map for dinner with your family, and this is all so stressful." I look out the window as we pull away from the curb and feel completely overwhelmed. And that doesn't even factor in the fact that I need to act like Jaxson and I are in a real relationship around our families — and simultaneously manage my attraction to him.

"You'll look beautiful even if you wear a big black garbage bag." He pats my hand, sending me a little spark.

"You say that, but your mom and sister might disagree."

Jaxson chuckles and then spends the ride to the airport on his phone. I glance at my email, but there are too many things to take care of easily. I know the plane will have Wi-Fi, and I'll end up working the entire five-hour flight. Why rush it?

"Are you excited to be going home?" Jaxson asks when he finally looks up.

I have to be honest, so I shake my head. "I have mixed feelings about my brother's relationship. Hannah, his fiancée, was a close friend in middle school. I was really hurt when she started dating my oldest brother in high school. Not because he was my brother, but the way she went about it."

"What did she do?"

I sigh because it sounds petty when I say it out loud. "We were at my house one day after school, and she announced that she 'totally believed in premarital sex' while Hudson was there."

Jaxson laughed. "How old was Hudson?"

"Seventeen and a virgin. My parents had hoped he was going into the priesthood. But instead she bewitched him with her magic pussy."

Jaxson snorts. "Magic?"

I sigh. "Hudson is super shy. She's the opposite. But he was a star football and soccer player, so he was a catch. She just threw herself at him. He went to Boston College so he could live at home, and they dated. Once she graduated from high school, they moved downtown so she could attend Northeastern, and he works for a bank. She's been driving the train from the moment they got together. I just worry he never had the chance to really explore his options and decide what he wants for himself."

Jaxson nods, but he doesn't say anything. It's possible that was too much.

Fortunately, we pull up to the private-plane terminal just a moment later, giving us a break from this conversation. This is only the second flight I've ever been on. My palms start to sweat.

"Have you ever flown on a private plane?" Jaxson asks.

I shake my head as I throw my backpack over my shoulder. "Never. My first flight was when I moved out here."

Jaxson's eyes widen, and he extends his hand. "Come on. Let me show you around."

The pilot meets us as we climb the stairs to the plane and duck our heads to get in. It has that new-car smell. Six blond-leather captain's chairs line each side of the shiny wood cabin, with plenty of room to maneuver around them and walk through the plane.

The captain opens his arms and shows me the cabin. "In the back is the restroom, and if you want to take a nap on the flight, your chair lays flat. The chairs also turn three hundred and sixty degrees."

Jaxson puts his things down in the first seat on the right. Christophe sits two chairs behind him and Wyatt sits across the aisle from him. That leaves me either sitting across from Jaxson or behind him. I decide it would look funny if I didn't sit across, so I stow my backpack and take my seat. Almost immediately, they close up the plane, and in seconds, we're taxiing down the runway. Easy peasy. *Why am I making this so complicated?*

But I can't seem to relax. I'm white-knuckling the armrests when Jaxson reaches over and holds his hand out. I take it and hold on. My pulse races as the plane speeds down the runway. I don't feel us take off, but then, the g-force pushes me back into my seat and the ground gets farther away.

Jaxson gives my hand a squeeze. "See? Not so bad."

I manage a nod. "That was so much faster than when I flew out here."

"Your parents never took you on a plane?"

I shake my head. "Ten plane tickets were too expensive, and hotel rooms would have been impossible."

"What about Hudson and Hannah? Have they been on a plane before?"

I don't let go of his hand. "They flew down to Disney World one year and had a great time, but Hannah said the flight was the scariest thing she'd ever been on."

"Are Hannah's parents teachers too?"

"No, her father repairs air conditioners, and her mom left when she was in elementary school. So it's just the two of them, but her grandmother lives with them to help out."

"Why did you leave Massachusetts?" he asks.

I knew he'd ask eventually. "I think you'll understand better once you meet everyone. But not many people know this." I take a deep breath. "My parents are beloved at their schools. They were always voted most popular, and they win awards for teaching. But when they come home, they've given their students everything. They're tired and have nothing left for their kids. My mother also has some depression, so by the time summer comes, she often doesn't get out of bed. I was raised by my oldest sister, Hazel, and I raised my little sister Hope. The expectations were that we would go to school locally, which I did, and get jobs locally so we could all take care of our parents. I didn't want to do that."

Jaxson nods, his face neutral. "San Francisco is about as far as you could get and stay on the same continent."

"That's right. So you'll hear a lot about how much they wish I still lived close by." I sigh. "But I think that's mostly because they think I should be doing more instead of letting it fall to my brothers and sisters."

"Tell me about them."

"Hazel, the oldest, is a nurse at the local hospital. She's told me she'll never have kids, and she wants nothing more than to be footloose and fancy free. She really held things together in the summers when I was growing up. I adore her, and she's the one who encouraged me to leave. She lives with and takes care of my middle sister, Harmony, who is on the autism spectrum and has OCD. They're in Quincy, which is very close to my parents. Hazel's been dating Paul for a few years, but my parents aren't crazy about him because he lives in New York City, and he wants her to move in with him."

"Ah, the Catholic thing."

"Exactly. Hazel is always the responsible one. She's more the mother in our family than my mom."

"Then who's next?"

"My brother Hudson, who is getting married. He works for a bank, like I told you, but he's been studying to be an electrician."

"Nothing wrong with that," Jaxson says.

"Nope. He figures it's the only way he can pay off his school loans."

"Little does he know..." Jaxson gives me a sly look, and I smile.

"Next is my older sister, Harmony, who has some challenges, as I mentioned. She's really smart but struggles socially. She isn't comfortable leaving the house. She can usually do family things, though, because we know her triggers. So you should meet her this weekend."

"That's a lot for Hazel to handle."

I nod. "My brother Hunter, next in line, is currently waiting to see if he can go into the seminary. He was turned down last year, so he's nervous."

"Why did they turn him down?"

"I think because he was honest and told them our parents wanted him to be a priest. He'd rather join a rock band and play drums."

Jaxson laughs. "I can see why they would be hesitant. But if he was a rock star and a priest, he would be the first."

"That's true." I laugh a little myself. "I'm next in the birth order, and you know about me. Then there's my brother Harrison. He studies finance at Holy Cross College and graduates next month. He has dreams of being a heavy hitter on Wall Street. The first two years of school, he lived at home and commuted, but with Hazel and me encouraging him, he finally moved to campus. He comes home many weekends to help out, though."

"That's kind of him."

I nod. "He's a good guy. It would just be nice if everyone felt a little more supported to live the life they want. Next is my little sister, Hope, who is almost eighteen and discovering boys. She wants nothing more than a fairytale wedding. She's been looking at Wellesley for after she graduates next month, and I hope she goes. The tuition is off the charts, even with all the financial aid, but she'd do so well there."

"Despite everyone at home she doesn't get enough financial aid?"

"Unfortunately, no. The herd has thinned, my parents make a decent combined income, they have good retirement plans, and they own more of the house than the bank does."

He nods thoughtfully. "Hope's the youngest?"

I shake my head. "No, Holden is the youngest. He's fifteen. He's a spoiled brat and lets everyone wait on him, but he's a good kid. He wants to go to medical school one day and study neurology. He says he wants to understand why Harmony is the way she is."

"That's very noble."

I shrug and look down at all the puffy white clouds.

"So everyone has a name that starts with H?" Jaxson asks, pulling me back to the conversation.

"Even my parents, Hailey and Henry. Everyone in town knows us, which I hate. It's like living in a much smaller tabloid world. In the beginning, I'm sure it was cute with us all having the same initials, but now, I'm embarrassed." I shrug. "What can you do?"

"Thanks for giving me the rundown," he says. "I want to be prepared when I meet them."

"Of course." I smile, but I don't know how to respond to that. I'm sure he means prepared to make our fake relationship believable.

The plane has leveled off, and I release his hand. After a moment, he turns and pulls out his computer.

"The wall behind you has a table. You can either turn your chair around, if you don't mind flying backwards, or you can change seats."

I turn my seat around, and he helps me put the table up. He rotates his chair as well, and we work like we would in the office — only without all the interruptions. We accomplish quite a bit sitting at the table together. The flight zooms by, and the landing is for some reason much less stressful than takeoff. We're on the ground at just after seven local time.

"Are you hungry?" Jaxson asks as we gather our things.

I pull my backpack onto my shoulders. "Thank you," I call to the pilots as we head down the stairs. "I'm famished. We're staying downtown?"

"Yes, at the Four Seasons off Boston Common."

"My favorite seafood restaurant is not far from there. It's called Legal Seafood, right on the water. It's a local chain if you don't mind that."

"Why would I mind that?"

"Being a billionaire and all."

Jaxson throws his head back and looks at the sky. "Wait until you meet my family."

There's a Cadillac Escalade waiting at the foot of the stairs, and the crew is already putting our luggage in. We climb into the backseat, and Jaxson introduces me to our driver, JR Woods. He works for the same company as Christophe and Wyatt do, but he's stationed here.

I call the restaurant and grab the eight o'clock reservation, and we head that direction. The traffic goes smoothly, and we arrive in plenty of time.

"What's your favorite thing on the menu?" Jaxson asks as we go inside.

"I love the stuffed lobster tail, but I'm going with the seafood stew. I can't eat that much this close to bedtime. I need to adjust my body clock."

"If I get it, will you share it with me?"

I shrug. "That should work."

127

We're shown to our table, and after the server takes our order and returns with a bottle of white wine, Jaxson looks over at me. "What do you miss about living here?"

"I miss my brothers and sisters. I know I complained earlier, but I do love them."

"Makes sense. What else?"

"Everything here is familiar. There are no surprises."

"Like what?"

"The menu here, the newscasters on television, the Boston accent. All of those things are the same."

He laughs. "And what don't you miss?"

"That's easy. Not once this winter did I have to trudge through dirty, ugly snow and gross New England weather."

"I understand. Like I told you, I grew up just outside of Detroit. I don't miss the long winter days, and I definitely don't miss the snow."

"Exactly."

We enjoy dinner, and I'm surprised by how easy it is to talk to him. Out of a work context, he's funny and surprisingly self-deprecating. Unless someone at home has Googled him, I don't think they'll know how fancy he is. He's very low key, and I like that.

After our meal, we return to the hotel, and Christophe meets us at the curb when we arrive. He says something to Jaxson, who nods, and then he escorts us to the elevator and in to a beautiful penthouse room with a sitting area but just one bedroom.

I take a deep breath and focus on the view from our suite, which faces the Charles River. I can see MIT and Harvard in the distance.

"I'll sleep on the couch," Jaxson announces after a moment.

I'm sure this suite is extremely expensive. There's a living room with a couch, loveseat, and two large chairs that face out to a sizeable patio. There's also a dining table where eight people could enjoy a meal. But there is only one bedroom. "Oh, that's unnecessary," I blurt. "We can share a bed and not have sex, can't we?"

What the hell just came out of my mouth? I said sex. Now, he thinks I have sex on the brain.

His eyes flash wide for a split second. "Are you sure? I'm fine to sleep on the couch. I want you to be comfortable."

I can't do that to him. "Of course. If anyone is going to sleep on the couch, it should be me. You're the one paying for the room." My heart beats wildly, and I'm sure he can tell I'm on the verge of a freakout. I'm not sure where Christophe and Wyatt are staying, but I have to believe they're close.

He shakes his head. "No. You won't sleep on the couch. For privacy, you'll sleep in the room. If you're okay with sharing, that's fine for me, but if you're not, I understand. There is no pressure."

"We can do this." I'm not sure if I said this for me or for him.

"Okay. You can use the bathroom first. I'm going to check on how things went in the office today and follow up with Gray and Nick."

I paint a grin on my face. "Great."

I grab my sleep shorts and tank and realize that they are rather sexy. I root around in my suitcase, but I didn't bring my flannel pants or a T-shirt. I need to hit Target or someplace and find something a little less revealing.

I quickly change, wash my face, and race into bed, where I turn the television on to watch the late news. Lisa Hughes and Dave Wade are bantering away. They're the same people I remember from long before I moved away.

I have the covers pulled up to my chin. I'm not tired. It's not even nine o'clock at home, and my mind is racing at the thought of sleeping in the same bed as Jaxson. I watch Stephen Colbert before turning the television off. Eventually, I can hear Jaxson talking in the other room, but I roll over on my side and try to relax.

There is a faint sound of traffic below, but that's not why I can't fall asleep. I try to clear my mind, but nothing helps. I'm excited to be here but also dreading it. I think about how I'll respond to the snipes and jabs about me moving away, about how they'll react to me dating my boss. And I'm sure my clothes will be a topic, too.

My heart sinks. Why did I bring Jaxson with me? We're not really a couple, and there's no reason for me to pretend with my parents. What are the odds that they'd see something in the media anyway?

Jaxson comes in and goes right to the bathroom. He walks out a few minutes later and, in the mirror, I catch a brief glimpse of his naked torso and boxer briefs. My heart skips several beats.

Twelve hours ago, I was fast asleep in his guest room, and now, I'm not even close to being tired.

Jaxson slides beneath the covers. "Goodnight."

"Goodnight," I whisper.

His breathing shortly becomes rhythmic, and I'm jealous. I lie awake for the longest time, staring at the ceiling and counting the time between the red blinks of the smoke detector.

When the alarm sounds, I find myself wrapped around Jaxson, and I jump away. "Sorry," I mumble.

"It's normal to have a hard-on in the morning." He chuckles.

"What?"

"Nothing," he says as he stretches.

I adjust my top so my boobs aren't hanging out and dash to the bathroom. "Why are we getting up so early?"

"You promised your mom we'd be at her house by nine for rehearsal prep."

I sigh. "Oh, right."

I grab a quick, scalding shower, and while my head is upside down as I'm drying my hair, Jaxson walks in naked. *Holy fucking cow.* He's beautiful, as if he was sculpted from marble.

He hops in the glass shower, and I try to pretend I don't see him. Right now, I wish I was the bar of soap he's using to touch every inch of his body. When he turns away, his ass is equally magnificent. I want to run my hands all over him.

In the end, my hair is not as dry as I'd like, but I can't stay any longer. I might drool all over myself.

Who am I kidding? I drooled.

I return to the bedroom and finish dressing. When I burst out to the living room of the suite, I find Christophe and Wyatt sitting at the table with breakfast.

I scoop myself a healthy portion of fresh berries and Greek yogurt, and while I eat, I study my email. I try to ignore Jaxson as he walks in. "Nothing much came in from work in either of our emails," I report.

I catch him out of the corner of my eye, and he's wearing a bold blue button-down shirt that oozes expensive with a pair of crisp gray slacks and fancy black loafers. I say a little prayer, asking for strength to make it through today without jumping him and yelling *yeehaw!*

"Did you sleep well?" Jaxson asks as he sits.

My head bobs up and down as I take a crispy piece of bacon. "And you?"

"I haven't slept that well in ages. You have a calming effect on me."

If that's what you want to call it. "I'm guessing we won't be back until after the rehearsal dinner tonight. I'm sure my family will have me doing all sorts of things today, so I'll pack a change of clothes. You look perfect. I mean...well, I'm...um... You're fine to wear the same thing today and tonight."

The corners of his mouth turn up. "You didn't mention whether you're in the wedding."

I shake my head. "I'm not. I'm not sure any of my brothers and sisters are." Hannah and I were close once, but once she had her claws in Hudson, she left me behind.

Jaxson takes a sip of coffee. "Let me know when you're ready to leave."

How can he be so calm? "I'll be ready in just a few," I assure him.

Finishing my yogurt, I zip back to the room and gather my clothes for this evening. I also try yet again to collect myself. Today is going to be difficult on so many levels.

CHAPTER 13

Harper

I take a deep breath as we arrive at my childhood home. It's always chaos. These days just four of my brothers and sisters live here, but I still expect nothing less.

"Are you ready?" I ask Jaxson.

He nods. "Should I be worried?"

I smirk. "Always when it comes to the Lockwood clan." I knock on the door and turn the handle. "Hello? Anyone home?"

"Harper!" Hope almost knocks me over.

I hold on to her tightly. "I've missed you so much."

"I can't believe you're finally here."

Everyone is home, and all my brothers and sisters come to the foyer. We're surrounded. Jaxson's eyes grow wide. There is no mistaking that we're all related. We all have dark brown hair and blue eyes, and we're tall.

"Everyone, this is my..." Suddenly, I don't know what to call him.

"Boyfriend," he supplies, and that gets a laugh out of everyone.

"Jaxson Bancroft," I add, so I'm not completely rude.

"You're dating your boss?" my older sister Hazel asks.

I shrug. "I'm dating my boss." I step over and put my arm around his waist. His arm wraps around my shoulders. *No, this isn't awkward at all.*

"Very nice," my older brother Hunter says. He thrusts out his hand and introduces himself. And then everyone introduces themselves.

"There will be a test later," Hope teases.

"I might get a few of you mixed up, but I promise I'm trying," Jaxson says. "Harper talks about you all the time."

Way to sell it. "Where are Mom and Dad?" I ask.

"They only took the afternoon off," Hope explains. "So they'll be home later."

I nod. My parents instilled an incredible work ethic in us, but it's typical of them not to give Hudson the whole day. I hate that I was always jealous of how much they gave their students and how little they had for us. Hazel always said we should be fine with it. Mom is usually in her room if she's home anyway.

The guys head into the dining room, and Jaxson goes right along with them. My sisters and I make our way into the kitchen, sit down, and catch up on everything going on around here. Hope practically sits on my lap.

"I think you should accept Wellesley," I tell her privately when we've both gotten up to get something to drink. "I will help you. I can give you part of my paycheck—about two thousand dollars a month."

Her eyes go wide. "Are you sure?"

"Positive. I have a little more money these days, so I've got you covered. You won't have to borrow as much."

"That will cover my rent, but I'll pay you back. Thank you." She gives me a tight hug.

"Just do well in school; that's all I ask."

She squeezes my hand. "I miss you so much."

"I'm always just a phone call away," I remind her.

"I know. I thought about applying to schools near you, but Mom wants me close."

"I'll support you wherever you decide to go, and I'll give you whatever I can."

She wraps her arms around me. "Thank you."

We return to the table, and my sisters catch me up on the gossip around the neighborhood and what's going on with the wedding while we wrap plastic silverware in napkins. They're excited that Hannah will be another sister.

"What about you, Hazel? Do you have a date for this weekend?" I ask. As the oldest, Hazel has given up the most for our family.

"Paul is coming up from New York," she tells me.

I tilt my head. "Reeeeeeally…"

Paul was her high school crush, and they've been serious for a while. I like him.

She leans in. "He's become more persistent about me moving to New York."

"When are you going?"

She shrugs. "I don't know that I am. Harmony needs a roommate to cover half the rent, so it's hard."

My heart breaks. If I was living here, I could rent the apartment, and she could move on. Harmony would be difficult for someone to adapt to, but she needs a roommate to split costs. "What about finding someone else to move in?"

"Mom and Dad would never allow her to live with a stranger," she says.

It's times like this that I feel conflicted about living so far away, but it's also the reason I chose to move. "I hate to see you put your life on hold."

"Not everyone can just turn their back on the family," she says.

That stings. I'd like to think she isn't purposely being mean, but it still hits me hard. "I'm sorry for the ways it made things harder for you, but I couldn't stay here any longer. You encouraged me."

She gives me a plastic smile. "I know." She slaps her knees and stands. "I should finish getting things ready. I'm hoping you won't mind helping me with the cooking for tonight."

"Not at all. How many people will be at the rehearsal?" I ask.

"About fifty."

That's a small gathering for us. "I'm here to help."

I look over at Jaxson, who seems entertained by my brothers. He catches my eye and grins. I hear Tessa Sky's name, and my stomach lurches. They know too much about Jaxson's past. I worry that's going to be a problem.

"What's on the menu tonight?" I ask Hazel, who's already moving around in the kitchen.

"I bought some frozen appetizers, so we'll need to heat them closer to time. If you could take the mini sausages and barbecue sauce and start them in the slow cooker, that would be great. After that, the bread dough should be ready for the dinner rolls. They need to be rounded and put in the pans for a second rise and then baked."

I reach for one of Grandma's old aprons. "Got it."

Hazel asks the guys to get the tent and tables up in the backyard and then help Holden get his DJ setup ready for tonight. Jaxson comes over and kisses me goodbye as they head out. It's a quick kiss, but I'm still shocked.

"If you would prefer to go back to the hotel, you can," I tell him. "I'm fine here, and we can catch up tonight."

He smirks. "I like being a regular guy. I'm good." He squeezes my shoulder and follows them out.

"He seems very into you," Hazel observes. "You hadn't mentioned him to anyone."

"It's happened quickly, but he was super enthusiastic about coming for this. We're stopping at his parents' in Michigan on the way home." I finish the sausages and begin working on the bread. "What about you and Paul?"

She shrugs. "He's getting impatient. If I don't join him soon, he's going to move on. His job isn't here; it's there."

My heart hurts. "How's Harmony doing?"

"She has her good days and bad. She has a good job working at home as a bookkeeper for a few small businesses. If she needs something communicated over the phone, though, I usually have to do it."

"And what about you?"

"Same old, same old. I get up each day and go to work at the hospital. Then I come home to cook for Harmony and me."

"She's able to cook," I remind her.

"If I want white rice and baked chicken breast every night, sure. But..." She shrugs.

I shake my head. That stinks. She's not Harmony's mother. "Tell me what to expect at the wedding tomorrow."

That gets Hazel talking about all the family drama that I don't miss — which aunts and uncles are coming, which aren't. Who's bringing what and particularly who *isn't* bringing something she thinks they should. Hazel is always careful not to criticize our parents, and when I ask how they're doing, she avoids the subject.

It takes three hours before I'm finished with the bread. My back is breaking and I'm hot, so I excuse myself and go looking for Jaxson. I find him in the backyard covered in mud.

"Oh no. Are you okay?"

He nods. "Harrison found me a pair of rubber boots, but a big part of the backyard is muddy. We rearranged the tent so people wouldn't walk in it, and we're making a run to Home Depot so we can make a stage people can dance on to cover the mud."

"Thank you. I know when I asked you to come, you didn't expect this."

He brushes flour from my hair. "I don't mind at all. It's been fun spending the day with your brothers. I always knew you were a rebel."

"They said that?"

He bounces his eyebrows. "I mean, when kids at school were told they couldn't wear suggestive T-shirts, you pulled your shirt off and walked around in a sports bra."

I fight a grin. "I planned that, so I'd have everything covered. You couldn't see anything important."

"I wouldn't have complained. They apparently had to fight off someone who was ready to take you home."

I nod. "Greg Hudson. He was captain of the football team and stealer of girls' virginity."

"Really? Did he steal yours?"

I'm not going to tell him that. "I didn't ask you about your first."

He moves in close. "Nicole Roberts, in my room when I was sixteen years old."

I shake my head. "It wasn't Greg Hudson."

"My mom taught me," he whispers in my ear, "that I was only ready to have sex when I was more interested in my partner enjoying it than myself. Nicole enjoyed it, and I learned how to get girls off. I'm ready to show you whenever you are."

I shake my head. "You're terrible."

"I'm actually quite good."

CHAPTER 14

Harper

"Harper!" Mom exclaims as she walks into the house. "My family is complete."

I smile. "Great to see you, Mom." I run into her arms.

"Where is that handsome man I've heard so little about?"

"He went back to the hotel to get showered and changed. They found a mud pit in the backyard, so he and the guys have built a stage for some dancing later tonight."

Dad wraps his arm around my shoulder and kisses my temple. "Good to have you home, Kitten. The neighbors are going to love a stage for dancing."

"Even if they don't, at least no one will be covered in mud."

"What did they do about the mosquitos?" he asks.

"They have those ugly mosquito coils," Hazel says from behind me. "And I put together the large planters with marigolds, lavender, and lemongrass, which should help. We have citronella candles on the tables, and everyone knows it's in the backyard, so they'll most likely wear Deet."

He nods. "Those planters are beautiful. Good call."

Hazel preens. She gets so little acknowledgement for all she does for the family.

"She's done an amazing job getting the food ready for tonight." I wrap my arm around her waist and give her a side hug.

"That's her job." Mom pats her on the arm.

I want to scream, *No it's not!* But I don't. Hazel deserves to move to New York and be with the man she loves. She doesn't need to be trapped here with our family, picking up the slack for things my parents should be doing.

I walk back to my old room and find Hope studying. "What are you working on?"

"I have a paper due next week. This weekend there's too much going on, so I'm trying to get ahead when I can." She closes her books. "But I guess I should get ready."

I place my bag on the bed and unpack my dress for tonight.

"Are you excited about this weekend?" Hope asks.

"I'm excited to be home. I've missed everyone."

She looks at me skeptically.

No family is perfect, and Hazel has shown me how to leave it at that. "Really. I've missed everyone. Even Hunter." My brother Hunter is thirteen months older than I am, and we were oil and water growing up. If I said the sky was blue, he'd tell the world it was purple.

"Will you have a date for tonight?" I ask Hope.

"No way. I wouldn't subject my worst enemy to the craziness of our family."

I change, feeling self-conscious about my expensive bra and panty set.

"Why didn't you tell me you were dating your boss?" Hope asks.

I slip the dress over my shoulders and turn so she can zip it for me. "I don't know. Probably because I didn't think he liked me that much. It's all happened pretty quickly."

140

"That man definitely likes you. He can't take his eyes off you, and he even bought extra twinkle lights for outside because he wanted it to be special."

I laugh. "It will be a good night for Hannah and Hudson."

"I think he wanted it to be special for you."

"Having him here is special. He knows that."

Hope pulls her dress on. She's really grown since I was home.

"You look beautiful."

"Thank you," she says. "So do you."

I help her with her zipper. "I hate to ask, but you're being careful right?"

Hope always has a lot of boys interested in her, and she doesn't have the brothers looking over her shoulder that I had.

"Yes," she says. "I still have my V-card, but I'm also on birth control. I'll always make sure we use a condom."

I'm relieved. "Good."

Hazel knocks on the door. "You both look lovely."

She's also cleaned up really nicely, and Paul and Harmony are behind her. I give Paul a hug as a greeting. I hold Harmony's hand a moment, and she squeezes it. It's the most I'll get from her, but I'm good with that.

"You both look fantastic." I turn to Paul. "Hazel did a lot of the work getting tonight organized. Make sure she has plenty of fun."

"That's my plan." He winks at Hazel.

"The rehearsal is finished at the church and people are beginning to arrive for dinner," she tells us.

We nod. The Lockwood sisters are ready.

We walk outside, and I'm talking to Paul when I feel Jaxson before I see him. Paul looks over my shoulder, and his mouth drops.

"Paul, this is my boyfriend, Ja—"

"Jaxson Bancroft," Paul finishes for me. He extends his hand. "I'm a huge fan. I was at your presentation on the Honeycomb trajectory and your plans as you prepare for your IPO."

"Great. What did you think?" Jaxson asks.

"It's a *buy* in my book." Paul turns to Hazel. "This guy is a legend in Silicon Valley." He tells her about what happened at Quick Reels, and what Jaxson and his partners have done since. "I swear, everything this guy touches turns to gold."

Hazel gives me a look. "Wow, that's great."

"He's also a fantastic kisser, and dances like Elaine from *Seinfeld*," I add.

Paul turns pink. "I'm sorry. I get a little overexcited."

Jaxson smiles. "No worries, man. I live in a bubble in San Francisco, so it's good to hear how things are playing outside the Bay Area. But I want to correct one thing. I'm a worse dancer than Elaine on *Seinfeld*."

Everyone laughs.

A few minutes later, my parents arrive with Hannah and Hudson, as well as Father Murphy.

They head over to me and Jaxson. Father Murphy hugs me first. "It's so great to see you. Your mother tells me you have a serious boyfriend."

I chortle. "Mom, Dad, Father Murphy, please meet Jaxson Bancroft, my serious boyfriend."

That gets a laugh out of everyone.

"Nice to meet you."

Mom gives him a hug. "We're so happy you're here. I'd be lying if I told you this weekend was not indicative of our family life. We're always this chaotic."

Mom and Dad spend the next fifteen minutes grilling Jaxson, and I hold his hand tightly, trying not to make any kind of scene. Harmony holds my other hand, and I know she's missed me. The rest of my family is flittering about, but they're listening intently to the Q and A, I'm sure. Jaxson is the new shiny object, I suppose.

Hudson and Hannah have been standing close by, so when they're ushered away to start dinner, Jaxson and I sit with Hazel, Paul, and my sisters Hope and Harmony.

Soon enough, we get our chance to eat, and the food is delicious. There are lots of appetizers, and then Hazel had been smoking a brisket, ribs, and chicken all day. After the ice cream sundae bar, my brothers shuffle things around and get ready for the dancing to begin.

Hudson and Hannah come over to raise their glasses to Hazel. "You really did a fantastic job tonight," Hannah says.

Hazel blushes. "I have an army of brothers and sisters who make it much easier."

I look over at my mother and recognize what I see on her face. She's not happy that they haven't thanked her or Dad. *That.* That is why I'm glad I don't live here.

"Would you like to dance?" Jaxson asks.

"Sure. Why not? Let's get this party started."

We're the first to get out on the dance floor, but we're soon joined by my sisters, and other guests trickle in. When a slow song comes on, Jaxson pulls me close. "You mentioned earlier that I was a good kisser," he murmurs in my ear.

"I did."

"I think we should explore that."

We rock back and forth, and Jaxson places a soft kiss low on the side of my neck. I can't help but sigh my appreciation, even as I remind myself he's doing this for show.

"You look so beautiful tonight."

"Thank you for coming this weekend."

"I'm glad I did. I've learned a lot about you."

I stiffen. "What did my brothers say?"

"Don't worry. You're fine. I've learned you can take direction. I've learned you make amazing rolls. I've learned why you live so far away. And I've learned that your family misses you."

"Okay." I sigh. "I somehow doubt our trip to your parents' will be so revealing."

He shrugs. "You never know."

We drink and celebrate, and when the night is over, Christophe drives us back to the hotel.

When we enter the hotel elevator, my tension level is high. Since meeting my parents before dinner, I don't think I've gone longer than three minutes without Jaxson touching me. Even now, his hand is at my back, and I feel like I might explode. Everything has been so emotional back at home, and it's been amazing to have him by my side. But it's also been *hella* confusing.

As we enter our hotel suite, Jaxson tells Christophe we'll be ready to leave for the wedding at noon tomorrow. Then he closes the door and turns to me. In a flash, he pulls me to him and leans down. His kiss is slow to start as he seems to savor every minute.

Adjusting himself, his hardness presses into my abdomen, and he clutches the fabric from the skirt of my dress. He leans far enough away to see my eyes, a question on his face. My heart races, and I'm a throbbing mess, but I know I want more. He leans in again, and our mouths collide. His kiss is firm and aggressive, and he reaches for my ass and squeezes. He moves down the side of my neck, and I see stars. He's erased the memory of any other man I've kissed.

When he breaks away, I nearly stumble.

Jaxson steadies me. "Are you okay?"

"Just a little lightheaded."

He smiles. "I'm glad it's not just me." He leans down and gives me one more chaste kiss. "Goodnight, my sweet. Go ahead and go to bed. I'll see you in the morning."

My heart flops on the floor like a fish gasping for water. He's left me speechless. That's not what I thought he was going to say — or do. I sit down on the bed and watch his back as he disappears into the bathroom.

CHAPTER 15

Jaxson

Waking with Harper laid across my chest makes me happy and very content. She didn't even move when I got into bed last night. I think she was out in an instant. That was a big day for her — and for me, I guess. Yesterday was surprisingly fun. Her brothers were protective of her, but they seemed to like me well enough. Hudson is the de facto father of the family, so I wonder how the dynamic is going to change now that he'll have a family of his own.

As I talked with everyone last night, it was easy to see why Harper moved as far away as she could get. And I heard her mother trying to talk her into coming back to Boston. She was resistant, and good for her. Of course, she loves these people, but there's nothing for her here. I suppose she can do what she wants once we decide to split up, but until then, she's going to be right by my side in San Francisco.

Not taking things even farther than I did with Harper last night was hard. I mean, I knew it would be, but I hadn't anticipated what a day of acting like a real couple would feel like. But I'm glad we're moving slowly. She'd had a few drinks, and I didn't want her to wake up and regret it. We've got to keep up our show for quite a while, so I have to make sure she's comfortable. But I'm definitely enjoying having her curled up with me.

Harper begins to stir, and watching her stretch reminds me of my childhood cat. Chester would go into almost a downward dog and then into a dolphin pose. I always figured he was probably a yogi in another life.

"Good morning," Harper murmurs as she lays her head back on my chest.

I kiss the top of her head, relieved that she didn't freak out when she realized where she was. "Good morning. How did you sleep?"

"Really well, actually. But I think I could sleep another ten or twelve hours."

I understand. I get so jetlagged from crisscrossing back and forth to New York. I'm used to being in a perpetual state of exhaustion. "You can sleep for a while longer," I tell her. "We don't need to leave for two hours."

She rolls away from me and does just that. I miss her body heat immediately but use that as my excuse to move out into the living area and get caught up on some work I missed yesterday.

Yesterday. That was fun. Those guys didn't care who I was. They weren't looking for me to fund their idea or for a handout in any way. I was just some guy who fell for their sister. Paul seems more like the guys I run into when we're at home. He was nice enough, but it gets boring when people are obsessed with how I must've gotten a lucky break. That plays a part in success, and I've certainly been fortunate, but having the right idea at the right time is also essential. I've worked hard for what's mine. But it also doesn't define me.

Our only job today, or so I've been promised, is to show up at the wedding. The bride's family is taking care of the reception in the church hall.

After knocking a few things out, I get showered and dressed so Harper can have the bathroom to do what she needs to once she wakes up again. As far as I'm concerned, she could go in a zombie costume and still be the most beautiful woman in the room.

Eventually, I hear her moving around in the bedroom, and she walks out wearing a simple light green dress with a delicate bow below the bustline.

"You're beautiful."

Her smile highlights her sparkling eyes. "Thank you. I'm so glad I'm not in the wedding. I prefer to choose my own outfit. The bridesmaids' electric blue silk dresses with lavender pumps are not my style."

I laugh. "Your dress really brings out the blue in your eyes."

She curtseys. "You look very good in a suit. But you always do."

"Thank you. I own several suits, but I usually only wear them when I'm meeting with bankers. The rest of the time I'm quite comfortable in my startup uniform."

"You wear jeans and high-tops well too."

I lead her out the door, and then Christophe and Wyatt walk us down to the car.

When we're settled inside, I reach for her hand and squeeze it. "I'm really glad you moved out to San Francisco, and even though the job isn't what you want it to be, I'm glad you ended up working for me."

"Me too." She smiles, but it seems a little plastic.

I can't even imagine all the thoughts running through her head while she's back here.

St. Francis Xavier Catholic Church is just down the street from Harper's parents' house. When we arrive, the four of us walk into the back. Christophe and Wyatt will stand in the vestibule while the wedding takes place. This should be plenty safe for us, so I'm hoping they'll just do a nice job of blending in.

The sanctuary is already full of people, easily five hundred guests. Harper has told me it will be a traditional Catholic ceremony with a full Mass. I grew up Catholic so I knew how to do church aerobics — stand up, sit down, stand up, sit down, kneel, stand up, kneel, walk to the front, walk back to your seat, kneel, stand up, sit down, and then walk out. It was a joke my sister and I had growing up.

The wedding begins, and everything is lovely. Harper and I follow along, and there's something comfortable about the familiar service. Usually, I avoid these things like the plague, but Hudson and Hannah do seem happy as they proclaim their everlasting love for one another.

Afterward, the reception is in the church hall. I didn't get to meet Hannah's family last night, but they are very kind as we meet them in the receiving line.

I lean over as we walk away. "What did we give the couple?"

"We got them something off their registry," Harper says. "I think it was sheets. I can't remember. There wasn't much left by the time I got there."

"Thank you for including me."

"Of course. We're a happy couple, right?"

She seems on edge. I'm out of my depth here, and everyone is going out of their way to talk to her, plus all the family pressure, so I know it must feel overwhelming. "Is everything okay?" I ask.

Harper sighs. "Yes. I'm just ready to go back to San Francisco. As you can see, my family is a lot."

"Whenever you want to leave, just let me know. We don't have to stick around."

She looks into my eyes. "Thank you."

"I wasn't lying earlier. You look beautiful today."

"Why did you kiss me last night?" she asks.

I'm a little taken aback. "Because I couldn't stop myself."

"But you could sleep with me in the same bed?"

"It wasn't easy."

She turns to me with a sexy look, but then her eyes move over my shoulder and her face becomes stoic. "Look out. Here comes trouble. Just ignore whatever shit he flings."

"Well, well, well. If it isn't Harper Lockwood returning to the scene of the crime."

"There was no crime, Jason. I just decided to move to San Francisco."

He crosses his arms and stares her down, or at least, he tries.

Harper takes a deep breath, and I grip her hand. "I'd like you to meet my boyfriend, Jaxson Bancroft."

"Oh, the whole place is buzzing about you landing a billionaire. I bet you spread your legs wide for him, don't you?"

What. The. Hell? "Excuse me? You don't talk about Harper like that."

Jason sways. He's obviously drunk. "She strung me along for years, and even agreed to marry me — "

"I was in tenth grade when you asked. You weren't serious. You thought that was how you were going to get into my pants."

I look over at Christophe, and he and Wyatt are making their way to us.

"Why don't you move along?" I suggest.

Jason rears back, and his fist is coming right at my face. I stop it with my hand. In an instant, Christophe and Wyatt have him locked between them, and they walk him out of the room.

It all happened so fast that most people didn't notice, but some did.

I lean in to Harper. "Are you okay?"

A tear falls down her cheek.

I put my hand on her back. "Why don't we walk outside for a few minutes and let everyone get back to whatever they're doing?"

Hunter, Harrison, and even her little brother, Holden, rush over. "Are you okay?"

"We're good," I assure them. "I think we're going to step outside a minute."

I wrap my arm around Harper and walk her to the exit. We go over to stand under the giant elm tree at the front of the church. The buzz of the traffic on the road is calming. Conflict crosses Harper's face, and I can tell she's trying to work something out.

I wait patiently. "Do you want to leave?" I ask after a moment.

She shakes her head. "No. I'm fine to stay. Jason was my high school boyfriend. He was best friends with my older brother Hunter, and our mothers are close friends. He tried to talk me into having sex with him for years. It was a high-pressure campaign, and I never did. Not because I was opposed to having sex, but because I found kissing him was like kissing my brothers. Yuck."

I chuckle. "And kissing me?"

She snorts. "You light every nerve on fire."

"You do the same to me."

Her eyes lift to mine, and they're smoldering. My dick stiffens.

Hunter rounds the corner and joins us under the canopy of the large tree. "I'm so sorry," he says. "But man, was that impressive. You caught his fist in your hand. Those two guys — do you know them?"

"They're my security detail," I explain. "They just walked him out and told him not to return, at least until he's sobered up."

Hunter's eyes grow wide. "You have a security detail?"

"I do. I never know what kind of trouble might find me."

150

"Wow." Hunter stuffs his hands in his pockets and shows no signs of moving on. "My friends and I were really impressed."

"We should go back in," Harper says.

"If you're sure." I search her eyes and see something I never have before, and that's desire. I want to take her back to the hotel and explore every inch of her body.

She nods.

"Okay, let's get back in there."

We walk in as Hannah's sister is giving her toast, followed by Hudson's best man.

It's announced that each table will be called to the buffet by number. We're sitting with her brothers and sisters toward the front, and we're among the last tables called. There isn't much food left.

"I think we'll want to stop and get something to eat on the way back to the hotel," Harper whispers.

"Agreed. Any recommendations?"

"I'm sure we can find a place close to the hotel."

"I'm fine with room service."

Her eyes light up. "That's so decadent."

"True, but we can get into our birthday suits and it won't cause a stir."

She looks me up and down. "You think you could handle me in my birthday suit?"

"I'd certainly like to try."

Hannah's father approaches us. "I'm so sorry we ran out of food."

"Don't worry about it." Harper reaches for his arm. "We're fine."

"I'm ordering some pies. That's pizza to you. They'll be here in a little over an hour."

"Don't do that for us. We had a big lunch. We're good," I assure him.

151

After dinner, Holden is the DJ again, and he plays a song for Hannah and her father to dance to, as well as Hudson and his mother.

A few minutes later, a nice slow song gets Harper and me out on the dance floor. "I really love dancing with you. I like having your body pressed up against mine."

"You're an easy man to please," she says.

We dance a short time longer, and then we watch the newlyweds cut the cake.

Harper turns to me. "Let's say goodbye to my parents."

We spot them deep in the mass of people. On our way over, several family friends stop us and tell me cute stories about Harper, who is a glorious shade of crimson by the end. When we finally get to her mom, she's surrounded by friends.

"Mom, Jaxson and I are headed back to our hotel," Harper says. "It's been a long day, and my feet are killing me. We'll be at the house for brunch tomorrow."

"We'll be going to ten o'clock mass. You're not going to join us?"

"After what happened tonight, no. We'll meet you at the house."

"What happened?"

Harper kisses her cheek. "See you in the morning after eleven."

"Aren't you going to tell me?" She reaches for her hand.

"I'm sure you'll hear about it," Harper replies. "Everything's fine."

Next, Harper walks over to her dad. "I'll see you tomorrow after church at the house."

He nods. "Have a good night, sweetie. It's great having you home."

"Thanks, Dad."

The ride back into Boston is slow, since it's Saturday night. But the air in the car is crackling. Harper and I sit close, our hands touching, but we both watch the road.

"Are you glad you came home for the wedding?" I ask.

"Very. But I'm really glad we're staying in a hotel."

It seems like hours, but it was really just a solid thirty minutes, door to door. I reach for Harper's hand as we cross the lobby. "Do you want a drink?" I ask as we pass the busy hotel bar.

"No. I'm good. I'd rather go upstairs."

"Lead the way." We enter the elevator with another couple who exit on the same floor we do. Christophe opens the door and scans our suite before exiting. I'm elated to be alone with Harper now.

Her lips find mine, and we kiss passionately, both of us heating up. One hand caresses her back, and the other frames her face. My dick tents in my pants, and I can see her nipples harden beneath her dress. She slides a hand up to massage my neck and tilts her head to give me better access to explore with kisses, licks, and nibbles. I find a few spots that make her squirm, and I file that away. I suck on her neck — not enough to give her a love bite, but enough to elicit a long, throaty moan of my name. And damn, if that doesn't get me hard as a lead pipe.

Her hand moves to my chest, and I slide my mouth a little lower. She purrs each time I venture farther. I explore her collarbone and play with the fabric of her dress.

Then, lacing my fingers with hers, I pull her into the bedroom of our suite and step back to take her in. She closes the distance between us, and we are back to kissing. My heart thumps so loudly I'm sure she can hear it. Her hands explore, and she's lighting everything on fire. Is she really telling me this is okay?

I step back. "What do you want, Harper?" I hold my breath, waiting for her to tell me. I'm worried she's going to deny me. I'm worried I should deny her, no matter what she says. I don't want her to regret this.

"I want this," she tells me.

I raise my brow, waiting for her to define what *this* is.

"I want you. I want you to make me come and to feel you inside me."

My heart races. My prayers have been answered. I've wanted this for so long. "I'm thrilled to hear that," I tell her. "You're sure?"

When she nods, I can't hold out any longer. I sit down on the bed and put my wallet on the bedside table, bringing her to stand between my knees.

My hands explore her body over her dress, touching and feeling as I memorize the look of ecstasy on her face. Harper purrs. I explore further, with feather touches and rough kneading over her arms, legs, and ass. Finally, my fingers brush the swell of her breast.

"Ohhhhhhh." Harper's sigh is full of desire. I trace around the side, following the contour. More purring. Harper leans down, and our tongues clash as I push her bra out of the way to cup her breast before rolling the nipple between my fingers.

"Yes," she groans into my mouth. I caress all around the underside as she writhes.

I stand and reach behind her to unzip her dress. Turning her around, I pepper kisses down her spine. My hands slide beneath the fabric and push it over her shoulders.

She steps out of her dress, and her lips crush into mine. She wants this. My head spins, and my hands are like magnets to her breasts. They feel fantastic—full, firm, and warm. I sit down, and she stands before me in a skin-toned, see-through bra and panty set. She takes my breath away.

As my fingers explore, I brush her nipple. She moans, so I brush it again. Her body language is hot and needy, so I close my fingers and gently massage.

"Oh God!" Harper's nipple swells and stiffens in my fingers.

My body is on overload. I've never wanted a woman more than I want her right now. Her lips press into mine, and she coaxes me to stand, rubbing my hard rod through my pants. She looks up, and her flushed gaze searches my face.

Her eyes trace my chest as I unbutton my shirt, and she licks her lips as I slide it over my shoulders. "Should I continue?" I ask.

"Definitely."

I drop the shirt on top of her dress on the floor. She reaches for my belt, but I step back to look at her. Harper is beautiful by any standard. I can barely process all the ways I plan on touching and tasting every inch of her body.

"Like what you see?" she teases.

"Without a doubt." I laugh. "You. Are. Beautiful."

"Stop. You're making me blush."

Her eyes move to my hand, which is pulling on my cock. I reach out and pull her close, feeling her breasts against my chest. We kiss and hug each other tight.

"Mmmmmm…" she purrs. "I really like you when you're like this."

And that starts a fantastic make-out session. Our lips crash together, our tongues duel, and our teeth clash. My hands frame her face, brush her neck, and move through her hair. Her kisses turn more forceful.

We caress each other's backs. Harper still wants more, so my hands migrate to her front and brush against the side of her breast.

"God, yes," she breathes into my lips.

I pop the clasp of her bra with one hand and slide it off her shoulder, adding it to our growing pile of clothes. I love the weight of her breasts in my hands. She moans. I caress the firm mound and feel her erect nipple dragging under my palm and fingers. She pushes herself into me. I love how responsive she is. Soon her body is writhing. I hook my fingers into the side of her panties, kissing, licking, and nibbling my way down as I pull them off of her.

"Leave the shoes on and lie down on the bed," I direct.

I lie beside her, and my pulse pounds. This body has tempted me for months. I trace kisses down to her neck. Her breasts tighten, and the flesh grows pebbled. I tease up to her lips for another kiss, then kiss along her upper chest until I reach her breasts. Having already warmed them up with my hands, I kiss her nipple and swirl all around with my tongue. Finally, I capture the straining nipple in my lips.

She gasps, and her arms come around to cradle my head at her breast. Swinging a leg over her, I look into her eyes. What I see is desire, and not a hint of hesitation. I kiss her again and move lower, every drop of blood in my body rushing to my dick.

I kiss along her tummy and play with her belly button. She squirms. The heady scent of her needy pussy hits me, and I move down to find the source.

"Oh, God!" she breathes.

She's in for a good tongue lashing. I tease her mound, moving across the tops of her thighs, reaching down to guide one of her knees outward, followed by the other. I look up, and her pussy is flushed with heat and moisture.

"You are amazing."

She moans in response, and I kiss up her thighs, finally moving to her slick slit and tasting her. She shudders beneath me and drives her hips down, pushing her clit against my tongue. I love how greedy she is.

Taking her clit into my mouth, I can feel her react. "Oh, my God!" she cries out, and I wonder if the whole hotel didn't hear her.

I reach up to her chest and palm a breast. A deep moan tells me I'm on the right track. I roll her nipple between my fingers, and I can feel the jolts of electricity through her body.

"Oh God, don't stop," she moans as she tenses under me. Then she bows her back off the bed. A shuddering cry announces the detonation in her body. Her pussy throbs against my tongue, matched by pulses in her nipple. I flatten my tongue and keep up the pressure as she jolts. When she finally collapses, I release the pressure and drink up her nectar. It's the best I've ever tasted.

"Oh. My. God. That was so good. Come up here."

I pull away from her swollen sex and kiss my way to her face. She fastens her lips to mine, swirling her tongue in my mouth. Her chest is heaving as she gasps for air, yet still she pulls me down beside her. "That was fantastic," she says. "Now, I want you inside me."

I raise myself and look into her eyes as I reach over and hand her a condom. She licks my tip, and I raise a brow at her. "I'm not going to last long if you keep looking at me like that." I won't last long no matter what, but I want to at least come inside her.

She smirks and kisses the tip of my cock. I nearly explode as she rips the foil packet and rolls it on. Her hand snakes down to place my cock at her entrance. "Fuck me."

Her hips lift toward mine, and the head of my cock enters a snug, liquid furnace. She circles her pelvis, and the first part of the shaft dives in. On the next circle, I'm deep inside. One more, and I slide home.

We groan together. She feels so good. Her pussy conforms to my shaft, each bit of my cock stimulated by tight, liquid velvet. And the heat. Her pussy is on fire.

I pull my attention up to her face. A huge grin animates her features. "This is incredible," I breathe.

"You feel so good," she replies. "And Jaxson, don't try to wait for me. Let yourself go. We have all night."

"Okay." I won't last long inside her fiery tunnel. Our lips connect as my hips pull back. I slide home again, and we both groan in pleasure.

We find a rhythm, and the pull of my orgasm seeps deep into my balls. She's everywhere around me, her hands caressing my back and face and her lips working magic on mine.

I don't fight my orgasm, and the pull grows until I know it's imminent.

"Come for me, baby." She pulls my head down for a deep kiss as her hips flex upward, driving me deeper. Fire radiates out from my cock, and I explode with a deep groan. Pulses blast out of my cock, filling the condom.

She cradles my head throughout my release, and then her hands wander all over my back. When I recover, she pulls my lips to hers and we kiss again, my cock still nestled inside her. There's a warmth for Harper that's infused my body, and I can feel the same in her. I pull back, and we look into each other's eyes, big grins on our faces.

We lie in each other's arms for a while, catching our breath. I don't know what to think, but I know I like this. Probably a lot more than I should.

"Thank you," she says.

I look down at her and smirk. "Are you hungry?"

She nods. "I need sustenance to do more of that."

"Sounds good to me."

CHAPTER 16

Harper

The heat emanating from Jaxson wakes me in the morning. To cool down, I roll over and kick my leg out from under the duvet. I'm sore. I can't believe what happened between us last night. How am I going to look at him? It was like he pulled the cork and I couldn't get enough. And he had me so needy and desperate. I squeeze my eyes shut. I'm so embarrassed.

Trying to not jostle him awake, I slip out of bed and wrap a towel around me in the bathroom. My reflection is like hell warmed over. My hair looks like a flock of birds nested in it, my eyes belong on a raccoon, my lips are swollen and red, and I have whisker burn all over, particularly between my legs and on my chest. I'm a mess.

With my mouth feeling like a cat dropped a hair ball inside, I dig out my toothbrush and start by brushing my teeth. By the time I've finished, I'm already feeling like a new woman. And just in time…

"How are you this morning?" Jaxson says as he wraps his arms around me from behind and kisses my shoulder.

I manage a smirk, but I don't know what to say.

He looks at me in the mirror. "Are you okay?"

I nod. "Of course. Just a little embarrassed about my behavior last night."

He tenses. "What do you mean?"

"I don't know. What do you think? I begged. I acted like I was insatiable." I look away. "That wasn't me. It was an out-of-body experience."

Jaxson laughs a deep belly laugh and pulls me close. Despite all the sweat and swapping of fluids, he smells fantastic. He turns the shower on and looks back at me. "Come on. Last night was amazing. I loved watching you, and you couldn't get enough of me. That's certainly nothing to be embarrassed about." His voice lowers. "It makes me want to stay here all day, pick up where we left off."

"I—"

He holds up his hand. "But, if we're going to get to your parents' on time for brunch, we need to get moving."

Somehow, my towel falls to the floor. He takes my hand and guides me into the shower. Then he wraps a towel around his waist and brushes his teeth. The warm water feels so good on my skin, and it soothes the sore parts. I carefully wash my hair.

"You're beautiful, and last night was incredible," he adds after a moment. "Thank you for sharing that with me." His face is now covered in shaving cream as he uses some fancy razor.

My heart skips a beat. *I got me some of that, and damn, if he doesn't look hot this morning.* "I've never been like that before. You know, you've probably ruined me for other men."

He shrugs. "I'm okay with that."

I rinse the last of the conditioner from my hair and the suds from my body before stepping out of the shower. "Don't let it go to your head."

He turns to me with a twinkle in his eye. "Too late."

I dress in the white pants and floral blouse I love so much, and while I finish my hair, Jaxson orders coffee and some fruit, which arrives just as I'm ready to face my family again.

"How do you think yesterday went?" Jaxson asks, looking up from the newspaper he's reading.

"It was good. I'm glad we came," I tell him. "Being here makes me miss them but glad I live in San Francisco."

Jaxson puts the newspaper down. "That's good."

I tilt my head. "Were you worried?"

"I suppose I was. You're obviously close to your family."

I sigh. "Yes, but I left to not be 'a Lockwood' but to be Harper. In San Francisco, I can be me. No one knows my mom and dad or that there are eight kids unless I tell them."

"So what do you think today will be like?"

"That's a good question. Growing up, after church and breakfast on Sundays Hazel and I did laundry all day while the boys did yardwork and cleaned the house."

"Wow, that's very structured."

"When you have a large family, that's the only way to keep the chaos at bay. I don't think those activities are on the agenda today, though, so who knows."

Christophe knocks on the suite door just before eleven o'clock. He escorts us out.

"Good morning, Mr. Bancroft," a housekeeper says as we move down the hallway.

As we walk through the hotel lobby, I realize how many people here call Jaxson by his name. I know we're in a large suite in the hotel, but it's surprising that everyone acknowledges him.

"Have a good day, Mr. Bancroft," the valet says as he closes the door to the Cadillac Escalade behind him.

"Does that happen everywhere you go?" I ask.

"What?"

"Everyone at the hotel addressed you as Mr. Bancroft."

His brow crinkles. "I've never noticed that before."

161

The traffic through the tunnel should be easy on a Sunday morning, but of course, they're doing something and have us down to one lane. I look at my watch. We're going to be late. We're just sitting here breathing in fumes from the cars in line. *Great*. I'll never hear the end of it. I look at my watch for the dozenth time and sigh.

"It's okay," Jaxson says. "We left with plenty of time. I don't think we'll be late, but if we are, you can call your family and let them know."

"We haven't moved for ten minutes."

Jaxson puts his hand on my leg, and it travels up my thigh. "I can take your mind off of it if you'd like."

Terror rushes through me as I push his hand away. I point with my eyes at the back of JR and Wyatt's heads in front of us. And Christophe is right behind.

Jaxson laughs. "Don't worry."

"Easy for you to say," I whisper.

Thankfully, the traffic gets moving again.

"See? I got your mind off of being stuck in the tunnel, and now, we're almost to your parents'."

I roll my eyes. "You're going to pay for that later."

"I look forward to it." He gives me a salacious smile.

As we pull up, I see Hazel walking into the house. I follow her into the kitchen as the rest of my family returns from church. They all surround Jaxson.

"How did it go last night?" I ask Hazel.

"I had to take Harmony home just after midnight, but Hunter said they were at the church hall until after two picking things up. Hudson and Hannah are out on the Cape now, starting their honeymoon."

"Wow. Did Paul take you home?"

"No. I'm meeting him this afternoon." She pauses a moment before she looks at me. "I'm going to tell him I don't think I can leave Harmony."

I reach for her arm. "No. Don't do that. Look, I've promised some money to Hope for Wellesley next year but let me pay your portion of the rent so Harmony can live alone."

"You can't afford that," she says.

"Hazel, you've done so much for our family. You've always put everyone else ahead of yourself. It's time you do what you want. Plus, I've moved in with Jaxson, so I'm shifting my money around. Hunter should be able to check in on Harmony at least once a week, and I'm sure we could order her groceries and have them delivered."

"Are you sure?" Hazel says with hope in her eyes.

"I'm positive. Let me do this. It will show Mom and Dad that Harmony can live alone."

Hazel pulls me into a tight embrace. "Thank you."

"Of course. I'm happy to do it." I hold on to her tightly. "Why don't you call Paul and see if he can come to breakfast? Take the day and spend it with him before he needs to return to New York." I can see the conflict cross her eyes. "Do it. What's one more mouth for scrambled eggs?"

She pulls her cell phone from her pocket. "Thank you."

I walk out into the dining room where everyone is sitting at the table, seemingly waiting for Hazel to make breakfast. I call over my little sister, and while I cook the bacon and sausage and the scrambled eggs, she gets the toaster going. A little while later everyone — including Paul — is sitting at the table eating.

"I have an announcement," Hazel says. She looks at Paul, and they're both wearing silly grins. I couldn't be happier for her.

She explains her plan to move to New York, and everyone seems excited for them. Well, almost everyone.

"What about Harmony?" Mom asks.

Hazel looks over at her. "She and I have been talking about this for a while. She wants to live alone. We'll figure out how to move her into a smaller space."

Harmony nods, and I swallow the snarky comment I want to direct at Mom. "I'd like to help by paying Hazel's part of the rent so Harmony won't be disrupted by having to move. I'm going to be living with Jaxson, so that will free up some money. I'm hoping Hunter will go over once a week to check on Harmony, and the rest of you too. And we'll teach her how to order groceries. Shaw's will deliver."

"What?" Mom gasps, panic on her face. "That won't work for Harmony. She needs Hazel."

I watch conflict move through Hazel's eyes. "No," I emphasize. "Hazel needs to put herself first for a change. She's given up enough of her life for the family. It's time."

"I forbid it," Mom says. "Both of you living in sin. What will God say?"

I take a deep breath. "Funny, you didn't care when Hudson and Hannah moved in together."

"Hannah wasn't my daughter, and Hudson assured us he was going to propose," Mom replies.

Paul clears his throat. "I've proposed to Hazel, and she's said yes."

"And I've proposed to Harper, and she's agreed," Jaxson adds. "We planned on telling you today."

I look at Jaxson, my eyes wide. It's in our contract that we'd get engaged, but I didn't expect that today or that he'd tell them I'd already said yes.

Dad smiles. "Congratulations to both of you!"

Mom stands as her eyes pool with tears, and she rushes out of the room.

Hope wraps her arms around me, and my brothers surround Paul and Jaxson. I watch Dad leave to go after Mom.

"Where's your ring? I bet it's beautiful," Hope asks.

"I left it back in California," I say. "This weekend is about Hudson and Hannah."

A part of me is fuming about what Jaxson said, but I guess I'm also grateful that both Paul and Jaxson have stood up for us. It's completely unreasonable that Hazel would put her life on hold for our sister. Now, I just hope Harmony can actually live alone.

We finish breakfast, and then Hazel and I do the dishes.

"You didn't tell me you and Jaxson were so serious," she says as she hands me the griddle to dry.

"I guess when it feels right, it's right. You must be excited to be moving to New York."

"I think so. The pace is very different than Boston, but I think I can find a decent job. That will make me feel better, and maybe you won't have to pay for Hope *and* Harmony."

"Don't rush. Put some money away and grow your nest egg. My job with Honeycomb Games has allowed me to do that, and for the first time, I feel like I can breathe."

"Wellesley is going to be expensive." She hands me the serving plate.

"I'm only paying a portion. I promised her two thousand dollars a month. Jeez. I didn't even ask what your half of the rent is."

"Two thousand is more than enough. And I started talking with Harmony about the possibility a few months ago. But when Paul told me what our rent would be in New York, I didn't know how I would make it all work."

Once we finish the dishes, I give Hazel a big hug. "Go spend the day with Paul. I've got you covered here."

"Are you sure?"

"Absolutely. I hear the guys are watching the Red Sox game, so I'll go check on Mom."

"Good luck. You're the only person she'll listen to."

I shrug. That's not true. I've always been her sounding board when she's frustrated. But she's never asked, so I never give her advice. "I moved away, though, so I think that's changed."

I look in the family room and see my dad, along with all my brothers, watching the game. Jaxson catches my eye and blows me a kiss.

I blow one back and wink. I know we're putting on a show for my family, but I could get used to all the attention he's giving me.

Taking a deep breath, I try to put Jaxson in the back of my mind as I walk to Mom's room and knock.

"Come in," she says in a quiet voice.

I shut the door behind me and sit on the edge of her bed. "I'm sorry you had to hear about Jaxson and me at breakfast. We didn't want to take attention away from Hudson's special day, so we were going to tell you and Dad today."

"First, you have to go all the way to San Francisco, and now, Hazel is going to New York. Hope is already telling me she's not going to live at home and go to Bridgewater State. What am I going to do?"

Hope's too smart for Bridgewater State, but I swallow that down and take Mom's hand instead. "We're all growing up. You raised us to be self-reliant. Don't be so hard on yourself. You should be happy for us."

"All of my friends have their kids close by. They spend all this time with their grandkids. Can you believe Hudson said he and Hannah don't plan on having children?"

I can because he and Hazel raised all of us. But I just smile. "They may change their mind. He's only twenty-seven, and Hannah is twenty-three. Let them enjoy some time together. But I bet if you bug them about grandkids, it will just make things worse."

She huffs. "Why didn't you tell me you were so serious about your boss? What about this woman he's been in the tabloids with?"

"He was done seeing Tessa Sky long before we started dating. Theirs was a brief relationship, but she's a publicity hound. She's making all kinds of claims that are lies, Mom. There's no need to pay them any attention."

"He travels in much bigger circles than we do."

I shrug. "He's smart, and he has good business sense, but he's from Detroit. We're flying to his parents' to have dinner with them tomorrow night."

Mom puts her arm over her eyes dramatically. "I don't understand why you had to move so far away."

"I love you, Mom. I just didn't want to be in the Lockwood shadow my whole life."

She lifts her arm. "What does that mean?"

"Have you ever noticed that everywhere you go, you're identified as a Lockwood?"

"That bothers you?"

"Yes. More than I can ever explain. I want to be myself, create my own life. I enjoy living in a city where people don't know my parents are incredibly popular teachers and have changed people's lives."

"That's ridiculous. And if it's true, why does it matter?"

"I like people not knowing that I have seven brothers and sisters. I don't have to explain that we're Catholic, not Mormon. I moved so I could be Harper."

"But you're settling down with a man who's been all over the tabloids for breaking up with a famous singer."

"It's hard to miss that part of his story," I admit.

"Do you love him?" she asks.

I should have known my mother would see right through me. "I do," I say, because that's what I'm being paid for right now. "And I know Hazel has loved Paul since she was in high school."

"I think she fell for him in elementary."

"That could be. But she needs her own life."

"I just don't understand what's wrong with what she has here. Why do all of my daughters want to leave me?"

I wrap my arms around her. "We're not leaving you. We're growing, like you've always encouraged us. And I would love it if you and Dad came out and visited me and Jaxson, maybe over spring break?"

"I don't know."

"Jaxson has two guest rooms that share a bathroom—you would be fine, and we could pretend you and Dad are sharing a room."

She gives me a look, but I'm done pretending I don't know what's going on. "He has restless leg syndrome and snores like a bear. It's the only way I can get any rest at night."

I nod. "Of course. All I'm saying is I'd love to have you visit San Francisco."

"Maybe over the summer."

"That sounds like fun. There's a lot to do and see."

After a few more minutes, Mom agrees to come out of her room, and we rejoin the group. I spend the afternoon talking to my siblings, and as dinner approaches, Jaxson and I say our goodbyes and go back into Boston for one last night in town.

We relax and change clothes at the hotel, and then I learn Jaxson has secured us a nice reservation at Woods Hill Pier 4.

When we're seated and settled, I admire the spectacular view from our private booth. The harbor makes me feel a little nostalgic for Boston and all it offers.

"What are you thinking about?" Jaxson asks as he sips his wine.

I sigh. "I suppose I'm a bit homesick. But only a little. The habba is so beautiful."

"Habba?" He looks perplexed.

"Yeah, the habba. Just like they call me Happa."

Jaxson snorts. "That's hysterical. Why didn't you move into Boston when you were ready to get away?"

"I thought about it, but it was still too close. I commuted to Boston for art school from home. When I tried to live close to campus, they dragged me back every weekend and periodically during the week. I knew it would be the same if I lived here. I'd have been knee-deep in Hudson's wedding planning, Harmony's care, and at every turn, they'd have been trying to get me to move home and take the T to work every day."

He nods. "That's a lot of pressure."

The waiter arrives to take our order, but once he's gone, Jaxson zeroes in on me again.

"You're going to help Harmony with her rent?"

I nod. "We need to find out if Harmony can live alone. Hazel and I have always thought she could, but she struggled when they first moved to Quincy. She doesn't adjust to change well. I'm also planning to help my little sister go to Wellesley next year."

"That's really great of you. I'm glad I'm indirectly able to help as well," he says. "And I'd like to add that once again, I'm very glad you moved out to San Francisco."

I look down at my bread plate and blush. "So, speaking of our work together, what are we going to do now?"

"What do you mean?"

"When we get back to San Francisco, what do we do? Do we change things up or do we pretend last night didn't happen and go back to the way we were before we left?"

Jaxson looks at me a long moment. "I think we change things up. You move into my bedroom, and at work, I'll try not to bend you over the desk and have my way with you. But at night, there's no reason not to enjoy one another and, most importantly, have fun. And perhaps we should think about birth control."

"I already have an IUD," I tell him. My voice sounds calm, but my mind is spinning. I want this...I think... But I don't really know what it means. The contract only speaks to what I get when Jaxson and I go our separate ways, and it's still not clear how long we'll be playing this game. I hope my heart can manage the ruse with a physical relationship added in.

"I always wear a condom, and I was tested the day we met. I'm happy to get tested again."

I nod. "Okay... Have you ever lived with anyone?" I ask. This is all new to me.

"Never. Have you?"

I shake my head. "What happens when you hate me again?"

"I've never hated you. *Hate* is such a strong word. If the time comes that you can't stay with me, just say so."

"And you'll do the same?"

He nods as our dinner plates arrive in front of us. He has a beautiful mahi-mahi steak, and I have shrimp and scallop scampi. We shift to lighter conversation and share bites as we eat.

"Tomorrow, we'll head out about eleven," Jaxson tells me. "I don't want to rush to Detroit. We'll grab some lunch after we land at Buddy's Pizza. I always try to get some good, square, Detroit-style deep dish pizza when I'm in town. It's better than Chicago deep dish. Then we'll go up to my parents' place. I promise my family will do a fantastic job of embarrassing me. I hope they won't bring up Tessa Sky, but it wouldn't surprise me if they did."

"Did they like her?"

He shakes his head. "They never met her. You're the only one I've ever brought home. But as you know, I've been all over the tabloids. Anyway, whether they mention her or not, they'll find a way to be embarrassing."

"That will be quite refreshing."

As we finish our meal, I enjoy what's left of my view of the habba and try not to worry too much about what lies ahead.

CHAPTER 17

Jaxson

Fifteen or so hours later, the server at Buddy's places a rectangular deep dish pizza — with the toppings on the top of the cheese — in front of us.

"Just wait until you try this," I tell Harper. "You'll understand how underrated Detroit pizza is. It's the best pizza out there." My mouth waters as I take a coveted corner piece. The cheese stretches, and a few toppings fall off, but I'm quick to gather them and pop them into my mouth. If Helen could figure out the recipe, I would have her make it several nights a week. And I'd be as wide as I am tall.

Harper looks at me, seeming bewildered. "Who are you and what have you done with my fake boyfriend?"

I beam. "I miss my family, and I miss this pizza." I look up as a woman approaches the table. She's wearing an apron, and her nametag says *manager*. "Jeannine?"

"I was hoping you'd remember me." She gives me a giant smile.

I look over at Harper. "This is Jeannine Wilson. We went to high school together, and I cheated off all her tests in English." I turn to Jeannine. "This is my girlfriend, Harper Lockwood." I'd rather say fiancée, but if Mom hears it from anyone other than me, I'll be in major hot water.

"It's so great to meet you. I can't believe you're here. Oh, and I got married. I'm now Jeannine Larson."

Harper extends her hand. "Nice to meet you. I bet you have some great stories about this guy."

Jeannine chortles. "We were nerds. And he's totally exaggerating about cheating off of me. He was too smart to need to cheat."

"You run this place?" I ask.

She nods. "After grad school, I worked for General Motors, but with layoffs, I ended up here, and I like it a lot better. My employees keep me young. I know all the gossip about you and Tessa Sky." She turns to Harper. "Sorry."

Harper shrugs. "I'm used to it."

"And I get to tell them all about my famous billionaire friend while still being around for my girls."

I smile. "Girls as in daughters?"

"Yep." Joy radiates from her. "Seven and ten, both going on twenty."

"That's fantastic. How are your mom and dad?"

"We lost my dad a few years ago, and Mom lives with me and helps me with the girls. She's a godsend. Oh, and Mary Elizabeth was just in town. She lives in New York these days and works for a fashion house."

"Really? That's great. She always was the most fashionable person in our class." I turn to Harper. "Mary Elizabeth is Jeannine's best friend."

Harper nods.

"How did you two meet?" Jeannine asks.

"We work together," I explain. I know Jeannine would never purposely sell a story about me to the tabloids, and I hate that I don't trust her, but I don't want to give her too many details either.

We talk for a few more minutes, reminiscing about our time together in school, and then she holds up her phone. "Can I get a picture of us? The kids don't always believe that I know you. You know, everyone in town talks about how they remember something you did with them."

I laugh. "I'd be happy to take a picture with you."

"Why don't I take it?" Harper offers.

I stand and we pose. Harper snaps away and then hands the phone back.

Jeannine looks at the picture and smirks. "Thank you."

"Jeannine, what did you do for General Motors?" Harper asks.

"I was an industrial designer. I really liked it," she adds wistfully. "I don't miss the crazy hours, though."

Across the room, someone waves her down. "The lunch rush is running long today. I better see what they need."

"It was great seeing you," I tell her.

She beams. "Enjoy your pizza. It's on the house."

"No. I can't do that."

"Too late. I did that before I walked over." She waves and moves toward the waiting table, greeting someone who's just walked in on her way.

I'm barely through my first piece of pizza when a guy walks over. "Jaxson Bancroft?"

I look over and notice Christophe, who's sitting close by, on high alert. "Yes?"

"I doubt you remember me. I'm Mark Chappell's little brother, John."

I stand and extend my hand. "Of course! How are you?"

Mark was my best friend in high school. After school, we lost touch when he went to Wayne State and I went to University of Michigan. He got leukemia and passed away a few years ago, and I snuck into the funeral because I didn't want to be recognized. It was awful that we lost him at such a young age.

"I'm great," John says. "We really appreciate all you did for us when Mark passed."

"I'm really sorry for your loss. Mark was one of my closest friends back in the day."

John smiles. "It would have meant a lot to him to know you set up a scholarship in his name at Wayne State."

"The least I could do," I tell him. "My visits home aren't the same without seeing him. Tell me, how are your folks?"

"Everyone is good. Just putting one foot in front of the other." He glances down at Harper apologetically. "I should let you get back to your lunch. I just wanted to say thanks."

"Please give your folks my best."

I've managed another bite when Mrs. Bosko stops by the table. "Jaxson Bancroft. You look much more handsome in person than in those silly supermarket tabloids."

"Mrs. Bosko." I wipe the cheese strings from my chin. "So good to see you."

She looks over at Harper, and I introduce her. "Mrs. Bosko and my mom are on the parish council together."

"It's nice to meet you." Harper smooths the napkin in her lap.

We talk a few moments, and she mentions that they're looking for a donor to pay for the repair of the back door of the church. I agree to take care of it.

Harper has finished her piece of pizza by the time Mrs. Bosko moves on and a young girl comes over. "Mr. Bancroft, I was wondering if you were open to interns in San Francisco?"

I look over at Christophe, and he hands me a card from his pocket. It's a generic card that has HR's information on it. "Here's my card. You should reach out to my Human Resources department. We do have some paid internships for certain positions, and they can give you the requirements and details."

She beams like I just made her year. "Thank you so much. This is fantastic. You've made my year."

"You have to impress the HR department," I remind her. "But I'm sure you can do that."

She walks away, and when I look down, the pizza is all boxed up.

Jeannine walks over. "If you make a break for it now, you can get out of here. I just got a call asking if the rumors that you're here are true."

I smile, grateful to her. "Thank you." I put two one-hundred-dollar bills in her hand. "Share this with your team."

Her eyes sparkle with tears. "You've always been too good to me."

I squeeze her arm and kiss her cheek. "It was fantastic to see you."

Christophe and Wyatt are out the door ahead of us just as three cars pull up. We jump into the center vehicle and are pulling away before anyone else spots us.

"Wow, you're a big celebrity here." Harper looks back as car after car arrives in front of the pizza place.

"I'm sorry. We should have gone to one of Buddy's other locations. I just wanted to show you where I hung out as a kid."

"I'm so glad you did."

In just a few minutes, we pull up in front of the house I grew up in. Mom has the door open before we've come to a complete stop.

"I heard you stopped for pizza at Buddy's," she calls as we get out of the car.

"Yep. Jeannine pushed us out the door just before the masses showed up."

Mom wraps me in her arms. "It's great to see you."

I squeeze her back and then turn to Harper. "This is my mom, Jess Bancroft. And, Mom, I'd like you to meet my girlfriend, Harper Lockwood."

Mom releases me and scoops up Harper. "It is fantastic to meet you."

"Great to meet you too," Harper manages, her eyes wide.

"Let's get you inside before the whole neighborhood comes over. I won't get any time with you otherwise."

"Eric?" Mom calls as we enter the house.

"I'm coming." Dad hobbles out to the entry way with his cane.

He's looking less and less sturdy, and it kills me. But he looks right past me to Harper. "What do we have here?"

"Dad, I'd like you to meet my girlfriend, Harper Lockwood."

He exchanges a look with Mom, and I can tell they have a thousand questions. He gives Harper a lingering hug.

"Okay, Dad, that's enough. She's going to think you're some kind of pervert."

Dad rolls his eyes. "That's a terrible thing to say about your old man."

He winks at Harper, and she grins. "It's great to meet you."

"How long did it take for people to discover you were at Buddy's?" Mom asks.

We move into the kitchen, and I pull a chair out at the table for Harper. "I thought I was unnoticed. We ordered, and no one bothered us until the pizza arrived and Jeannine came over. What the hell happened at General Motors?"

"Watch your language," Mom warns. "As I understand it, she was working on one of the truck lines they closed down. They laid her off, and because it wasn't a union job, she got a lousy package. She was married to Tommy Larson, and he bailed, leaving her with those precious girls. Without any real income, while she was looking for work, she got a job at Buddy's. Gary Ross wanted to retire, so he sold her the franchise. I think she likes being her own boss."

"Anyway..." Mom turns to Harper. "What can I get you to drink? I have iced tea or a slew of pops and all kinds of liquor if you'd like something stronger."

"Iced tea would be fantastic," Harper says. "Your home is lovely."

I look around at the house I grew up in. It's certainly cleaner now that I'm not living here. We moved in when I was in second grade, and it's stuffed with pictures of my childhood and some antiques that were my grandmother's. It looks the same as it did when I went to college. So many good memories.

"Thank you. I know it's not as shiny as Jaxson's apartment in San Francisco."

Harper giggles. "His place is a little contemporary."

"Hey!" I act wounded. "I paid good money for that shiny, contemporary look."

Harper pats me on the arm. "I'm sure you did."

"We rarely get to meet Jaxson's girlfriends." Dad takes a sip of his coffee. "In fact, you're the first."

"Actually, she's my fiancée," I tell them. "I asked Harper to marry me, and she said yes."

Mom looks at Dad, her eyes wide. Then she jumps up and hugs us both. "I can't believe it! That's fantastic. Oh, that's so wonderful."

"Will you do it here?" Dad asks.

"We haven't discussed that," Harper says. "We just came from a weekend at my parents' where my older brother got married."

178

I reach for Harper's hand and give it a gentle squeeze. "Mom, I just asked her. Don't scare her off."

"This is so exciting." Mom is practically bouncing in her seat.

I know it wasn't Harper's intention to announce our engagement on this trip, but it happened, and if it gets to the tabloids, Mom would be irate that we were here and didn't tell her.

The back screen door slams, and I turn to Harper. "Buckle up. It's about to get interesting."

"He stopped at Buddy's before coming home. I mean —" Ava, my older sister, stops short. "You're here."

"Yes, we stopped for the best pizza in the world on our way over. I had to show Harper what good pizza tasted like."

Ava launches herself at me and wraps her arms around my neck. "It's great to see you, baby brother."

I break away long enough to introduce Ava to Harper as my overbearing and meddling older sister.

"They're getting married!" Mom announces.

Ava looks at Harper. "It's not too late to change your mind."

Harper's lips curl in amusement. "I'll keep you posted."

"Are you doing this because of Tessa Sky? I mean, that woman doesn't seem to want to let you be."

I sigh. "We've officially been in the tabloids longer than we ever dated."

Harper stands. "May I use your bathroom?"

Mom walks her to the bathroom. While Harper is gone, I turn to Ava. "Do you think we can skip talking about my ex in front of my fiancée?"

She holds up her hands. "You're right. Sorry. But I don't like that she's making you out to be such a creep. I mean, turning her fans on you is bullying to an extreme."

"I get it," I assure her. "It's started a boycott of our games and that could affect our IPO."

"Do you need your shares back?" Dad asks.

"No!" I narrow my eyes at him. "Those are yours. Sell them off if you want. Take Mom on a fantastic trip around the world. Buy a big house with tons of help. Whatever you want."

"She's not interested in any of that."

"I bet if you offered to take her to Rome, she'd go," Ava urges.

He shrugs. "We don't need your money."

Mom returns and sits down at the table, but she doesn't look at me.

"You realize I wouldn't be where I am today without you," I tell them. "I know you would never let me buy you a bigger house, but the shares I gave you are a small fraction of what I have. I'm happy to share them with you."

"I don't want to talk about it," Mom says dramatically.

"We ran into Mrs. Bosko," I warn.

Mom sighs. "What did she talk you into doing?"

"I'm repairing the back door to the church."

"She has no shame," Dad says as he looks at Mom.

"It's okay," I placate. "I don't mind."

"Every single parish council meeting, she wants me to ask you to donate." Mom throws her hands in the air. "You can't be our only funder."

"This was fine," I assure her. "I also ran into John Chappell. He thanked me for setting up the scholarship in Mark's name. How are his parents doing?"

Mom tells us all about the Chappells and how they're coping after losing Mark. As her story winds down, she stands. "I need to do some prep for dinner."

"Can I help?" Harper asks.

"You're a guest the first time you visit. I'll put you to work next time."

"I have to show you my new workshop," Dad tells me.

Ava stays at the table. "I'm going to tell her about the time you had Christy Swensen here at the house."

I point my finger at Harper. "Don't let her fill your head with lies."

Everyone laughs, and I follow Dad out to his workshop. He was in an accident working an assembly line at General Motors when I was in high school. He's been well taken care of by the union since then, but he still has a lot of problems, and it's hard for him to get around when it's cold. I know Mom would like to go to Florida for the winter, and I'm hoping the stock options I gave them will be used to do that.

In the meantime, to keep himself busy, Dad makes beautiful wooden slab tables and has started a YouTube channel, thanks to Ava, showing off his skills. I have one of his tables in every conference room at Honeycomb, and people often ask about them.

The workshop is the size of a three-car garage. I whistle as we enter. Every time I visit, it gets nicer.

"The floors are heated, which helps keep the aches away," Dad tells me.

"Very nice." I look over at the seventy-inch television, which I'm sure only shows ESPN. "When are you going to make me that table I want for my dining room?"

"I'm guessing you'll need a crib first."

"What? Why?"

"You haven't been dating Harper very long. I assume she's pregnant, and that's why you broke it off with that pop-star girl."

I shake my head. "First, Tessa broke it off with me because she likes being in the tabloids, and I want to live a low-key life. We've been apart for quite a while now; she just won't let the story die. And second, and most importantly, Harper isn't pregnant. I love her. She's the first woman in my life in a long time that makes me feel like she likes me for me, not my money."

As the words come out of my mouth, I'm not even sure I'm lying. Dad has always been critical of the way I treat women. He's not exactly wrong, but he also doesn't understand that their appreciation never felt genuine. They liked me because I was popular in school. They liked me because I had a startup with venture-capital funding. These days, they like me because my company is successful. It's never because I'm a regular guy from Detroit.

My dad studies me. "I'm glad to hear it. She seems like a nice girl."

"She is."

I spend the afternoon helping Dad do a few things around his workshop, and we also watch the Tigers play the White Sox. It's a close game, and they're a big rivalry, so we even see a few fights in the stands.

Mom calls us in for an early dinner about four thirty.

I sit next to Harper at the table. "How are you doing?"

She nods. "Just fine. I've mostly been watching. They wouldn't let me do much."

"That's my mother for you." I squeeze her leg, and she smiles a genuine smile that makes my heart speed up. I'm the luckiest guy in the world right now.

"Like I said, the first time you visit my house, you're a guest," my mom says as she bustles in. "Next time, I'll put you to work. When will you all be back?"

"Hard to say," I tell them. "Honeycomb is only a few months from going public, and the only reason I was able to leave this weekend was because we were going to a wedding."

"You didn't tell me Harper has seven brothers and sisters," Ava says.

"I didn't tell you she's a fantastic graphic designer either," I counter. "But she is."

Harper blushes.

As we eat, Ava tells Harper about some of my escapades from high school. She gripes about living in my shadow, but growing up, Ava was the one everyone adored. She was two grades ahead of me and the most popular in the school, and I still think some of my guy friends only hung out with me to see her.

When we finish, Harper and I clear our plates, but Mom won't let us help with cleanup.

"I know you have a plane to catch," she says.

"I'm glad we could stop by. There will be a big party when we go public. I'm hoping I can fly you out to be there."

"I don't like to fly," Mom says.

"Well, this is a big deal. Maybe if I send a jet, you can give it a try."

She pulls me in for a tight embrace. "We'll see."

Ava hugs me. "I'll get her on the plane if I have to dose her. We won't miss it."

I hug Dad, and everyone hugs Harper, and then we're out the door.

Christophe has us zipping down the road toward the private plane terminal when Harper turns to me. "Your parents are wonderful."

"It was hard after my dad's accident, but they're very supportive."

"And they're protective. I love how your mom doesn't want you to be everyone's cash machine."

I nod. "After I lost Quick Reels, I moved home for a few months. I had money but I needed a break from Silicon Valley so I slept at Ava's to avoid all the attention and tried to lick my wounds. They were my foundation. Without them, I wouldn't have made it."

"While you were hanging out with your dad, the phone rang nonstop. Your mom finally had Ava unplug it. I think she served dinner early so she could send us off before people started showing up at the door."

I sigh. "That's what I think too."

"She wants a Catholic wedding," Harper adds after a moment.

"How do you feel about that?" I ask.

She gives me a look. "I didn't think we were actually going to get married."

"Oh, of course." I cover quickly, but my heart sinks a bit. It surprises me, but I'm disappointed that Harper doesn't even want to pretend we'll get married.

CHAPTER 18

Jaxson

I stretch my legs out as I wait for my drink. I feel like I've barely stopped moving today — or the last few days, actually. I'm early to meet Gray and Nick at Bourbon and Branch, as I knew if I didn't leave work when I did, I'd be late. Harper and I have been back from our trip for a week, and I'm just now getting my feet back underneath me. Taking four days away from the office was a lot with the IPO looming, not to mention that my friends and I have just bought a significant position in nine companies. That's what we're gathering here to talk about tonight.

The server places my bourbon in front of me. She gives me a suggestive smirk and a peek at her cleavage. But I'm not interested. We've bantered in the past, but I won't do anything that could jeopardize my road to image rehab and whatever we want to call this thing with Harper.

When Gray arrives, he's got Mason with him. This is a bit of a surprise. I like Mason, but he's on my board, and I wanted to talk to my friends about my feelings toward Harper. I feel like I'm deep in the forest and can only see the vast number of trees around me. I need them to identify some of the leaves. But that will have to wait.

We shake hands, and the server returns to get their orders. She looks over at me. "Still good?"

"Yep."

Her face contorts. I've been too direct.

"What happened with her?" Gray asks after she retreats.

I put my best confused face on. "What?"

"Did you yell at her before we got here?"

I shake my head. "No. I ordered a drink, and that was it. In the past, we've chatted a bit more, but I'm not interested in going there right now."

Gray purses his lips but says nothing.

Then Nick plops down next to me. He catches the server's eye and points to my drink. She bobs her head.

"See? She's fine," I tell them.

"What's going on with you and Harper?" Gray asks.

I can feel Mason's eyes on me. "Everything is great. We had a good time with her family. She has a big bunch of brothers and sisters, but it was nice being a regular guy."

"No one knew about you?" Nick asks.

"Well, they knew a little about me — I got plenty of Tessa Sky questions — but I wasn't recognized on sight. Her parents weren't too excited to learn I was Harper's boss, but they expected me to pitch right in. Unlike when we got to my parents'." I roll my eyes. "I wanted to show Harper where I hung out growing up, so we stopped for pizza. But we couldn't get through lunch without a thousand interruptions, and when we got to my mom's, she had to unplug the phone."

"You mean people stop you and ask for — what? Autographs? Selfies? Money?" Gray asks.

"I'm repairing the back door to the church." I tick off my fingers. "I got hit up for an internship. And I was thanked for a scholarship I provide in a high school buddy's name. Don't you get stopped when you go to your hometown?"

Gray and Mason shake their heads, but Nick nods. "All the time," he says.

I don't want to talk any more about Harper with Mason here, so it's time to move things along. "Where are we with our investments?"

Mason shifts in his seat and pulls out some notes. "There's been a bit of a development," he says. "SHN may purchase Technology Startup Fund. Their operations, which include about two hundred and ten billion dollars in assets, fifty-six billion dollars' worth of customer deposits, and about seventy-two billion dollars' worth of business loans, are all in need of someone to take over and protect them. Dillon, Cameron, and our other partners are working together to purchase them and put them under the SHN umbrella. Dillon is working with the Financial Industry Regulatory Authority to hash out the deal. And right now, we're expecting a discount of about sixteen-and-a-half-billion dollars from the face value of the loan portfolio."

My jaw drops. "What does this mean?"

Mason leans back in his chair. "With FINRA's help, we'll move the Fund to much stricter regulation. Sara, Dillon, and our finance group are digging through all the contracts. Eventually, we'll figure out what we want to keep and what we want to sell, but right now, Villefort is grateful we haven't taken his house, his bank accounts, or the equity in his investments."

"Does he know it's SHN bailing him out of the mess he created?" I ask.

Mason nods. "Definitely. It hit the wire today, so it's common knowledge. I would have told you regardless but in a less-public place."

"How will this affect our recent investments?" Grayson asks.

"You have some assets in the Fund, but…" Mason leans in. "Our plan is to remove Villefort, so it won't be an issue for you shortly."

My heart sings. "I can't wait to watch that happen."

"What are you going to do with the companies you don't feel are viable?" Gray asks.

187

"Well, some of Villefort's investments were not very strategic, but the market always determines profitability if they can IPO," Mason says. "Several won't, so we'll help their investors either sell to companies that can benefit or let them crash and burn."

"Will you be investing money from TSF?" Nick asks.

"Eventually, but at least until Villefort is no longer involved, we'll be using our own finances to do SHN business, as we always have."

This sounds like a wise approach to me. I nod along as Mason explains a few more things, and then we say our goodbyes when he needs to leave to meet Caroline and some friends.

"Sorry I brought him along without telling you guys," Gray says once he's gone.

"Not at all," Nick says. "It was good to hear what's going on. SHN taking over Technology Startup Fund is great for us." He picks up his drink to toast.

"I agree," I add.

"So let's get back to what happened with Harper," Nick says.

I look away. "I don't know. This is a contractual relationship to show my board some stability, but I have to say, I'm personally concerned about her situation with her family."

"What do you mean? They want money from you?" Nick asks.

"No. Nothing like that. All families have their challenges, but her family seems to take Catholic guilt to a new level. It's a little manipulative."

Grayson raises his brow.

"Her parents are not happy that she lives so far away. Her oldest sister, Hazel, has been taking care of a sister who has some health challenges, and now Hazel's moving to New York to be with her fiancé. I have a feeling the others are going to put a lot of pressure on Harper to come back and take care of her sister."

"Can you move the sister out here?" Gray asks.

Maybe I could… But I'm not sure Harper wants that. It still makes her responsible for someone she shouldn't have to be. I sit back and try to articulate what's been racing through my mind. I explain that ultimately, I'm afraid they're going to take her away from me.

Gray leans forward. "That sounds like your relationship has changed. Are you worried about that because of the contract and the situation you've created?"

"Well, of course," I assure him. "I don't want to have done all this for nothing. There's still the IPO to think about…" I trail off, and neither he nor Nick looks particularly convinced.

"Right. Okay," Gray says cautiously. "Have you talked to Harper about this?"

"I'm not sure saying negative things about her family is going to go over well, considering our situation."

He nods. "Why did she move so far from her family? Did she move here with someone?"

"No. She moved to get away from them. That's what she's told me. She wants to live her own life. It makes sense. While we were there, they gave her constant reminders about how she'd left them behind in every conversation." I sigh. "However, despite all that, we had a really nice time while we were gone." I think back to the first night we had sex. It was the best I've ever had. By far.

"You got laid," Nick announces.

Several people around the bar look over.

"Shush," I admonish. "I've had sex since I broke up with Tessa."

"But now you've had sex with Harper," he says in a low voice.

"I'm not saying."

He looks at Gray, who nods. "He did. And you said she wanted none of that. I guess the romance of a wedding changes things."

I shrug. "We had fun, and she was a great sport when we told our families we were getting married."

"Wow, you moved into that phase of the plan already?" Gray asks.

"When are you getting her a ring?" Nick asks.

Now, I'm feeling a little overwhelmed. "We need to go shopping, but I know when I do it will make the tabloids."

"Isn't that what you want?" Gray says.

I don't know how to answer that. I mean, that is the point of this whole thing, but I'd rather it be more intimate. That's probably silly.

"Caroline Sullivan has a guy," Gray tells me.

"A guy?"

He grins. "Yep. He helped me with Scarlett's ring."

I don't know what to say to that, so we shift gears and talk a bit about Honeycomb's impending IPO. The guys each have the same number of shares as Harper will have, so they're invested in my success too.

When we part ways, we agree to catch up next week, and I head for the car.

Christophe is waiting for me at the curb. "Ms. Amy Brighton is at the house with Harper."

I nod but feel a bit disappointed. I guess I was hoping to have dinner with her. "Thanks."

As we drive back home, I open my email and go through the financial records our attorney sent us earlier today to check up on our new investments. I need more time to really look at it, but when I walk in the house it smells like something burned. I follow my nose to the kitchen, rather than my office like I'd planned, and it's a disaster.

"Oh my God!" Harper jumps up. "I didn't expect you so early."

"Why does that matter?" I look over at the Dutch oven on the stove that has definitely boiled over with some sort of red sauce. "What are you making?"

Harper looks at Amy. "We were working on Amy's mom's sauce. I told Helen we'd be making a big pot. But our pot wasn't quite big enough. I'll be up half the night cleaning red off of everything."

"Is that what I'm smelling?"

Amy smirks. "No, that's probably the bread. In all the craziness, we forgot the bread in the oven, and it is a charcoal briquet. Then the noodles boiled over."

I laugh. "So nothing from your dinner is salvageable?"

Harper looks close to tears. "I'm a good cook. I got distracted telling Amy about our trip, and everything went downhill from there."

"So what are you going to do for dinner?"

"I'm admitting defeat," Harper says. "We were talking about making grilled cheese and reheating some of Helen's tomato soup."

While that sounds good, that's not what I want. "What about takeout from Fog City?"

"What are you thinking?" she asks.

"They have a pretty mean barbecue brisket over polenta. I think that's what I'm in the mood for. "

"It's nearly eight o'clock." Amy looks at her cell phone. "I think I'll head home."

"You're welcome to stay," I urge.

"I have a five-a.m. appointment with my trainer tomorrow, but thank you."

While Harper walks Amy to the door, I quickly order two briskets and look over the kitchen. Helen won't be happy, but we'll do our best to make it right.

When Harper returns, I help her clean up while we wait for dinner.

"You don't need to help me," she insists.

"I don't mind. Growing up, Ava and I traded off days doing the dishes. And I did them when I was living with her after the Quick Reels debacle. I like to think things over while I do them."

"What's giving you anxiety these days?" Harper asks as she makes a space for me at the sink.

I shrug. "The same old stuff—Spy Game's issues, the loss of users with Chocolate Crush, the IPO, you—"

"Me? I don't want to be a stressor for you. I'm sorry about the mess. Honestly, I'm not used to such a professional kitchen. I won't let this happen again. I promise."

"I don't care about this." I wave my arm around, and we've made a good dent in the mess. "I'm enjoying our time together, but after our visit to your parents, I'm worried about you."

"Why?"

"I guess I'm worried they're going to manipulate you into going back to Massachusetts."

She sighs. "I will admit, I worry about that too. They're relentless, and that's a good part of why I'm here. I don't want to sound selfish, but I want my own life. I loved spending time with them last week, but I've had my fill for the time being. Don't you worry."

The doorbell rings.

"Saved by the bell," Harper says with a grin. "Or is that saved by polenta?"

CHAPTER 19

Harper

Since we got back from our family visits, we've been crazy busy at the office. I've hardly seen Jaxson this week. The last time I saw him was the night I destroyed the kitchen. I'm asleep when he gets home, and I barely recognize that he's in bed with me. And then he's gone in the morning by the time I get up. Christophe and I have run the stairs a few times, but I don't know what Jaxson is doing for exercise. This is crazy, and I worry it's only going to get harder as we approach the finish line for the IPO, which is in less than six weeks.

I'm sitting at my desk outside Jaxson's office on Friday morning when I look up to find a tall, distinguished gentleman in front of me, with two bodyguards standing behind him, both wearing visible bulletproof vests.

"I'm here to meet with Mr. Bancroft," he says.

I pull up Jaxson's calendar and don't see any time blocked for a meeting. "I'm sorry. Do you have an appointment?"

He nods. "My name is Robin Friedman. He's expecting me."

I point him to the seating area across from my desk. "Please have a seat, and I'll let him know you're here."

He nods, and as he sits down, I notice his giant silver briefcase. The two bodyguards remain vigilant. I'm not too sure about this guy… Is he mafia or one of Tessa Sky's lawyers?

I knock and enter Jaxson's office. "There's a Mr. Friedman here to see you with two of the biggest bodyguards I've ever seen."

Jaxson looks up. "Oh good. Send him in and join us, please."

My eyes must show my surprise.

"It's nothing to worry about. I asked him to come. My bad, I completely forgot to put it on my calendar."

I nod and take a deep breath, not sure what this could be about. This is not the way Jaxson typically does things, and if this guy is up to something illegal, I'll walk out the door and not even look back. I'm not interested in wearing orange, no matter what the show says.

I return to the waiting area and paste a smile on my face. "Mr. Bancroft will see you now."

Mr. Friedman stands, and the two bodyguards position themselves outside Jaxson's office.

"Can I get you anything to drink? We have water, coffee, tea, and a large assortment of soda."

"I'm fine," he says. I watch him approach Jaxson with what seems like it could be trepidation. "Mr. Bancroft, it's so nice to meet you. Caroline Sullivan has so many nice things to say about you."

I relax. Caroline would never get Jaxson involved in anything shady.

After retrieving a pad of paper and a pen, I try to return to Jaxson's office, but the bodyguards block the door.

"Um, Mr. Bancroft has asked me to attend the meeting."

They step to the side and allow me to pass, but by the time I'm through the door, they've already blocked entry for anyone else. I don't know what to think.

Mr. Friedman has spread a black velvet tablecloth over the table in Jaxson's office, and Jaxson has a grin spread wide across his face as he crosses the room and holds my hand. "Mr. Friedman is a private jeweler here in town."

The black velvet makes some sense, but not much else.

"I've brought an array of stones and settings we can go through," Mr. Friedman says. "Per your request, I've brought flawless or very, very slightly flawed stones that are colorless or nearly colorless. Do you have a preference on the setting?"

Both Jaxson and Mr. Friedman turn to me. Finally, it clicks. *We're engaged.*

"Uh, I'm fine with a gold band," I tell them.

"We can't get engaged without a nice ring." Jaxson squeezes my hand and looks at Mr. Friedman. "Let's look at what you suggest."

Mr. Friedman looks at my hands. "Hmmm... What do you think about this setting?"

He slips on a platinum band with the center stone missing, but there are two large sapphires on each side.

Jaxson looks at me. "What do you think?"

"Too big."

Mr. Friedman studies my hand. "The size seems correct."

"No," I clarify. "The two sapphires are too big, which means the center stone would be even bigger. Someone would cut off my finger for that ring."

Mr. Friedman's face contorts. "I would hope you're not anywhere that would be a risk."

I take the ring off my finger and place it on the velvet.

He puts it aside and picks up another setting. "This is a cushion setting, and there's a matching wedding band."

I look at Jaxson, who seems to nod. "Is this what you think would work best?" I ask.

"This is my gift to you," he says, looking in my eyes. "You will always have this ring."

That sounds romantic, but I hear what he's telling me. After our relationship has run its course, the ring will be mine to keep. He keeps forgetting that I don't want his money. I just want to send my siblings to school and pay off their debt.

"I don't think this is it." I look over what Mr. Friedman has brought, and they're all very ornate. "Do you have just a solitaire setting?"

"I do. What kind of stone would you prefer?" Mr. Friedman clasps his hands in front of him.

I shake my head. "Maybe a typical diamond shape that's not very big? Like a half-carat size?" Mr. Friedman seems horrified, and I feel like I've said the wrong thing.

Jaxson looks at me, bewildered. "That's it?"

I nod. I'm not sure how to get out of this. This is so much more than we ever discussed.

Jaxson looks at Mr. Friedman. "Can you excuse us a minute?"

He opens his mouth, but it's clear he doesn't know what to do. He can't leave all his stones and settings.

"We'll step out," Jaxson says.

Mr. Friedman's shoulders relax, and Jaxson grabs me by the hand and opens his office door to two giant shoulders. "Excuse us, gentleman. Can you step into the office with Mr. Friedman and give us a moment?"

They nod and leave us standing with most of the staff on the floor staring at us. Jaxson pulls me into a small conference room.

"Harper, think of this as your retirement fund. Get as big a diamond as you can."

I cross my arms. "Do you know what happens to children in Africa with conflict diamonds?"

The corner of his mouth turns up. "Is that what this is about?"

"Not entirely, but they're overpriced for what they are."

Jaxson nods and runs his hands up and down my arms. "You're perfect. You deserve the most beautiful diamond my money can buy."

"I don't mean to sound ungrateful because I'm not. I just don't feel comfortable with something like that on my finger."

"I need you to have something that someone in my position would give you. This needs to be realistic, remember? Do you think you could wear something like that for special occasions and a few pictures?"

I reluctantly nod. I am doing a job here. "I suppose so."

"Good. I'll have a talk with Mr. Friedman, and we'll get it figured out."

"Great. I have plenty of work to keep me busy."

I turn, but Jaxson takes my hand and pulls me close. "Tonight, we're going out for dinner—just the two of us. I have special reservations. Be ready to leave the house by six."

"Should I dress up?"

"I've had Catherine from Nordstrom send you something, and it's at the house. Christophe will be here at four to take you home."

My brow furrows. "I have so much to do. Can't we leave here together later?"

"I'll meet you at the house at six."

I return to my desk to wondering looks from those in proximity to my desk. Jaxson goes back into his office, and I focus on my work.

A little while later, Mr. Friedman leaves with his two bodyguards. "Thank you, Ms. Lockwood."

"We appreciate your help," I say with a tight smile.

One of the office interns walks up after they've gone. "Who was that guy? He had some seriously hot bodyguards."

I just shrug. The office will know soon enough. Tomorrow, we have our engagement photos, and the PR team will announce our engagement in next week's issue of *People* magazine. That's when life is going to get interesting.

I manage to keep up with my day until suddenly Christophe appears at my desk. "Are you ready?"

I shake my head. It can't be four already. "I'm drowning. I can't leave. The work doesn't stop."

Christophe just looks at me.

I put my pen down. I'm not going to win this. "Fine. Let me shut down my computer." I save what needs to be saved and explain that I'll see everyone Monday morning. Then I follow Christophe to the waiting car.

As Wyatt drives us across town to the house, I begin wondering what Jaxson has planned. "Do you know where we're going for dinner tonight?"

"Yes," Christophe replies.

I wait for him to expand, but he's silent.

"Can you tell me where we're going?"

"No."

I take a deep breath. I need to prepare if I'm going to have to deal with the paparazzi. We've been dodging them since we returned from our trip. I let out a deep sigh.

Wyatt pulls the car into the garage, and I don't get out until the door is closed behind us, as they've instructed me.

Helen meets me at the door. "Catherine just left. She has an outfit for you tonight and one for the morning, but she'll be at the photo shoot tomorrow."

"Okay," I say, a little confused.

"The hairdresser will be here in an hour to do your hair and makeup."

Now, I'm really confused. *What are we doing tonight, and where are we going?*

Walking upstairs, I find a beautiful blue dress with silver heeled sandals, along with a light blue bra and panty set. Catherine left a note. "The blue will show off your eyes. Wear the pearls tonight to accent your beauty. You'll look fantastic."

Butterflies flutter in my stomach, and I have to sit down on the bed.

I have roughly an hour before the hairdresser arrives. I take a cool shower and then lotion myself up from top to bottom. Since the hairdresser is doing my hair and makeup, I just put on lingerie and a bathrobe and touch up my toes with a bright pink polish.

The hairdresser arrives and looks down at my toes. "Did you do those yourself?"

"Yes, I did." I don't think they look half bad, but I gird myself for her criticism.

"You're pretty good at that. Most women in your situation would have had a pedicure set up for tonight."

I shrug. "I'm not most women, I guess."

She snorts. "I've seen your boyfriend. He's pretty hot."

"He's not my boyfriend," I respond reflexively. But that's not a lie. He's my boss and my fake fiancé. We seemed to jump right over boyfriend. But in another week we'll be in *People,* and my life will change forever.

The hairdresser blows out my hair until it's shiny and straight. Then she does my makeup with a pretty smoky eye.

When she's done, I slip into my dress and make my way downstairs. I'm only ten minutes late, but Jaxson is nowhere to be seen.

"Have you heard from Wyatt?" I ask Christophe.

He shakes his head and picks up his phone. "It looks like he's still outside the office."

I pull my phone from my bag and call Jaxson.

"I'm sorry. I'm leaving now," he says when he answers. "Shit! I can't believe I did this."

"That horrible woman who manages your calendar slacked off today and got her hair and makeup done, leaving you to your own devices."

Jaxson laughs. "She's my ruthless guard dog."

"What would you ever do without her?" I tease.

"I hope I never have to find out."

My eyes grow wide. "You mean you haven't started a countdown?"

"Never."

I roll my eyes. I know better than to believe this banter. "I'll see you when you get here, or would you prefer I meet you wherever we're going?"

"I need to put a suit on. I'll be there as quick as I can."

"Okay."

We disconnect our call, and I don't know what to do with myself. I don't want to sit down and put wrinkles in my dress. Helen appears. "Would you like a drink?" she asks.

She's read my mind. "That would be great. What's your favorite?"

"I'm afraid I'm not a big drinker, but I like a vermouth cassis. It has vermouth, crème de cassis, and club soda. But we have a full bar, and I'm happy to make you whatever you'd like."

"I think the vermouth cassis would be perfect. What is cassis?"

"It's a black currant liquor—gives the drink some color and smooths out the edges of the vermouth."

"I don't know what Jaxson has planned for tonight, but I think a lighter beverage would be best."

It seems like seconds before I have a drink in front of me. I take a sip and my eyes grow wide. "This is fantastic!"

Helen beams brightly. "It will be our favorite together."

"Definitely."

Jaxson comes running in and kisses me on the cheek. "You look truly beautiful."

"Thank you."

"Catherine picked a dress that makes your eyes intense."

I blush from head to toe. "I like it too."

He steps away. "I'll be right back. I want to take a quick shower and change. I'll be down in fifteen minutes, tops." He races out of the room.

"He'll be the talk of the restaurant with fifteen minutes' prep. This—" I motion to myself. "—took all afternoon. Men have it so easy."

Helen laughs. "I have a feeling all the eyes will be on you tonight."

"I don't suppose you know where we're going?"

"I wouldn't want to spoil it."

"I'll remember this," I mock threaten.

Helen laughs. "Would you like another drink?"

I sit back in my chair. "I'd better not. I don't know what he has planned."

"Just make sure you have fun tonight," Helen reminds me.

Jaxson reappears in a navy suit, a crisp white shirt, and a tie that complements my dress. I shake my head in wonder. "You look very handsome. You'll be shooing the women away."

"I only have eyes for you."

We walk out to the garage and get in the back of the Land Rover. Wyatt jets us across town.

"Are you finally going to tell me where we're going?" I ask.

"Bernal Heights."

"Isn't that a neighborhood?"

He gives me the side eye. "Look at you, learning all about San Francisco."

"Anna Hill from marketing lives there with her family."

He nods but says nothing more.

A few minutes later, I ask, "What time is our reservation?"

"It was at seven, but I wanted to walk around beforehand. Now, we'll be a few minutes late, but I let them know."

"I'm sure wherever we're going will be fantastic."

He looks amused and reaches for my hand. "I owe you so much for doing this for me."

"Well, what you're going to do for my family will be more than enough."

We pass a park that despite the late hour is full of families — kids playing with soccer balls and riding the swings. People are walking their dogs, and it's like a public square with the neighbors all congregating to talk to one another.

Our car stops at the top of the park in front of an elegant restaurant — *Marlena,* reads the script across the front. As we approach, a man opens the door. "Mr. Bancroft. Welcome."

"Daniel?"

He nods. "Yes. We have the restaurant ready for you."

The walls inside are a soft gray. The kitchen is open, but the dining space is empty.

"Oh, did you open just for us?" I blurt.

Jaxson squeezes my hand. "They closed for us."

A single table in the central dining room is covered with a warm gray tablecloth, two white cloth napkins, and a pair of candles.

"We can set you up to face the kitchen or to look out at the park and the view of San Francisco," Daniel offers.

Jaxson looks at me. "It's up to you."

"Why not enjoy the view of San Francisco?" Out the large windowfront, the Bay Bridge connects downtown to the East Bay and the evening lights are coming on.

We sit down and Daniel immediately brings us a bottle of wine that Jaxson has evidently already chosen. "Tonight, we have a six-course tasting menu," he explains. "I'll let you get settled and have some wine before I bring you the first course, a tuna tartare with golden tomatoes and radish in a lime dressing."

"Thank you," Jaxson tells him.

I shake my head. "This is really too much."

"Caroline helped me secure the reservation," he says. "They were very kind to reserve the restaurant for us."

I hear soft music playing overhead, although I can't make it out, but the lights are low and dinner is going to be spectacular. "You'll spoil me," I warn.

"Isn't that my job?"

I sigh. "I'm going to live this lavish lifestyle and not want to give it up." I smile at him — it was meant to be a joke — but I can't quite sort out the look on his face.

"I got the evaluation for our IPO this afternoon," he says after a moment.

I look at him expectantly.

"We think the initial bids for our stock will be at just over forty dollars a share, and by closing they'll have split twice."

"What does that mean?"

"Well, you have five thousand A shares. And we've been issuing B shares to our new employees, which means they've split before we even go live. Today, they're worth roughly four hundred thousand dollars."

My eyes widen. That's more than I thought.

"When they reach two-hundred dollars a share, we'll do another split, so by the end of the day, that means your shares will be worth at least two million dollars."

I put my wine glass down. "That's too much. I told you I didn't want the shares."

Jaxson chuckles. "I'm ignoring what you crossed out. And they're worth that much because the company is that exciting."

"I changed the contract," I remind him.

"I know you did, but I promised you I'd cover your siblings' education but I'm also sticking with the original contract. You'll still get your own company, all the clothes and jewelry we buy, and the stock options."

I sit back hard in my chair. "Why would you do that?"

"Because you're giving a lot up to do this for me, and you're an excellent assistant on top of that. It's the least I can do."

I don't think arguing is going to get me anywhere, and it's certainly not pleasant dinner conversation, so I force myself to move on — for now. "You mentioned when we were visiting your family that they have the same number of shares I do. Do you have any shares or have you given them all away?"

"Mason's company owns twenty percent of the original shares of Honeycomb. I gave five-thousand shares each to Gray and Nick — and they've given me five-thousand shares in each of their companies. I gave you, my sister, and my parents each five thousand shares. Combined, you all own about ten percent of the business. Even with what SHN has and the other shares we've provided to employees, I still own fifty-four percent."

My jaw drops. "What happens if the IPO doesn't do what you think?"

"What I've told you is the conservative estimate. We think it will continue to grow. The only thing you need to know is that you can only sell five percent of your shares at a time, because it has ramifications for the health of the company and, more than that, is forbidden by the Securities and Exchange Commission."

"I just don't understand this," I tell him. "Why are you so generous with me?"

He smiles, his eyes warm. "Because I knew you'd never ask for it."

CHAPTER 20

Jaxson

The food and wine are spectacular as course after course arrives to dazzle us. Having Marlena to ourselves makes tonight extra special. And the more time I spend with Harper, the more I realize that this woman next to me is extra special. She's different than anyone I've ever dated. A gold band? That's the ring she asked for earlier today. Even if it's just a contractual marriage, no way is the woman I'm with only going to wear a gold band. I mean, maybe for everyday wear, if that's truly what she wants, but when we go out, I want the world to know she belongs to me and is worth everything I can give her.

That thought stops me in my tracks for a moment. Sometimes, I can't tell what's for show and what I believe.

I think that's part of why this afternoon I ended up picking out a ring with an oval-cut eleven-carat diamond and two three-carat trillion-cut sapphires on each side. It set me back about two and a half million, and I know it's bigger than anything Harper would even allow herself to look at, but it's beautiful. And when our charade is done, she'll have the ring to sell or maybe keep as a fond memory.

I smile at Harper and look around the restaurant again. The public relations company we're working with to launch this engagement has hired a photographer. I know he's taking pictures from afar tonight and will sell them to the tabloids after the article goes live in *People* magazine.

We've eaten our amazing dinner, and they'll be bringing out the dessert shortly. That's when I'll propose. I'm actually nervous.

"Are you ready for your world to change?" I ask her.

Harper shakes her head. "No way. But don't worry, I'll do this anyway." She gives me a saucy look. "I've never aspired to be famous. I moved across the country to be anonymous, and now, a big part of the population is going to know who I am — or who they think I am, anyway. So much for anonymity." She rolls her eyes.

I have to smile. Harper is so sweet. I really hope this hoax we're perpetrating doesn't change that. "We're going to do this together. We have a strong group of friends to help us, and in the end, you'll be able to live wherever you want. If it's an island in the South Pacific, far away from everyone, so be it."

The server sets dessert down in front of her, and I look her in the eyes. "There's a photographer out there capturing the moment, so I'm going to make this look official."

I get down on one knee. "Harper, thank you for being wonderful enough to do this for me and for Honeycomb. There will never be enough ways for me to show you how much this means to me. Will you marry me and stay until you can't stand me anymore?"

Harper's shoulders relax. "Yes, I will marry you."

I lean in and kiss her lips softly. "Thank you."

I pull the ring from my jacket and hold it out to her. "I know this is more than a gold band, but Robin Friedman assured me that the diamond is a Canadian stone, so it's not from a conflict area. And the sapphires are from conflict-free Sri Lanka."

She looks down, and the color drains from her face. "That's a lot more than a gold band."

"And you deserve it. It is your ring forever."

Her hands go to her mouth, and her cheeks go pink. "It's too much."

I slip the ring on her left hand. "It's just right for a billionaire's wife."

She leans in and kisses me, and it isn't a chaste kiss like I expect, but a deep kiss that has her tongue dipping into my mouth. She holds me close.

"If you're not careful, I'm going to want to do all sorts of things to you on this table in front of that window."

She giggles. "How about you hold that thought for when we get back to your house?"

I lean in and kiss the tip of her nose. "Our house."

I feed her a bite of chocolate mousse and follow it with a kiss. "I think I have a new favorite flavor—you dipped in chocolate."

She bounces her brow. "I could go for that."

"There are lots of things we can explore together."

When all the chocolate is gone, we leave the restaurant hand in hand and sneak into the back of the Land Rover. I clasp her hand as we drive across town.

"What time do we meet the photographer tomorrow?" she asks.

"Hair and makeup are coming to the house for you early, and the photographer will be at the Clear Security offices at eight. They want morning light for the photos."

"I can't believe they have a park on their roof."

"I think you're going to be impressed."

When we arrive home, I pull her to me in the kitchen. "I don't know what you did, Ms. Lockwood, but you've completely bewitched me. You've gone out of your way to help me when you could have walked away. I know this isn't what you wanted for yourself, but know that we're in this together. So if things are upsetting, you need to tell me. I may be very blind to it all."

"I'll tell you what upsets me, right now," she says with a twinkle in her eye.

"What? I'm all ears."

"That we're down here talking when we should be upstairs."

I look up at the ceiling. "What did I do to deserve you?"

"You asked."

I chase her upstairs, and we're not even fully into my room before I push her up against the wall. My cock has been rigid and ready since the moment I saw her in that dress.

I break our kiss. "Clothes on the end of the sofa, if you please, Ms. Lockwood."

"Yes, sir." Harper nods with a sexy grin. She turns around and pulls her hair to the side. "Can you unzip me?"

Her neck looks delicious, and I leave a trail of kisses as her skin is exposed. She lets the top of the dress fall to her waist before she pushes it over her hips.

"Turn around," I growl.

She stands before me in a light blue see-through lingerie set. "Do you like what you see?" she asks.

I stop breathing as I take in her perfection. "Don't stop on my account. I'm ready for more dessert."

She blushes and unclasps her bra. Her breasts are full and high. God, I love them. I drink in every new inch of flesh Harper exposes. I've seen it all before, but I can still see a bit of embarrassment and insecurity in her. Whoever told her she wasn't perfect is an asshole and completely wrong. She is every man's wet dream.

When Harper finishes, and her clothes are neatly folded on one of the sofa's arms, I walk over to the dresser and pull out a box of toys I bought for us. I pick out a riding crop and swing it fluidly. Harper sucks in her breath. We may never be ready for that, but just in case…

"Legs together, Ms. Lockwood," I say, tapping my hand on her thigh. She rushes to follow my instructions. "Hands crossed behind your back."

She does what I ask.

"Good girl."

"Thank you, sir," she says. She watches me carefully as she waits for what will happen next.

I circle her. "The second you step into our bedroom, you are no longer Harper Lockwood, my assistant." I run my hands around her breasts, fighting the urge to play with her nipples. "You're my soon-to-be wife, and your only purpose is to serve me. Your wants and desires come second to mine. And my desires are to make you a very, very happy woman." I toe out of my shoes and pull off my socks and tie. I hold the tie in my hand and consider tying her hands together but decide to save that for next time. I unbutton my shirt and pull it off before draping it over her clothes.

Her eyes dilate with lust as I stand in front of her, barefoot and shirtless. We were made for this. I lean in and salve her nipple before closing my teeth around it and pulling. She moans her appreciation as her hands lace through my hair.

I step away. "Hands behind your back, holding your elbows," I say.

Harper does as she's told.

"You like nipple play, don't you?" I catch her chin and turn her face to me.

"Yes," she says softly.

My dick is so hard. Without warning, I twist each nipple. Harper's soft moan turns to a grunt, and she shivers. I slide my fingers through her folds, and she's very wet. Her hips move, looking for the friction she's craving, but I'm not going to give it to her yet.

I hold up a set of nipple clamps. "Have you ever used these before?"

She shakes her head.

"Do you want to try them?"

She nods, and the corners of her mouth turn up.

"God, you're sexy when you're like this." I lower my head and pull Harper's left nipple in my mouth. She moans, and her disappointment shows when I pull back.

I open the pincher and clasp it to her right nipple. She inhales sharply.

"Is that okay?"

"Yesssssssss," she hisses.

I do the same to her left nipple, and she moans.

"Let me know if they become too much," I warn.

She nods, rotating her hips.

"Spread your legs," I say, my cock almost ready to break my zipper.

I reach for the Lilo vibrator in my toy box and bring it to her lips. "Open up and suck it like you want to suck my cock."

She licks the silicone cock before taking it deep in her mouth, her eyes on mine.

Fuck, I need her mouth on me. But I want to see her come several times before I finish, and right now, if I don't stop, I'm going to shoot my jizz in my pants and be done for the night.

I remove the Lilo from her mouth and turn it on. I use it to trace her breasts, and she slowly inhales.

"Tell me, do you like your engagement ring?"

"Uh-huh," she moans.

"Use your words."

"Yes," she says as I creep the vibrator closer to her prize.

"Are you going to wear it?"

She doesn't respond, so I stop moving the vibrator and turn it off. She's so close to the edge of the cliff. This slows us down, but I want her to know that I own her orgasms, and in return, she'll wear my ring.

"Will you wear your engagement ring?" I ask again.

She looks at me, and I can see the fight in her eyes. I remember what she told Robin Friedman, but she'll have plenty of security. I wait for the answer I want.

She closes her eyes and her chest heaves. "Yes," she finally moans.

I turn the Lilo back on and move it farther down, the tip working around her hips and down her thighs. "Tell me, Harper, are you going to be an adoring wife or a distant wife?"

"Adoring. Definitely adoring if you can make me come."

"Are you asking for permission to come?"

She looks at me, and the corner of her mouth turns up. "Yes," she breathes.

I kneel between her legs and press the vibrator gently into the folds of her exposed, wet pussy. The cool silicone tip makes her shiver, and her legs shake. She looks up at the ceiling as I move the vibrator over her hardened nub.

Beads of sweat sprout as the heat of her impending climax courses through her. Goose bumps ripple her skin, more and more popping up the longer I hold the Lilo to her sex. Her breathing becomes rapid as her orgasm builds.

I'm ready to see her fall apart.

I push the toy deep inside her and pivot in and out as the clit massager rubs furiously.

"Now, Harper. Come for me."

The first wave of her orgasm hits, and she screams my name. Damn, if I don't feel twelve feet tall. I keep the vibrator moving, and as the first climax ends, I watch a more intense one begin.

Her legs tremble, and she grips my shoulders. I try to steady her as she nearly collapses from the release of back-to-back climaxes.

211

I move her to the bed and rip off my pants. My cock stands proudly at ninety degrees from my body. "Are you ready for this?"

"Yes, please," she breathes.

She reaches for my cock and licks from base to tip before wrapping her tongue around the head. Taking my cock deep down her throat, I look up at the ceiling and I see stars. If she doesn't stop, I won't get to come inside her and that is all I want to do.

I pull out of her mouth and look at her. "Are you okay if I don't wear a condom?"

She nods. "You've put a ring on it. I think we're okay."

With that, I push into her, and her warm, soft insides hold on to me. I'm finally home.

I know I'm not going to last, and I don't want to. It's just too good. My mouth is on hers, and I'm tasting myself on her tongue. I'm swallowing her moans and she strokes me harder with her tongue and her pussy.

My head is spinning, and I'm groaning her name. I'm about to explode. I'm about to come into the most beautiful woman I've ever known. I don't care what she thinks. I don't care what anybody else thinks. This is mine. "Harper, I'm coming."

"I'm coming with you," she whispers.

I thrust into her, again and again, just wanting to stay inside her forever.

Our orgasms flood our senses, and we ride a wave of pure bliss together.

I lose track of how many times she climaxes, only stopping when her clit becomes too sensitive for the vibrator, and her nipples too sore for the clamps. She falls asleep, spent and exhausted, and I'm floating right along with her.

It's just before six in the morning when the alarm sounds, and I seriously consider canceling our photo shoot as I look at Harper's naked body splayed out over me. But I can't. Eyes on the prize. We have to do this.

"We need to get ready," I tell her, rubbing her shoulder. She moans.

I get up and get in the shower. When I return, Harper is sitting up, but still in bed, the sheets pooled around her waist.

I groan. "You can't tempt me."

She chuckles. "Honestly, I'm not trying. This is just as far as I've gotten. I need to shower, but I need some caffeine before I can do much of anything."

"I've got you covered." I quickly dress and head downstairs just as I hear the doorbell.

I let in the woman who is going to blow out Harper's hair and do her makeup. "She should be out of the shower in just a minute," I tell her. "Let me take her some coffee, and I'll call you up when she's ready."

The stylist nods, and I take the stairs two at a time.

When I open the bedroom door, Harper is already out of the shower. Her hair is wet, and she looks beautiful from the glow of her many orgasms.

"The stylist has arrived."

"Oh good. We have less than an hour to make me presentable."

I step in and hand her a coffee. "If it was up to me, you'd have your hair curly and no makeup at all."

She beams. "Good to know you like the real me."

"Always."

I step out and go back down to let the hairdresser know Harper is ready for her. Then I sit in the kitchen to check my email and make sure there isn't anything I've missed.

I've barely gotten through the messages that arrived overnight when Harper comes downstairs. She's wearing tight jeans and a soft blue sweater that sets off the color of her eyes, and of course, her hair and makeup are flawless.

"Are you ready?"

"One more cup for the road and I will be." She heads straight for the espresso machine. Once she has her latte in hand, we head out.

In the back of the car, she scrolls through her phone and then gets stuck staring at her email. Her face changes, and it seems like something is upsetting her.

"What's up?"

"Nothing."

I put my hand on her leg. "What is it?"

She sighs. "Hope graduates in a few weeks, and she's doing all these fun things. I'm a little sad I can't be there."

"Why can't you be there?"

"Um, I think that's obvious." She looks over at me. "We're just a month from IPO. You've given us eight million dollars for this party, and even with a planner, it's stressful."

"You don't have to go for a week," I counter. "You could take a NetJet into Logan with Christophe. He'll get you to the graduation, and you can stay for some after-graduation activities and then take a redeye back and sleep the whole way."

She makes a face. "That seems a little extreme."

"But it's family, and I know how important Hope is to you."

"You wouldn't mind having a temp for a day?"

"Not for something like this. Plus, it will be a great way for you to see how Harmony is doing on her own."

She looks at me like I've hung the moon and wraps her arms around me. "Thank you. Tonight, you're getting special treatment."

"I got that last night." I waggle my eyebrows.

She blushes. "No, I got the special treatment. I want to make *you* happy."

"Trust me, watching you unravel over and over was special treatment for me. But I'm happy to do a repeat tonight."

"It's a good thing we didn't have this conversation yesterday or my knees would be all sorts of messed up for the photos."

My cock goes hard in my pants. "Do you know how sexy that would be?"

She smirks. "It's not too late. But I think that would run counter to the publicist's plans."

I snort. "I think you're probably right."

When we arrive at Clear Security's warehouse-looking building, she takes a deep breath. "I apologize in advance if you have to remind me to have fun today."

"We're going to have a great time. Don't worry about it."

We park in the garage and head up to the top floor. The elevator stops in Jim Adelson's penthouse apartment, and we step out into chaos. His twin boys shoot past, running after one another. Jim's wife, Kate, grabs the leading one by the waist. "Okay, you two. That's enough. Company is here."

Jim smiles and extends his hand "Saturday mornings are crazy right now. We're on the way to a little league game, so we'll be out of your hair soon. Just use our place as you need."

Kate releases her son and extends her hand to Harper. "I'm Kate Adelson. Welcome to our crazy house."

"I grew up with seven brothers and sisters. This is nothing."

"I knew there was another reason to like you." Kate beams.

Just then the elevator pings and in walks Catherine and two racks for clothes — one for me and one for Harper.

"Thank you so much for doing this for us," Harper tells Jim and Kate. "I'm sorry if we've put you out."

Kate waves that away. "You're fine. It gave us a reason to clean up the garden upstairs. It's now ready for summer."

A woman appears from nowhere. "The photographer and your publicist are already upstairs."

I open the door to the stairwell and hold it for Harper. "Let's go meet them. Catherine, when you're ready, come on up. You can talk to the publicist about what she wants while we work with the photographer."

"No problem," she says as she pulls the racks over and starts unpacking mirrors and other things I'm not interested in. "I'll be up in a few minutes."

We wave goodbye to the Adelsons and go upstairs. When I open the door, Harper stops short. "Holy shit!"

I can't help but laugh. The entire roof is a private park, which the Adelsons have instead of a yard. There's a full basketball court, a swing set, a large vegetable garden, a flower garden, and lots of grass for the boys to play in.

"This is incredible."

"I agree. I'm super grateful Jim is giving us the space," I say.

Megan Bates, the publicist, rushes over. "Hello! Welcome. We're just about ready." She hands us a clipboard. "We've mapped out a few pictures and have three clothing changes. The weather looks like it's going to hold, so it should be perfect for today."

Four and a half hours later, Harper and I are both exhausted and ready to go home. We must have taken more than a thousand photos. Harper has radiated joy and happiness all morning, and she's been amenable to all the photographer's requirements.

"You guys did fantastic today," Megan gushes. "I'll reach out once I pick the photos I'm going to send to *People*. There's a good chance you'll have the cover of the magazine."

I nod. "That sounds great. Let us know."

With my hand on Harper's back, I guide her downstairs where Catherine has wrapped all the clothes in garment bags and Christophe, Wyatt, and another one of Jim's people are loading them up and will put them in the back of the Land Rover.

"Thank you so much for being here today," I tell Catherine.

"I work on commission, so it wasn't an issue." She gives me a wink. "Let me know if you need anything else."

"We will."

When we get to the garage, she walks one direction, pulling the now-empty clothing racks with her, and Harper and I walk to our car.

"When we get home, I'm going to take a long nap," she announces as we climb in. "When I wake up, I'll take a luxurious bath. After I'm relaxed, I'll eat whatever Helen left us, and then I'm going to watch a movie tonight in your media room."

"That sounds like a solid plan. And tomorrow, when you're rejuvenated, we can go for a run and hit the farmer's market for Helen."

Harper rests her head back and shuts her eyes. I'm not even sure she heard me, but that's okay. This is the last weekend we'll have the cover of anonymity for a while.

CHAPTER 21

Harper

This week has gone by in a blur. The peace and quiet of our lives is going to explode when the magazine comes out tomorrow. I hardly know what to do with myself. Fortunately, there's plenty of work to keep me busy. But Jaxson seems to have other ideas.

"Go home," he encourages. "Have fun with Amy. I'm going to meet up with Gray and Nick for a drink at Rockwell on Fillmore, but I don't think I'll be too long. Nick has a date, and Gray has dinner plans with Scarlett."

I nod. "Helen made pizzas for us to put in the pizza oven for dinner."

Jaxson narrows his eyes. "Can you work the pizza oven?"

"Just because I make a mess in the kitchen doesn't mean I can't follow the directions she leaves."

Jaxson holds up his hands in surrender. "I was only going to offer to do it when I get home."

"Oh. I like that idea. We're also going to go through the package Megan from the PR agency dropped off earlier."

"She will be worth the cost if we actually pull this off. Have you looked at it?"

I shake my head. "No. I didn't want to chance anyone seeing it."

He looks around, secret-agent style, before he opens the manila envelope on my desk and slides out the magazine. Sure enough, we're on the cover. I'm sitting on a swing in the fancy dress, looking up at him like he's the center of the universe. "Aw, look at us! Megan is beyond thrilled that we made the cover," he notes.

"Tonight is the last peace we're going to have for a while." I'm still getting my head wrapped around that.

"I know that scares you, but remember, we're not handling this alone. We have Christophe and Wyatt to manage anything that gets too crazy."

I nod, but my stomach rolls. I can already feel how life is going to change. This is so much more than being a Lockwood in tiny Weymouth, Massachusetts. "I know. I just never thought I'd be on the cover of a magazine."

"Did Megan tell you she's talking to *The Knot* and a few other wedding-planning magazines?"

My heartbeat kicks up. "No. I don't think I can deal with that."

"That's what I told her." He smiles. "The party planner for the IPO would be great as a wedding planner too. You can set it up so she does the work and we just appear on the right day if you want."

I don't know what to say to that. *What is he thinking?* We never agreed to actually get married. And anyway, a wedding, even if it's for show, is going to require a lot of time and attention to detail. You can't just hand that off entirely. But it's not worth explaining that to him, so I paste a smile on my face and give a polite nod.

I look down at my watch. "Oh shoot. I'm going to be late. See you at home in a few."

I say that loud enough that Louise Harvey, assistant to Honeycomb's VP of operations, looks up at me with surprise from the next desk over. But at this point, it doesn't matter. The magazine is going to get the word out, and it's guaranteed to blow up long before I get back to the office tomorrow.

I pull my bag from my desk drawer. "Have a good night, Louise. See you in the morning."

She squints at me as I pass. Whatever. That's one thing that will be a little freeing. In the few photos that have been taken of Jaxson and me so far, my face has been obscured, and I'm never identified. Jaxson has been so careful about that, and I know it's because he's trying to shield me from publicity as long as he can while still starting some buzz that he's seeing someone. I appreciate that, but I've agreed to do this, so it will be refreshing to be out in the open with it. At least I think so.

Once I've reached the car, I slip on my engagement ring and text Amy to let her know I'm on my way. I haven't seen her since I got my ring, and she's going to lose her mind as we go through the magazine.

Amy: I'm just hanging out making pizzas with Helen. See you in a few.

I look up at Christophe through the rearview mirror. "Did Jaxson tell you we were flying out to my sister's high school graduation in a little over a week?"

"Yes."

"We'll stay the night and then take the redeye back."

"Yes," he replies, always so formal these days.

"And if you want to sneak off with one of my sisters for some down and dirty sex, you can do that."

His eyes move to mine.

I make a face. "I was checking to see if you're listening."

"I always listen, and your privacy is always my first thought."

I take a deep breath and smooth out imaginary wrinkles in my pants. "Thank you. I think it's about to get very busy soon."

"You'll be safe."

"I'm not worried about that. I've never had anything to fear. I'm just nervous about losing myself. I'll no longer be Harper Lockwood. Instead, I'll be Jaxson Bancroft's fiancée, girlfriend, rebound, or whatever label they want to put on it."

He shrugs. "I think you'll be just fine. Maybe being called Mr. Bancroft's whatever will guarantee that you won't lose yourself."

I look out the window. "If I'm lucky."

Christophe pulls into the garage, and once the door has closed, I walk in the back door, drop my coat in the coat room, and get a bear hug from Amy.

"I want to see it." She steps back and grabs my left hand. "Holy hotness. That's a giant ring."

"It's way more than I wanted, but Jaxson wanted to make sure it was appropriate for his status."

"Wow. That must have set him back a bit."

I shake my head. "I'm not sure many things set him back."

"Will you keep the ring after your contract is over?"

I don't want to get into that. It's too much. "We'll figure that out when the time comes."

"Well, it's fantastic, and you deserve it." She sits down with an exaggerated sigh. "This is a nice place to hang. Thanks for having me here."

I pull the magazine from my bag and hand it to her. "No problem. I'm glad you don't mind. I know it's a step down from my last place," I tease.

When she doesn't respond, I turn to look. She's completely absorbed in the magazine and doesn't seem to hear me as she flips the pages.

"You look so beautiful," she gushes.

"Thanks."

She begins to read the article. I haven't even done that. They didn't really interview me. They sent me a questionnaire, and I responded.

"Your meet cute is captured so well here," she says.

"What does it say?"

"That Jaxson propositioned you the first time he met you because he knew as soon as he saw you that he was in love."

I snort. "At least it's half true."

While she reads, I walk into the kitchen, leaving my shoes behind in the mudroom. "Jaxson has kindly offered to run the pizza oven when he returns."

She looks up and smiles. "It's not that hard."

"I know, but I think it gives him an excuse to come home when all his friends have plans tonight except for him."

Helen bustles in. "That sounds like as good an excuse as any."

I smile at her. "The magazine announcing our engagement hits the newsstand tomorrow morning."

Helen nods. I can tell she doesn't approve. She probably thinks I'm in this for his money. That's what everyone is going to think.

"I'm sorry in advance for all the inconvenience this is going to cause you," I tell her.

"Me? You're the one putting your life out there." She pauses. "Whatever he's paying you, it isn't enough."

I open my mouth but then close it. Helen's never confirmed that she was in the know before. "He's hard to say no to."

She smiles. "I agree. But none of the other women he's dated compare to you. I'm glad you're the one."

"Well, thanks."

"And for what it's worth, whatever your agreement, Mr. Bancroft definitely likes you. He's always checking on you."

Amy comes up for air from the magazine. "This is so cute. Have you read the article?"

I shake my head. "You've spent more time with that magazine than I have."

She opens it up and takes me on a tour, pointing out all the highlights. The photos show us laughing and smiling, and there are plenty of smoldering looks.

"All this tells me that despite what you say, you have feelings for one another," she concludes.

I feel like a deer in the headlights as I try to formulate a response to that. Thankfully, Jaxson comes in and saves me from having to say anything.

He looks over at the magazine on the counter. "It's good to see all the money I'm spending on PR has convinced you, Amy."

Her brow creases. "I don't think you're being fair. These photos show something."

He flips through the spread. "They show some serious airbrushing," he says, shaking his head. "Also, the building that was behind us is gone, and they moved the Bay Bridge. But I imagine they did that for our protection."

I look down at the picture. "You're right! I didn't catch that before."

Jaxson claps his hands together. "Who's ready for some pizza?"

"I am!" I didn't have lunch today, and I'm hungry. "I'm thirsty, too. Do either of you want something from the bar?"

"I'll take one of Magnolia's IPAs," Jaxson says.

"That sounds good. Do you have two of them?" Amy asks.

"We sure do. I'll make it three."

Magnolia Brewery is right here in the City, close to where we were photographed. It's a great place to hang out.

I walk into the entertainment room to the bar and pull out three bottles. I pocket one of the dozen openers over there before returning to the kitchen. Jaxson has walked outside to start the pizza oven, so after giving Amy her beer, I leave her to talk to Helen and walk the beer out to Jaxson.

"Here you go. I didn't expect you so soon. I thought you were having drinks with the guys."

"Grayson had to work late, and Nick ended up with better plans."

"That drives me crazy about California," I say. "Everyone jumps on to the next thing. On the East Coast, we're a little better at keeping our commitments."

He shrugs. "Or maybe you hung out with better-mannered people. I'm from the East Coast, as is Nick, and he dumped me for a date with his girlfriend." He drapes his arm over my shoulder and kisses my temple. "I'll try not to leave you stranded too often, but it happens."

"I was getting mad for you, not for me."

He grins. "I've been hungry for Helen's pizza all afternoon, so I wasn't too disappointed that they canceled."

"Her pizzas are good." I turn, leaving him to play with the heat of the oven. "Thank you for coming home to do this."

His face softens. "Happy to do it."

We spend the evening enjoying our pizzas, and eventually, we put in a movie, but none of us is paying attention. We have a spirited conversation about politics, and I'm grateful to find we all agree on the big-picture things. We just quibble a little over the small stuff.

Jaxson's phone rings just after nine, and Amy uses that as her excuse to head home. "Enjoy tomorrow," she tells me. "Don't let any haters upset you."

I give her a big hug. "Thank you for hanging out tonight. It means a lot to me."

She puts her hand on her heart. "Are you kidding? I'll be able to tell everyone at work tomorrow that I saw an early copy of the magazine."

I chuckle. "If you buy your own copy, maybe you can get Jaxson to sign it."

She gives me an all-teeth smile. "He already said he would."

I shake my head and open the front door, just as Christophe arrives behind me. "How are you getting home?" he asks Amy.

"I was going to catch a bus," she replies.

"May I drive you? There are a few photographers around. They may think they can join you on the bus and harass you into telling them something as you ride home."

Her eyes grow wide. "In that case, I'd love a ride."

She comes back in, and they disappear into the garage instead. I begin to clean up.

"Where's Amy?" Jaxson asks when he reappears.

"It's a school night, so she went home. I guess Christophe was concerned about photographers so he's driving her."

"That's smart thinking." Jaxson runs his hands through his hair.

I've noticed he does that when he's nervous.

"What is it?"

"The story is live, and the hits on the website are bigger than they ever were with Tessa."

I take a deep breath. "I haven't read the article, but Amy said it was really sweet. The PR agency did a good job."

He nods. "I figured Megan would. She's the best in town."

"Those pictures of us are really good too."

"My family will want them. We'll have to get some prints from the photographer."

I smile, but knowing those photos aren't real, despite how they look, makes this moment bitter.

My cell phone pings.

Unknown: Jaxson Bancroft doesn't love you.

I snort to myself. Whoever got my cell number is more accurate than they know.

213-555-1289: He can't marry you. He can only marry me.

Number blocked: You will die before you marry my Jaxson.

My hands start to shake. This is exactly what I didn't want to see.

"What is it?" Jaxson asks.

I shake my head, fighting off tears. I can't tell him what they're doing and how it makes me feel.

He reaches across the counter and takes my phone out of my hands. He reads through the text messages and his face goes grim. "I'm sending these over to Jim Adelson."

"I'm going to take a bath."

"Do you want company?" he asks.

I sigh. I think I just need space. "I'll be okay. Do what you need to. I'll be ready to run the stairs tomorrow morning."

Jaxson reaches for my arm as I walk out of the kitchen. "Remember, we're going to handle this together."

"I know, and I'm grateful for that."

I give him a reassuring squeeze before heading up the wide, winding staircase to the second level.

I dump almost an entire bottle of bubbles into the jetted tub and immediately they billow up tall. I quickly undress and sink into the tub, letting the water cover me as I think about those ugly text messages. How do people know my cell number?

I lay back and shut my eyes until I hear Jaxson. "Are you in that sea of bubbles?"

I laugh and swipe the bubbles away from my face. "I got a little carried away, but I'm here."

"I just spoke with Jim, and he's going to have someone come by and make a clone of your phone."

I sit up more fully. "Is that really necessary?"

"It's a precaution I'd like them to take," he says. "They're going to monitor calls from numbers that aren't in your phone directory."

"Okay. I figure my sisters will call and maybe my mom tomorrow afternoon, but I doubt anyone else will."

"He thinks it's best for you to mute your phone tonight. If you have this many texts when the article posted less than an hour ago, it's going to be busy by morning."

"Okay. I'll send a text to my family tonight to let them know I'll talk to them tomorrow after work if they would like."

"Great idea." Jaxson tilts his head to the side. "Are you sure you can manage all those bubbles yourself? I can always wash your back."

He's so kind, and he looks so delicious standing there. I can't refuse him. "There is one spot... I'm sure if you rub hard enough, you can take care of it."

Within seconds, Jaxson is naked and climbing in behind me. We spend the night intertwined, and he takes my mind off of what's on the horizon.

Before falling asleep, I finally send a group text to our family chat.

Me: Guess what? I'm on the cover of *People*. The magazine dropped about midnight your time and my phone started blowing up. I'm going to have it off for most of the day tomorrow, so if you need me, call me at the office or on the home phone. Love to you all. XOXO.

I wake up just after seven on Friday morning, feeling very disoriented. "We're not climbing the stairs?" I ask.

Jaxson kisses my head. "Nope. The crazies are out today. There are about two dozen people outside who pretty much camped on the street last night."

I sit up, suddenly very alert. "Are you kidding?"

He shakes his head. "I wish I was."

"What does that mean?"

"Jim's team has sent over another person to help us out. And we're going to be sticking around the house or the office for a few days."

My stomach sinks, but I try to put on a brave face. "What's the overall reception to the article? Can you tell?"

"It's very positive," he says with a smile. "I'm quite surprised."

"Why is that surprising?"

"I was concerned that Tessa Skye's fans wouldn't like me moving on."

I sigh. "Right. That. Now, I remember." I manage a smile. "I guess we should get into work. You have the announcement?"

He nods. "It was sent overnight to all Honeycomb employees. You'll see it in your inbox. And we're going to take this one day at a time."

"Okay." I walk into the bathroom and turn the shower on. As the room fills with steam, I shut my eyes and say a small prayer that I haven't made a mistake by agreeing to help Jaxson.

When I'm dressed and ready, I head downstairs.

"You have your ring?" Jaxson asks.

"Right here in my pocket."

"Go ahead and put it on. The team is going to take us in. You'll have someone with you all the time today. Don't let that be alarming."

"No problem there," I assure him. "And I'll be too busy to notice. I have plenty to do for the IPO party."

The crowd outside the house is growing by the second, and San Francisco police are here. Jaxson's neighbors must love us. We get into the car, and the ride over to the office is like any normal day, except we're in a larger vehicle.

When we arrive, they drop us into the garage and we're escorted up to our floor. As promised, Wyatt is stuck with me all day. He takes a seat in the waiting area just beyond my desk.

"I'm really sorry about this," I tell him.

He waves me off. "It's not your fault, and this is what I do for a living."

I guess no matter who Jaxson talked into being his wife, it would be like this. He was voted one of the sexiest men in the USA last year, mostly because of Tessa Skye's PR team, but fans don't know that.

When Louise gets in, she's visibly upset. "I suppose all the chaos downstairs is your fault?"

I look up. "My fault?"

"No," Jaxson says, stepping out of his office. "It would be my fault. If it's too much trouble for you, you're welcome to work from home today."

Louise turns a bright shade of crimson. "No, Mr. Bancroft. That came out harsher than I intended." She turns to me as she heads back to her desk. "I apologize."

CHAPTER 22

Harper

After fighting our way into the office Friday, we've spent our weekend around the house. I would have preferred to go outside, but there are still plenty of photographers camped out there. And more than that, the fog has rolled in, so it doesn't seem as inviting.

Jaxson worked yesterday while I spoke to my family, and then it felt positively decadent when I started and finished a book the same day. I haven't been able to do that since moving to San Francisco. Jaxson worked a little more this morning, and I caught up on a few things, but then we took a break and caught up on several shows. He grilled us steaks for dinner, and we ate them with Helen's amazing twice-baked potatoes and roasted asparagus.

I'm feeling pleasantly full as I swipe my last bite through the sauce on my plate, and the evening unfolds before us. "What are you up for after dinner?" I ask Jaxson.

His eyes move to my chest. "I'm sure we can think of something to occupy our time."

"I'm sure we'll get there, but I mean besides clearing the table and having sex on every surface of your house —"

"Our house."

"Semantics. I was thinking we could play a board game." When I moved in, I spotted a closet full of them.

"Do you have one in mind?"

"How about Scrabble?"

He looks at me. "That's pretty dull. Would you like me to make you dessert and we can try to break our record for number of orgasms?"

I narrow my eyes. "We're going to leave this house again eventually, and I want to walk — not hobble. What if we played Scrabble with different rules?" We played a lot of Scrabble growing up, and we'd use it to trade chores and other things.

"We could play strip Scrabble," he suggests.

I chuckle. I should have guessed. "How would that work?"

"For every ten points your opponent makes, your remove an article of clothing."

I make a face. "No. That's too easy. What if we play dirty Scrabble?"

Jaxson leans in. "What is dirty Scrabble?"

Now I have to figure that out. "Well, every word needs to be naughty."

"And if it isn't?"

"Then you have to take off an article of clothing."

"What happens when you're naked? Do I get my dessert?"

"Maybe I want mine."

"Isn't that what you're getting when I eat you out?"

I shiver with anticipation. "I enjoy eating you, too, you know."

Jaxson's smile turns dark. "I'm up for your game of Scrabble."

We take our dishes to the sink and move into the game room. I tell him I need to go to the bathroom, and I run upstairs and put on another T-shirt and a pair of socks. I want the game to last longer than three words.

When I return, he's set up the game. He laughs when he sees me. "You've added a few items."

"I was cold."

"I'll turn the fireplace on."

He lights the flames with a flip of a switch and sits across from me. "You draw first."

I pull the L out of the velvet bag. "Middle of the alphabet. Your turn."

He smiles and pulls the Y. "I guess that means you'll go first."

We trade the velvet bag back and forth until we both have seven tiles. I have a good first word, W-H-I-P, and I place it on the board. "Twelve points!" I write it down and wait for him.

There's a twinkle in his eye. "I think I'm going to love this game." He adds a P-E-D to my whip and looks at me. "I believe with the double letter score, I'm at twenty-one."

"Don't celebrate too quickly." I use his D and make the word *hard*.

He looks down at his crotch. "Whenever you're ready."

By the time we're done, we've got *ass, succumb, cock, dick, daddy, yes, blow*, then *blowjob, penis, tease, eat,* and *tit*. I had to pass twice, and he had some great three-letter words. In the end, Jaxson is the winner. He reaches for me, and his arms tighten around my waist, drawing me against him.

I love his hardness against my softness. Pushing up on my tiptoes, I match my lips to his, and heat gathers in my center. His mouth moves over mine, sucking and biting before drawing me deeper. Every nerve in my body is on alert and begging for his touch.

He pulls away from me. "I would like to take a shower," he whispers.

"Do you need any help?" I ask.

He reaches for my hand and walks me upstairs. The tension between us is sizzling hot as I watch him undress. The naked male form doesn't always do much for me. I mean, I love a good dick, but more often than not, the hint is more exciting than the reality. However, that is not the case with Jaxson. His abs are hard and rippled, his pecs well defined. Truly, the man's ass is a rock, and his dick is a work of art.

"Are you joining me?" he asks.

I bite my lip.

"Get naked."

I slip off my shirt and bra, and his eyes are glued to my breasts. I lift them and watch his cock jut ninety degrees from his body. Pushing my yoga pants to the floor, I step past him to turn the shower on. Standing beneath the warm water, I wet my hair and crook my finger at him. The cool air hits me as he opens and shuts the glass door.

He turns me to the wall and reaches for the loofa. The smell of lavender-scented body wash fills the shower.

Slowly, he circles my back, massaging in the soap as he kneads my muscles. I moan my appreciation, and he uses the shower wand to rinse me. His lips graze the back of my neck, which sends little shivers of pleasure down my spine.

He turns the shower wand to massage and positions it between my legs. The water pulses against my clit as he leans down and suckles my breast. My stomach coils tighter and tighter until it springs free and I explode, moaning his name.

He gives me a conceited smile. He knows he's wrecked me for all other men. I hate that, but I've vowed to enjoy what I can for as long as this lasts.

When it's my turn, I take my time, lathering soap over his body. I love the way his muscles twitch and ripple under my hands.

As I wash the suds away, I leave little kisses on his skin. Then, with the wall to support me, I sink to my knees. I rub the loofa between my hands, creating a thick lather, and wrap my hands around his beautiful cock and balls. I work the soap into his hardness. Our eyes lock until he braces himself, lets his head fall back, and moans.

I stroke and make sure the suds are rinsed away, but his cock is hard and begging for more attention. Licking the underside of his balls, my tongue moves up the shaft all the way to the head, lapping around and making it a different kind of wet. He's hard and soft all at once.

His hand cups the back of my head, and his fingers lace into my hair. I work his head deeper into my mouth. His cock pulses.

Jaxson pulls my head back, forcing me to stop. "Not yet." He offers me his hand and helps me to stand. His lips find mine, and he tastes like good Kentucky bourbon. I taste like him.

Turning me to the water, he wets my hair thoroughly and massages shampoo into my hair. I'm somehow both relaxed and turned on. Jaxson rinses me thoroughly, and I wonder if he's going to give me another shower-wand climax, but instead, he nudges me to place my hands against the wall of the shower.

His fingers slide up my slit, and I moan. He spreads me apart, and the head of his cock pushes against my entrance. I sigh in anticipation, but Jaxson takes his time entering me. My muscles grip him, trying to hold him in place. I tilt my hips down and backward. Jaxson wraps an arm around my waist and pushes harder, filling me deep. Slowly, he pivots in and out, the veins of his cock creating a delicious friction.

His foot spreads my legs wider, and I get tighter around him. My breasts rock back and forth as he pushes in and out, hard and fast. His free hand winds its way into my hair, and I gasp as his teeth scrape my neck.

Juices drip, coating our thighs. Jaxson rolls his hips, teasing me. I moan, wanting more. He pumps in and out of me slowly and sucks on my neck, placing his mark on me. His rhythm picks up, marked by the steady slapping of skin. We're both breathing hard as we build to our pinnacles.

The freight train is coming, and there's nothing I can do or say to make it stop. I see white lights, and my body pulses around Jaxson. He keeps to his rhythm, allowing me to ride the waves until he follows right behind me, groaning my name.

"Fuck, what you do to me," he says between gasps.

Before the water can turn cold, we exit the shower, and he dries me off.

We crawl beneath the sheets, and Jaxson pulls me close. "I have a board meeting in the morning. I'm sorry to be leaving you to face the office alone."

"I'll just keep my head down and get my job done. I think having Wyatt close by will keep them in check."

Jaxson nods. "I like that he's close by, but I forgot to tell you, Wyatt's not working this week. His wife had their first baby last night. But I think we can find you someone else. Actually, I should call Jim about that..."

"Don't bother him now. I'm not worried about my safety at work. There's a team downstairs to keep the photographers out, plus the office already has tons of security measures in place. I'll be fine. Wyatt hardly has anything to do anyway." I roll over to face him. "But you skipped right over Wyatt's wife having a baby. You knew this for many hours and are only telling me now?"

"Why does it matter?"

"We need to make sure she has some meals when she gets home, and let them know if they need help, we're just a phone call away. They need time to bond with that baby. Do you know if it's a boy or a girl?"

"I didn't ask."

My heart sinks. "Jaxson, I know you worry about me, but we need to make sure Wyatt feels appreciated. We need to at minimum give him a gift."

"I like when you get all worked up like this."

"You're not getting laid again tonight after that comment."

He crosses his arms across his chest. "You don't have to be mean about it."

"I'm not being mean. I love that you're all about my safety. Just don't do it at the expense of those around us — or anyone, for that matter."

He sits up, reaches for his phone, and types into it. I turn over and settle in to sleep.

"Jim says they had a little girl," he reports after a moment. "She was seven pounds, three ounces, and they named her Renee after his mother."

I roll back toward him. "So you bothered Jim anyway?"

"This was important." He winks. "Thanks for bringing it to my attention."

"I'll reach out tomorrow to send a baby gift."

Jaxson nods and kisses me softly as his hands begin to explore. Suddenly, I'm not so tired anymore.

I wake in the morning as Jaxson heads out. He doesn't wear suits often, but today, he's wearing my favorite dark gray one with a crisp white shirt and a lavender paisley tie. He kisses me goodbye, and I know I should get out of bed, but I'm a little bit dreading going into work today. I can tell by the bite in the air that it's cold outside, and the fog is still here. It's so warm underneath the duvet, but eventually, I manage to get up and moving.

When Christophe returns to the house after dropping Jaxson, I'm ready to go. He does the circuit again and drops me off. Then he moves on to shadow Jaxson.

Nothing seems out of the ordinary as I go inside, but once I'm settled in at my desk, I have to ignore the whispers.

"Congratulations on your engagement," Louise says without looking at me.

"Thank you."

"I always appreciate people who keep their personal lives out of the office."

"I do my best," I reply. I'm grateful she's not making a big deal of it.

I reach out to Stella from Clear Security, and we decide to order flowers and a week's worth of meals to be delivered to Wyatt's home. It feels good to have that taken care of before I move on to focus on my real work—the IPO party prep.

The invites need to go out next week, but I'm still waiting for a few things to be finalized. I open up the file to review the various logos I've created for the IPO party. The current logo is very rigid and uninspiring. I've created two logos I like better than what the in-house graphic designer for Honeycomb did, and there's a third that's kind of a compromise. It uses the old logo and evolves it. I guess I'll present them to Jaxson and he can decide.

As I swap each of them in and out of the invite, a shadow crosses my desk. I look up, and my eyes go wide to find a six-foot, lithe blonde with cornflower blue eyes standing before me. It's Tessa Sky, and four giant men stand broad shoulder to broad shoulder behind her.

"Can I help you?" I squeak.

"No. I'm here to see Jaxson." She looks me up and down, and her eyes fall to my left hand. She doesn't react.

Maybe she doesn't recognize me, or more likely I'm lower than a snake's belly in her pecking order. "I'm sorry. He's at a board meeting. Do you have an appointment?" I know for a fact she doesn't.

She brushes her beautiful blonde locks off her shoulder. "I don't need an appointment."

Every eye in the office is on Tessa Sky and me. I don't want to make a scene. "You can wait for him in the seating area, though I'm not sure when he'll be back." I do my best Vanna White impression and show her where to go.

Her eyes become laser beams. "Look, I know who you are, but you're just a rebound for him. He loves me and needs me. I'm here to get him back."

"Well, he's not here. And as I've said, you're welcome to wait if that's what you'd like."

She turns on her heel and heads to his office door. But when she turns the handle, it's locked.

"Did you lock his door?" she demands.

"No. He keeps it locked when *he's not here*." I'm running out of polite ways to say that.

"Unlock this, please."

"I'm sorry. I can't do that." There's absolutely no reason for her to be in that office.

"You're his secretary," Tessa screeches.

My eyes widen, but I take a deep breath. "I'm his assistant," I clarify. "But my title is not particularly relevant, right now."

She rolls her eyes. "When is he due back?"

"I honestly don't know. The board meeting started a while ago, but there's no set length of time they last."

She's quiet a moment, and then her face changes. "I get why you hooked up with him. He's a good kisser, isn't he?"

My stomach curdles, and I give her a tight smile, saying nothing. There's no way I'm going to make a scene.

When I don't respond, she sits down on the couch and her entourage stands beside her. I return to my desk and try to focus on the logos and invitations. But then it becomes clear that people know she's here. It starts as a trickle, but then a line of Honeycomb employees seeking autographs and photos or just looking to gawk at a mega star forms. The executive floor is chaos.

I send a text to Jaxson.

Me: Tessa Sky is here in the office, impatiently waiting for you to return. What do you want me to tell her?

Jaxson replies moments later.

Jaxson: Fuck! Why couldn't she have shown up when Wyatt was there to scare her off?

I don't have anything to say to that. I wonder why she felt the need to show up at all. Well, I'm sure it's because of the magazine spread. And if that upset her, she's going to be really pissed when the tabloids drop pictures of the ring and his proposal. I find it incredible that after all the crap she's dished at Jaxson, she thinks he's going to take her back with open arms.

My phone pings again.

Jaxson: I'm gone all day. If she won't leave, I'll have Christophe come over and escort her out.

Me: She's enjoying attention from just about everyone in the company right now. There's a line for autographs and photos.

Jaxson: I'm sorry. Don't let her distract you too much.

I've just put my phone away when Louise slaps her hands on her desk. "That's it!" She stands, and her desk chair rolls back and slams into the wall. "After everything you've done to Mr. Bancroft, do you think he wants anything to do with you? Move on and leave us to do our work. This is a place of business."

I give Louise an appreciative look. She said what I would have loved to be able to say.

Tessa lets out an audible sigh. "You don't have to be rude about it." She stands and comes over to my desk, all eyes on her. "Did you ask her to be your pit bull?"

My jaw drops at the accusation. "People think for themselves around here. But she's right that you're making it hard for everyone to work."

"I saw you over here on your phone."

"I texted Jaxson to ask when he expects his meeting to be over."

She rights herself. "And?"

"I'm sorry, but he's not planning on coming in today."

"You're lying!" she yells.

I stand so she can take in all five-foot-ten of me. She may be taller, but she can't intimidate me. "We run a business here. This isn't a place to play. You're welcome to sit here as long as you'd like, but he won't be back until tomorrow morning."

She leans in. "He doesn't love you."

"Does it make you feel better to tell me that?"

"We had an immediate connection that will never be broken, and nothing will ever compare to that."

"So that's why he hasn't spoken to you since you dumped him?"

"I didn't dump him. I left and expected him to follow."

"He's not a dog. He's a grown man." I force myself to stop there. She just sets off every single nerve in my body.

Her face flushes pink. "I'll be back tomorrow, and we'll get this all settled."

My stomach turns. I want her to go away, but I don't want another scene here at the office. "Actually, let's get this taken care of sooner rather than later. Why don't you come by the house tonight? You can join us for dinner." I paint a fake smile on my face.

She scowls, but I can tell she's intrigued. "What time?"

"I would hope he'd be home by seven."

"I'll be there. And please tell Helen to make my favorite dish. She knows what it is."

"Oh, I will."

With that, she signals her entourage and flounces back to the elevator.

The crowd of employees races to catch the next car, and some of them head for the stairwells. Eventually, the floor returns mostly to normal. I take a few deep breaths and try again to focus on the work I need to do.

Louise looks over. "Thank you for getting rid of her."

I shake my head. "I'm sorry she was so disruptive. I didn't want to cause a scene, but I did anyway."

"You handled her well."

I smile at her unexpected graciousness. "Thank you."

Picking up my phone, I call Jaxson.

"Hey, beautiful. How are you? Everything going okay? I'm so sorry about the mess with Tessa."

"Well, I got her to go away, but she'll be at the house tonight at seven. I didn't want her to come back here tomorrow and cause an even bigger scene. Please tell me you can be there by then."

Jaxson groans. "I should have just left the meeting and dealt with her today."

"Well, you can do that tonight without all the onlookers." I tell him everything she said to me, so he's prepared. "You can't run and hide. You need to talk to her."

"I'll be there." He sighs. "What a mess. This is way more than you bargained for. I really am sorry."

"To make it up to me, you get to tell Helen that Tessa wants her favorite meal." I laugh, but I'm serious. I have no idea what it is. Snake livers? The blood of an innocent?

"She won't be staying for dinner." Jaxson's voice says he's preparing for a fight. "In fact, why don't you see if you can meet Amy for dinner?"

It is tempting to avoid the rest of this entirely. "I don't think that's a good idea," I tell him. "If I'm not there, you won't have a witness, so later she can say anything happened. Plus, that might give her the idea that you want to get back together."

"She may say terrible things about me," he warns.

I snicker. "I'm sure she will, and I'm looking forward to it. Maybe she and I can form the Jaxson Bancroft ex-lovers' club next year."

"Just the thought of that turns my stomach."

"You know I'm teasing, but I won't let Tessa Sky upset me. I won't let her win that way."

"You're amazing. You know that?"

"You just want me to do naughty things with you later." I look over at Louise. She has a headset on now and thankfully seems to be ignoring me.

"Do you promise? We still have some toys left to try."

"I'm game if you are, but let's be sure Tessa doesn't cut your balls off first."

"Okay. Listen, I'll take care of security. But can you please call Helen?"

I sigh. That does make more sense. "Yes. But do you know what Tessa's favorite meal is?"

"No clue. I never paid attention. You, however, love any kind of fish that's well prepared."

"You know me well. A girl could get used to that kind of attention." *Okay, Harper. Get yourself in check.* "How are things going with the board?"

"Our meeting is just about finished, and they're happy about the magazine spread. I'll be home early so I can work before Cruella arrives."

That makes me laugh.

We say our goodbyes, and then I call Helen and explain the situation. I relay Tessa's request. "I'm hoping she doesn't end up staying, though."

"She'll stay," Helen warns. "Mark my words, she'll try to stay in a guest room tonight."

"You think she'd do that?" I shake my head. "I'm positive Jaxson is going to tell her to pound sand."

"Well, I'm sure you're right, but that woman doesn't listen to any voice but her own."

"Helen, I adore you."

"Good, because I adore you. And don't you worry, dear. One way or another we'll get this sorted out."

"Thank you, Helen. I should be home by six."

"I'll see you then."

CHAPTER 23

Jaxson

Well, this move from Tessa Sky is one I did not see coming. The more I think about it, the angrier I get. Poor Harper. I can't believe she has to be part of this now. It's bad enough what Tessa's done to me, but this tells me she's completely off her rocker. I plan on making sure she knows exactly how I feel.

When I get home, I head into the entertainment room and pull out the expensive bourbon. What I told Harper about the meeting wasn't a lie, but it wasn't the whole story either. Today was kind of a shit show. The board did like the positive press with the announcement of my engagement, but they're still concerned about Spy Game.

I've been working with Julia Willis, the head of development for Spy Game, and we're determined to crawl into the code ourselves and see what the problem is. It's crashing like crazy with our testers, and that doesn't make sense.

Harper walks in looking absolutely beautiful in a dark pink pencil skirt with her floral blouse untucked. She's barefoot and looks sexy as hell. "I thought I heard you," she says. "Has it been that kind of day?"

"It was a little rough, and I've got my work cut out for me so we can get Spy Game up and running, but I need this drink because of our dinner guest. You probably need one too. I know I was difficult when you told me what you said to her, but I think you're right about doing this at home, rather than at the office."

"Should I jot down the day and time so we can memorialize my superpowers?" Harper teases.

"You could. But we already know you're right most of the time."

She smiles. "So I don't forget, I'm meeting with the party planner again in the morning, and I have some suggestions for the Honeycomb logo on the invitation, which you will have to approve."

I nod but shut my eyes a moment. I know it's important to her, so I need to make some space in my brain for that, even if it feels minor compared to getting the damn game working.

"Come on into the kitchen," she says. "I figure Tessa will be here early."

She's probably right, and I should change, but I don't feel like it yet. I'm waiting for the bourbon to kick in and kill a few brain cells. I'd like to be a little numb before Tessa arrives. Still, I pick up my drink and follow her.

"Here are the designs for the IPO party." She sets three images down on the table. "Which one do you prefer?"

The first is our current logo of mostly hexagons, with some filled in yellow to symbolize honey. It shows that we're efficient and strong. The second is a beehive that almost looks like a shit emoji, and the bee has a smile. It's a little too cute for the games we produce. Then I pick up the third, and it incorporates the hexagons with the addition of an uncomplicated bee. That makes a difference.

"Where did you get these?" I ask.

"The artists are on the back. But before you look, you should choose one. And if you prefer David's design, we'll run with that." David did our original logo.

"Did you do one of these?"

"No," she says.

I'm disappointed, but I have her so busy as my admin and with the IPO party, she probably doesn't have time to do graphic design. I pick the one I like best, with the honeycomb and the bee, and flip it over. It has a heart on the back.

"What does the heart mean?"

She breaks into a smile. "It's me. I lied when I said I didn't do one. I wanted you to make an honest pick."

I turn the design over. "I really like this."

"I thought it went with the IPO. It's the bees—our investors—who will help to fill our honeycomb and make us all more honey."

I nod. "This is fantastic, and what a great story to tell at the party."

"Just don't tell them it's mine. I don't want them to know. They'll think you just chose my design because of our relationship."

I step in and kiss her deeply. We only break when I hear a commotion, and then a throat clears. Tessa has arrived and is standing in the doorway to the kitchen. Christophe stands behind her. He was briefed on what happened at the office today, and I told him she'd be stopping by. He looks like he's passing a kidney stone.

"Tessa," I say as my boner deflates.

"Hello, my love." She walks over, ignoring Harper, who pulls away from me.

I miss her heat immediately.

Tessa wraps her arm over my shoulder and leans in to kiss me. She attempts to push her tongue into my mouth.

I jump back. "What the hell, Tessa?"

"Come on. I can see that you did all this to get me back, and it worked. I'm back." She reaches for my hand. "Let's go upstairs and get reacquainted." She gives me a salacious smile.

"What are you talking about?"

"I'm back, so you can stop this charade of a relationship with your secretary."

I look over at Harper, who has moved to put the kitchen island between us. "Tessa, we only dated a few months. Then you left, and I fell in love with Harper."

She scoffs. "I only left so you would chase me."

"I'm too old to play games," I tell her. "And you leaked story after story to the tabloids, the thing I hated most, and you knew that."

"Sweetheart, I only wanted you to come to me so we could be tabloid darlings and live happily ever after."

I run my fingers through my hair. This is karma for all the women I didn't call after I slept with them. Breathing in deeply, I gather my wits. "I didn't chase you because I don't love you. I need you to understand something." I pause until she meets my eyes. "I fell in love with Harper, and we're getting married."

Tessa's eyes become pinpoints. I've seen her do this before, just before she explodes. "You don't love her. You love me."

"No. I don't love you. I never did."

"You told me all the time," she insists.

I shake my head. "That's not true. I cared for you, but really, our relationship was only physical. You were busy with your songwriting and preparing to go into the studio, and I was busy getting my company ready to go public."

"No. I don't believe that." Tessa shakes her head.

"I'm sorry." I cross the room and wrap my arm around Harper.

Harper pulls me in tight, and I feel immediately better. We're fighting this together.

"Would you like a drink?" Harper asks. "Helen made veal parm for dinner."

"I told you to have Helen make my favorite!" Tessa yells.

"I...I did tell her." Harper's face is indecipherable. "We can order something instead."

"I'm a pescatarian," Tessa shrieks. "I won't watch you eat baby cow."

"Tessa," I say sternly. "Why are you really here?"

She slumps into a kitchen chair. "I was at an airport and saw a magazine with you on the cover. I thought you were cute, and I read your story. It spoke to me, so I made arrangements to meet you. I immediately felt a connection with you I've never had before. When we were dating, I could tell you were hesitant because of my job and success, and I thought if I left you, you'd realize that you really love me."

"I'm sorry, but that's never how I felt. We had fun, but now, we're—"

"Fun? What do you mean, we had fun? I gave you a part of me I've never given anyone else. How can you say it was just fun?"

Suddenly, I know this will be all over the papers tomorrow.

"Why can't you love me?" Tessa bangs her fist on the table, and tears form in her eyes.

I shake my head. "It doesn't work that way. And you don't really love me. You love the idea of someone chasing you, and that isn't who I am."

"No! If you don't break up with her right now, I'm going to make you regret it."

I work to keep my growing anger in check. "I will always be grateful to you. Because of you, I met Harper." I look over at Harper and smile, and she gives me a smile of encouragement. "I miss her when she's not standing next to me. We're meant to be together. I'm sorry this isn't what you want to hear, but I hope one day you'll understand."

She stares at Harper. "You need to break it off with him."

Harper's eyes grow wide, but she just shakes her head.

Tessa paces and stops with her finger in Harper's face. "This is all your fault. You're going to pay for this!"

"She's done nothing wrong," I warn. "And if you continue to behave like this, you're going to find yourself on the wrong end of a very public lawsuit."

Tessa gives a wild and chilling scream before she stomps out of the room, with Christophe on her heels. He'll make sure she actually leaves the house.

I fold Harper into a hug. "Are you okay? I'm really sorry about that."

Harper picks up a glass of water, and her hand trembles slightly. "I'm fine. Honest. And I told Helen that Tessa asked for her favorite meal."

I throw my head back and laugh. "Helen always hated Tessa. She did it on purpose. I'm sure she knew it would make Tessa leave."

"I like Helen more and more every day."

"Once again, I'm really sorry. That was beyond the pale." I pull her into me again. She smells like cinnamon and vanilla, which is quickly becoming my favorite scent.

The front door slams, and we both jump.

"I'm glad we didn't have that conversation at the office," Harper says.

I nod. "Yep. You were right about how to handle her."

"Yeah, we don't need any more of what happened at work today. There were a lot of people at the office excited to see her, and Louise flipped out."

The hair on the back of my neck stands up. "What do you mean?"

"People throughout the building had filtered up to see Tessa, and it became difficult to work. Louise lost it and demanded that she move on. I think that's what finally triggered her to leave."

"Why did you let her up, knowing I wasn't there?"

Harper shakes her head. "I didn't let her up. She just arrived with a bunch of bodyguards."

"Why didn't you stick her in my office?"

She gives me a look. "Does that seem like a good idea to you? I don't open your door when you're not there, and I certainly wouldn't want her in there without someone with her. We're too close to going public to risk something being leaked."

I nod. "You know, on my desk is a folder outlining all the problems we currently have with Spy Game. If that leaked, that would sink us for sure. I don't know what I would do without you. Thank you for always making the right call."

She smiles at me. "I'm sure after dinner you'll think of several ways to thank me."

"I'm up for the challenge."

Tonight, Harper and I explored spanking with our sex, something I've never done with anyone before. Now, she's here in my arms, her bottom a delightful shade of red. I hope that the Tessa Sky situation has resolved, once and for all, though I'm a little unsettled by her anger today. And I'm still more than a little unsettled about the problems with Spy Game. As soon as they fix one thing, something else doesn't work. And for our IPO to be successful, I need Spy Game's release in four weeks to go smoothly.

I ease myself out of Harper's arms and go to my home office. I can't bother Julia Willis at this hour, so I pore over the code myself. But I'm missing something. I send a message to Cameron Newhouse, the tech guru at SHN, about my concerns. If anyone can help me, he can. Hopefully, he'll see my note first thing in the morning.

Then up pops a Slack notification.

Cameron: I saw your message. I'm happy to look at it. Send it over.

Me: I don't want to interrupt anything.

Cameron: Hadley and the girls are at some dance competition in Southern Cal, and I can't sleep when the house is this quiet.

With a few clicks of a button, I send him the link he'll need to get into our servers.

Me: I sent it to you. I'm just not sure why the game is so buggy. We're four weeks from launch, and I feel like we fix one thing and then something else doesn't work. I don't want to strip it down and start over.

Cameron: Let me check it out. I can meet you at your office tomorrow, early afternoon.

I check my calendar, and I'm booked solid, but I'll move whatever I have at the time he arrives.

Me: I'll be there. Thank you.

Cameron: This is what I love to do. You don't have to thank me.

I feel a giant weight off my shoulders. Cameron is the genius behind so many successful software programs. I'm sure fixing a game doesn't compare to perfecting centrifuge software that identifies the kinds of cancer cells in someone's blood, so I'm very appreciative.

Pouring myself three fingers of bourbon, I sit back and think about what Tessa said this evening. I've never seen her as manic as she was today. I followed the script Harper and I have created and said what I needed to so Tessa would understand we were through. But as I think back over it, nothing I said to her about Harper seems off-base or scary to me. I think I spoke so clearly because I spoke from the heart.

I'm falling for Harper. It's as simple as that. She understands what I need and gives it to me before I even ask, and I love taking care of her. Sometimes, I watch her outside my office during the day. When she's thinking hard, she bites the end of her pen. When she's mad, she throws her shoulders back, and I swear her eyes turn steely gray. When she's happy, she has a melodious and infectious laugh. And I know there is still so much to discover. What am I going to do when it's time to let her go?

I look up to see Harper standing at the doorway in my shirt from earlier today. I smile. "Did something wake you?"

"I woke and you weren't there. Is everything okay?"

I push back from the desk and pat my lap. "I sent Spy Game off to Cameron Newhouse over at SHN to review. He's a genius for that kind of thing, and I can't figure some stuff out."

"That's good, isn't it?" she asks, still in the doorway.

I take another sip of my drink. "Come over here."

She curls up on my lap.

"Are you sore?" I ask.

"A little, but I don't mind. It will remind me of the fun we had earlier."

"Wear your favorite dress to work today."

"Why?"

"Because I'll love knowing that each time you move, it's rubbing against your ass and you'll think of me."

"You're insatiable."

"Only with you."

"Not with Tessa?" Harper asks after a moment. I can hear the vulnerability in her voice.

"Never repeat this, but Tessa was a dead fish in bed. She just laid there and let me do all the work."

"I feel like that's all I do. You don't even let me reciprocate."

"I do too. Trust me, you are an active participant in our incredible sex life."

"What else is bothering you?"

"Nothing." I don't want her to know that I'm conflicted about what's happening between us, that this fake relationship is feeling dangerously real to me. Once things settle down, I have to let her go back to her own life. But I'm not ready to think about that.

"Can I talk you into joining me in bed?" she asks.

I close my eyes, grateful for every minute Harper allows me to be this close to her.

It was after three when I finally got back in bed, and the alarm at six thirty comes entirely too early.

I roll over on my back. "I'm going into the office early. Cameron's going to come sometime this afternoon. I'm not sure when, but maybe we should cancel my appointments."

Harper yawns. "I can move them around. It's mostly updates with your direct reports, including me. But I can give you the information you need tonight or in a memo."

"Okay, thank you. That's a good idea. Don't tell anyone who I'm meeting with, but if you could, ask them to write up what they want me to know, and I'll Slack them with any questions I have."

She nods, her eyes closed. "I'll say that a little nicer, but I'll get it done for you." Then she looks up at me. "Do you still want to meet with Julia or have her join your meeting with Cameron? She's freaking out a bit. It may calm her down."

"No. I want to hear from Cameron what's going on before I talk to her, and I don't want her to know I'm checking her work behind her back."

"Got it." Harper stands, and she winces as she walks to the bathroom. "I'll try to be ready to leave in a half hour."

"You don't have to be ready," I call after her. "I'm not expecting you to come in with me."

"Don't you think the paps saw Tessa arrive yesterday? They'll look to see what's happening between us this morning."

I sigh. She's right again. "Okay. But take whatever time you need. I'll wait."

She heads into the shower, and I follow her into the bathroom to shave. When we're both dressed and coiffed, we walk downstairs to find Helen has made egg sandwiches to go.

"Your veal parm was perfect last night," I tell her.

Helen lights up. "I hope it was okay. I heard Tessa Sky was coming for dinner, but I knew she was only trying to intimidate Harper."

"If she was, it didn't work."

Helen smiles at Harper.

"Sure, it did." Harper walks over to the espresso machine and starts a cup. "She told him to break up with me so they could go upstairs and do the horizontal mambo. I was shaking in my boots."

There's a deep crinkle between Helen's eyes. "That woman is crazy."

Harper shrugs. "I wouldn't argue with that."

As we climb into the car in the garage, I kiss Harper on the temple. "You are perfect for me."

"Of course I am. I have an expiration date."

That flippant comment is a slap in my face. My breath leaves me for a moment. "Not really," I finally manage. "We can do this as long as we want to."

"I know that," she says, patting my hand. "But you're making progress toward your goals all the time." She won't meet my eyes, so I can't quite tell what she means. "Anyway," she adds after a moment, "the party planner has agreed to help me start planning the wedding after the IPO party, so it looks real. She'll fly out to Boston and meet with locations and get things together so we can do a weekend and make some decisions."

I nod. "I'm down with whatever you want."

"You want me to decide without you? I guess that makes sense if we're not really doing any of it," she adds.

My heart lurches again. I have no idea how to tell her what I really think. "I'm happy to chime in wherever you need me."

The day is nonstop, and Harper has sandwiches delivered for lunch. Just as they arrive, Cameron does too. Harper brings them in and places a sandwich in front of him as well.

I look at her, bewildered.

"I called and got his lunch order," she explains.

"Do you see how efficient she is?" I marvel.

"And overqualified," Cameron notes.

"Thank you," Harper says as she sashays out of the room.

"What did you learn?" I ask. I can't even wait until we've finished eating.

Cameron takes out his laptop and brings up the Spy Game code. "I've made a copy of the code and color coded each of your developers' work," he says. "That makes it easier to spot where the flaws are. I also pulled all the history so we can see what changes have been made, and they're on the side here."

I take a bite of my sandwich and watch as he shows me where things have been altered and by whom. I can see the team has been all over the various bugs he points out.

"What I found most interesting is that someone has blacked out a trojan horse in your code."

I stop chewing. "What do you mean?"

He highlights two lines that are below an if:then query. If the player does one thing, then the game responds this way. The two lines look like they're a pause in play, which can be normal. But in this case, the code can't be seen on the black screen, until Cameron highlights it and makes it all red.

I read the code and understand immediately why my software isn't working and the giant vulnerability that's going to kill the game.

Someone on the team is behind this sabotage. But these lines aren't color coded, so I can't tell who. "What do we do?" I ask him. "Can you tell who did it?"

Cameron nods. "Jim Adelson and Gage Easton should be here shortly. I've left your software on the server so your team can continue to work on it. But between you, Gage, and me, we're going to clean this version and get it ready for release."

I'm numb. "Who's behind this?"

"Gage is going to have his team confirm my suspicions."

"Tell me who you think it is."

Cameron shakes his head. "Not yet."

My blood pressure rises and heat flushes my body. "Because…"

"It could be a frame job, and I don't want to ruin your relationship with any member of your team." He looks at me, his face serious. "But that also means you can't tell anyone what we're doing."

"I'm telling Harper," I inform him.

He sits back and picks up his sandwich. "That's fine. But stress to her that she can't tell anyone. I'm going to have Gage get involved in a few things that will either validate my suspicion or point us to who's behind it instead."

"I don't know what to say." I push my sandwich away. I've lost my appetite. I suppose I feel a small glimmer of hope, since we've identified the problem but another betrayal at work? Why is my career perpetually cursed? I squeeze my hands into fists. I'm going to punish the person behind this mess. "What do you think was their goal?"

"To make sure you didn't have a successful launch and sabotage your IPO."

I take a deep breath. "The person behind this is going to pay."

"I'm on board with that."

"But also, I can't thank you enough. You're saving me here."

"Happy to do it. This is a win for SHN as well, as I'm sure you realize." He gives me an easygoing smile.

Cameron and I talk a bit longer, and we agree to meet up when he's ready to discuss next steps.

When he leaves, Harper walks in. She immediately looks at the sandwich left on the table. "What did he say that made you lose your appetite?"

I shake my head. "You know me better than anyone in the world."

She waves that away. "I just know how you work."

"Close the door, would you?"

She does so, and then after she sits down, I tell her what Cameron said.

Her eyes become saucers. "Someone on the Spy Game team is out to get us?"

I nod, wondering if someone is listening. "It appears so."

CHAPTER 24

Harper

Flipping through the stack of tabloids that Megan from Bates PR dropped off at the office is horrifying. They're worse than what's been posted on the internet. Most detail Jaxson's sordid history with multiple women, and a couple explain how I trapped him in to marrying me because I'm pregnant. Or there's my personal favorite—I'm blackmailing him. I sigh as I toss them on my desk.

There's also an article saying Tessa was seen at the house. It says she fled in tears, and they're blaming me. I roll my eyes. If any of the articles is going to gain traction, watch it be that one.

Jaxson waves me into his office. "Are you okay?"

"My mom is going to love that we're getting married because I'm pregnant."

His mouth curls up. "We can make that true."

"Uh, no, we can't." I sigh and sit down. "Should we bet money on which of the articles is going to stick?"

"The pregnancy will stick. They'll report on a nonexistent baby bump forever."

I scoff. "There goes my peanut M&M obsession. I figure the one where I'm the horrible person you left Tessa for is going to play well. It gives her the ability to play off everyone's sympathies and gives them a villain—me!"

"Where was that one?"

"*The National Examiner*. They saw her leaving the house last week."

Jaxson reaches for my hand. "I know this isn't easy. But I promise this will fall off as soon as someone who's actually famous does something stupid. I promise."

I groan. "I know, but jeez. It's not even real. If they keep telling people I'm pregnant, and in the end, I don't have a baby, how are they going to explain? It's all lies."

"Let's get out of here early tonight. We can make pizzas and watch a movie, or I can let you beat me at Scrabble."

"You let me win?" The last time we played I wiped the floor with him. He was naked in four words, and I just took off my socks.

"Not on purpose," he says innocently. "I just had bad luck picking tiles."

"I don't know if I believe you."

Jaxson stands and pulls me in for a chaste kiss and a hug. "You know if we could frost these windows, I'd bend you over my desk and—"

"I know," I try to smile at him. "Thank you." I hear my cell phone ring and race back out to my desk. It's Hazel.

"Hello," I say, sounding much more chipper than I feel.

"Hi. You're famous," she says. "I've told all my new coworkers that you're marrying Jaxson Bancroft. Half of them hate you because they want to be you and the other half want your wardrobe."

I chuckle. "Did you tell them Mom and I make most of my clothes?"

"I think they're referring to the ones you're wearing in your magazine spread."

"Those were just for the photos," I assure her. I don't want her to know all the things Jaxson is doing for me. "How is living in New York City?"

Hazel sighs. "It's fun, terrifying, and lonely."

I put my elbows on my desk. "What do you mean, lonely?"

"I don't have any friends here. Most of the women I work with have worked here for years, and I guess they don't trust me enough to be friendly."

"It's their loss," I say spitefully.

"Why do you think I'm letting them know you're my sister?" she teases.

"Use it if it works." I giggle. "How's Harmony?"

"I went home on my last weekend off. She's doing okay. She needs to eat better, but Hunter and Harrison are stopping by at least every other day."

"What about Mom? Has she stopped by?"

"Nope. I guess she's been busy with year-end things."

"What's happening for Hope's graduation?"

"That's why I'm calling. Are you going to be there?"

"I am. I'll fly in on Monday afternoon and leave on a redeye after the ceremony. It's not ideal, but we're four weeks from going public, and I'm organizing a party for all the employees and investors. Plus, this mess with the tabloids makes moving around difficult."

"Okay..." She sighs. "You're in the same boat as I am."

"But what do you need help with?"

Hazel sniffs, and I realize she's crying. "There's been nothing done to prepare for the party. And I don't know how —"

"I'll take care of it," I say, cutting her off. "We don't have to cook anything. I'll order food. We can order a dozen pizzas from Mamma Mia's; they'll deliver. And the guys can make sure the house is picked up. And I'll call Katy Williams from high school. I've seen on PeopleMover that she's decorating cakes these days."

"Are you sure?"

"Absolutely. I'll call them both right now and get everything ordered. I found a pretty necklace I'm giving Hope for graduation. Have you found anything?"

"No. I was leaning toward a gift certificate to Macy's for clothes. You know, I still have the paperweight you gave me for my high school graduation—a rock that was covered with tissue paper and glue."

"I made that rock," I remind her.

She laughs. "I know. That's why I still have it. Also, it was the only graduation gift I got."

"No way. You got nothing else?"

"Nope, I was pretty much forgotten, which is why I'm always such an advocate for celebrating."

"It's a milestone."

We talk for a few minutes, and as we hang up, Hazel's voice softens. "Don't let the tabloids bother you."

"Thank you," I mumble. "I'm sure Mom is having a conniption because they're saying I'm pregnant, which is not true at all."

"Darn it. I was hoping you'd make Mom happy with grandchildren."

"I'm not sure that would work. I don't think she liked Jaxson. He'll keep me far away here on the West Coast."

"You live your life wherever you want to," Hazel says, resolve in her voice. "Don't let her talk you into something you don't want."

"I like San Francisco. You, Harmony, and Hope are the only things I miss."

"Okay, thanks for all your help," she says. "I've gotta run, so I can get to the hospital on time. Love you and can't wait to see you on Tuesday."

"I can't wait either."

I hang up, call Mamma Mia's, and put in an order for twenty pizzas—two of every kind—for the graduation party. Then I call Katie. She's friendly and chatty, so we catch up a little, and then I order a giant vanilla cake for Hope. Katie's going to put strawberry preserves between the two layers.

"That sounds amazing," I tell her.

"Well, I'm happy to do it. Promise me that if you get married at St. Francis, you'll let me do your wedding cake."

"I promise," I assure her, feeling a little guilty. "But we've just gotten engaged, and I have no idea about the location."

She laughs. "Your mom told my mom that you were getting married at St. Francis."

"You can't see me right now, but I'm rolling my eyes. We have quite a few things to get through before I can start thinking about my wedding."

"From everything I've read, I like Jaxson Bancroft," she says. "And Tessa Sky is a little off her rocker."

"Well, maybe, but I think I can relate," I tell her. "She liked someone who didn't like her back."

"That's the story of my life!" Katie squeals.

"Mine too, until I met Jaxson. I have faith the right guy will be coming your way one of these days."

"From your lips to God's ears."

"And so it will be. Thanks so much, Katie."

When I hang up, Jaxson motions for me to come in.

I grab my pad and pen. "What can I do for you?"

"Is everything okay at home?" he asks.

"Why?"

"I heard you talking to Hazel."

I sit down across from him. "Just the same old stuff. Hazel is expected to organize everything despite not living in Boston anymore, so nothing has been done for Hope's graduation. I'm not arriving early enough to do the decorating or make food, but I ordered twenty pizzas and a cake, and I only had to promise that if we get married at my family church, the baker can do our cake too."

"Did you use the credit card I gave you?"

I look at him, almost offended. "Of course I didn't. These are personal expenses."

Jaxson tilts his head to the side. "That's what it's there for."

"I can afford pizza and cake."

Jaxson shakes his head. "But you don't have to. I don't mind paying for pizza and cake and decorations and whatever else you need. My money is your money."

I shake my head. "You earned your money, and you're more than generously compensating me."

"We can talk about this at home." He gives me a look. "I may have to resort to using the methods that got you to wear your engagement ring every day."

My eyes grow wide. "That was cruel punishment."

"Then you should spend my money." Jaxson drops his voice. "You're even staying at your parents' rather than a hotel."

He has to be crazy. "It's only me and Christophe for one night. One of the girls' rooms is empty. He said he didn't mind. He'll have his own room, and I'll stay with Hope in her room."

"But wouldn't you be more comfortable in a hotel?"

"I don't want to commute to the house when I'm barely going to be in town."

"This is what I'm talking about." Jaxson stands.

"I don't want this to become a fight. Christophe is in the next room. We share a bathroom with him, so he can get to us several different ways if there's a problem."

Jaxson looks up at the ceiling. "I don't understand why you're being so stubborn."

"This is my family, and I want to spend time with Hope. I want to show her she can move away and it doesn't mean she can't come back for visits. Plus, I'm hoping to get some time with my mom to see if she and Dad will come out for the IPO party. That's okay, isn't it?"

"Absolutely. Any of your brothers and sisters who want to come are welcome. We can send a plane for them. I have access to a plane that will seat twenty-four people."

This man is generous to a fault, but I manage not to smile at him. "I'll find out and let you know."

We worked all weekend getting things ready for the IPO, so I'd be ready to fly out this morning. The amount of paperwork needed to validate our public offering is a giant pain in the butt, but the SEC wants to make sure our numbers aren't too different from what they reported when Honeycomb applied for the public offering.

But we made it through, and even though the flight has eaten most of my Monday, Christophe and I are here now. I'm so happy to be home, even if only for a little more than twenty-four hours.

I follow Hope down the hall with my suitcase. She was here to meet us, since she's done with classes, though everyone else is still at school this afternoon.

"Thank you for coming to stay with me," she says.

I nod. It's both familiar and unfamiliar to be back here. "Are you nervous about tomorrow?" I ask.

"Not really. I'm ready for it to be over, though."

"Is your valedictorian speech done?"

She chuckles. "Of course. It wasn't too hard, and I'm so ready to be finished. I do feel bad for Holden bringing up the rear, though. He'll be the last of the Lockwoods to finish at Weymouth High School, and with everyone else gone, all the focus will be on him."

"He's not struggling in school, is he?"

"No. He'll definitely be valedictorian. His scores blow mine away. I bet they give Mom and Dad an award."

We both giggle. Our parents are beloved, and they've kept that high school in business for a while now.

"When do you have to be at Wellesley?" I ask.

"The first week of August. I'm going to keep my job at Dunkin Donuts and transfer to a local store just off campus."

"I'm sorry you have to work while going to school."

She shrugs. "You did it. Everyone has done it."

"I know, but I often wished I didn't have to."

"Tell me about Jaxson," she says, changing the subject. "How is the sex with him?"

"Hope!" I act shocked. "I'm not going to tell you that."

"Well, you live in his house."

"We live together, and we're getting married. I like him, probably more than I should."

She looks at me strangely. "Shouldn't you like him a lot if you're going to marry him?"

I breathe out a big breath of air. I need to watch myself here. "He's not a normal guy."

She narrows her eyes. "Does he have two dicks? That would be awesome."

I laugh. "No, only one. What would you do with two dicks?"

"You co—"

I hold up a hand to stop her. "No, you couldn't. One is more than enough."

"Who are you, and what did you do with my sister?"

"I'm still me. It's just that… His life is very different from growing up here. He never worries about money. He insisted on paying for the food tomorrow. And he has decorations coming, too. I only hope they're not over the top."

"I think that's great. And your engagement ring is gorgeous."

I look down. It is beautiful. "I worry someone will cut off my finger for it."

"They'd have to get through Christophe first, and that man is worse than our brothers. He sneers at anyone who accidentally gets near you."

"What about you?" I ask, trying to redirect the conversation. Again. "Who will you miss after graduation?"

"I don't know. Everyone's already talking about meeting up for the ten-year reunion, but you already say you won't be going yours."

I shrugged. "It's not my thing."

"Hazel told me it was all about people walking around trying to make themselves sound more important than they are."

I have to laugh at that. "Welcome to life. You can choose to get on that train — whether you attend the reunion or not. But one step at a time. What about Corey? He's going to school locally, isn't he?"

She nods. "He's going to Bridgewater to study accounting. His parents met in high school, and his sisters met their husbands in high school, so no matter how many times I've told him I'm not interested in any kind of long-term thing, he makes me feel bad because I don't want to marry him."

"Never feel bad about that. Marriage is hard, and it should be with someone who's not only your friend, but your chemistry is off the charts."

"You have that with Jaxson, right?"

"Sure, but there are other complications you also have to consider."

"Do you regret getting engaged?"

I sigh. "Sometimes. I mean, I expected to show up in the tabloids, but not with a pregnancy countdown. And the ones that say I'm blackmailing him are a lot."

She shakes her head. "None of that matters. He's very handsome. You looked so happy in *People*."

"I am happy. He makes me smile, and I'd love him if he didn't have two pennies to rub together."

"But he has a lot more than two pennies."

"That is definitely correct."

After the graduation ceremony the next day, we're all standing around at home, chatting about how well Hope did today with her valedictorian speech.

Hudson sidles up next to me. "I heard you're paying for part of Hope's college."

"We have an arrangement, and I'm going to help her out, yes," I reply evenly.

"Must be nice to get engaged to a guy with so much money. All you got me and Hannah was a set of sheets."

Are you kidding me? "First of all, you're *my* family, not Jaxson Bancroft's. He came to your wedding only because I asked him to. Second, I chose something from your registry, which I assumed you wanted. And I paid for it—me. I'm making my own living, and I'm helping out my siblings as much as I can. That's something you've never volunteered to do. What's stopping you? You have a good job and so does Hannah."

Hudson holds his hands up in surrender. "You don't have to be all bitchy."

I shake my head. "I'm not your bank, Hudson. You did nothing for me—nor did I expect you to—but don't act as if you're being robbed."

Hudson gives me the evil eye and walks away.

I turn back to Hazel, and I can't quite read her expression. "I'll apologize to him later."

"You don't need to apologize," she says. "He was being an ass. You don't comment on the gift someone gives you, no matter who they are. You're helping out, which is more than he ever did. He's had Hannah in his pocket from the beginning, and he could barely help, let alone contribute."

"I don't want to fight with anyone."

Hazel reaches for my hand. "You're helping two of your sisters. None of us had any help except from each other. I think it's great that you can do that."

"There are many ways to help that don't include opening your wallet," I remind her. "And you did them time and again."

"I don't miss being in charge of everything."

"I'm glad your situation is better now."

She smiles. "Anyway, Paul and I are so excited to be at the bell ringing for the IPO, and I can't wait to explore San Francisco."

"I don't know how much I'll be able to show you around, but there's so much to see and do. You're going to love it."

"Paul's boss wanted to know if he could come to the party, and Paul shut him down."

"If it's important, I'll get him in the door as a guest, but I can't fly him out or put him up in a hotel room."

She shakes her head. "He's not as wealthy as Jaxson, but he has money. I'll let Paul know, but I think he wants to enjoy this on his own."

"That makes sense. When we were in Michigan visiting Jaxson's family, everyone seemed to want something from him. It's not fun to be liked for your money."

"I don't hate you for your money. I hate you for your boobs."

"What?"

She nods. "You got good boobs."

Hazel's are maybe a little smaller than mine, but they're not small. She's being silly. After a moment, she dissolves into giggles.

"You're too much."

She shrugs. "I try."

I look at my watch, and Christophe and I need to leave in less than an hour. "I should go talk to Mom and Dad before I need to go."

She steps in and gives me a tight hug. "Thank you for all you did for Hope today."

"Happy to do it, and it wasn't that hard. I only hope she doesn't feel slighted."

"She doesn't. Look at her. She's all smiles." Hazel squeezes my hand, and the distance between New York City and San Francisco never seemed so far.

I weave through the crowd until I spot Mom, busy talking to a woman I don't recognize.

"Here she is," Mom says and reaches for me. "Harper, this is Melissa Scalia. She works with me."

Melissa smiles. "So nice to meet you. I'll let you two chat. I'm very thirsty."

She walks away, and I turn to Mom. "School's out, so I suppose your plan is to sleep for a few weeks?"

"Yes," she says dramatically. "Every year it gets harder and harder to recover."

"Teaching isn't for the faint of heart." I shake my head.

"No. It's hard work." We stand together looking out at our family and friends. It feels like she has something to say, so I wait.

"Why can't you stay longer?" she whines.

"Because I'm busy at work, planning an enormous party. I'm hoping you and everyone will come to San Francisco for it. Hazel and Paul will be there, and there's a private plane you all can use to get there — even Harmony."

"I don't know," Mom says.

"Please think about it. I could show you where Jaxson and I live, and we'll have some time together."

She still doesn't commit, but she gives me a hug. I know my family doesn't understand what I'm in the middle of, but a successful initial public offering is a big deal. I just hope I get the chance to show them.

CHAPTER 25

Jaxson

Throughout the day, Harper sent photos of what they were doing and from the graduation ceremony. I missed her last night, and I didn't sleep well. Tonight isn't looking so good either. I'm staring at the ceiling, thinking about her.

Harper has really surprised me. I enjoy spending time with her. It's easy. And now, I miss her when she's gone. "What are you going to do?" I say aloud to no one.

I haven't a clue. I'm not usually a good partner when it comes to the women I date. In fact, I don't usually want to be a partner. I love sex, but they're never a priority. But Harper takes care of me and is helping me shepherd my company through the IPO. I don't know how I'd do it without her at this point, and I think I mean personally and professionally.

I turn over and look at the glowing red numbers on the alarm clock. She's probably over Kansas or maybe Colorado about now. She'll be here in the morning, yet that isn't soon enough.

Sometime later, I feel a warm, naked body slip into bed with me. "You're here," I murmur. It's now just after six. I did fall asleep at some point. "This is my favorite kind of wake-up call."

"I slept the entire way back, but I'm still exhausted." She yawns for emphasis.

"Take the day. We'll be fine."

"No. I'll be in, but maybe closer to nine. If I can get a few hours of sleep, I'll use an IV pump for caffeine and be right as rain."

I hold her close. "I missed you," I say, just above a whisper.

She strokes my cock and brings me to life. I like when she's assertive.

"I missed you." She groans.

Our foreheads meet, and her cinnamon-and-vanilla scent calms me. She kisses me sweetly as she guides me to her opening and sinks onto my hard rod. Damn, if she doesn't feel warm, soft, and inviting.

She rocks her hips until she has me fully seated inside her. Her eyes close as she finds the spot that gets her so excited.

Licking my thumb, I rub her clit. I can feel her pulse strumming a fine beat.

"Tell me what you want," I whisper.

"More," she groans as she starts a rhythm, moving up and down languidly.

While one hand circles around and over her bundle of nerves, I reach for her nipple and play with it.

"Harder," she breathes.

Up and down and up and down.

"Right there," she mewls. "Don't stop."

Her slow and sensual movements have me following her down the rabbit hole, and each time her channel grips my cock, it pushes me closer to the edge.

She grabs my pecs, and her nails sink in. The pain and the way she's clutching my cock like a vise send me rocketing to my peak.

Her chest heaves as we come down. "I needed that."

I give her a lopsided smile as she curls up against me.

"I don't know if I want this to end," I whisper.

But her breaths are steady. She didn't hear me.

Maybe that's for the best. Once the IPO is over, we can talk about it, discuss how we feel. Maybe we could make it real between us. I want to believe she has feelings for me, just like I do her.

I reach over and set the alarm for her, and I swear I'm going to get up and get to the office. But I close my eyes for just a second, and then the alarm sounds.

"You stayed." Harper yawns.

"I wasn't planning to…" I sit up and confess the truth. "I didn't sleep well without you here."

Her hair is all mussed, and she looks so sexy. She kisses me chastely. "I'm so glad to be home. I talked to my mom about coming out for the IPO, and she's on the fence. But I think if all my brothers and sisters are going, my parents will go with them."

"Good, we can introduce our parents that weekend too."

She sighs. "You don't think we're setting everyone up for disappointment?"

"Maybe. We'll figure it all out after the IPO. Maybe we can get away and spend some time together, figure out what we both want."

She looks over, and the crease between her eyes is deep.

"Stop worrying," I assure her. "There's nothing to be worried about."

"Okay."

We get to work shortly before ten, and Harper orders us lunch. Tessa calls a few times—as she has the last few days—but I decline the calls. I said everything I wanted to say to her the last time I saw her, almost three weeks ago at my house.

When my phone pings, I almost ignore it. But the successive pings grab my attention.

Grayson: Scarlett and I have the night off. Drinks, anyone?

Nick: Sure. Where are you thinking?

Grayson: Bourbon and Branch? 6ish?

Nick: That works for me.

Mason: Caroline and I will be there.

I motion Harper into my office. "Do you want to join me and my friends for drinks tonight?"

I can see conflict in her eyes.

"Grayson is bringing his wife, Scarlett, and Mason and Caroline will be there."

She shrugs. "Okay. I can sleep after the IPO."

"That's what I keep telling myself."

We work through the afternoon, and before I know it, Harper is standing at the door to my office. "Your friends are already at Bourbon and Branch."

I look at the clock and notice it's dark outside. "Okay. Let me save my work and I'll be ready to go."

As Christophe drives us over, we talk about the issue with Spy Game and the new plan.

"Does this mean you'll have a successful launch of Spy Game?"

I rub my fingers over her knuckles. "I think so. The in-house team will think they're doing the upload, but really, the new plan is to have Cameron upload the final version from his offices."

"Are you relieved?"

"Surprisingly, yes. The success of the game could affect the initial public offering, so a smooth rollout takes precedence over figuring out the staff problem for now."

She smiles at me across the darkened backseat. "I'm thrilled for you."

I bring her hand to my mouth and kiss it. "I owe it all to you."

"I had nothing to do with it. I've just entertained you for a few months."

"You've done a lot more than that."

Christophe stops at a corner, and we hop out to ring the bell outside the bar.

The door opens. "Do you have the password?"

"Booklover," I reply.

The hostess allows us in and points us to our table in the library.

Harper and I take the last two remaining seats at the table, and they're not together. I'm disappointed but feel better when I see the smile on Harper's face as she sits down between Caroline and Scarlett.

"How's it going?" Gray leans in and asks softly.

"Very well. Cameron Newhouse has stepped in on the Spy Game project and is making it all work. Someone on our team is a saboteur."

"What?" Nick says a little louder than I would have liked. I didn't even know he was listening. "Who is it? Do you think Villefort is behind it?"

I shrug, trying to seem nonchalant. "They're still investigating, so they won't tell me, which is not helping my anxiety."

Mason sets his glass down and turns toward us. "Gage Easton, one of Clear Security's top technology security analysts and one of Jim's partners, is working on it. Plus, it's better not to know until after you go live and the game is a roaring success."

Now, everyone is listening. So much for being discreet.

"How are you sleeping?" Gray asks.

"Better when Harper is here."

Gray and Mason exchange a look. They understand. I've decided there's something to be said about the calming effect the right woman can have on you.

Mason leans in. "The Honeycomb board had an unofficial meeting today."

276

I perk up. "And why wasn't I told about this?"

"Grantham Wilks invited everyone over to his law firm for lunch. He wanted our thoughts on the publicity."

"I hope he's happy."

"He's happier than he was, but until you go public, he won't be completely confident."

"Why did you talk me into having him on my board again?"

"Because, despite being difficult, he's an excellent lawyer, and you're going to need him when it comes to fighting Villefort."

I think about how direct Grantham can be. I'd rather he be on my side than my adversary's. "He's not my biggest fan."

"Yes, he is," Mason assures me. "He wanted to be sure everyone else was happy. I promise, he's even worse when he doesn't like you."

"Did you tell him or the board about the sabotage?"

"No, I'm leaving that for you to tell them in your wrap up after your successful IPO."

I nod. "Thank you. I appreciate that."

"This is your party," Mason says. "We're just grateful to be invited."

Grayson snorts. "It's a party you made happen, for all of us."

Nick nods. "To SHN!"

We lift our drinks and toast.

CHAPTER 26

Jaxson

A knock at the bedroom door wakes me. "Yes?"

Christophe is at the door. "Megan Bates is here to see you."

I rub the sleep from my eyes. It's not even five o'clock. "Did she say what she wanted?"

"Just that she needs to see you right away. I had to physically restrain her from racing up the stairs."

"This can't be good," Harper mumbles.

"Tell her I'll be right down. I need to use the bathroom."

Christophe backs out of the room, and I look at Harper. "I have no clue what this could be."

She pulls the covers back, walks over to her dresser, and starts opening drawers. By the time I finish in the bathroom, Harper is dressed and has her toothbrush in her mouth.

"You're mighty fast this morning."

"Growing up I learned to be quick." She smiles and winks at me.

I get dressed, and we head downstairs. Harper laces my fingers with hers. This is not going to be a fun meeting if the PR agent has come here unannounced at this time of the morning.

We find Helen in the kitchen with Megan, who is drinking an espresso. Helen looks at me questioningly and gestures to the coffee machine.

"Yes, please. For both of us. I have a feeling we're going to need a lot of caffeine today."

Megan takes a deep breath. "The press is already accumulating out front."

"Great. The neighbors must love that," Harper mumbles.

Megan places her phone on the countertop, and a bouncy melody begins to play.

I can see it in your eyes, you don't love her like you love me
I know you're about to marry, but I'm begging you, can't you see?
I broke up with you to make you realize
That I'm the one you need, the love of your life

I can't stand to see you marry her when I know you love me
It's tearing me apart, can't you see?
I'll marry you, don't marry her
I'll love you forever, don't let her be the one you prefer

Harper gasps, and Megan nods, but the song is nowhere near over.

I remember all the good times that we shared
But now you're about to marry, and I'm feeling so scared
I'm convinced you're making a mistake
You should be with me, for heaven's sake

I can't stand to see you marry her, when I know you love me
It's tearing me apart, can't you see?
I'll marry you, don't marry her
I'll love you forever, don't let her be the one you prefer

279

You don't have to do this, don't make this mistake
Just look into my eyes, you'll see the love we can make
I'll be there for you, through thick and thin
Just say the word, and let our new life begin

I can't stand to see you marry her, when I know you love me
It's tearing me apart, can't you see?
I'll marry you, don't marry her
I'll love you forever, don't let her be the one you prefer

Don't go through with this, it's not too late
I'm here for you, just let fate
Bring us back together, where we belong
With a love so strong, we can't go wrong.

Finally, the lyrics stop, and the music fades out. I feel sick to my stomach.

"You've got to be fucking joking," Harper exclaims. "What is wrong with her?"

I take a few breaths. I think Harper is exactly right. There is something not right with Tessa Sky. "What does the press want?" I ask.

"They'd like a comment," Megan explains. "They know you're the person she's referring to."

I shake my head. "Unbelievable. My first instinct is to have no comment, but what do you suggest?"

Megan takes a sip of her espresso. "I think we need to make a statement that essentially says you're in love with Harper, and you wish Tessa Sky nothing but the best."

"I wish we could tell her to go jump in a lake," Harper says. "What is she hoping to accomplish? Does she think a song will make Jaxson dump me and go to her? That he'll cave to the pressure? Why is that even what she wants? That's not a real relationship." She throws her hands in the air. "In what world is that okay? People shouldn't treat each other that way."

It warms my heart to hear Harper agitated about this. I smile at her. I think she has real feelings for me.

Megan smiles sympathetically. "I think we can leak to a few of the tabloids how upset you are that she would treat another woman this way and expect so little from a man."

Harper sighs. "I'm sorry. I'm just venting. She showed up here and tried to dry hump him right here in the kitchen in front of me. She is not okay."

"No, she isn't." Megan pulls out a laptop and starts typing away. She then retrieves a cylinder that she feeds a piece of paper into, and it prints out a press release. "What do you think of this?"

I look it over. It's clear and to the point, and I guess it's the best we can do in this situation. "I'm forever going to be synonymous with this song," I lament.

"I think you're right. But a more muted response is still your strongest option."

I reread it. "How many copies of this do you need?"

"I'll send it out across the wires, but if you'd like, we can also pass them out to the press outside. I can do fifty copies from my little gizmo."

"If you email it to me, I can print them in my home office."

She perks up. "That would be great." In a few clicks, there's the whoosh sound of the email being sent.

"I'll print them," Harper says.

She disappears down the hall, and I look over at Megan. "The only thing good about this is that Tessa admits to breaking things off with me." I scrub my hands over my face. "I don't like what this is doing to Harper. If you want to plant some stories, I have text messages where Tessa has threatened me. But this isn't just about my personal life. My board is watching. I want to be very careful how we handle this so it doesn't snap back at me when we IPO."

Megan purses her lips in thought. "Tell me what happened when Tessa showed up—that was three weeks ago?"

I nod and tell her the story about Tessa coming to the office, Harper moving the meeting to the house, and what happened here.

"That woman has a serious set of balls on her." Megan drains her espresso. "And she's also a little unhinged."

I look out at the fog-covered Golden Gate Bridge. "Can we get this out there as soon as possible? I know she'll be doing press on the song."

Megan nods. "She's going to be out there telling the world that you're really in love with her."

"I was never in love with her. We dated for less than three months." I look up at the ceiling. "This is going to create trouble for our families, too. They're not equipped to handle this. What do you suggest?"

"I've got that. We can't stop anyone from selling a story—"

"My family knows better, but I'll send an email right away warning them to not say anything to the media."

Harper returns and hands a stack of papers to Megan.

"Thank you. We were just talking about the fact that the press may contact your families," she tells Harper. "Just let them know that they should say you both seem very in love and leave it at that. And they need to be very careful about speaking with friends who might then sell something to the tabloids as an inside source."

Harper nods. "I need to get to my family via email and text message right away since they're on the East Coast."

"Smart."

Harper thanks Megan on her way down the hall, and I thank her as well.

"Of course," she says. "We've got this. I'll get this to the crowd out front, and let's touch base at the end of the day. You and Harper please refer all calls about this to me."

"Okay. And I'll send a note to the company with the press release so that's covered."

Megan heads out, and Harper and I spend the morning working on this from the house. I get supportive texts from Gray and Nick. And I make a point of calling Mason to give him the update.

"Man, who would have thought spending time with Tessa Sky would leave you with so much drama?" Mason asks.

"I dunno. I kind of feel like I should've seen it coming." I manage a laugh. "Harper tells me it's because she's an artist. This is how she's working out her feelings."

"Why can't she do it like a normal person — less publicly over a bottle of wine?" Mason asks.

"That would definitely work for me," I tell him.

"How is Harper holding up?" Mason asks.

"She's amazing. She's almost more upset that a woman would do this to another woman than anything else."

Mason snorts. "Caroline said the same thing."

By the end of the day, Tessa's song is at the top of the charts, and Megan has warned us that she believes it will linger there for a few weeks.

I pull Harper into a hug in the kitchen as we prepare dinner. "I'm really sorry about all of this."

"It's not your fault. Though it would be nice to have your ex-girlfriend a little less in our face."

"I'll remember that for next time."

Her eyes flash, and I know right there I screwed up.

"Well, I mean —"

"I know what you mean," she says. "We're good. This is a business arrangement." She gives me a plastic smile.

My heart sinks at her comment. We were having such a great day, in spite of all this — working together as a team toward the same goal — but I had to put my fucking foot in my mouth. I want to scream at the top of my lungs at my stupidity. *Why did I say that?*

It's definitely a Monday morning, and I pour my third cup of coffee, determined to get moving as I head out to the car. I'm exhausted. Tessa Sky's new song dropped a week ago, and it's been in the number-one spot ever since.

Tessa's fans have shown up at the office and attempted to get in the building a couple of times, but we've hired extra security, and they're keeping them out.

There's been some backlash to Tessa's song from women's groups, but for the most part, her fans seem to think she can do nothing wrong. Last week, Caroline sent Harper a giant bouquet of pink flowers she called cabbage roses.

Harper has been a little distant since my cock up about my next girlfriend, but when I asked her about it, she told me we were fine. Things will be better after the IPO. We just need to get over the final hurdle.

Today, Honeycomb has a board meeting at the Fairmont Hotel, one I'm invited to. We do them outside our offices so there's an element of security and privacy. Harper and I head over together, though we don't say much. I'm distracted, and she seems lost in her thoughts. As we pull up outside, I'm prepared for a tough discussion, but I've not heard anything negative from the board members since the song dropped. Either way, this will be our last meeting as a private company. While we've always taken notes and tracked our conversations, we don't have to share them with stockholders, and we're accountable only to us. After we go public, that will change.

I'm already settled in my seat at the table when Grantham Wilks walks into the conference room. "Good to see you, Jaxson." He gives me a nod.

"Glad you could make it."

Right behind him, Veronica Vance and Dominic Valente arrive, and after them come the other board members and part of my team. Harper gets herself a coffee before taking her seat.

Soon there are twelve of us sitting around a large table, munching our continental breakfast. "It's good to see you, Ms. Lockwood." Grantham comments.

She nods in greeting, and I look up and smile. "Wouldn't do this without her," I tell him. "Harper has spent hours with SHN and the lawyers getting the IPO paperwork squared away. She's also organizing the party, which I think you're going to love."

"You both have done so much to get this over the finish line," Grantham says.

Mason straggles in, uncharacteristically late, which actually just means he's on time, rather than early. He waves in apology, and with that, we're ready to go.

My heartbeat picks up, and I pull out my copy of the file each person has at their place. "Now that we're all here, we can talk while you eat. We'll also have lunch served at noon, and if we remain on time, we should be out of here by four."

Everyone nods.

"Let's start with Corey Craven, Honeycomb's CFO, who will walk us through the profit and loss statements."

Corey is a petite Black woman who has probably spent her life being underestimated, but as soon as she begins her presentation she commands the room. She was my first hire, and I'm convinced there is no one stronger.

After Corey has answered everyone's questions, we hear from Stacy Bragio, VP of operations, who updates the board on each of our games, both active and in development. She notes the loss of Chocolate Crush users and explains what we're doing to get them back or replace them. She ticks through the four games we have in development and then spends an hour talking about the launch of Spy Game. She ends her presentation indicating confidence that we'll have a successful, on-schedule release.

Only Mason and Harper know that Cameron and his team have removed the trojan horse and fixed the game and that we'll upload his version for release. In all the craziness, I haven't followed up with him to get the latest. But Mason has assured me that I shouldn't be concerned. He and I still think it's best to hold off on telling the board what's happened until after the launch and IPO.

After lunch, Mason and I share our plans for the cash infusion we should receive from the public offering. Mason gives a report on four of our competitors who've gone public in the last five years, the gaming market's growth, and what he and his team feel is realistic for where Honeycomb will end up after IPO. It's almost twice the figures I gave Harper. And that has the board ecstatic.

"That's wonderful news!" Grantham says.

"I'm so happy for all of us," Veronica adds.

"Uh, well, my accounting has it at about half that, so I'd prefer we set our expectations to be happy with a little less than what Mason's sharing," I caution.

"Have some faith," Mason says.

The board laughs.

As a wrap up, Harper and I spend the last hour talking about the IPO events. She gives each of them a lavish invitation to the IPO on the floor of the stock market in New York and then to the party here in town a few days later. "We hope you'll be there to celebrate with us," she concludes.

"We're looking forward to it," Veronica says.

Grantham clears his throat. "I'm very happy you took our recommendation of settling down a bit before the IPO. You and Harper seem to work well together. We hope that despite how your relationship started, it will continue for as long as you're both happy."

I feel like this is the conversation my dad had with me about sex, and I can feel my face getting hot. "Thank you." I smile over at Harper. "Harper has been a great sport, particularly where Tessa Sky is concerned. I'm sure you've all heard her new song." I roll my eyes, which gets laughs around the table.

"You've handled it with dignity and grace," Veronica says. "I think if I'd been in that situation, it would have been very difficult not to lash out."

Harper smiles. "Trust me, that was my first instinct. The song is tacky, but her fans love it."

"You're wise beyond your years," Veronica says.

"I guess Jaxson was always destined to be famous," Harper says with a twinkle in her eye.

CHAPTER 27

Jaxson

Harper and I walk up to the front door of the Sullivans' home. It's been a crazy week since our board meeting — full of pre-launch of the IPO details — and the weather is crazy too. Despite it being early July, we're decked out in jeans and wool coats. The fog often makes the summer rival a cold winter's day, and everyone's quoting Mark Twain — "The coldest winter I ever spent was a summer in San Francisco."

"It's days like today that make me want to go hide on the Cape," Harper says with a shiver.

"It's just three days until we're in New York City," I remind her. "You can soak up plenty of heat, humidity, and sunshine."

Harper laughs. "I can't wait. I've never been to the Hamptons before."

"You'll love it." I pull her close on the doorstep, kiss her on the forehead, and ring the bell. "It will be great to have some time alone before everything goes crazy —"

"Come on in!" Caroline opens the door and ushers us in with a giant grin on her face.

So much for our conversation, though this wasn't the best time anyway. I know now that I want to tell Harper my feelings for her are real. We just need some focused time alone together. Everything is so busy right now, and I think that means it needs to wait. I have to do this right.

Harper hands Caroline a bottle of sparkling wine. "I thought we might want to do a private celebration for the Spy Game release."

She nods. "Thank you. Yes! We're going to be doing a lot of that."

In the living room, Cameron, Grayson, and Nick are already seated, and I'm surprised to see Jim Adelson come in from the kitchen. I wave to them in greeting.

Scarlett ushers assorted kids downstairs and swipes her hair off her face. "I cannot wait to have a few days away without the kids."

Caroline nods enthusiastically. "It's been so long since we did something like this. I'm so excited."

We're all flying to New York on Wednesday, and we'll take a helicopter to Mason and Caroline's home in the Hamptons. They have a large estate in Quogue on Dune Road. I've been one other time when the board did a retreat there, and it was amazing. This time, we're going to celebrate the launch of Spy Game with several Wall Street muckety-mucks, and then on Monday we'll be in New York City to open the Stock Exchange and celebrate our IPO. Then we'll be back to San Francisco by midweek to prepare for the giant party. But tonight, Cameron is giving us a preview of what to expect from Spy Game.

I join the guys for a predinner cocktail in the sitting room.

"Have you heard from Tessa Sky?" Cameron asks as he plops down with his drink.

I shake my head. "No, thank goodness."

"I heard she released a remix track of the song with your recorded conversations interlaced."

I groan as I nod. This fucking song is going to chase me forever. "My lawyer got that version taken down immediately. It was recorded without my knowledge. Every time it's played, she'll have to pay graduated fees starting at a quarter-million dollars."

"Hopefully, that will be a deterrent," Gray says.

"We hope so too."

We chat a while longer until Caroline calls us to dinner.

She's set up a spread of fajitas with beef, chicken, shrimp, and tilapia and all the fixings. It's perfect for tonight, under this chilly blanket of fog. We all fill our plates and take seats at the table.

Then, with a margarita in hand, Cameron clears his throat. "I'm only saying this because it has to be said, but everything mentioned this evening needs to stay between us. Please don't discuss this with anyone outside unless you get specific permission first."

We all nod as he looks around the room.

"I'm not sure who knows what, so I'm going to start at the beginning. After repeated issues with bugs and glitches in the Spy Game code, my team and I copied the code from the Honeycomb server and set up a version on SHN's private server. From there, we fixed the bugs, and as I've already let you know, Jaxson, there was a trojan horse embedded that we removed. We also found and closed a back door that would have given outside sources access to your game."

My stomach sours as if I've just chugged a half gallon of spoiled milk.

"Once we made the repairs, we moved on to identifying who placed the trojan horse and when. We found that the same person was responsible for the back door."

I've stopped eating, just listening to Cameron.

"We traced payments, which we believe came from Zack Villefort, to a private account this person owned at the now-defunct Technology Startup Fund."

My fists are white with rage. "You know for sure that Villefort paid the money?"

"We're tracing the money through multiple shell companies and accounts. We have all the breadcrumbs that lead to him, but we haven't connected the dots just yet. We will though."

"No fucking way," Nick bellows. "What does he think he's doing?"

"I'll get to that," Cameron promises.

"Who's taking the payments for this?" I ask, as calmly as possible. Harper is looking at me with wide eyes. Calm must not be the vibe I'm giving off. "And when can I fire them?" I try to keep my rage at bay.

Sara Arnault, SHN's attorney, hands me a file. "Julia Willis accepted three payments, each for two hundred and fifty thousand dollars, and we suspect a fourth and final payment will arrive after the game goes live."

My pulse quickens. *Not Julia.* "Is there any chance this is a frame job? She's been the lead on the game since the beginning. I...I don't... She's smart, and some people feel threatened by that."

"That was our hope when it was first uncovered," Cameron says.

"But she's purchased a very expensive Tesla and a condo in the East Bay," Mason reports.

I feel utterly defeated, like I shouldn't be in charge of anything. Am I a really horrible judge of character? When I think of all the trust I had in her, to find out she's betrayed me is an enormous blow, to the company as well.

I look around the table, my blood boiling. Harper places her hand on my thigh. "What could be her motivation to sabotage the game? She has at least a thousand shares of Honeycomb stock, which are worth much more than a million dollars. She's only hurting herself if she tanks the IPO."

"I have a few theories, but it doesn't matter why she did it, only that she did," Cameron says.

"The only bright spot in all of this is that she left her money with TSF, so it's gone," Mason points out.

I snort.

"And no one's going to replace the funds," Gray adds with a twinge of bitterness.

"Are we sure she's the only one?" I ask.

Cameron looks down at his plate a moment. "Right now, she's the only one who's received any payment, but that doesn't mean we'll stop monitoring things after the game goes live. Villefort may have a backup plan."

I look at Mason. "What do I do?"

He nods at Sara.

"We suggest you take the information in the file I gave you to the FBI. We've worked with Duncan Snow there in the past. They can make an arrest for corporate espionage if they deem the evidence complete. Or they can investigate on their own. It should be up to you to determine whether you want that done quietly or at the office in front of everyone."

My desire to punish Julia is great. But I want to be a better man. I don't want anger to consume me. I look over at Harper. I need her to guide me.

"It's up to you." Her voice is soft. "There are merits to both sides. If it's done quietly, it may not alert Villefort, and he won't know you're on to him. But if it's done loudly, it can send a message to anyone else who might be tempted by something like this."

So many things are running through my head. I want to cause Julia pain for betraying me, but what would that look like? She's already going to be out of a job, and she'll lose all her stock options. I remind myself that I have a strong and competent funder who helped me avert the disaster and solve the most immediate problem. Regardless of what I do, Villefort is probably going to know we're on to his shitty scheme.

"What do I need to do?" I ask.

We decide that tomorrow morning, Sara, Jim Adelson, and I will meet with the FBI at my house. From there, we'll develop a plan for the best way to proceed with Julia.

During the remainder of our dinner, we discuss what to do about Villefort.

"He's weak right now," Gray says. "His money is mostly gone. But he still thinks he can come back from the Technology Startup Fund collapse. Maybe it's time to see how much you're propping him up with the money you've got in his companies and go for the kill."

The table erupts in various points of view on what "going in for the kill" should look like, but it seems everyone is ready to do this.

Nick clears his throat. "We saw the way he tried to undermine Firefly's purchase of Hearst Transportation. And now, we know what he's done with Honeycomb. I wonder what he's done that I don't know about at PayFriend?"

The room goes silent.

Cameron sets his glass down. "I think we should probably go through your code and determine what he's gotten his greasy hands on."

When we return home, Harper leads me upstairs and undresses me before undressing herself, down to her fabulous underwear. "Don't let Villefort steal anything else from you," she says, kissing me softly.

She's giving herself to me. I can make tonight what I want and what I need, but it's her simple statement of support that sends my heart soaring. Other than my family, Gray, and Nick, I've never had someone so solidly in my corner. I love her.

Her hand wraps around my cock, and her arm wraps around my shoulders. She looks up at me. "Tell me what you want."

She's my angel. I'm crazy about her and so grateful she's here with me right now. "I want you."

Her lips travel up my neck to my mouth. She pulls herself close, her soft breasts pillowing against me.

My heart races as she rests her head against my chest. I reach for her, cupping the sides of her face and kissing her fiercely. She tastes like Boston cream pie and espresso, our dessert earlier this evening.

She presses her body against mine. "Take me the way you need to," she breathes.

I don't need to be asked twice. She's wearing black see-through lace boy shorts and a matching bra, her nipples straining. I swear her seam is glistening. "I need to send Catherine a huge tip."

She smiles. "You like?" She twirls around, and damn, if she doesn't have the perfect ass.

"Come here," I demand.

Goose bumps ripple across her arms.

With a single flick, her bra comes unclasped and her tits spill out. I lavish each one with a thorough tongue lashing. Her hips grind against me, hoping for more.

I pull away. "Get on the bed and lie back."

She moves into place and looks at me, her eyes hooded with desire — desire for me, not the money in my bank account, not the doors I can open. Just me.

She licks her lips, and my cock weeps for her.

"Spread those legs wide," I demand.

She's so wet; I can see it through her panties. I fall to my knees and pray to her pussy, smothering it with my tongue through the lace.

Harper groans, and I have to tug on my cock to give it some release or I might spill before the fun even begins.

I slip her out of her panties and savor her in a long and languid lick. She tastes so good. I stop and look at her.

"Don't stop," she begs. "Make me come."

I put her knee over my shoulder and suck her clit into my mouth as my tongue flicks the hard nub. With two fingers, I stretch her wide and find her special spot. Her chest heaves and muscles tighten. She's getting close. If I was a cruel man, I'd stop. But I want to make her happy. So I lick, suck, and fuck her pussy with my fingers and mouth. I reach for her nipple and give it a squeeze. She moans my name and comes all over my face.

I lap it all up as her breath steadies. Then I lie next to her and see her blissful smile. "You're fucking beautiful."

She smiles at me. I think I fucked the words right out of her. We move up the bed and settle our heads on the pillows.

"Will you make love to me?" she asks after a moment.

I kiss her again and climb over, my weight balanced on my arms and my knees between her legs.

"Are you ready?"

"Yesssss."

I align myself and slowly enter her. As we kiss, our bodies meld into one. I rock in and out of her, peppering her with kisses. I fondle her breasts and massage her clit — all while moving in and out of her with deep and passionate thrusts.

I can see her body building toward another orgasm, and my balls tighten.

Her legs clench, and her nails dig deep into my back. The slight pain releases my seed deep inside her, and she follows right behind.

I've never made love to a woman before. I've had lots of sex, and most of it was good, but making love is something new. Tonight is perfect.

After, we lie together, wrapped in each other's arms.

I want to tell her about my growing feelings, but I'm still not sure this is the time. I don't want her to dismiss it as a euphoric proclamation. When I tell her how I feel, she has to know I mean it.

Soon enough, her breathing evens out, so this isn't the time anyway. My sleep comes in fits and starts, but when the alarm wakes me, I feel ready to meet with the FBI agent today.

I kiss Harper's shoulder, and she moans. My dick is awake and wants nothing more than to stay here and make love to her all day. But we have important things to do.

I take a quick shower and kiss her again, finding her still in bed. "Agent Snow from the FBI will be here any minute."

I hear a muffled "Good luck," from under the covers.

Or at least that's what I think she said.

Christophe is downstairs waiting for me and with an espresso in hand. "Are you ready?"

I take a sip of the glorious dark roast he hands me and savor the bitterness. "I think so." Just in case, I sit down and read through the entire file several more times before Duncan Snow arrives.

When the bell rings, I meet him at the front door. He looks fifteen years old, dressed in jeans and a T-shirt. He doesn't look like any FBI agent I've ever met, but thankfully, I've not met many.

We greet each other, and he extends his hand. "Nice to meet you."

"Thank you for coming."

"I've worked with Cameron for a while and trust his judgement."

I smile. "Me too, and this find really saved my bacon when it comes to the release of this game and my IPO next week."

I walk him into the kitchen. Harper is standing in front of the espresso maker, drinking her coffee.

"What can we get you?" I ask him.

"I'm good. I had a Monster drink on my way over – lots of sugar and caffeine."

I shake my head and smile. "I can't do those anymore."

He laughs. "I probably shouldn't, but I drink them by the case. My wife is trying to wean me off of them."

Jim suddenly appears in the doorway. It's almost as if he teleported in. The guy is all stealth, and Christophe didn't announce him. "Thanks for coming," I tell him. "Coffee? Espresso drink?"

"Espresso, please."

"With a twist or sugar?"

"Neither."

Sara breezes in just as Harper places a double espresso in front of Jim. She returns to the machine and makes Sara a cappuccino, which she gratefully accepts.

Sara and Jim know most of what I'm telling Agent Snow already, but they listen intently as we talk about Julia's development of the game and her involvement from the very beginning, as well as how upset I am.

"She's ready for the game to be a failure," I tell Agent Snow. "So our plan is to let her believe she's uploading the bug-filled version while we actually load Cameron's cleaned-up version. Then we'll see what she does when the launch goes off without an issue." I take a sip of my coffee. "Also, we think Zach Villefort, the person who funded her espionage, is working on something involving another business as well."

Agent Snow looks intrigued all over again.

I explain what happened with Quick Reels and Villefort and then what he did to Firefly. I conclude by telling him we're researching to discover what he's doing with Nick's company, PayFriend.

Agent Snow nods and seems lost in thought for a moment. "Back to Ms. Willis and the Spy Game espionage. It will take us a bit of time to make sure all the evidence is in order before we can make an arrest. But the only risk I can see with your plan is her going underground once she realizes you're on to her."

"If you can't put someone on her, I will," Jim says. "We won't lose her."

"That would be great," Agent Snow says.

We end up agreeing that it makes sense to wait for Julia to upload her version of the game and accept her final payment before the FBI arrests her anyway. Hopefully, the timing on their verification of the existing evidence will work out perfectly with that. And in the meantime, Clear Security will cover Julia's tracks and make it look like she's run off with Villefort's money without sabotaging Honeycomb. That last bit is kind of diabolical, and I love it.

We talk a while longer, and Agent Snow promises to confirm with us as soon as possible about whether the FBI is prepared to move forward with an arrest.

After everyone leaves, Harper gets her coat and gets ready to go in to the office. "How are you feeling about all of this?" she asks.

I let out a deep breath. "I think this betrayal has hit me as hard as what Villefort did to us with Quick Reels."

"I'm sorry."

I hold up a hand. "It's not your fault."

"I know, but I'm sorry you're feeling bad. You can't let these two shade your ability to trust people," she adds, looking at me intently. "Last night, everyone there supported you and was ready to back you up, whatever you need. There may always be someone you shouldn't trust, but take solace in the fact that there are so many you can."

I smile, knowing she's right. She's the best example of all. "You've been a real gift through all of this."

"And just think, you get to fund about a half-million dollars in college educations for it."

"That's a bargain." I reach for her. "I'm happy to do it. Thank you for your unyielding support. This means more to me than I can truly admit. I didn't see any of this coming when we made our deal."

She looks at me a bit strangely, and I force myself to stop talking. I still don't know quite how to tell her how I really feel.

CHAPTER 28

Harper

On Sunday evening, those of us who've gathered at the Sullivans' house in the Hamptons hold up our glasses to toast to the successful release of Spy Game on Friday and prepare for Honeycomb's IPO tomorrow. It's been a crazy weekend, and what a ride this is. I'm so happy for Jaxson and Honeycomb Games.

Spy Game is off to a resounding start with over a million downloads already, and the average player is spending over a hundred dollars a day at the moment. For comparison, Chocolate Crush was the most downloaded game in the app stores last year with 138 million users, and the average daily spend per person was right at fifteen dollars.

Spy Game's income will likely drop off, but nearly all the reviews have been favorable, leaving the game at a four-point-eight-star average on a five-point scale.

"To Honeycomb Games," Mason says with a slight slur.

He's had a few cocktails and has been happier than Jaxson all day. Jaxson is still reeling from Julia's deceit. I want to scratch her eyes out.

"I just got an update from Jim," Jaxson reports, looking at his phone. "Julia Willis left early on Friday, and they think she cleared out her desk."

I raise my brow. "Really? Can she exercise any of her options on Monday?"

Jaxson shakes his head. "Employees have to wait a week, and then they can only be sold at the lowest price they were offered. She has a thousand shares she could cash in, and with the success of Spy Game today, I'm not expecting the stock to dip below the initial offering."

Hazel puts her arm around me. "I attribute that to Harper's hard work. Isn't my sister the greatest?"

I blush and roll my eyes.

"I agree," Jaxson says. "She's the greatest. The best thing I ever did was hire her and then move her into my house."

"That's not very romantic," Hazel admonishes.

"Trust me," I tell her. "It's very romantic." I smile at Jaxson.

Megan whispers in Jaxson's ear and whisks him away to talk to a reporter.

"I really like him for you," Hazel says once they're gone.

"Good, because I like Paul for you."

"He wants to have children," she whispers.

I turn to look at her. "What do you want?"

"I don't know. I feel like I've raised seven kids already. I want to be footloose for a while."

"Then you should do that. Have you explained it to him that way?"

She gives me a noncommittal look. "Does Jaxson want kids?" she asks.

"We haven't talked about it," I tell her. "I'm on the fence." Across the room Jaxson is being grilled by the reporter, but he seems cool as a cucumber. *As you should be.* I silently send him good vibes.

I turn back to my sister. "How is Harmony doing on her own, and I don't want it sugar coated."

Hazel opens her mouth but doesn't say anything.

"I won't ask you to move back, and I won't ask that she move home," I clarify. "I just need to know."

Hazel nods. "She does better when she lives with someone. Her mental health suffers when she works at home and lives alone. There's no one for her to interact with."

"She loves dogs. What if we got her a dog, and she could take it out for walks or something?"

Hazel shakes her head. "She doesn't really love dogs. They're too unpredictable for her."

"Do you think she'd move to San Francisco?"

Hazel shrugs. "She'll be out there later this week. You can talk to her about it."

"Is that your way of saying she won't move?"

Hazel smiles. "I don't think she'll move, but I also think that's okay. I remember when this wise woman told me that raising my brothers and sisters was not my job and I needed my own life. That's good advice."

I smile because *I* said that to her. "She is a wise woman. But you never know what lies in store."

Jaxson catches my eye and gives me a panty-melting smile that makes my heart race. There's no clean way out of this for me. I tried to keep a wall around my heart, but I couldn't. Getting to know him and going through the intensity of prepping for Honeycomb's IPO has torn the walls right down. Once we go public and settle the terms of our deal, I'll have to find a way to repair my heart, probably by caring for my sister Harmony.

Hazel gets up to get herself some snacks and check in with Paul. After his interview, Jaxson walks back over and sits down with me. "Why are you looking so serious?"

I shrug. "Just thinking about my sister Harmony. Hazel says it's not the best for her to work from home and live alone. How did that interview go?"

He smiles. "It was fine, and I'm glad it's over. Listen, I'm sure there are some things we can do to help Harmony. After everything calms down, let's sit with her and your parents to figure out a plan."

I appreciate the thought, but autism has no cure. And Harmony is not warm and fuzzy. But she's my sister, and she's doing the best she can. "Thank you."

"Great. Now, let's go upstairs and I'll show you my appreciation for all the things you've done to get me here."

"Just paying for my siblings' education is all I ask."

He nods. "I've already set that up. Most of the lenders got their money last week, and I set up a trust for Hope and Holden."

I look at him, eyes wide. "But we haven't gone public yet."

"I know we're going to," he says with a laugh. "There was no reason to wait. You've been amazing through all of this." He takes my hand. "I've really loved spending time with you at work and at home."

I can see the breakup coming. I take a deep breath and try not to get emotional. He warned me not to fall in love with him, but I did. And now, that's my problem.

"Tomorrow we can figure out our life plan," he adds.

You mean the one where we navigate my disappearance from your orbit? The thought sours my stomach, but what is there to say? I manage a smile. "Sounds good."

"Are you ready?" I ask Jaxson as we arrive on the NASDQ trading floor with Mason and Caroline. Honeycomb has brought breakfast for everyone, and each of the floor traders will get a mason jar of a local honey. That was the planner's idea for a favor at the IPO party on Friday, and Megan thought it would be great to do here as well.

Jaxson smiles. "I've been ready for this for a long time."

He leans in, and his lips capture mine. As our tongues tangle and dance, I can't help but miss this already. I love the way he takes control and kisses just like he has sex — hard, fast, and with purpose.

He breaks away and walks off with Mason to press the flesh with the traders.

"You look sad," Caroline says, appearing next to me.

I shrug. "I can't believe how quickly today came. When I met Jaxson in March, I thought today couldn't come fast enough. But time has flown by."

"I know you had an unconventional start, but he absolutely adores you."

I can't let the hope of her comment come in, or I'll be crushed. "He's a great guy. I mean, women literally write songs about him."

Caroline laughs. "Who would've thought she'd turn out to be such a mess?"

I understand her better than I can let on. Jaxson's done a number on me as well. "She seems so kind and friendly, but I assure you she was not that way to me."

Caroline laughs. "Unbelievable, isn't it?"

Soon enough, Jaxson is ringing the bell, and the day goes by in a whirl as we watch the stock prices climb and split repeatedly. By the end of the day, the original shares have split five different times because the demand was so much higher than what was available to be sold. It's a good day for Honeycomb Games.

That evening, Hazel and Paul meet us for dinner at Eleven Madison Park. Caroline knows the owners, and they've set us up in a private room.

"You wouldn't believe how jealous my teammates were that I was on the floor with you this morning and invited to be here tonight," Paul gushes. "*And* flying back with you guys to San Francisco for the party. I can't thank you enough."

"We're glad to have you," Jaxson says.

We enjoy a delicious plant-based meal, though you'd hardly know it. I never realized I loved mushrooms so much.

After dinner, a whole parade of vehicles lines up to drive us to the airport, and everyone moves with polished precision to get us and all of our things loaded and settled onto the private plane.

When everyone is in their seats, Jaxson leans over from his spot next to me. "Too bad we've not made it into the mile-high club."

"You've had plenty of opportunity," I tease.

"Do you think anyone would notice if we went into the back room together for about an hour?"

"I do. Particularly because right now Mason is in there having a phone conversation with someone."

"Hmmm.... Good point. Besides, I'm not really into letting anyone see you as you climax."

"Before long, I'll be only a memory."

He laughs, but he doesn't correct me.

I pull the blanket up and my eye cover down and try not to cry. It's my own damn fault for falling for him. I have no one but myself to blame.

When we land, it's just after five thirty on Tuesday morning in San Francisco, and the sun has just broken the horizon. It's a beautiful day, or at least it seems so until I see the look on Cameron's face at the base of the stairs.

As we disembark, Jaxson steps aside to conference with Cameron, Gray, Nick, and Mason before meeting me at the car.

"It's about that thing," he says as he approaches. I know he's referring to Julia. "I'll try to be home early tonight, but you should spend the day with Hazel and Paul. The party planner has it all under control. Just enjoy your family and prepare for everyone to arrive."

He kisses my temple and gets into a waiting Suburban. I'm already feeling lost, but I paint a smile on my face and turn toward Hazel and Paul. "Let's get to the house. Helen will have breakfast for us, and I can give you a tour of the City."

Hazel claps her hands. "I can't wait."

As we drive into town, my sister puts her hand on my knee. "Don't stress about us being here. If you need to go to work today, I get it. We can find our way around."

"According to Jaxson, the party planner has everything under control, so there's no need."

"Great."

After breakfast and dropping our things at Jaxson's house, we spend the day walking around Golden Gate Park. We visit the aquarium and Japanese Gardens, and then Wyatt drives us down Lombard Street.

"I totally get why you live here," Hazel says with awe on her face.

We have dinner reservations for four at Sotto Mare, but Jaxson doesn't show, and he doesn't respond to my texts. I'm embarrassed but try not to worry or read into it. They just went public, and doing damage control for the aftermath of Julia probably has him hopping. But I can't deny that ever since the IPO, I've felt him pulling away.

We go to bed early, but between jet lag and sleeping on the plane last night, I can't sleep. I try reading, but I can't concentrate. After a while, I realize I've read the same paragraph a dozen times. I try to call Jaxson again, but the phone goes to voicemail.

"Hello, sweetheart," I say. "It's getting late, so I'm going to bed, but I was hoping to convince you to come home. I can help you fall asleep. This big bed is very empty without you."

He's always been great at letting me know what he was doing and when I'd be seeing him. How could it all change so quickly? He told me he'd fulfilled the requirements for our contract. I guess that's how. I sigh. He wants to talk after the IPO party, and it's clear he's ready to move on.

I want that to be as painless as possible. We've had fun together, and I've done a great thing for my family. I need to focus on that. But my heart is heavy and my eyes leak as I chastise myself for making Tessa Sky's new song my anthem too.

I wake the next morning, and Jaxson's side of the bed hasn't been slept in. It doesn't look like he came home last night. The writing is on the wall. I should be celebrating that we thought our arrangement might require years, and it ended up being less than six months. But nothing about this feels celebratory. After showering, I dress for another day of playing tour guide.

The kitchen is quiet, and I've just started an espresso when I see a note in Jaxson's handwriting.

Have fun showing your sister and Paul around. You earned this time off. I don't know when I'll be home tonight.
XOXO,
Jaxson

So he came home at least long enough to leave the note, but he never got in bed with me. And there's no apology for standing us up for dinner.

I shouldn't care. But I do.

It's after nine when Hazel comes downstairs. "My God, this view is incredible."

"It's easy to get used to, that's for sure."

Hazel sits across from me. "What's wrong?"

"I don't know." Tears fill my eyes, and I look away.

"You can tell me." She reaches for my hand, and I hold it like a lifeline.

"Only if you don't tell anyone — not even Paul."

She nods, and I take a deep breath and tell her about the agreement and why Jaxson and I are together. "In exchange, he's paying off everyone's student loans."

She shakes her head and doesn't say anything for a long time. "Wow," she finally manages. "You didn't have to do that. We would have been just fine."

"It would have been selfish to just take a bunch of money from him for myself. This way, I could help all of us."

"That's quite the gift." She looks into my eyes. "That may have been the agreement, but I can tell he's crazy about you."

"He's already told me he wants to talk about our next steps. I wanted a job with the graphic design team, but he keeps telling me it would be too messy. He wants to set me up with my own company instead."

"That sounds like a better deal," Hazel agrees. "You'd have clients and be able to do the work you love. Mom says you did the new Honeycomb logo and all the party invites."

I nod. "After the IPO party, we'll talk and I'll move me out, but I'm realizing that everything I do in San Francisco will be a reminder of him. I'm not sure I can stay here."

Hazel's eyes soften. "You can always come to New York or even go back to Boston."

I shut my eyes and wish for calm. I need the weekend to go well and be drama free. "Everyone arrives tomorrow," I remind myself as much as her. "I need to focus on that, and then I'll decide what to do."

Hazel puts her arms around me. "I know it doesn't seem like it, right now, but you're going to look back and love that you went on this adventure."

I hold her tight and let the tears fall.

"Sorry to interrupt," Paul says.

"You're not interrupting. I'm just getting all weepy," I say with a smile. I wipe my face and take a deep breath. "What do you guys want to do today? We can wander around Pier Thirty-Nine. It's a bit of a tourist trap, but you can get clam chowder in a sourdough bread bowl, and you can buy all the T-shirts and San Francisco crap you could ever want. Or we can head over to Union Square and check out the expensive stores and pretend to buy some things before having lunch in Chinatown. When we're ready to come back, we can take the cable car to this side of town. Your choice. Tell me what sounds good."

Hazel looks at Paul. "We were thinking about going for a walk around the Palace of Fine Arts and then maybe walking to the middle of the Golden Gate Bridge."

"Okay then." I slap my knees.

"We can manage that, though. Why don't you enjoy your day?" Hazel puts her arm over my shoulders. "Once everyone arrives tomorrow, it's going to get pretty hairy around here."

"Oh!" I realize they want to be alone. "Of course. That's a good suggestion. Have a great time."

They have a quick breakfast and then head out, leaving me by myself. Today is Helen's day off, and we're going to Fog City for dinner tonight, so I'm at a loss as to what to do to keep myself busy.

I open my laptop and look for graphic-design jobs in Boston. A few catch my eye, so I apply and send over a digital copy of my portfolio. I'm not confident that anyone will want to interview me, but if they do, it will be fate telling me it's time to move home.

Then I spend an hour on the phone catching up with Amy about what's been happening with her, which includes yet another failed date. "I promise I'll introduce you around at the IPO party."

"I can't wait," she says.

After that, she has to go be productive at work. It's not even ten, and I have nothing to do. Under normal circumstances, I'd be loving this and would curl up with a good book or go for a walk and do a few sketches. But none of that sounds appealing, so I peek my head into Christophe's office. "I think I'm going to go into the office for a while today."

"Sure. When you're ready, I'll drive you over."

I look down at my jeans and sweater. It's more casual than usual for me, but it's the uniform for San Francisco. "Let me get my bag, and I'll be set."

Christophe stands, and by the time I have my bag, he's ready to walk me out to the garage. "We've organized four Suburbans to pick up your family tomorrow," he tells me. "We'll keep in touch with the pilots so we know when they'll be touching down."

"That's great. When are Jaxson's parents and his sister's family arriving?"

He gets into the driver's seat and looks back at me in the rearview mirror. "Their flight will come in around dinnertime. If your family's flight comes in that late, we have a plan."

"Thank you. The house is going to be full."

He nods. "Helen's excited. She has some help coming to make it easier."

"I'm happy to help too," I remind him.

He shoots me a look. "You're not the help."

His eyes return to the road, so he doesn't see my face crumble. "Christophe, you know as well as I do that I'm the help. We're all paid to be here to support Mr. Bancroft."

"You're selling yourself short," he says as he pulls up in front of Honeycomb's building.

I open the door and give him a sad smile. "We have dinner reservations at seven."

"Wyatt will be here to pick you and Mr. Bancroft up at six forty-five, and I'll drive your sister and Paul over to meet you there."

"Thank you." I open the car door and dodge a bike messenger on the sidewalk before I enter the building.

"Hello, Ms. Lockwood. I saw you on television earlier this week." Seymour, the security guard for the building, smiles broadly as I badge my way in.

"I hope it was before the humidity attacked my hair." I make a face to let him know I'm joking.

"You looked beautiful at Mr. Bancroft's side. He's one lucky man."

"You're very kind. Thank you." I know he means it as a compliment, but this whole exchange just makes me feel tired.

I get into the elevator with Megan Bates and several Honeycomb employees. Everyone praises me for all the work I did to take the company public. When just Megan and I are left, heading to the top floor, she rattles off all the things she has to get done for the party.

"Please let me know how I can help," I tell her. I'm not sure if that's what she's getting at.

But she waves me away. "You've done all the heavy lifting. Now, it's up to us to put a shine on it. You can relax."

Why does everyone want me to relax?

Jaxson's door is shut when I arrive, so I boot up my desktop computer and start going through my email. When lunchtime comes, I look at Jaxson's calendar, and it's straight meetings, so I order his favorite pastrami sandwich and when it arrives, I knock on his door and walk it in.

He's on the phone. "What are you doing here?" he mouths.

"Working. Hazel and Paul wanted to explore alone today."

He gives me a thumbs up, and based on his side of the conversation, I can tell he's talking to Cameron Newhouse.

I eat my turkey club at my desk and continue to sort through all the mail that came in while I was out.

By late afternoon, I've gone through my email and my desk inbox, and I finally feel like I can breathe again.

Jaxson's hardly come up for air, and his phone line has been busy all day. I send him a Slack.

Me: I'm finally caught up. What do you need help with?

Jaxson: You don't need to be here today. Human Resources has a temp for your desk for the rest of the week. Go have fun with your family.

Me: OK. See you at Fog City at 7.

Jaxson: Shoot. I can't make it. Apologize to Hazel and Paul for me.

Me: You missed us at dinner last night too. Is everything OK?

Jaxson: Yep. Just trying to make up for being out of the office for a few days.

I turn off my computer and tell Christophe I'm ready to go home and can take a rideshare. He shakes his head and tells me Wyatt is at the curb waiting for something to do.

On the drive home, I think about what I'm going to do with all our family here on Thursday. They won't want to spend too much money, so a walk down Union Square, Chinatown, and the Ferry Building are right up their alley. We can eat at the food trucks, and the fish markets are always fantastic. Then I decide to buy tickets for everyone to go out to Alcatraz. I haven't done that tour yet, and I bet it's interesting.

I have a great time at dinner with Hazel and Paul. They show me some fun pictures they took as they crossed over the Golden Gate Bridge, including one of them snuggled together and surrounded by the fog.

When we get home after dinner, I find Jaxson in bed, completely zonked out. I could bring a marching band in here, and he'd sleep right through it. I crawl in behind him and he rolls over to spoon with me.

I breathe him in and commit his scent to my forever memory. I love the way he fits perfectly with me and the way he wraps his arms around me. It makes me feel safe and cared for.

When I wake up, I'm alone. I check my email as I make coffee in the kitchen, and AdVenture Works, an ad agency in Cambridge, has responded to my application. They would like to meet next week for an in-person interview. I stare at the request for a few minutes. It would be an easy ride into town on the T from Harmony's apartment. I decide to tell them I'll be there next Wednesday for the interview.

Hazel and Paul are up and out the door for another morning of exploring together, and Christophe reports that it looks like everyone made the flight with no issues. They should be here about one. Helen is going to put out a taco bar for anyone who's hungry. As she prepares the dishes for her buffet, I become more and more hungry, but I distract myself by doing research on AdVenture Works so I can prep for my interview.

It's chaos the second my family walks through the door. "Sweetheart, you're here!" Mom says as she brings me into a hug.

"Welcome to San Francisco." I open my arms to the view of the Golden Gate Bridge, Alcatraz, and the North Bay.

"This is truly beautiful," Mom says.

Helen places a large bowl of guacamole on the island.

I introduce her to my family and give them the lay of the land on food. "There's a taco bar for anyone who's hungry now. Dinner will be about seven, and we're grilling steaks."

My mom's mouth opens. Growing up, we only had steak for special occasions, and it wasn't anything like what we'll have tonight. Helen picked up a beef tenderloin from the butcher and had them cut it into filets. I saw them this morning, wrapped in thick slices of bacon. We'll have baked potatoes and all sorts of other sides.

"I can't believe you live here!" Hudson says as he looks around.

"I'm very lucky," I agree. "So, what do you want to do?" I tell them my ideas, and Pier 39 is the agreed-upon winner for this afternoon and Alcatraz with both families tomorrow.

We spend a few hours walking up and down the pier and then walking to the Ferry Building.

The sun is shining, but the wind along the waterfront is brisk. I look up at the Bay Bridge as we approach, and my heart is heavy. I hate that I'll be leaving soon.

Dad wraps his arm over my shoulder. "I can see why you love it here. It suits you."

I agree, but I'm surprised he thinks so. "What makes you say that?"

"You're blossoming here and becoming the woman I knew you were always meant to be."

I blush right down to my toes. "Thanks, Dad."

My cell pings.

Wyatt: I have the Bancroft clan, and we'll be at the house momentarily.

That was really sent more for Jaxson than for me, but I want to be at the house before they get there.

"Jaxson's family has landed, and they're making their way to the house. I should be there when they arrive."

"We can go with you," Mom announces.

I can see the disappointment on my siblings' faces.

"Anyone who wants to come back certainly can, but if you want to stay and continue wandering, feel free. You can take a rideshare back to the house. It'll cost about twelve dollars from the Ferry Building."

Hazel and Hudson look at each other and conference with their partners before agreeing to stay, and the rest of us return to the house. We arrive just as Wyatt is pulling into the garage.

"Harper!" Ava says, her arms wide. "We're here!"

"I'm so happy to see you."

I hug everyone, and Ava introduces me to her sons and husband. I introduce my parents and the brothers and sisters who are here. "There are a few more, but they're wandering around the waterfront."

"Isn't it just beautiful here?" Jess, Jaxson's mom, says to my mom.

Helen directs Wyatt and Christophe to where they should take the luggage.

"I think this will be the first time my house has been so full," Jaxson says, as he enters behind them and kisses my cheek.

The evening is crazy with so many people. After dinner, some of my brothers and sisters go out to have fun, and the rest of us get out the board games.

I pick up the Scrabble game to tease Jaxson, but he doesn't notice. He's distracted.

"Is everything okay?" I ask.

"No stockholder issues yet." He smiles, but it doesn't reach his eyes.

In all the craziness, I go in search of Harmony and find her alone in the library. "There you are," I say with a wide smile. "Are you hiding?"

"Not really. I like books."

I slump into an overstuffed chair and put my feet on the matching ottoman. "This is my favorite room in this house."

"Mine too. I've looked at many books, and someone has read them, so it's an actual library."

I sit down by her, and as usual, Harmony doesn't make eye contact with me.

"So how are you enjoying living alone?"

She leafs through a big book on bridges. "It's lonely."

"Do you think you could move here to San Francisco?"

She shrugs. "Not sure. My work is very important."

"But couldn't you do it from here?"

Harmony glances my direction and taps her chin. "Not sure."

"What if I were to move back to Boston and live with you in Quincy?"

Her head turns toward me, but she still doesn't meet my eyes. "But what about Jaxson Bancroft, billionaire, entrepreneur, and handsome man?"

I love that she has so many descriptors for Jaxson. I shrug. "I'm getting close to being done with helping him. Now, I need to find something else to do. I was thinking about working in Boston. Maybe I could live with you — in Hazel's old room."

"I'd like that, but what about Jaxson Bancroft, billionaire, entrepreneur, and handsome man?"

"He has his company here. He'd probably stay here."

"He loves you, and you love him." Her head tilts, and her brow furrows.

I look around the library. He doesn't love me, but I can't explain that to her or even myself.

"You pay half of the rent," she says after a moment. "You can live in Hazel's room."

Hazel joins us in the library and looks between me and Harmony. "Sounds like you're ready to move home."

I sigh. "I'm thinking about it."

CHAPTER 29

Jaxson

The Honeycomb offices were closed today, and we celebrated with all our employees. For this evening's events, we've bussed the staff over to Oracle Park, and we're now a total of just under five thousand people on the field for our official IPO party. The liquor is flowing freely, and though the night is still young, many people are tipsy and excited. Our initial public offering created more than two hundred millionaires within the company overnight. Their wealth is tied up in their stock options, which they can't sell outright because of Securities and Exchange Commission rules, but a lot of people are probably buying condos, homes, vacations, and fancy cars with those options as their guarantee.

I'm working my way through the crowd when I spot Harper's mother. "Hello! Welcome," I greet her. "Do you know where Harper is?"

She looks around, but she appears to be alone. I don't even see any of Harper's brothers and sisters. "She's around here somewhere. I just saw her."

I nod and tell her to have a great time as I move on. This is not a night when I'm going to have meaningful conversations with anyone. Still, it's an amazing event. Harper did such a fantastic job. Even David was impressed with the way she adapted his old logo into the new logo for the occasion.

I need to make sure to tell her that. Since we've been back from New York, things have been crazy with our plans for Villefort. Cameron and his team at SHN are pouring through millions of lines of code for the program that runs Nick's company, PayFriend, to see if they can find anything out of place. And Jim Adelson is going through the employee background checks, with particular focus on financial records. We all know there's something there. We just need to find it.

I've missed having Harper at her desk, but she deserves this time to be with her family. And anyway, she shouldn't have to be at the office twelve or fourteen hours a day, like I have been lately. But once her family's gone and this party is behind us, we're going to have a serious conversation about the future for the two of us. I've decided I can't settle for anything less than us working on a genuine relationship. But for now, I'm biding my time.

When it's time for me to speak to the crowd, I bring my board, the management team, and Harper up to the stage and thank each of them. I give my board members each an exclusive bottle of scotch that I imported from Scotland. For my management team, the men get Honeycomb-logo cufflinks covered in pave diamonds, and the women get a similar pair of earrings. I spend the longest time thanking Harper, and I choose my words very carefully, wishing once again that she knew everything I'm saying is true, even without the contract.

"Many of you know that Harper and I are engaged to be married. Without her, today would not be possible. She was behind me, picking up all the pieces I was dropping. She's made sure we had something to celebrate *and* she set us up in this place for this wonderful party tonight. While so many of you here played a part in the success of our IPO, without Harper, we wouldn't be here at all."

I hand her a jewelry box, and inside is her own solid-gold bee, along with a disk engraved with the date we met on a chain she can wear as a necklace. I wrap my arm around her shoulder and kiss her temple.

The crowd goes crazy, and Harper turns a glorious shade of crimson.

"Staff members, please pick up a gift bag before you leave," I announce to the crowd. "And thank you for being the best team I could ever ask for."

The crowd goes crazy again, and I'm confident they'll be even more nuts when they pick up their party favors. Each gift bag has a beautiful jar of honey and a bunch of cool swag, including a one-of-a-kind Apple Watch with our logo on the band.

As I step down from the stage, I'm besieged by people wanting to express their appreciation, and I lose track of Harper in the crowd.

An hour or so later, I finally spot her, surrounded by Amy, Sara, Caroline, and Scarlett. She looks happy. I break away from the crowd surrounding me and approach her from behind.

I wrap my arms around her waist and kiss her neck. "Here's my beautiful fiancée."

She turns and smiles, but it doesn't reach her eyes. The other women excuse themselves.

"Everything okay?" I ask.

She nods. "I think so. No one's come to me with any problems."

"That's not what I meant, but I'm glad to hear it. I asked the party planner to limit the interruptions since our families are in town."

"Ahh." She nods and then gives me a little squeeze. "How are you? You're the man of the hour. I've seen so little of you this week."

"I know. It's everything all at once, isn't it? I've been burning the midnight oil at the office because the FBI arrested Julia Willis trying to flee to Mexico."

Her eyes light up. "Anything from Villefort?"

I shake my head. "They arrested her as she made her way down the jetway, so if someone was watching, they likely still think she boarded the plane and left. The FBI has offered her immunity for testifying against Villefort, but she won't do it."

Harper gasps. "What? She'd go to jail for that asshole?"

I lean in close. "You know I love it when you turn all angry."

The smile that doesn't reach her eyes returns. "I'm really sorry she won't testify against Villefort. Did she tell them why she did it?"

"All she's said is that Spy Game was her idea, and Honeycomb sold her out."

Harper's brow furrows. "Most often, if I'm doing work for a client or my employer, they own what I create when it's all said and done. I'm creating it for them. Isn't it the same for employees of a game developer?"

"It is." I wrap my arms around her and kiss her forehead.

"Then why is she mad?"

I throw my hands in the air. "We don't understand it. She was trying to sabotage her own work, and if she'd been successful, it would likely have affected the value of her stock options. She'd received three-quarters of a million dollars from Villefort and was due a final payment. But she sacrificed her options, which would have paid her four times that at least."

Harper makes a face. "She's not very bright."

"I can't imagine what Villefort was putting in her head."

"What about Nick's company? Any word on possible sabotage?"

"As of this morning, no. They haven't found anything amiss. But listen, none of that is important right now. We should be celebrating with our families. Oh, and your mom has been putting pressure on me to set a date for the wedding. We'll have to tell her something soon," I tease.

Harper nods, her face serious. "I'll figure it out. Don't worry."

I wish I could lighten her mood. "I don't worry about a thing, thanks to you. I'll never be able to repay you."

"My siblings all know you've paid off their school loans now. Their plan is to thank you in person."

I nod. "I've talked to most of them this evening. I told them it was something you wanted to do."

"You didn't have to share the credit with me. It was the compensation for our agreement."

I shake my head. "I don't mind. Your family is my family. And my sister wants to cart you off to some design expo. I told her no more white rooms."

Harper continues as if she hasn't heard me. "It isn't about what I want. Only what you want."

I look at her a moment, trying to figure out what's going on. "Well, then it's a good thing I want you."

She wraps her arms around me and holds me tight, as if she's on a sinking boat. "We don't have to keep lying," she whispers.

"Is everything okay?" I ask. My heart sinks as I realize she doesn't believe any of what I've said about her tonight is real. And I guess this isn't the time to delve into it since there are five thousand of our closest friends around.

She brightens a bit. "Everything is great. Look around. This turned out to be a great party."

"As long as you're here, I'm happy as can be."

She smiles but looks away. "Did you catch that Amy and Grantham from your board are talking?"

"No. I haven't seen them. What's going on there?"

"They have plans this weekend."

"I think that's great." He's about ten years older than her, but I won't give him too hard a time about their age difference. Unless he comes up with some other ridiculous demands for my personal life.

Megan, our PR agent, walks up with a giant grin. "Jaxson, I'd like to introduce you to Christian Schultz from *The New York Times*. He'd like to talk to you about Honeycomb."

This is a perfectly reasonable request, and a great opportunity, but I feel a little panicky. I'd really rather just keep talking with Harper. I feel her slipping away, but I'm trapped in quicksand... *You're not going to solve this problem tonight*, I remind myself.

"It's great to meet you," I say, turning to Christian Schultz with my practiced smile.

"Harper, can you introduce me to your parents?" Megan asks as she begins to guide her away.

But I don't want to let go of her hand.

Harper pries her fingers from mine, looking at me strangely. "Of course."

They step away, and I turn to face the reporter, who asks me mostly the same questions everyone else has.

"I understand you had some pretty serious bugs in Spy Game and were sweating the release," he says after we've been over the basics of our IPO.

I shrug and try my best to be nonchalant. "There are always bugs in software, and trust me, everyone sweats the release. You can have your game in front of hundreds of people who love it, but if the wrong person doesn't, it can be a flop. But we are thrilled with the way things turned out."

"We understand that your lead developer on the project, Julia Willis, ran off to Mexico, leaving the game a mess."

I school my face. *How does he know any of that?* It's not common knowledge. "Julia's in Mexico?" I look out at the party, trying to collect myself and come up with an appropriate answer. "She gave notice a few months ago. Her plan was always to leave after we launched the game, but I thought she was going to a competitor. If she's sitting on a beach sipping margaritas, good for her. She deserves the break. She worked very hard for Honeycomb."

His brow furrows. Seems that wasn't the answer he was hoping for.

Now, I feel antsy. I need to talk to Agent Snow and SHN and let everyone know that someone — probably Villefort — is leaking information.

After I finish with Christian Schultz, I look around for someone I can speak to about this, but I can't walk two feet without someone stopping me. I chat with several party guests before I finally see Nick.

I grab his arm as he passes. "While being interviewed for *The New York Times*, I learned something big. Can you grab the team to meet as soon as we can?"

He nods and disappears into the crowd, which is finally getting a little smaller. It's almost two o'clock in the morning, and I realize Harper and the families probably left a while ago. They've got a big weekend of sightseeing planned before they all fly out Monday morning.

I say goodnight to several different groups and receive three impromptu hugs from people who are thrilled with the contents of their gift bags — I'll have to tell Harper — and finally Nick reappears, with Gray and Mason in tow. We decide to meet at Nick's loft, which is in the financial district, since he lives alone. Olivia left the party earlier, so he doesn't have to worry about her.

Forty minutes later, I've left the last of the evening in the hands of the party planner, and the gang has gathered in Nick's living room. I drink ice water as I tell Mason, Nick, Gray, and Cameron about what Christian Schultz asked me during our interview.

"Who do you think is his source?" Gray wonders.

"Villefort." I quip. "He wants us to know that he knows Julia's gone to Mexico."

"That's a big accusation," Mason says.

"Who else could it be?" I roll my eyes. How come I'm the only one who can see this?

"Could someone from your team have told the reporter?" Cameron muses.

"When Julia cleared out her desk, we already knew she'd likely be arrested. But the team seemed truly shocked when they learned she'd quit, and I don't think they're that good of actors. They don't know she's the one behind all the bugs, and they couldn't understand why she'd walk away from her stock options."

"I think you need to call Agent Snow once the sun comes up," Gray suggests.

I nod. This is shitty timing with all the family here. If this turns into something, I'll have once again stuck them all with Harper. I'm going to owe her big time. I already do.

"Harper and the families are heading out to see all the sights around town this weekend, and they all leave on Monday. I have to get a few things done and ready so I can take Harper to Fiji. I've reserved a private beachfront villa at Emaho Skeawa. Nick sold me on the idea."

"Does this mean what I think it does?" Mason asks.

"That I want to be with her for real? Without a contract? Yes. Without a doubt."

"Pay up," Nick says to Gray.

"Why? I agreed," Gray says with scorn.

"But I said he'd figure it out this week."

"I'd say he figured it out weeks ago but is only facing it now."

"Well, you still owe me."

Grayson stands, pulls out a handful of change, and selects four quarters. "Here. Now, you have the bragging rights and everything."

Nick happily takes his four coins and grins. "We think it's great. Olivia will be thrilled when I tell her."

"Where did she go tonight?"

Nick sits back in his seat. "She's leaving early tomorrow to go wedding planning with her sister up in Napa this weekend."

"Did you get engaged?" I ask.

Nick looks a bit sheepish. "Not exactly. I haven't asked her, but she's doing some preplanning so that when I do, she'll have the groundwork in place. I guess you'd say we're engaged to be engaged."

"We have a bet about you and Olivia," Gray tells Nick.

My brows shoot to my hairline. I'm not sure telling him about that is a great idea.

Nick shrugs. "I know our relationship is unconventional and you think she's marrying me for the money, but I already told her she has to sign a prenup."

"Has she signed it yet?"

He shakes his head. "I need to give it to her. She wants a monogamy clause."

"What's that?" Mason asks.

"If I cheat, it nullifies the agreement."

"Have you cheated on her before?" I ask. I think I would know if he had. He's always been loyal to Olivia. But none of us can stand her.

"No," Nick replies. "But her sister just found out her husband had a side piece, so Olivia wants to protect herself."

"Make it a two-way street then," Mason warns.

Nick's look of triumph is gone. "We're likely getting married next spring. I just want it all to go smoothly."

"We want that for you too," Gray says.

The sun is rising, and it's after five. Nick looks at his watch. "Should we call Duncan?"

I reach for my phone. "We might as well. Who needs sleep on a Saturday morning anyway?"

We speak with Agent Snow, and he immediately agrees to meet us at FBI headquarters. He's going to interview Julia again, and I want to hear how it goes right away, so I text Harper and include my mom.

Me: Something big happened with Villefort last night. I'm going to be stuck at the FBI offices today. I'm so sorry, but have fun seeing all the sights. I'll meet you for dinner.

At half past eight o'clock, Duncan finds Gray, Nick, and me waiting in a conference room at FBI headquarters. He's talked to Julia for over an hour and a half.

I look up from my phone as he enters. "What did she say?"

He shakes his head. "She promises she said nothing to anyone at Honeycomb about what was going on. She was too terrified they'd figure it out and tell you. She seems to have a lot of anger toward you, by the way. She's not your biggest fan. But anyway, she believes someone in-house figured out the sabotage anyway, and that's why the bugs didn't make the final version of the game. In a way, she's right, but she doesn't seem to realize Cameron and his team intervened."

"Well, that's good," Gray says.

I sit back, but there's a nagging voice in my head. "I have to believe Villefort used *The New York Times* reporter to find out what I know."

"Do you think he'd be that stupid?" Nick asks.

"Zack Villefort is a lot of things, but dumb is not one of them. He gave Julia a lot of money, and what he was hoping for didn't materialize. The reporter's question was his way of letting us know he's behind this," I reply.

"He's on the ropes. Why would he tell us? He's already losing," Mason questions.

"He doesn't know we're aware of his pending bankruptcy," Nick says. "So this is his last stand. He may never spend a day in jail for what he's done, but his identity is all wrapped up in his net worth and his influence. He ruined his own net worth, but we'll get our revenge when we take all his influence away."

We hash things out for a while longer, and Agent Snow promises to continue working on this. He says he has some additional questions for Julia after our conversation.

When I look at the clock again, it's nearly ten. I need to go home so I can spend some time with our families and get some sleep before I surprise Harper with our trip.

"If Villefort was behind that question in your interview, then you telling the reporter Julia Willis had given notice really fucks with him," Gray says with a smirk.

I nod. "He'll be chewing on that for a while. But I don't think the article will be published until Tuesday when they do their technology roundup."

We thank Agent Snow for his help.

"Are you heading home?" Gray asks as we all walk out of the FBI building.

"I'm going to stop by the office while it's quiet and get a few things done first," I tell him. "I should go home — I haven't seen the families much at all — but I worry I'll just sleep. I really want to clear my desk before we leave."

"Have a great time in Fiji."

I give him a mock salute. "I can't wait to get to that part. My plan is to sleep, make love to my girl, sleep, and repeat, with a bit of nourishment in there."

Nick pats me on the back. "After this week, you deserve the time off. You've really knocked it out of the park."

On my way back to the office, I call Harper to check in.

"What are you guys doing?" I ask when she answers. There's a lot of noise around her, and it's hard to hear.

"We're in Union Square. Everyone has shuttled off in different directions. Some are getting food, others are shopping. I think my brothers are in the Apple Store drooling over the latest devices."

"I wish I could be there. I have a lot to tell you about what's going on."

I hear people talking around her.

"I'm sorry. What did you say?" she asks.

It's too hard to bring her up to speed right now. "I just said I'm done with the FBI, but I have a few things to get done at the office. I'll meet you for dinner."

"Okay. I know your family would love to see you."

"I'll be there." We disconnect, and I go upstairs to my office. Everything is so quiet. I open a package I find outside my door, and it's the leather sketchbook I ordered for Harper, along with the colored pencils she liked at the fancy art store in Boston but wouldn't buy. I want to give her something special. She's been so amazing, and with these, while we're in Fiji, she can draw all the flowers and whatever else suits her fancy. I can't wait to see what she creates.

I get a few hours of work done, and I consider leaving now, but with everyone on the move, it seems too tricky to try to catch up with the families while they're out and about. So I decide to take a power nap on the couch here before meeting them for dinner.

Only when I wake with a start, it's dark outside. I sit up and find my phone, and it's after eleven. My head falls back. *Shit.* I missed dinner. I missed everything.

I see eight missed calls and realize my phone has been on mute since I was at the FBI offices. There are four calls from Harper and a call from my mom and my sister. I call Harper, and it goes to voicemail. She must already be in bed. I scramble and send everyone a text, just to make sure they know I didn't get kidnapped or anything.

Me: I'm sorry about tonight. I laid on the couch to take a power nap and that was the end of it. I just woke up. I'll make it up to you all. I'll be home for breakfast.

I'm now ready to push through and get a few more things off my plate. I work until the sun comes up and then head home.

When I arrive, it's not even seven but the house is crazy.

"There's my long-lost son!" Mom comes over and hugs me. "I saw your text, and I can't even imagine the hours you've been keeping. Your dad and I are so proud of you. But we'd have been proud of you if you worked a line at General Motors."

I shake my head. "I would never have worked in the place that crippled my father."

She smiles and hugs me again. "Everything works out for a reason."

In the kitchen, Harper is flipping pancakes on a griddle while Hazel fries sausage links, and Hope is scrambling a gigantic bowl of eggs.

"Wow, you ladies have it down to a science."

"Many years of practice," Harper says with a smile.

I kiss her temple. "Sorry about yesterday."

"Did you work through the night?"

"I did. I want to get away for a bit after all this is over."

She nods. "You've worked so hard; you deserve it."

"What's the plan for today?" I take a sip of juice someone handed me and look around at everyone.

"We're going over to Alcatraz," Harper says, a crease in her brow. "I didn't get you a ticket. I'm so sorry. But you can go in my place so you can spend some time with everyone."

I shake my head. "I don't think I should be that far out of pocket with how crazy things are. You go have fun."

My dad pats me on the back. "You can have my ticket."

"No," I insist. "I can take Harper and go another time. Please. You don't get out here very often, so enjoy the tour. Just don't let them keep any of you."

"Not a chance," Harper's brother Harrison says.

After breakfast, they all head out, and I lie down again. I've just drifted off when my phone rings. It's Agent Snow, and he has something to discuss with Gray, Nick, and me. He wants us all together.

I listen for a minute. "Okay, I'm on my way." I leave a note for Harper and my family, telling them I'm headed back to the FBI offices. *Maybe they've broken Julia and are preparing to arrest Villefort.*

When I arrive, Gray and Nick are already there, along with Cameron and Mason and a woman I don't know.

"What's going on? Did Julia agree to testify against Villefort?" I ask.

Cameron shakes his head. "We found what he's done with PayFriend."

I look over at Nick, who is clearly shellshocked. "What happened? What did he do?"

Agent Snow appears and shows us to a conference room. Once we're all seated, Cameron and one of his developers, Tammy Summers, explain what they've found.

My jaw drops.

"Whoever is doing this is skimming a few cents off of business transactions. So far we've looked at the last seven months, and the losses are at twenty million dollars. That could grow," Cameron says.

I cringe for Nick. This is a big-deal fraud, and he is potentially liable. This could cost him his company and possibly his freedom if someone tries to pin it on him.

"How could they do that?" Nick asks, panic in his voice. "I need more information."

"They set it up so the person initiating the transaction is being charged between two and eight cents in additional fees. It's never the same amount, which made it difficult to identify. The deposit account was at Technology Startup Fund, but it was moved to AmericanBank before the Fund shut down."

"That's where my accounts are," Nick groans.

"Does that mean we finally have the evidence to trace this to Villefort?" Gray asks.

Cameron shakes his head. "The account isn't in Villefort's name. It's owned by a shell corporation that we've traced to fifteen other companies. We're still digging."

"But you can't trace it back to Nick either," I note.

"Yes, but that doesn't clear him," Agent Snow counters.

"What does this mean for me and my company?" Nick looks away from us and out the window. His chest rises and falls, and I can see anxiety wrap around him like a blanket.

Cameron clears his throat. "We're going to claw back some of the money they've taken, but it won't be all of it. Tammy is going to start figuring out who is owed what, and we recommend you pay the money back."

Nick nods, his knuckles white. "Of course. I wouldn't want it any other way."

"And we're going to continue to trace the fraudulent fees," Cameron assures us.

Agent Snow crosses his arms across his chest. "We'll look from our side too, and hopefully, we can find Villefort's connection quickly."

"So what you're saying is that unless you find Villefort holding the smoking gun, there's nothing we can do," Gray scoffs, throwing his hands up.

My stomach drops. *How does this asshole continue to get away with everything?*

Agent Snow looks back over the information. "As of right now, we can't arrest him, and if we make any other moves, we risk him knowing we're on to him. But we'll work with Clear Security to get this figured out so we can take some sort of action."

After the meeting, the three of us return to Nick's place, feeling angry and powerless. Villefort is making us miserable all over again.

And I realize I've missed dinner.

Me: I'm an idiot, and time got away from me again. I'm sorry about missing dinner. I promise I will make it up to all of you on your next visit.

Harper: We missed you but know you've got a lot going on.

After a little while, Gray leaves to go home, but I stay with Nick. He's really upset.

"Nick, this is on Villefort, not on you," I assure him. "We're going to be able to prove that."

"Why does he keep targeting us? He took Quick Reels from us. Wasn't that enough?"

"I've thought a lot about that." I take a deep breath. I've never shared my theory, but this might be the time. I think back to the beginning of our relationship. "When we came out to the Bay Area with our idea, we were the three Musketeers — you, me, and Gray. It was us against the world. Then we got in bed with Villefort, and one night, I remember him telling me how he made his fortune. He had two business partners. They came in with the money, and he was the workhorse."

"Where was I when he was telling you this?" Nick asks.

I shrug. "Probably off with some chick getting laid."

Nick walks over to his beer fridge and pulls out two longnecks of his personal brew. He hands me one as he sits back down.

"After their first colossal success," I continue, "he said he squeezed them out, pitted them against each other, and they took each other down."

Nick looks at me. "Where are they now?"

"I've always wondered, but I don't know their names." I take a pull on my beer. "I think since the beginning he's been trying to turn us against each other. And he hasn't given up. Maybe he thinks if one of us isn't as successful as the others, that will be a wedge."

Nick seems to consider that a moment before nodding.

"But right now, he doesn't know what we know about Julia Willis being in FBI custody," I point out. "He's most likely preparing to leak details of the PayFriend transaction thefts to those who've been ripped off in an attempt to sink your IPO. Remember, he doesn't know we have an interest in each other's companies. He also doesn't know that we have a controlling interest in over a dozen of his companies. We're going to get through this, and after your IPO, we're going to tell the world what a fraud he is."

Nick finally looks a little better. I can see the usual spark in his eyes. "Amen, brother." He holds his beer bottle up.

I clink my bottle against his. "Amen."

CHAPTER 30

Jaxson

I wake and the house is dark, so I roll back over, prepared for more sleep. I can't remember ever being this tired. Then I realize Harper isn't next to me. I should go find her. I'll do that in just a minute.

Sometime later, I wake again. It's lighter now. My stomach growls, and I smell coffee. That brings a smile to my face. When I open my eyes, there's a cup next to me on the nightstand. I pull my pants on, tuck my phone in my pocket, and go downstairs. Helen is in the kitchen making something, but I'm not sure what.

"Did I miss saying goodbye to everyone?"

She looks up at me. "They left on Monday. It's Wednesday."

"What?" I pull out my cell phone, and she's right. It's late Wednesday morning. *What has happened to me?* "Where's Harper?"

Helen looks at me, confused. "Didn't you see the note next to the bed?"

I shake my head as I take a deep pull of hot coffee and think about all the things I want for breakfast. I'm starving. "Did she go in to the office? I'm surprising her with a trip to Fiji. We were supposed to leave yesterday, actually..." *Good thing we're not flying commercial.* "I'm sorry I didn't tell you. I just pulled it together last minute. I figured after everything she's done, she deserves a break, and I want us to have some time to figure out what's next."

Helen studies me. "You need to go upstairs and read her note."

"Okay, but I need to eat something. It seems I slept for more than two days straight. How did I manage to do that? I'm starving."

Helen nods. "What can I make for you?"

"How about a three-egg omelet with cheese, bacon, mushrooms, and peppers?" In the meantime, I pull out the peanut butter and smear a big dollop on a slice of bread.

"Would you like some potatoes with that?" Helen asks.

"Sure." I take a big bite of the peanut butter sandwich, and I'm sure I've never had anything better. "I didn't even say goodbye to our families. I must be a real schmuck in their eyes."

I'm still standing around waiting for breakfast when Christophe walks in. "When are we leaving for Boston?" he asks with a strange smile.

"Boston? No, we're going to Fiji. I have no desire to go to Boston."

Christophe's face morphs into surprise, but then he nods, all business. "Of course. When would you like to leave for Fiji?"

"We missed what I scheduled, and I don't know the timetables, so check with the pilot to make sure we can land when we arrive. Nothing worse than showing up in the middle of the night when the airport is closed."

Helen is chopping vegetables for my omelet. "You need to read Harper's note," she says again.

"Oh, right." She's awfully concerned about this note. What could be the big deal?

I walk upstairs in a fog. I think it's a too-much-sleep hangover. I can't believe I slept that long. I've never done that before.

I find an envelope next to the bed, and then I see the ring. My heart stops. She couldn't have. *No...*

I tear the envelope open.

Jaxson,

Thank you so much for everything you did for me and my family. I will always treasure the time we spent together. You are an amazing human being and will be successful at anything you put your mind to.

I know we talked about this relationship being a minimum of six months, and we're not yet at that threshold, but your board is happy, and your IPO was a giant success. I need to go home and take care of Harmony. She's struggling. I've left the clothes and ring. I'm sorry to do this so quickly, but Honeycomb is rock solid, and no one will even miss me.

Never change.
Harper

But I'll miss you. Panic rises in my chest. I practically run back downstairs, and Helen and Christophe are waiting for me. "When did she leave?" I demand.

"She left with her family on Monday," Christophe says. "She didn't take much. Just her suitcases."

"How come you didn't tell me?" I'm fighting back tears.

"We didn't know she hadn't told you." Helen shakes her head. "I only realized it when I found you in bed and saw the note on the table this morning."

I turn to Christophe. "Okay, now, I want to go to Boston. Do we know where she is?"

He nods. "We have JR from the Boston team monitoring her. With her name in the tabloids, we wanted to keep an eye on her until you said otherwise. Currently, she's staying with her sister, Harmony, and she interviewed this morning for a graphic design position in Cambridge at AdVenture Works. They've started a background check, which indicates they're likely going to extend her a job offer."

"Let's go. I need to talk to her."

Christophe nods. "The jet is waiting for us at SFO."

I race upstairs to throw a few things in a suitcase. I grab my laptop bag, which also has the sketchbook and pencils. I'll use everything I can to talk her into this.

At least she left for Harmony, I rationalize. I can't expect her to do anything for herself without figuring out a solution to that problem. Do we find her in-home care? What about one of her brothers? Would she feel better in a house with a yard? With a dog or cat, maybe? Maybe a one-bedroom apartment is better. What if we found someone to stop by? Maybe her parents could retire, and she could move home with them. I don't know what to do, but I need to get it figured out.

It's after nine o'clock when we land in Boston. The sky is ink black, with barely any visible stars. My mind has raced the entire five-hour flight, but once we land and I get in the car, a calm comes over me. I'm ready to go, and I have a plan.

Traffic is light through the tunnel and into Quincy. When we stop at Harmony's five-story, new-looking apartment building, I can smell the ocean. It must be close. I'm out the door with Christophe right behind me.

"She's in apartment three twenty-three," he calls.

I trot up to the front door, ready to buzz her apartment with the keypad on the side when I see that the door is ajar.

The lock is broken. This must be fixed. This isn't safe. What will happen once the press finds out she's here? But for now, I'll take it. I step inside and scan for the elevators. Once I find them, I must push the button twenty times.

Christophe leans in. "You know, I've heard that the more you push elevator buttons, the slower they are."

I sneer at him, and he smiles.

It finally arrives, and inside is a short brunette. "Hello there, hot men," she says. She sways a little as she passes us. "I have to go out now, but later, you can come find me in four-oh-seven."

She's drunk. I shake my head and restrain myself from pressing the three button more than once as we enter the elevator.

When we arrive on the third floor, the elevator doors shut behind us and I look around, trying to figure out how to find 323. The building is shaped like an H, and the elevators are in the middle. I finally find a sign with directions, and we head down one leg of the H. When we're standing in front of 323, I rap quickly on the door. There's some rustling inside, but no one answers.

I knock a second time. "Harper? It's me, Jaxson. Please open up." I lean my head against the door, praying.

After a moment, Harmony opens the door. "Jaxson Bancroft, billionaire, entrepreneur, and handsome man."

I smile at her. "Hello, Harmony. Is Harper home?"

"She's moved in to take care of me. I told her I didn't need her. She cries at night, and I don't like that." Harmony rocks back and forth and runs her thumbs over the pads of her fingers in a circular motion.

"I miss her, and I came to tell her that."

Harmony steps aside. "You can come in. I know you — Jaxson Bancroft, billionaire, entrepreneur, and handsome man."

"Thank you. This is my friend Christophe. Are you comfortable with him coming in too? Or would you prefer he remain in the hall?"

"Mrs. Ellsworth across the hall doesn't like it when we loiter."

"Are you okay if he comes in, then?"

She nods. "He's a handsome man too."

Christophe turns bright red.

I turn to look at him. "I suppose he is."

"Harmony—" Harper comes down the hallway wrapped in a towel. Her eyes go wide when she sees me. "What are you doing here?"

"I came to see you. I...I didn't know you'd left. I fell asleep, and no one woke me when you were leaving."

She shakes her head. "It took your mom and me a good twenty minutes to get you out of your clothes and under the covers. You were pretty out of it."

"I'm sorry. I hadn't really slept in weeks. I just woke up this morning."

"You slept all that time?"

"Crazy, right? I came as soon as I read your note. Can we talk?"

She looks over at Harmony, who is mooning over Christophe. "Harmony? Can you get everyone a glass of water with ice?"

She looks just past Christophe for a moment. "Yes. I can get water with five cubes of ice. Four melt too quickly and six make the glass overflow."

"Thank you," Harper tells her. She looks at Christophe. "I'm sorry."

"Are you kidding? A beautiful woman who thinks I'm handsome? We're all good."

Harper smiles. "Thank you. I'm just going to change. I'll be back in a minute."

340

I want to follow her and help, but that's not what the situation warrants. Instead, Christophe sits in a chair, and I sit on the couch. Harmony returns with glasses of water for both of us and takes a seat in a chair next to Christophe.

"Did you have fun at the party in San Francisco?" I ask.

Harmony shrugs. "There were many people."

"Yes. It was busy. I'm sorry if that upset you."

"I had my own room, and Hazel and Harper were with me."

"You did have your own room," Harper says over my shoulder. "And we had some good food and even danced to some of the music."

Harmony smiles. "That was fun."

I look at Harper, and my heart hurts. I realize what's happening here. Since Hazel has left to marry Paul, she's stepping in. I want to fix this and not just because I want her in my life.

"Did you like being in San Francisco?" I ask Harmony. "Did you enjoy seeing all the sights?"

"I like that it doesn't snow in San Francisco."

Christophe smiles.

"No, it doesn't snow," Harper says. "It's cold in the summer, though."

"It was nice."

I stand and look at Harmony. "Do you think it would be okay if I took a walk with Harper while you stay here with Christophe?"

"Yes! Definitely," Harmony says, looking at the carpet.

Harper gives Christophe a questioning look.

"We'll be fine," he assures her.

"Don't let her try anything."

"Promise," he says.

Harper turns to her sister. "Why don't you get some cheese and crackers out for us for when we get back? I have the salami you love."

Harmony nods.

"You're safe with her," Harper tells him. "She has recently decided she likes men. And I have to say, at least she has good taste."

Christophe smiles. "Thank you. Are you sure we shouldn't go with you? Is this a safe neighborhood?"

"We'll be fine," I assure him, already headed for the door.

CHAPTER 31

Harper

"Why are you here?" I ask Jaxson as soon as we hit the sidewalk out in front of the building. He's ignored me since his company went public ten days ago, except for a few public performances, of course. I was prepared for that, and I've made my plans to move on. What could he possibly want from me now?

"Why did you leave?" He runs his hands through his hair. "I mean, I get that Harmony needs you, but why didn't you talk to me about it?"

"Because it's none of your business." I stop and put my hands on my hips. I take a breath and remind myself to remain calm and not sound upset. "I'm so grateful for what you did for me and my siblings. But we went into this knowing it was going to end. That time has come."

He looks completely perplexed. "I thought we were going to talk about that?"

What? He's been focused on moving on for weeks. "You belong with someone like Tessa Sky, someone who enjoys announcing their engagement in magazines. That's not me."

He steps in close. "You know that's not me either." His shoulders fall. "Look, I stopped looking for anyone else the minute I met you. You were a beautiful mess and the only one I wanted. I know we started this as a contractual, business arrangement, but I'm crazy about you. My plan was to take you to Fiji this week so we could talk about throwing out the contract and starting a proper engagement."

That doesn't make any sense, and it's nothing I want, screams an indignant voice in my head. I stand straight. "Jaxson Bancroft! I don't need saving. That's why I didn't want your stock options or some kind of company. I'm perfectly able to make it on my own."

"Stop it!" he yells. "I know that, but I want to take care of you anyway. I'm not saving you from anything. I just want to be with you. Everything that is mine, I want it to be yours, and everything that is yours be mine. If you need to take care of your sister, let's take care of your sister. But let's do it together. I'm not ready to give up on us."

I can hear the desperation in his voice, and it would be so easy to say yes. Because that screaming voice in my head from a minute ago is a liar. He is what I want. If only what we had was real.

I know in my heart of hearts that I'm really just a crutch. Everything has been easy between us because it was fake. But he'll find another good assistant, and he'll find plenty of women to keep his bed warm now that the board is happy with his IPO. I have to let him go before he decides to do it to me.

"You're amazing..." My voice cracks. "But I can't."

There's a wildness in his eyes I haven't seen before. "I love you," he declares. "I know I should have said it before, but I do. And even if you don't feel the same way yet, I love you enough for both of us. Please don't do this. I want whatever we have to grow. What do I have to do? Please don't give up on us. Look, I know I've been busy and made a mess of things these past few weeks, but once Villefort is out of my life, I'll do whatever you want. Please don't leave me."

I'm falling apart inside, but the only way I know to go is forward. I can't stray from the choices I've made. He thinks he loves me, but he doesn't. How could he? Everything hurts, but I need to be strong for myself and for my sister. "I need some space," I tell him. "I'm sorry."

We've circled the block, and as we approach the entrance, I walk back into my building, leaving him on the sidewalk. I'm broken, but at least, I see us for what we are.

When I return to my apartment, Christophe is still sitting in the same chair. He's listening to Harmony sing.

"Where's Jaxson?" he asks when she finishes.

"He's downstairs waiting for you."

"You're not coming back with us?"

I shake my head. "No, I'm needed here."

"Is it something Tessa said?" Christophe asks.

I look at him a moment. "No, I think for myself, thank you. Though I do think she has some perspective on this situation." I take a deep breath. "Jaxson no longer needs me. His board is happy, and his company is doing well. My sister needs me here now, so it's time to move on. That was always our agreement."

"I think you're selling yourself short," Christophe says. "He's crazy about you."

I smile. "Please tell Helen I will miss her. She taught me so much."

"You should tell her yourself."

"Maybe I will someday. Goodbye, Christophe."

With that, I turn and walk back to my room, where I fall completely apart. This has to be the right choice. It's the only explanation that makes sense. So why does it feel so awful?

I feel the bed dip, and Harmony's hand settles on my back. She rarely touches or shows affection. "I'm sorry about Jaxson Bancroft, billionaire, entrepreneur, and handsome man."

I roll onto my back and look at her. "Thank you, Harmony. We're going to be okay."

"You know, I can live alone."

"I see that, but right now, I can't. Do you mind if I stay for a while?"

"You pay half the rent." She stands and walks out the door.

The phone wakes me on Friday morning. I fell asleep crying again last night, and my eyes are crusted from the salt of my tears. I shake the cobwebs from my head and answer, realizing I'm a sweaty mess. It's like a sauna in my room this morning.

"Good morning, Harper. This is Mark Brown at AdVenture Works."

My heart races. "Good morning." All evidence that I was asleep moments ago is gone. I'd been hoping I would hear from him.

"I'm calling because we really enjoyed meeting you on Wednesday and would like to offer you a position as a junior graphic designer in our products group."

Junior? I've worked for two years as a graphic designer, and my portfolio is impeccable. The Honeycomb logo alone should move me to senior designer.

"So what do you think?" he presses. The hair on the back of my neck stands up.

Before I met Jaxson, I would have taken the job and just been disappointed that I was underpaid with a crappy title. But I know my value, and I've seen what I can do. I'm standing up for myself. "I'm a bit surprised by the offer of junior graphic designer. I interviewed for a senior position."

"We filled that role with another candidate, but we still believe you'd be an excellent addition to our team. Right now, we only have a junior position open."

"I see. I, um… Can I think about it and let you know?"

"We're the largest ad agency in Boston with strong ties to New York City. This is an excellent offer."

He's so aggressive. I'm really not sure I'm comfortable with him.

"I know that, but I have another offer I'm considering," I explain.

It's not exactly lying, and I don't want to be pushed into a job where they'll use my experience and pay me crap.

"You told our human resources department you had nothing else going on."

"It just came up last night."

"If this is a negotiation tactic, it won't work."

My hackles rise again. "Right now, I don't see anything to negotiate. I need you to understand that I'm not a junior-level designer."

"I see. Well, take the weekend to figure out where you want to go. We only hire the best talent, and we think you're one of them. I'll expect a call before ten o'clock on Monday morning if you're going to accept our offer."

"I appreciate the call, Mr. Brown."

He barely says goodbye before hanging up. He's not happy with me.

He may be right. I could be turning down the best opportunity out there. But I won't be forced or coerced into doing something foolish. I can always hang my own shingle and start a business. I open my laptop and go to my bank's website so I can do the math to figure out how long I have before things get desperate.

When I open my account, it reads that I have two hundred and fifty million dollars and some change — and the eleven-thousand dollars of change is what's mine. The rest? Well, that's Jaxson Bancroft's money.

Jaxson, what the hell?
I immediately text him.

Me: Why is there $250,000,000 in my bank account this morning?

Jaxson: I promised you 5K shares of Honeycomb, and that's what they're worth.

Me: I don't want the money.

Jaxson: It's in the contract.

I slam my phone down, fortunately into my mattress. There's no use arguing with him. I'll have to figure out how to return it on my own. But I need coffee before this day throws anything else at me.

Out in the living room, it's even hotter than my bedroom. "Harmony? What's going on?"

She looks like someone dumped a gallon of water on her head. She's soaked to the bone with perspiration. "The air conditioner here is bad."

I place my hand over the floor vent, and it's blowing hot air. The thermostat reads ninety degrees.

"Have you called the management company?"

She rocks back and forth. "Hazel always did that. He scares me."

I throw open every window, hoping some of the hot air will filter out, and get Harmony a tall glass of ice water. I then text Hazel for the number, and she quickly replies.

Hazel: That place has so many issues. This is the third time that's happened this summer. If I could break that lease, I would. Here's Kevin Walsh's number.

Thankfully, the number is highlighted as a hyperlink in the text. I push the button.

"Hellllloooo?" a chipper voice says.

"Mr. Walsh? This is Harper Lockwood. I'm in unit three twenty-three. Our air conditioner has gone out, and we were hoping you could come fix it."

"It's in the high nineties. What do ya expect?"

"I expect the air conditioner to pump out cool air."

"You-a one of those." His Boston accent grates on me.

"If you mean one of those bitches who pays nearly four grand a month for an apartment that comes with air conditioning, then yes. That's exactly who I am."

"Jeez, you don't have to get ya panties in a wad."

"When can we expect you?" I ask in a sugary sweet voice.

"Ya like eighth on the list."

I hold back on the expletives racing through my head. It's hard, but I manage. "Great. We'll see you in a half hour then?"

He snorts. "Not likely. Mowa like fowa days."

I close my eyes. "Okay, then I'll reach out to the renters' board and see what they say I can deduct from our next check."

I disconnect the call and take a cold shower, trying all the while to assure myself that I'm ending things with Jaxson for both our sakes.

As soon as I step out, sweat pools under my arms, and my hair becomes a giant frizz bomb.

As lunch approaches, I talk Harmony into walking to a neighborhood spot that's air conditioned. But when we arrive, it's overcrowded with people like us escaping the heat.

"Should we see a movie?" I ask her, trying to think of other air-conditioned options.

"I need to work."

"I'm sorry. What would Hazel do?"

"She'd go to work."

We return to the apartment, and Harmony settles in at her computer while I go to my bedroom and look for more job openings for graphic designers. I'm not finding anything. Maybe I should take the junior position and work from within to show the ad agency I'm worth a senior position.

The person to talk to about this would be Jaxson, but he'll just focus on getting me back. I can't.

My phone rings, and it's a Bay Area number, but I don't recognize it. I let it go to voicemail. They can leave a message, and I won't have to hang up on anyone I don't want to talk to.

I go out to check on Harmony, and it's even hotter than it was. She's closed all the windows again.

"Harmony, you need to leave the windows open. It's too hot for you and too hot for the computers."

"It's too loud."

"How about we find your headphones? That way you can work with the windows open."

She rubs her fingers together. I reach for her tentatively. I don't want to make her more uncomfortable. "It's okay. I'm here. You're going to be fine. I can work at the kitchen table if that makes you feel better."

She gives me a single nod, and before getting my computer from my room, I open the windows and get her more water.

What would she have done if I wasn't here? Would my brothers or my parents think about checking on her?

My phone lights up with another Bay Area phone number, and I once again send it to voicemail.

I sit at the kitchen table with my laptop and surf through YouTube. I'm mesmerized by people who cut wood into small pieces and then glue them back together in a fancy design. They then put it on a lathe and make incredible pieces of art.

A little while later, the refrigerator begins to make noise, and I throw in the towel.

"Come on, Harmony. Let's go camp out at Mom and Dad's for a few days. We can sleep in our old room and tell stories like we did when we were growing up."

I call a rideshare to drop us at our parents. We pack a few things, and Harmony seems good with this plan, but on the drive over, she becomes agitated.

"What's wrong, Harmony?"

"Why didn't Jaxson Bancroft, billionaire, entrepreneur, and handsome man come back after your walk?"

"He had to fly home."

She watches the road. "Why did he come see you?"

I shrug. "I'm not sure."

"I like him. He is always nice to me. I really like his friend Christophe."

"Christophe is very handsome."

She nods. "He's funny too."

"Did he tell you some jokes?"

She nods. "What is a cracker without cheese?"

I shake my head. "A saltine?"

"No, silly. Crackalackin." Harmony laughs really hard, and I can't help but join her. I'm so impressed that while Harmony was making a cheese tray, Christophe told her jokes.

When the car drops us at our parents' home, Mom greets me at the door. "Thank goodness you're here. We were just wondering what we were going to do for dinner."

I shake my head. "It's Friday. Don't you make pizzas?"

"Yes, but Hazel is the only one who can make the dough."

I don't even know what to say to that. These are grown, fully functioning adults—at least outside their home. I put my things in my old bedroom and explain what happened at our apartment. Mom nods along but doesn't offer any real suggestions to help. Finally, as she sits there looking at me, I go into the kitchen and begin making the dough. It's not that hard. It only takes some time.

"Who all will be here for dinner tonight?" I ask.

351

Mom looks at me like I've grown horns. "Everyone. Like always."

This is why I left.

CHAPTER 32

Jaxson

I can't stop thinking about why Harper left. I keep trying to put her out of my mind, to consider that this is what's best for her, and I should accept it. But I just can't. I don't believe it's true.

After an excruciating weekend — divided between worrying about this and meeting with the team about Villefort — on the drive in to work Monday, Christophe asks me a question I hadn't considered. "Do you think Tessa Sky said something to Harper?"

If I were a cartoon, a lightbulb would have lit above my head. "There's a good chance she did." I shake my head. Yet another horrible part of Harper's experience with me. "But I don't think that's the key to all this or anything. Harper seems to have lots of reasons why us being together is not the right thing."

Christophe hesitates. "I know it's not my place to say anything, but wouldn't it be the *best* thing? I mean, she glowed around you, and I know you want her back."

"That's all true," I say. It's what goes through my head a thousand times a day. "But she seems to think I have an ulterior motive, or it can't possibly be real. And she's committed to being with her sister."

"That's a cop out."

I meet Christophe's eyes in the rearview mirror. He seems to have strong feelings about this. "It may be, but that's her thinking, right now."

"I'm sorry." Christophe shakes his head. "I know it's tearing you up inside."

I should have told Harper how I felt about her a long time ago. I had so many chances, but I was so worried she'd leave... And then she left anyway. I'm so angry with myself — and with Villefort. If he wasn't such a destructive ass, I wouldn't be tied up dealing with Julia Willis or *The New York Times*.

I sigh. But I probably wouldn't have Harper in my life either.

I arrive at work, and there's another temp in Harper's seat.

"When is Harper going to return?" Louise demands as she follows me into my office. "I spend too much time training your temps. I can't get my work done."

I sit behind my desk and look at her. "She's not coming back."

Louise looks utterly defeated and sits down hard in a chair. "Why not? I liked her. She was good at her job."

I nod. "I agree, but she's moved on. She went back to Boston to be closer to her family. It's what she felt was right for her."

Louise shakes her head. "But what about your engagement? Are you moving to Boston?"

I dismiss the thought outright. "No. Honeycomb is here."

"I don't know how long I can take this nightmare."

I suppress an eye roll. Louise is being dramatic. "You and me both, Louise."

She stands to leave.

"Louise?"

She turns back to me.

"I need someone as good as Harper was. Would you or anyone you know be interested in working as my executive admin?"

Her mouth opens. "I wouldn't want to put Stacy in a bad position. I can't just abandon her."

"I would need to talk to Stacy, but maybe you could find your replacement. I need someone who can keep my calendar and get me out of the office at a reasonable time."

Louise seems unsure. "I'm not as young as Harper. I'm not able to work the long hours she worked, and I don't have any graphic design experience."

"I understand. The graphic design was more her passion. It's not essential to this role. Plus, there are a few things going on that should soon lessen our workload, so we can have more regular hours."

She finally nods. "I'll let you talk to Stacy about the move."

"I'll do that, and I'll have HR be in touch about a replacement."

I email Stacy, the VP of Operations, and let her know I'm stealing her assistant. Hopefully, that won't be too disruptive. Then I bury myself in reports on Spy Game and the notes I've gotten from Cameron and his team regarding the hits we're getting on the corrected back door and attempts to signal the trojan horse, which is long gone.

When I look up, the office is empty.

I pick up my phone and find the voicemail I've saved. I listen to it when I really miss her.

"Hello, sweetheart. It's getting late, so I'm going to bed, but I was hoping to convince you to come home. I can help you fall asleep. This big bed is very empty without you."

I need to get her back, and I think the first step is managing the situation with Harmony.

CHAPTER 33

Harper

Ten o'clock has come and gone this Monday morning, and Mark Brown at AdVenture Works did not get a phone call from me. I don't know what I'm going to do, but it's not going to be that. I'm not going to take a step back in both job title and money. I'm an excellent graphic designer, and I can keep looking. One day, I may regret it, but I talked to my brother, Hunter, over the weekend and he agreed. Of course, he also thought I was a fool for walking away from Jaxson.

He may be right.

Somehow, I also have eight voicemails. I went for a walk to clear my head this morning, and evidently, I missed quite a bit. Harmony seems settled at her desk with her computer out in the front room, so I pull out a pad of paper and play the first message.

"Harper? This is Melissa Scalia at NexTech. We saw the logo you did for Honeycomb, and we would love to talk to you about our IPO rebranding. You can call me at..." She rattles off a San Francisco-area number.

My eyes go wide as I frantically write down her name and information.

Then the second message begins. "Harper Lockwood? This is Elliot Tomov. I'm with TechVantage. We saw the rebranding you did for Honeycomb Games, and we're interested in talking to you. I did our first logo, and I know it's terrible. When you have a minute, please call me." He rattles off his Bay Area number, and I scribble it down.

The next five messages are also people looking for rebranding. I'm overwhelmed by the work. Even if half of these pan out, they can hold me over until I find a regular job with benefits.

The last message is from Jaxson. My finger hovers over the button for a long time, but finally, I press play.

"Hello, Harper. I just thought you should know I'm thinking about you. There was a piece in the *Silicon Valley Business Journal* about our logo, and as people call, I'm referring them to you. I miss you."

Tears fill my eyes. I can't take his continued kindness.

After lunch, I take the afternoon to return the calls and set times to meet with my new prospects. Most of them would like me to come for in-person meetings, but I push them to Zoom, at least for the time being.

I need to figure out a contract and get things in writing, once I'm sure I'll be able to do what they're asking.

At the end of the day, I feel like a heel for not reaching out to Jaxson to let him know I appreciate all he's done for me. But he also needs to know that he should stop. I pace around my room, trying to figure out what to say that doesn't make me seem like a raging fool or that I'm ready to take him back.

Harmony knocks on my door. "You got a package."

I immediately know it's from Jaxson. I thank her and accept it from her, but I debate whether to open it. I don't even last five minutes.

Inside the shallow box is a binder. I open it up, and inside are incorporation documents for Bright Brain Marketing, with me as the sole owner. It includes a website address and email address, with meticulous directions for how to get things started, and contracts I can send to clients. Jaxson also included a quote from him to use on my website.

I close my eyes. He's done the other thing he promised he'd do for me. He gave me a company.

Beneath the binder is a beautiful leather-bound sketchbook. I saw these at the art store we visited together on our trip here. It makes my heart stop. The leather is so soft. There's also a wooden box of seventy-six Caran D'Ache colored pencils. These come from Switzerland, and they're considered the best in the world. I bought just one years ago for more than ten dollars, and it was so creamy to work with. I loved it and dreamed that one day I'd have a set just like this.

At the bottom of the box, Jaxson has tucked an envelope with a card inside. I take a deep breath as I lift it out.

My beautiful Harper,

My goal was to give this to you after the IPO party. I've made many mistakes in my life, but you were never one of them. You're the best thing that ever happened to me. I know you loved this sketchbook and pencils. I hope you will use them and think of me.

Always and forever,

Jaxson

I wipe the tears that fall with the heel of my hand.

Harmony appears at my side. "Why are you sad about presents?"

"I'm not sad about the presents. They're very special to me." I run my hand across the leather again.

"They're very pretty," Harmony says.

I wipe the tears away. "I agree."

Now, I need to actually call him, and I need to do it before I can change my mind. The phone rings and goes to voicemail. I can't decide if I'm happy or sad not to talk directly to him.

"Hey, Jaxson," I begin after the message. "Thank you. Thank you for giving me the space I need and for giving me a company with clients as you always promised. The sketchbook and colored pencils are so generous. But please don't do anything else. You're making this too hard."

CHAPTER 34

Jaxson

Christophe meets me in the kitchen. We're heading out to run the Lyon Street stairs. We've been coming every day, and we're up to four circuits each morning. It's a grueling workout, but it's the only way I can get through the day. Truthfully, it makes me too tired to care about anything.

A little over forty minutes later, we've finished. "Next week, we'll try to add another round," I tell him.

Christophe is walking around me with his hands on his hips, breathing hard. "Have you talked to her?"

"Who?"

He gives me a look and tilts his head to the side.

"I've tried a few times, but it always goes to voicemail. No matter how hard I try, I can't make her listen to me." *And the one time she called me, I was wrapped up in a board meeting and missed it.*

"You have the means to show up at her apartment," Christophe notes.

"I'm aware of that."

He shrugs. "What's keeping you?"

I turn and start the walk back to my house. Bonnie Raitt's "I Can't Make You Love Me" plays on repeat in my head. I don't even like Bonnie Raitt.

When I return to the house, I head for my bedroom but find myself in the room Harper first stayed in. It's still all white, and it's terrible. After Harper left, I couldn't look at her clothes in my closet so I moved them here. Sometimes, I come in just to smell her perfume. As I'm walking out, I spot a bright green hair tie partially under the bed. I reach for it.

It has a strand of her hair tangled around it, another piece of her she left behind. I look up at the ceiling. I'm never going to move on. She was in my life for such a brief period, but she's left a mark so deep in my heart that I can never fill it again. With her by my side, I knew no matter what happened with Honeycomb or Villefort, I would be okay. She was such a support for me. Now, she's supporting her family.

What could I have done differently? I should have been more honest with her, but I feared she'd run away. I mean, the woman I met after that awful introduction at the Fairmont had fire in her eyes. She was my equal. No, she was better than me. And my cock was at full attention.

But when it really comes down to it, I've never met a woman who wanted me for me the way Harper did.

I slip the elastic over my wrist and get in the shower. I have a full day of meetings, and then it's a long weekend for Labor Day. Grayson and Scarlett are going up to their house in Lake Tahoe and invited me to join them. But I don't think so. They're entirely too happy, and I'm not up for playing uncle and watching them moon all over each other right now.

Nick and Olivia are going to some island I've never heard of to spend time together. They're still not engaged but have changed the date of their wedding three times because Olivia can't decide on the venue. That can't be a good sign, but what do I know?

All that means is I have nothing to do this weekend. I've made no plans. The City will be full of tourists, and it'll be difficult to get around. I could hole myself up at my office and work, but when I look out at the empty chair outside my office, it reminds me of Harper, even though Louise has held the job for over a month now.

As the water pounds against my back, I wonder if maybe Christophe is on to something. Maybe I should go knock on her door again. But what if I fly all the way to Boston and she's not there? I guess that beats staying home. Helen's going to her sister's in Sacramento, so she won't even be here to cook for me.

I'm still thinking about it as we drive to work.

"I want to go see her," I announce suddenly as we approach the office. Fuck this sitting around and waiting for her to figure it out. If I want her, I need to fight for her. "I'll see if it's too late to get a flight out."

Christophe meets my eyes in the rearview mirror. "I can ask Helen to pack your bag and be ready to leave as soon as you're set."

"Slow down. It's a holiday weekend. Chances are I won't be able to get a plane."

"Let me know." Christophe returns his eyes to the road.

When I get inside, I check availability with NetJet before my first meeting. By some miracle, there's a plane. I can take the redeye out tonight and arrive in Boston first thing tomorrow morning. This has to be a sign.

I let Christophe know, and my mind fills with plans as I go to the conference room for my meeting. I don't expect that Agent Snow has anything new for us, as Julia is still resisting cooperating, but I'm determined not to miss a thing this time. Villefort will not succeed again.

I take a deep breath and prepare for battle on all fronts in the days ahead. I'm going to make my case with Harper one more time, and I'm going to succeed there too.

I gather myself as I exit the car. I didn't sleep a wink on the flight out, but now that we're here in Boston, I'm ready. It's just after eight, and the sun is bright. I figure Harmony is up, so maybe she'll answer the door.

The door to the building is open — again. Why have an entrance with a lock and security pad that never works? It's certainly not very safe. I take the elevator to the third floor and ring the bell. I have a box of a dozen Dunkin' Donuts and four cups of coffee. Christophe is standing behind me, ready to witness Harper calling the police on me for harassment.

It's fine. I've got lawyers.

After a moment, Harmony opens the door in shorts and a T-shirt. "Jaxson Bancroft, billionaire, entrepreneur, and handsome man."

"Hello, Harmony. Christophe and I brought donuts and coffee. Is Harper here?"

"She's sleeping. Go back and make her happy."

I freeze on my way into the apartment. "Is she still crying at night?"

"Yes, ever since she moved here. She cries at night."

My heart breaks at the thought. I hope she'll see that together, we can make everything better.

I leave Christophe with Harmony in the kitchen. They're already telling each other jokes and laughing. I walk back to Harper's room and knock on the closed door. The apartment is hot, and the humidity makes my T-shirt damp as I wait. I wish I was wearing shorts rather than jeans.

I knock again and announce myself. "I'm coming in."

Harper sits up in bed, her hair a beautiful, tangled mess. "What are you doing here?"

"I'm here to tell you I'll move here. I'll come to Boston and do whatever you need so we can be together. I can't be without you any longer. Tell me how we can make this work. I will buy your parents a new house. I'll pay for twenty-four-hour care for your sister. Hell, she can move in with us. I don't care. Whatever you want, I will do it. But I won't go away."

"Jaxson?"

I pace, ignoring her protest. "I've tried it your way. I've been miserable the last four weeks. I've given you everything I promised, including the space you needed, but I can't anymore. I can't be great without you standing beside me. Please," I beg. "Please be with me. I'll do whatever it takes." I feel tears threatening, but I can't read the look on her face.

"You are not moving here," she tells me as she pulls the covers aside. "Why is it so hot?"

She steps past me and out to Harmony. "Is the air conditioning out again?" She pivots. "Hey, Christophe. Sorry. We've been having problems with our air conditioning. I will not go back to my parents again," she announces to the room. "The last time, I got stuck cooking and cleaning all weekend. No thanks!"

"They think she's like Hazel, but she hates it," Harmony explains.

Harper holds up her hands. "Everyone just stop!"

I hold my breath.

She turns and stares me down. "Why are you here, Jaxson?"

"I love you. I've been in love with you since I came to your apartment that first day. I will do whatever you need if you'll just try to love me back. I'll be patient, but we have to try — no contract, just because we want to."

Harmony rushes over and wraps her arms around me.

Harper is dumbfounded. I've never seen Harmony express emotion like this, and based on the look on Harper's face, neither has she.

After a moment, she steps aside and turns to Harper. "You can be happy now."

Harper's face softens. "But what about you?"

"I have an idea," I interject. "Harmony, I know you'd like to live alone. I have a two-bedroom apartment over the garage behind my house. It has its own entrance, and you'd be living alone, but we'd be close by, so you would have company."

She nods.

"But it's not here," I add, wanting to make sure this is clear. "It's in San Francisco."

She nods again. "Okay. I can go to San Francisco."

My heart sings.

"That's an awful lot of change," Harper warns her. "What about your job?"

"I asked my boss after I visited San Francisco, and she said it was okay. My friends are on the internet, and I'll be close to you."

Harper narrows her eyes. "You won't be close to Mom and Dad."

She shrugs. "That's okay. I want to meet Christophe's little girl. She has autism too."

I turn to look at Christophe because I had no idea. He just smiles.

Harper was right about me. I need to pay better attention. No wonder he connects so well with Harmony.

Turning to Harper, I smile. "I guess it's up to you. Will you come back to San Francisco and give us a try?"

Her face is still unreadable. "On one condition," she says after a moment.

I feel like I can't breathe.

"I want to hear you tell me you love me often and enthusiastically."

I race over, wrap my arms around her, and spin in a circle. "I love you!"

She leans in and kisses me, a bit chastely. "I love you too, but I need to brush my teeth."

Right now, I don't care. I'm just happy. I kiss her deeply until Christophe clears his throat. I give him a look, and he fans his face with a magazine. At first, I think he's reacting to our PDA, but then I realize what he means.

"I have an idea," I tell Harmony and Harper. "I have a two-bedroom suite at the Four Seasons downtown. Their air conditioning works. Why don't we go spend the weekend there, and we'll make plans to pack up your apartment. We can fly back on Monday with the items we need, and we can have the rest put in a moving van."

Harper smiles. "I love that idea, but before we just leave town, we're going to need to tell my parents."

I nod. "Of course. We'll do it all together. Who is Harmony's legal guardian?"

Harper looks at me, confused.

"Who is legally responsible to make decisions for her?" I ask.

"My parents, I suppose. I don't know that we've ever set up anything else."

"Well, let's do that. We could make it you and me together. I will make sure she's financially taken care of, and you can make sure she's medically and physically fine."

Harper turns to Harmony. "How does that sound to you?"

"I can be responsible for myself." She rubs her thumb on the underside of her fingers.

Harper reaches for her hand with a smile. "I agree. But if we have some paperwork, that makes sure you have help, if you ever need it when making decisions."

Harmony nods. "I like that."

CHAPTER 35

Harper

Jaxson's chest rises and falls as he sleeps. I can't believe I'm here in his arms at the Four Seasons. Harmony is happy as a clam doing her work out in the main room, and I can see my life opening up before me. But telling my parents is going to be tough. They were so happy when I returned to Boston. They won't take me leaving with Harmony very well.

I sigh as I wonder how I can best broach the subject with them.

"Stop thinking so hard," Jaxson mumbles.

"What do you mean?" I feign ignorance.

He opens an eye and looks at me. "We'll go see them today."

He's read my mind. "What if they refuse to let Harmony go?"

"We'll talk it through. Harmony can tell them what she wants. She's an adult. And it's not like she'll be living in a strange city all alone."

He's right. I'm not responsible for their feelings, only for making sound decisions. We can do this. It will be best for all of us. "Thank you."

His dick twitches, so I reach down and play with my favorite joystick.

"You are so fucking sexy," he says.

I don't think I can ever hear that enough. Before I can tell him I'd like to add that to the list of things he says enthusiastically and often, Jaxson rolls me on my back and nudges my legs open. He stares at my wet center, stroking his long, hard pole. I reach down and circle my hard nub.

He shakes his head. "That's my job."

Crawling over me, he leans down and takes my nipple into his mouth. His teeth grasp it, pulling, and my back arches off the bed.

Kneeling between my legs, his fingers slide down my stomach to my center. I quiver with anticipation. No one has ever touched me like Jaxson. It doesn't matter what he does. He enters the room, and my body responds.

He kisses, licks, and nibbles his way across my chest, pulling again on my nipple as he works his way down. His hands hold my legs wide as his flattened tongue starts at the bottom of my slit and curls around my hard nub.

My fingers lace through his hair as I tip my head back to the ceiling. *Exquisite.* "Jaxson," I breathe.

He licks me slowly at first, and then his tongue lashes around my nerves as his fingers stretch me wide. His whiskers burn as my body rides his face. "Oh... My... God... So... Good..." I groan.

He moves my legs over his shoulders and pushes me right to the edge of my precipice. I'm so close. My hands pull at his hair, and I rock my hips into his mouth. "Yes," I gasp. "That's it."

He tweaks my nipple hard. "Come for me. I want to taste all of you." He slides two fingers into me, and that spark building deep within my stomach bursts into flames. I explode and shudder deep within as I hold on to him for dear life, convulsing from one of the most intense orgasms I've ever had.

He laps up every bit of my juices before he sits back on his knees. I'm blissed out, and he chuckles. "You're so beautiful right now."

He leans down and kisses me. With our eyes locked, he lifts my legs around his waist and slides in so deep he knocks the air out of me.

"So fucking tight," he groans.

He pulls out and immediately pushes back in. He feels so good. I've never been with anybody like Jaxson Bancroft.

We have an emotional connection, beyond the obvious physical one. He circles his hips while he's deep inside, and it's like he's pushed a button. Suddenly, I'm shaking as I reach another climax. He leans forward and pivots in and out of me. He grunts and groans, and I'm sure we're going to break the bed.

Then he freezes and groans my name. "Haaaaaaarper."

He falls down next to me, covered in a sheen of perspiration and gasping for air.

I will never get enough of Jaxson Bancroft.

The heat emanating from Jaxson's body next to me wakes me as the sun rises. *Oops.* So much for talking to my parents yesterday. My thoughts then transition to Harmony, and I nearly leap out of bed before I remember Christophe is keeping an eye on her. I roll over and smile. Not having to do everything myself is pretty great. Jaxson is still asleep, his face serene and relaxed. So handsome. We had an amazing night.

I prop myself on my elbow and watch him. His hair is messy, his big rosy lips are slightly open, and his eyelashes are long and beautiful.

His eyes flutter open, and he smiles. "Good morning, gorgeous." He caresses my hip.

I lean over and kiss him. "Good morning."

I reach for my phone and see there's already a text message from my mom.

Mom: Can you pick up a gallon of milk, two loaves of multigrain bread, and whatever you're making for lunch.

I lie back. Maybe I'm better off just calling her from San Francisco to tell her what we've decided.

Jaxson tilts my hand so he can read Mom's text.

"Just tell her you're picking up lunch. What do you want to get? Something for the barbecue? Or order pizza? I'm happy to get some grinders."

"We call them spuckies," I correct with a smile. Sighing, I look away. "Maybe we should just go and tell them after we get back to San Francisco."

"Your mom doesn't mean to be demanding. She —"

"I know. I just wish she'd ask and say please and thank you."

"That's fair. And when we get back to San Francisco, she won't be able to be as demanding."

"Okay, we can pick up spuckies from a place not too far from the house."

Me: I'll pick up some spuckies. Have everyone send me their order. And Harmony and I won't be there tonight for dinner.

Mom: Are you sure? I'm hoping for some alone time with you.

Me: I'm sure, but I'll take some alone time with you this afternoon.

Mom: Okay. Are you stopping at Spuckies on Park Ave?

Me: Yes.

Mom gives me a long list of sandwiches, and we slowly get out of bed.

Harmony is dressed and out in the living room when we emerge. "We're going to go to Mom and Dad's, and we'll tell them we're going back to San Francisco today," she announces.

Jaxson nods. "Okay."

"Are you sure you're okay with moving?" I ask.

"It was a nice visit," Harmony says. "I can always move home if I don't like it. But I'll have to not like it a lot if I move home."

"If you're unhappy, we'll figure something out," I assure her.

"Let's get going," I tell them. Jaxson looks in danger of settling in on the couch for a nap. "We have twelve spuckies to pick up."

"I want an Italian," Harmony announces.

"Me too," Jaxson agrees.

On the drive to my parents', we stop at a small spuckie shop. There was a time when I always knew someone behind the counter, but not today. I give them our order, and Christophe adds his favorite.

As we watch them put the enormous sandwiches together, Christophe groans. "That is so much food."

"You can always take it home," I reply.

He nods. "You can count on it."

Before I realize what he's doing, Jaxson pays for our lunch.

"You didn't have to do that."

He waves me away. "Don't worry about it."

We get to the house just before noon, and Mom stops short when she sees Jaxson and Christophe with us.

"No!" she announces as we enter.

I cringe. "Mom, Jaxson bought lunch for everyone today."

"Did you get the groceries I asked for?" she counters.

"We did. Christophe has them," I assure her.

"We're moving to San Francisco," Harmony announces.

My eyes widen, and I stifle a laugh. *Thank you, Harmony. No time like the present.* Mom and Dad stare at me as we move into the living room. "I love him. We want to be together, and he has a guest house on his property that will allow Harmony to live alone but have help nearby."

"She said I can move back if I don't like it," Harmony adds.

"You don't have to go," Mom insists. "You can always live here."

"No thanks." Harmony pulls her spuckie from the bag and turns away from them, heading for the kitchen.

I try not to giggle at her brutal honesty.

"I think it's fantastic," Hudson says.

"Me too," Hannah chimes in.

Jaxson turns to my parents. "When you want to come out for a weekend or a holiday or just because you miss your girls, call me and I'll get you a plane. And they can always do the same."

Mom's eyes pool with tears. "I'm going to miss seeing you girls all the time."

"We won't be very far," Harmony calls.

Mom gives me a hug. "I'll come visit as often as I can."

The Four Seasons has been a great spot for all of us this weekend, and today we've spent the holiday on a long walk through Boston Common. We even fed the ducks and rode a duck boat. We have arrangements made to move Harmony's things, and we've packed a bag for her in the meantime. We're flying home tonight.

"What's on your mind?" I ask Jaxson as we wander the tree-lined paths. He hasn't had much to say for a few minutes.

"I could have made it work here."

My heart softens. "I appreciate that, but I think I'm looking forward to being back in San Francisco. Maybe one day we can reevaluate. But for now, I'll be happy to return to the life I had."

"Wherever we are, I want you to know my goal is to step back from work. I want to be there for you and Harmony, and I want to live my life more fully."

"You are amazing." I wrap my arms around his neck and kiss him. "Thank you."

CHAPTER 36

Jaxson

Harper straightens my tie and stands on her tiptoes to kiss me softly. "You're going to do great today."

I blow out a breath of air. This is my first official board meeting for my now publicly held company. After I update them on Honeycomb's status after three months of public holdings, I'm finally going to tell them about what happened with Spy Game.

"Thank you. I know you've told me, but what are you doing today?" I learned a long time ago to feign forgetfulness rather than get pegged with not listening.

"I'm meeting with NexTech and showing them my ideas for their logo. I've got to convince them the colors are right. The most popular colors right now are a cobalt blue and orange. She keeps leaning toward pink and blue. I'm beginning to wonder if she's pregnant."

"Ha! I've heard it does take over your brain."

She shakes her head. "No, thank you. I need all of my brain I can get right now."

"Well, I suppose we'll just stick to practicing, then. No rush on anything else."

"That's true. We can continue our process in sunny Fiji next week."

I had to adjust the timing on our Fiji trip, and it's not a surprise anymore, but we're still going, and I'm calling that a win. "Yes, please." I kiss her on the nose.

What she doesn't know is that I'm going to propose again. I have the ring I gave her before, and I'll promise her the gold band for everyday wear. "Good luck with NexTech. I know they're going to love the logo," I tell her as I head out.

"Call me after the meeting," she yells after me.

"I will." I go downstairs where Christophe is waiting to take me to the Fairmont. "Wyatt is taking Harper to her meeting, right?"

He nods. "Helen will be here if Harmony needs her. She already has plans to make her a grilled cheese with tomato soup for lunch."

Lucky her. "I wouldn't mind one of those too."

"I think the hotel is serving you salmon."

"The grilled cheese sounds so much better."

"I agree," Christophe says.

It's a pretty smooth drive to the Fairmont. When we arrive, Christophe walks me to my board meeting and leaves me at the conference room door. I see Jim Adelson is already here, and I know he's brought a team from Clear Security today. We've been cautious since Nick announced that there was a flaw in the PayFriend system and they've returned all the skimmed money to the accounts it came from.

Nick has been beat up pretty good in the press, but most of his users are thrilled. Most of them never knew about the issue, and they've acknowledged how honest he was to reveal it and return the funds before it was discovered in an official audit. I'm hopeful it will actually help his IPO.

He, Gray, and I have discussed how we all wish we'd been a fly on the wall when Villefort found out he'd been discovered. We're sure he's boiling in rage.

I find a seat and notice Mason talking to Grantham. Louise is running around, making sure my computer is working on the projector and directing hotel catering on what she was promised. She's not Harper, but she's good, and she found the perfect gentleman to work with Stacy and be her backup for me.

After a moment, Louise gives me a go-ahead nod.

"Okay everyone, let's get something to eat and get started." I clap my hands and rub them together as I walk to the buffet. Everyone follows me over.

Once everyone is sitting around the table, I bang a gavel softly. Louise sits down off to the side so she can take notes.

"Let the first official board meeting of Honeycomb Games begin." I glance at my watch. "It's eight nineteen a.m. on October tenth." I look up at them and smile. "If everyone is okay with the agenda, let me get started."

I begin with a recap of how our stock has trended since going public. It has continued to do well. And our games are performing well too. "You'll see a strong uptick in users for Chocolate Crush, and as we have an average of five million people playing Spy Game at any time, the average spend has dropped from an opening-day high of a hundred dollars a day to twenty-four dollars a day. That's still a higher daily rate than Chocolate Crush, though we expect that to eventually fall to a little less than fifteen dollars a day."

Veronica Vance looks up at me. "If I'm doing the math correctly, you're bringing in one hundred and twenty million dollars every day?"

My heart beats crazy fast. "That's correct. As we get more downloads and more people playing, that number will go up, even as the average player spend drops."

"Whoever said games weren't profitable hasn't met Jaxson Bancroft," Grantham Wilks snipes with a grin.

After I take my seat, Corey Craven, our chief financial officer, gives her presentation on our profit and loss. She is hammered with questions about how we're storing our cash. The board is jittery after Technology Startup Fund's collapse.

"We were never invested in TSF, as we choose more risk-adverse options," she explains. "Some cash is locked away for the next two years, and some is more liquid."

"But you're not in anything too crazy?" Dominic Valente presses.

"The liquid assets are in American Bank," Corey explains. "It's spread across several accounts, with the most fluid one being our payroll account."

As she's finishing up, I watch Duncan Snow and two other FBI agents come in and take a seat along the wall in the conference room. Grantham gives me a funny look.

After everyone has clapped and celebrated Corey's good news on Honeycomb's financial health, I stand again and move to the front of the room. "The next item on your agenda is Spy Game." I introduce Agent Snow, and he introduces the people with him. I then tell the board the full story of what happened with that game's development and the lead designer.

"Why didn't you tell us this was going on?" Veronica demands.

"We were working with the FBI." I point to Agent Snow.

He stands. "We asked that it not be shared outside of SHN and Mr. Bancroft's former co-partners and friends."

"Why did your friends know?" Grantham asks, agitation in his voice.

"They were also being attacked," Snow says. He outlines what we believe Villefort perpetrated with Firefly and PayFriend.

Grantham Wilks puts his coffee cup down. "Why hasn't Zack Villefort been arrested?"

"Julia Willis won't testify against him," Snow shares. "She's accepted a plea and is being moved to Metropolitan Detention Center Los Angeles. If the judge approves, she'll be there for fifteen years."

"Has she said why she isn't interested in testifying against him?" Veronica questions.

"We've offered her every protection, but she's holding firm," Agent Snow says.

"And won't we have enough evidence to take Villefort down without her?" Dominic says with frustration.

"He's sheltered himself behind better than seventy shell companies," I say. "Please know that I'm frustrated more than all of you combined. I believe, one day, he'll get his just desserts, but right now, this is incredibly disappointing. I wish I had better news."

"Are you positive it's him?" Grantham asks after a moment.

I nod. "We are."

"If we can't arrest him and put him in jail, we should do the second-best thing and go after him civilly."

My ears perk up. "What do you mean?"

Grantham sits tall in his seat. "We can sue him for corporate espionage and fraud in civil court. There we only have to convince the majority of the jury that he's behind the plot, and once we paint him as the asshole he is, that shouldn't be a problem. This won't put him in jail, but he'll have a hard time working with anyone in the industry after that. And sometimes, for a guy like him, that's worse than being in jail."

Mason sets his pen down. "He's gone after a dozen companies and pushed the founders out, just the way he did with Grayson Blackwell, Nick Maywood, and Jaxson at Quick Reels."

"I think this is an option we should explore," I say, trying not to sound giddy.

Everyone around the table is nodding their agreement.

"It looks like we have consensus," I announce.

Grantham nods. "I'll be in touch."

The meeting continues smoothly through the afternoon, and after we officially close our proceedings—and before my board tries to leave—I make an announcement.

"I wanted to thank all of you for pushing me to settle down. I'm taking Harper away next week, where I hope to propose to her again, without a contract this time. I want you all to know that I'm grateful for the push."

The room explodes with congratulations.

When we break for the day, Grantham tells me he'd like Mason and me to be in his office with Gray and Nick to get started on the civil case as soon as Harper and I return from our trip. "I never liked that man, but if he attempted sabotage at Honeycomb and has succeeded elsewhere, we need to address it."

I nod. "One thing to remember, though, both Firefly and Honeycomb have had successful IPOs, and we expect the same will be true of PayFriend."

"Yes, but it took money out of all your pockets to get this fixed. And you didn't get to benefit from your work at Quick Reels. I'll pull in someone from my office to help us decide. Just find a time to be at my office together." He shakes my hand and disappears out the door.

Mason nods after him. "If Grantham Wilks thinks he can nail Villefort to the wall, I say go for it."

"I doubt I'll need to work too hard to convince Gray and Nick. We can also bring in the others whose companies he's stolen."

"I have that list, and I'll bring it with me," Mason confirms.

I can't wait to tell Harper.

Thank you so much for reading Harper and Jaxson's story. I loved telling their story. Do you want more of Harper and Jaxson? Down load the bonus content at https://dl.bookfunnel.com/47r4pakrm7 to take a look into eleven months into future. It will add you to my mailing list, which you can opt out at any time or stick around and hear about what I'm reading and working on.

Made in United States
Orlando, FL
30 July 2023

35576263R00212